Plumcake

a novel

Sarah Gray

Plumcake

ISBN: 978-1-960326-81-2

Copyright © 2024 by Sarah Gray

All rights reserved. No part of this book may be reproduced or transmitted in any form or by any means, electronic or mechanical, including photocopying, recording, or by any information storage and retrieval system, without permission in writing from the publisher.

Tehom Center Publishing is a 501c3 non-profit imprint of Parson's Porch Books. Tehom Center Publishing is an imprint publishing feminist and queer authors, with a commitment to elevate BIPOC writers. Its face and voice is Rev. Dr. Angela Yarber.

For my parents, whose love has been everything to me.

She began to look for her plumcake. She tried in Downes's bag and then in the pockets of her raincloak and then on the hallstand but nowhere could she find it. ... At the thought of the failure of her little surprise and of the two and fourpence she had thrown away for nothing she nearly cried outright.

Clay

James Joyce

"I DON'T RECALL."

When the lawyers questioned Faye, many details refused to materialize. Even so, she knew so very many things that a girl in her position should not have known.

Faye knew that Doctor Edward Vogel scraped his leftover dregs of food into the trash can under his sink instead of washing them down the chute like every other person she had ever known. Faye had never seen a house that didn't have a garbage disposal or a dishwasher, but she knew now that Edward's house lacked both these basic appliances.

Faye knew that Edward let the shower run while he shaved in the growing fogginess of the steam. She knew, too, that Edward used an actual razor and clouds of puffy cream. (Her father had only ever used an electric razor, its buzzing disks moving so innocuously they seemed not to move at all.)

Faye knew that Edward ate dinner with his back to the VCR in his front room and that the television in the garage was black and white even though, for God's sake, it was almost the 21st century.

Faye knew that Edward slept in a long, plaid nightshirt like the one Ebeneezer Scrooge wore in *A Christmas Carol*.

Faye knew that Edward called his sister "little Millie," even though his brother Glen was the youngest of his parents' four children. Edward talked nostalgically about his youth on the family farm in Kansas.

Faye knew that Edward wore glasses. No other students at Aquinas Prep Catholic High School could possibly know this. Faye and the Aquinas Prep choir had performed in four states, on two continents, in five countries, and at too many hotels and conference centers to count. Never once had they suspected that Edward's penetrating blue eyes were in fact thinly covered by contact lenses. Edward, Faye learned that summer, removed them at the night's absolute last minute, dragging himself to the bathroom to exchange his contacts for humorously large glasses. In the summer of 1998, Edward Vogel kept watch in the dark over the sins of Citrus County, California. He stared out from giant spectacles with the omniscience of a God and conferred judgment on Faye, the teen-aged girl striking the pose of a prayerful supplicant.

Donovan Presley pulled back the veil. When at twenty-four, he stepped forward to say that Fr. Mick had *done things* to him back in 1987, he forced the unfathomable images of his own abuse into the unwilling minds of Citrus County Catholics and all who coveted their affiliation with Fr. Mick and with Aquinas Prep High School. A few years prior, stories of altar boy abuse had surfaced here and there, but mostly *there*, in the old Catholic communities of Boston, Philly, and Milwaukee. Priests had been molesting boys in traditional immigrant neighborhoods back when Citrus County still consisted mostly of lemon groves that sprawled south and west between Los Angeles and San Diego. Donovan's charges outraged and confused everyone. There was no sense in it. Surely a sixteen-year-old boy could fight off a priest at a bustling school in the middle of the day. The world did not know yet, would never understand, that love had made him stay. Donovan and all the abused had stayed for love of God, for love of Aquinas Prep, and for love of the men who abused them. To their young, faithful hearts and their soft, sacred bodies, these were three parts of the same divine force.

To be clear, very few locals had actually watched Donovan's press conference and even fewer believed Donovan's accusations. Over her father's shoulder at the breakfast table, fifteen-year-old Faye had learned of Donovan's shocking ordeal by way of a grainy photo and confusing headline in the *Citrus County Sun Times*: *Local Man Claims Improper Relationship with School Administrator, Priest*. Faye's eyes scanned the photo. The man still looked teen-aged at twenty-four. An ill-fitting second hand suit engulfed his slumping shoulders. The boyish-looking man held his hand defensively to his forehead, protectively avoiding the photographers' gaze.

Faye's father had folded his hands together and then rubbed them back and forth, a nervous habit. He let out a long sigh of frustration (with Donovan or with Fr. Mick. Faye could not be sure). A freshman at Aquinas Prep, Faye did not know Fr. Mick. He had been principal at Aquinas Prep in the 1980s during her brother's time there. Now, ten years later, the principal was just a regular guy. In fact, very few priests walked the halls. Lay teachers had largely taken over, their movements governed by powerful hands at the Fulton Diocese.

"I don't know that I believe all this," her father had said with deliberate skepticism. "Not about Fr. Mick."

Faye's father turned to B3 and re-creased the paper with visible angst.

"Wait until mom sees this," he had said. "She's going to be absolutely devastated."

Faye noticed, then, a small black and white photo of Fr. Mick in the article's bottom corner. The man was clean-shaven with a shock of wavy, light-colored hair and a wide smile. At first glance, she had thought it a photo of the editor. A pullover sweater patterned with geometric shapes covered the priest's Roman collar. His name was typed neatly beneath the photo: Fr. Timothy Heald.

"Fr. Timothy Heald?" Faye read with surprise. "I thought his name was Fr. Mick."

"Oh," Faye's father chuckled. "His name is Fr. Tim. They call him Fr. Mick because he's so popular—a real rockstar, like Mick Jagger."

Faye squinted and took in the photo once more. Indeed, there was a charismatic glint in the priest's eye.

Inside the Fulton Diocese, tempers had flared and anger had surged up through the chain of command from Fr. Mick to other Aquinas Prep administrators, Diocesan Human Resources, and, ultimately, to Bishop Jim McCaulley himself. Outside those walls, denial had been swift and thorough. Back channels of Catholic society had quickly smeared Donovan's character. Aquinas Prep alumni organized parades and galas in Fr. Mick's honor, their effusive praise just loud enough to cover the doubts clawing their way in. When, by the year's end, there had been no trial and no settlement, Citrus County Catholics eagerly filed the scandal away. Three years later, when Fr. Mick had been defrocked and had slipped away from California to New Orleans, his devotees looked away as the Bishop paid Donovan a seven million dollar settlement.

Faye's parents, neighbors, friends, and all those whose children had passed through Fr. Mick's care at Aquinas Prep brushed off the horrible business of that misunderstanding. How could they be sure that anything had happened? If the boy were telling the truth, wouldn't the priest have been arrested? A generation of Catholics so eager to personalize the Church and to find their way into the center of its mystery now held more fear and doubt than they could handle. The personal had been let in and the secrets had been let out, and there remained the messy business of being Catholic in the world, of raising families, participating in liturgy, and pretending the Church was as they had always believed it to be. But there was Donovan Presley—young but weary, his eyes sunken and sallow—humble and insistent that their Church was of men, not of God.

Fifteen was no age to decide who was telling the truth. Though Faye had neither believed Donovan nor believed Fr. Mick, the newspaper photo of Donovan Presley—so fragile yet so brave—had whispered a secret that Faye tucked away in the back of her mind. While she saw the shimmering luster of Aquinas Prep's exterior, Donovan Presley had seen something darker, something dangerous. She had been too embarrassed to ask either her parents or her friends what they thought had happened. Walking the outdoor corridors at Aquinas Prep, she easily imagined that young man as a bumbling teen-aged boy, his face shiny with adolescent perspiration and pimples like the faces of her classmates. *What had Fr. Mick done to him? How,* fifteen-year-old Faye wondered, *was it even possible to rape a teen-aged boy?* Thoughts of the priest and the boy haunted her. Faye imagined the priest ushering Donovan into the darkened chapel, his hand on the boy's shoulder. Her conjuring stopped there. The act itself was unimaginable. She saw Fr. Mick flash his signature smile (the same from the newspaper photo). Then, the image faded. Like a film scene, the camera of her imagination zoomed tightly to the bright shards of stained glass on the chapel windows, Donovan's and Fr. Mick's voices now audible only as muffled sounds from a place she could not go. Eventually, unable to solve the mystery, Faye stopped thinking about Donovan Presley and opened her arms wide to all that Aquinas Prep offered. Certainly she would not have thought then that Donovan would emerge from the Citrus County Catholic smear campaign a successful attorney and fierce advocate for victims' rights. Even less likely, she and Donovan would be fast friends upon meeting ten years later and, ultimately, would be colleagues in activism, their adult lives spent buffing away the gilded exterior of so many dazzling institutions and conmen.

I

ON THIS SPRING MORNING IN 2019, while CNN's B-roll of angry senators ran silently along commentary from the previous day's Supreme Court hearings, Faye prepared press statements announcing Sunset Bluffs' speaker series on teen suicide and appropriate language for addressing transgender students. As the Title IX coordinator for Sunset Bluffs Unified School District, Faye Collins was a paid champion for equality, compassion, and the general well-being of the teenagers whose loud voices bounced off the walls of Citrus County's wealthy public high schools. When, three months prior, Sebastian Murray had hanged himself from a tree at a nearby park, Faye felt such a crippling emotional blow she thought she might never recover. A sophomore at Newport East, the largest school in Sunset Bluffs Unified, Sebastian was not a quiet kid whose suicide should have been foreseen by a watchful community. President of the unofficial *Newport East Queer Friends Alliance*, Sebastian was the out and proud voice for marginal kids confused about sexuality and for all who faced bullying and pushback against the school's efforts to teach inclusion and sensitivity. His visible swagger was a beacon for the weaker kids, a sign that queer could be strong and that *different* could mean exceptional. Because he had seemed so secure, because he had risen above the vitriol of parent groups who threatened to cease donations if the district formally recognized *QFA* as an official student group, Sebastian's loss opened a deep cavern of grief among the queer student population and even the broader student body. Kids with ashen faces from lack of sleep walked the halls with eyes cast down, shaking their heads each time they remembered that Sebastian had actually *done* it. Faye's office had responded swiftly with counseling and education initiatives, but she knew more than most that her essential job in the aftermath was to save the lives no one realized were at risk. In quiet corners, other kids were turning Sebastian's suicide over slowly and methodically in their minds, not wondering why Sebastian had done it but if they, too, could find the courage to follow his lead.

A light knock on her open office door raised Faye's eyes from her computer. Paul, her weary colleague, stood in the shadow of her door frame.

"I'm already getting press inquiries about a parent group pledging to protest outside the evening event," he said. "They're calling it inflammatory. They are saying the event will," he paused, scanning the document in his hand, "the event will cause gender confusion and promote lifestyles that are dangerous and unhealthy for adolescents."

Faye pushed her chair back from the desk and spoke with derision.

"They can protest all night long," she said. "Studies across the board show that the best deterrent of suicide for children of all genders and sexualities is open dialogue about mental health."

Paul raised one hand defensively. "You certainly don't need to convince me. I do think, though, that we should establish some kind of perimeter to keep protestors off the property. The kids don't need to see angry parents scowling at them."

"What's it going to take," Faye responded, "for these parents to learn that kids are literally killing themselves because the people closest to them are making them feel perverted and hopeless?"

"It's not *their* kids," Paul said flatly. "At least they hope to God it's not their kids."

"But they are somebody's kids," Faye said with an exasperated sigh. "They play football with their kids and carpool with their kids and do lab projects with their kids."

"Not these kids," Paul shot back. "You're being naïve. These parents," he said, waving the press inquiry in his hand, "keep their kids apart. You won't find them sharing lab stations or locker rooms with anyone these parents don't approve."

"And so their own kids go underground," she responded, more sadly still. "No support. No one to confide in. Their crises will come in five years, if they make it that long."

Faye had tried for years to understand, but the logic eluded her. The insensitivity of "concerned" parents had shocked Faye at first. Then, their callousness had begun to offend her. Their easy dismissal of her concerns— their active defiance against education and healing for struggling and traumatized students—showed their real intent. The parents who left nasty voicemails and resentful emails were not actually concerned. They were combative, ready for war with any idea or experience that threatened the pre-delineated path they saw for their own wealthy, white, carefully coddled teens.

In her first few months on the job, Faye had instituted sweeping changes to the handling of Title IX complaints and had created new, safer reporting guidelines for gender-based bullying and inter-partner violence. The backlash had been swift. School board protestors complained that Sunset Bluffs was demonizing teen-aged boys and pushing a "gay agenda." In those early years, Faye feared the vitriol would jade her and would lessen her satisfaction at the good she was doing. Over time, the opposite had proven true. Faye poured herself into the work with untiring devotion. Angry parents thought Faye worked for some nebulously identified liberal machine. The news media considered her an arm of the state, representing California policies filtered down through the Citrus County Department of Education and ultimately Sunset Bluffs Unified. Faye never thought herself an institutional agent. She worked for the kids. Before an administrator, she had been an educator. Faye still saw herself as a teacher. She knew that for so many high school students, education was possible only after the clearing away of puberty's real obstacles—fear, angst, self-loathing, emotional neglect.

As Faye rose from her seat, beginning to gather papers into a file, she glimpsed her boss walking resolutely toward the office. Paul turned just as Marilyn arrived at Faye's door. She seemed alarmed.

"The press inquiry?" Faye asked. "It's the same script every time. I don't think there will be a problem tonight."

"It's not Queer Alliance," Marilyn said. "We have a much bigger problem."

Paul stepped into Faye's office. Marilyn followed behind and closed the door. As Assistant Superintendent of Student Life and Culture, Marilyn worked beside Faye on most of her projects. Though Marilyn slightly outranked Faye, their roles diverged mostly in kind rather than degree. Marilyn handled a much wider variety of student issues and was glad to hand any Title IX related concerns to Faye after a first glance. Marilyn was seldom rattled. Faye noticed a downturn in the corners of her mouth, her lips pursed together as if stifling some outcry.

"I just took an initial phone report of a sexual assault," she began. "An assault of a student by a group of students. The reporting party was a parent, not the student himself."

Almost in unison, Paul and Faye straightened up with renewed curiosity.

"The victim is male?" Paul asked.

"Yes," Marilyn confirmed. "The parent reported that her son had been sexually harassed and assaulted by a group of his male teammates. Apparently the boys have been harassing her son for a few weeks." Marilyn scanned her handwritten notes as she talked. "Hanging dildos in his athletic locker, leaving lipstick kisses on his shoulder guards, writing obscenities on his undergarments."

Faye bit her lip slightly. She could tell the worst was still coming.

"According to today's complaint, last week a small group of boys—possibly three or four—attacked her son from behind in the locker room. They strapped him to a chair using exercise bands, blindfolded him, and dribbled semen on his head from a plastic bag."

Faye's stomach dropped. *That poor boy*, she thought.

Every assault and affront she had seen, every attack and side-glance and social media blast had one thing in common. They aimed to humiliate. Humiliate *that* kid before someone humiliates you.

Paul seemed stunned. He shook his head so slowly the movement was almost imperceptible.

"Sweet Jesus."

Life experience had taught Faye that people hurt each other over and over again. Education and advocacy could dent the ever-growing tower of pain, but pain there still would be. Each puny-looking victim who appeared in her office reminded Faye that her work often failed and that she could not give up. Title IX coordinator was a tough business. As a young woman, she had planned to teach high school English at Aquinas Prep. Instead, she had begun teaching Gender Studies at St. Anne's. Research and teaching had taxed Faye intellectually; her work at Sunset Bluffs drained every well of human spirit she had. She was meant for it, though. Faye felt that surety in her bones after a long trek from adolescence to the shiny glass administrative building at Sunset Bluffs. After graduating from Aquinas Prep Catholic High School in the late '90s, Faye had left southern California for Sacred Heart University in Potato Creek, Indiana, a planned four-year Bachelor degree stint that turned into six years and a Master's degree before Faye moved on, a husband now in tow, to doctoral study at the University of Illinois's flagship campus in Tolono. Faye became Doctor Collins, then, a three-hour Uhaul drive bringing her back to Potato Creek to teach at St. Anne's Women's College and to begin her work cultivating the next generation of women intellectuals.

Oh, how the small towns of the Midwest changed over thirteen years. Faye's parents had left her there in 1998, the sticky Indiana August turning slowly to a blank icy wasteland into which she had felt abandoned. Meeting Daniel had changed all that. The towns opened to Faye then with possibility and community, revealing beneath the bucolic strangeness a warmth that embraced and lulled her. Faye matured as the fields did, the cycle of seasons sustaining in Faye a belief that her life could indeed begin anew with each revolution of the Earth. Upon the birth of her first child—that first feel of Teague's hot, slippery skin against her own—love and God and all the ecstasy rushed over Faye, bringing with them the knowledge, finally, that so much more joy awaited her if she dared to keep reaching for it.

Eleven years into the new century, Faye had two babies and was ready to go home to Citrus County. Because Teague and Louisa had been born in Tolono, the humidity, openness, and lush green farmland of the Midwest had taken root in Faye's heart. For the rest of her life she would think of those spaces, the bright sun making cloud-shaped shadows on the harvested cornfields, as a homeland that held all the energy of her budding womanhood.

Maybe it was she, and not the towns themselves, that had changed over that time between her flight from Aquinas Prep High School and her return, a bit of a prodigal daughter, to the streets of her childhood in Osage Park, California. Daniel at the wheel of their sensible SUV, Teague and Louisa alternately napping, sucking lollipops, and spotting livestock in between cities with criss-crossing cement freeways, the Collins family drove toward a new start in an old place, arriving in Citrus County to find everything slightly off kilter, familiar as a home movie, the sights and sounds both expected and eerily foreign.

Four years after their return, Wyatt was born in Citrus County as Faye, herself, had been, the only California-bred child and, for that, a special place in his grandparents' heart. Faye liked to think her time away from southern California had given her enough distance for fresh perspective. While she had racked up degrees and built a career in midwestern university towns, the rest of her family and most of her high school acquaintances had stayed firmly planted in Citrus County, bar crawls and Sunday morning Mass bringing renewed contact year after year with the same classmates who now looked like puffy, balding versions of their former selves. Aquinas Prep still stood strong, a bastion of athleticism, Catholicism, and elitism despite years of alleged misconduct and a cost of attendance so exorbitant that most Aquinas Prep alumni could not afford (as they had dreamed they would) to push their kids off to school in the same scarlet polo shirts and plaid pleated skirts they had worn. Aquinas Prep had bloomed bigger and bolder, its growing footprint eating up full neighborhoods of modest family homes summarily bulldozed for the expansion (with hefty payouts to families of Mexican immigrants whose American Dream had suddenly been realized). Shiny new facilities popped up amidst modular classrooms, graying and old after decades of use. In the back windows of beat up sedans, flashy sports cars, sensible minivans, and high tech electric vehicles, AP decals zigzagged Citrus County freeways, showing through various stages of sun-worn use the pride of successive generations of AP families. Not only because she had moved away but because she had dared to criticize Aquinas Prep in her work and in her activism, Faye had been forced outside of the fold. Though she nursed a secret desire to find a way back in, the truth was clear. Faye had changed; most of Citrus County and Aquinas Prep had not.

Growing up Catholic in Citrus County had meant entrenched conservatism and cutthroat tribalism. Everyone Faye knew had been *with* Aquinas Prep (not against it), pro-life and proud of it, suspicious of public schools, determined to keep their gay family members in the closet, and against interracial marriage because oh! what difficulties would be foisted on interracial couples! Better to stick with your own kind. And Faye had, it was true, stuck with her own kind—Catholic education at Sacred Heart, a Catholic husband, and three Catholic children, Mass on Sundays, and crucifixes above each door. Faye laughed, musing to herself as she sat in her office at Sunset Bluffs. She was a Kennedy Catholic now, a social justice Christian in the vein of Sister

Helen Prejean at a time when most Citrus County Catholics looked more like Bush family evangelicals. Inside, Faye was no longer the Faye they all had known. She had flown away from Citrus County and had come back a different woman. The trickle down misogyny of Faye's childhood had produced in teen-aged Faye a firm belief that the smartest woman could best serve by standing behind a powerful man. This pervasive sense of proper social hierarchy had infected Faye so easily she had hardly noticed it. After she had read so much and had seen so many people—had really gotten out there and met them in the past thirteen years—Faye could still blend in, but she didn't quite fit.

Leaning back in her office chair, Faye scanned the full bookshelves crowding the walls. The texts reflected a history of her own evolution. In fifteen years' worth of study, her consciousness had been piqued then pricked then stirred to unbelievable ardor in the face of injustice toward women and girls based on their perceived inferiority and the fear that their assent in the halls of power might disrupt the success of the men around them. Professor Carol Psomedietrich's undergraduate course at Sacred Heart had started it all. From her seminar on Victorian Society and Faye's reading of *On the Subjection of Women*, Faye's adolescent training had begun to erode. Next came Professor Sue Ellen Baldwin's Illinois graduate course in 20th Century American Women, Nella Larsen's *Passing*, and Betty Friedan's *The Feminine Mystique*. By the time Faye wrote her dissertation on the queering of masculinity in the Irish Free State, Faye had caught both the Church and the patriarchy in her crosshairs. From there, it was a quick leap to recognizing the shameless hypocrisy of the Catholic leaders she had revered in her Aquinas Prep and Sacred Heart days. On the surface, Church leaders were losing their luster, Church misogyny pushing through Vatican II's exterior gilding. Inside, the Church still lived in Faye, its mysteries warm and nourishing.

Professor J. Hansen's convocation speech for the 2009 Women's Day at St. Anne's College had pushed Faye into her current role. His talk on MacKinnon's searing text *Sexual Harassment of Working Women* had come at Faye with an irresistible call to trade academic inquiry for the trenches of real-world suffering. And though she may have fancied herself a burgeoning Gloria Steinem, she soon found that the powerful, assertive women she had long associated with gender abuse—the Anita Hills and Monica Lewinskys who spoke truth to power with razor sharp bite—represented the exception, not the rule. Here at Sunset Bluffs, she was mired in an endless parade of despair, teen girls and boys being ushered into young adulthood through unimaginable trauma. Faye's phone rang incessantly; on the other end, there were reports of children losing the fight with a world that rolled over anyone who did not measure up. Faye's work demanded thick skin and a strong stomach, neither of which, in truth, Faye had.

Teague breathed a deep intake of fresh air as the empty driveway of his house came into view, his mom's station wagon nowhere in sight. Junior high let out an hour before elementary and preschool, so Teague's siblings were likewise absent. The afternoon was his to do anything he wanted, and to do it *alone*. Seventh grade was shaping up just fine. Seventh grade meant riding home from school with the wind on his face and his favorite tunes pulsing from the phone in his pocket. Seventh grade meant his own terrarium and pet iguana (named Avocado) and his own room. His dad had even helped Teague paint one wall deep purple, Teague's favorite color. Teague couldn't believe now how nervous he had been about leaving elementary school. Because he was changing school districts as well, he had started seventh grade knowing only one other kid. The past few months, though, he had discovered several other boys he got along with and had learned, with relief, that junior high was just big enough that everyone could not be watching everyone all the time. After some initial skirmishes, Teague settled into a routine with a few other boys and largely flew under the radar of the cool kids and the bullies. Sure, Eddie Costanzo had made a dumb joke about Teague's project in 1st period art that morning. "Check out Teague's gay pride flag," Eddie had yelled, a reference to Teague's use of rainbow-hued lettering, but hardly anyone had laughed. Teague's best friend had made an even more biting comment about the acne sprouting on Eddie's chin. Nothing could have brought Teague down this day. At lunch, Maya had given him half her Twinkie. The only thing Teague liked more than Twinkies was Maya.

William came tearing onto Teague's driveway just as Teague removed his bike helmet.

"Swimming or Battle Bonds?" William asked.

Both tempted him, but Teague was looking forward to a few hours alone to sip an orange soda and draw. And to think about Maya.

"Not today," Teague responded, wheeling his bike toward the garage. "I've got some drawings to work on."

"Saw you talking to Maya today," William said. "Maybe she likes you back."

"I don't know," Teague mused. "Maybe."

William prepared to ride off, his house a mere two blocks west of Teague's.

"Call you later for some Battle Bonds?" William asked.

"Not tonight. Tomorrow, though, for sure."

Teague dropped his backpack in the entryway and relished the silence. Two little siblings meant a lot of noise at the Collins house. For years, Teague had been the loudest of all, everybody said so, but in the past few months, he had started to enjoy any quiet time he could get. He loved most of all to wake up early on Saturday mornings and make himself a hot chocolate to savor before anyone else got up. Being home alone made him feel older and more in charge. Teague's first seeds of independence were blossoming. This opening of adolescence brought exciting discovery. Teague could feel himself cleaving slightly away from his family and forging his own path. Nothing felt better than this duality: the comfort of his house, where the towels smelled like his mom and his collection of stuffed animals lined the bedroom shelves, and the sense that he was old enough and strong enough to take care of himself, to decide how to spend his time.

After quickly finishing a bowl of cereal, Teague rinsed his dish in the sink, plucked an orange soda from a shelf in the fridge, and headed to his room with his backpack in tow. He dropped a piece of lettuce in Avocado's tank and sat down to draw. His room felt warm and cozy. He liked feeling closed in, his room hugging him like a cocoon. Whenever Teague's mom passed his room, she opened his door and window wide to let in the light. *It smells like boy in here*, she would say with derision. Teague took no offense, though. His mom complained about everything—his messy room, his arguing with Louisa, the backtalk, too much time spent staring at the television or game console—but Teague could tell in his core that she loved every minute she spent with him. Always, without her saying it, Teague had believed that he was her favorite. Sometimes when they argued, his mom had a way of guilting him that was absolutely heartbreaking. Even then, he felt between them an invisible tie that said everything would be okay as long as they had each other.

Sketching the crude outline of a spiky-skinned reptile, Teague thought of Maya. Teague had always liked girls. He learned early that boys mostly wanted to *play* something; Teague liked that girls always wanted to talk. Teague liked to talk, too. Maya was unlike any girl he had ever met. The other kids probably found her shy, but when Maya talked with Teague, she told long stories about her horseback riding expeditions and funny stories about her pet guinea pigs. Maya felt uncomfortable around most adults, did not like sharing personal information with other kids, and loved animals of all kinds far more than she liked people. They had started talking in English class after Teague had written a poem about Avocado. Maya wanted to know more about Teague's pet and to regale him with facts about iguana diets and habitats. Teague had seen Maya talking with her friends during lunch hour. When she spoke to other kids, Maya shifted her weight back into her heels as if trying to fold herself away from them. When she talked to Teague about wolf rescues and ocean life protections, he felt her leaning in toward him, her voice getting louder with excitement and purpose. None of the other kids cared so much about anything. Of course he thought Maya was pretty, too. In stark contrast with Teague's paleness, Maya's skin was a rich brown color, a shade darker than the caramel-colored brown of her eyes. When it wasn't wrapped up in tight box braids, her hair poofed out because it was thick, wavy, and cut just below her ears. *Warm*, Teague thought when he saw her. Maya looked like her skin would feel warm against his. He hoped maybe, some day, she might hold his hand so he could find out.

The crash of Louisa's helmet in the entryway announced her arrival before she appeared at Teague's bedroom door. A twinge of annoyance pricked at Teague's skin. He didn't mind his little sister, though lately he had not been particularly happy to see her. The two kids frequently argued, their conversations escalating quickly into one-upmanship and angry accusations. It seemed the older he got, the more Teague's mom expected him to give in and keep the peace, a role Teague was certainly more suited for but one he was beginning to resent. Teague kept his eyes focused on his artwork while Louisa spoke.

"Teague, Teague—"

His mother was right, Teague suddenly realized. The kids said each others' names *a lot*. Like, unnecessarily a lot. Teague sat right in his sister's line of sight, but Louisa kept repeating his name, waiting for him to look up. Teague tried not to sound brusque, though he was already annoyed at the breach of his solitude.

"Louisa, I hear you. Just say what you want to say."

"*Pasqua Peaks 4* is being released tonight. Do you think we can have a movie night?"

Without looking away from his drawing pad, Teague shook the paint down in a bright blue marker.

"Mom and dad are going out tonight, but we can still watch it. I saw the trailer. It looks like they're bringing back that old man from *Pasqua Peaks 1*, the one who chased the kids after they threw the oranges at his house."

The tension dissipated as both kids thought about their favorite animated movie series and became more animated themselves.

"That guy was hilarious. Oh, that's great. I can't wait to see it."

"And Louisa—Louisa—remember he had that dog that kept trying to push over all those trash cans."

Both kids were laughing now. Teague felt good. Really, Louisa was an okay little sister when she wanted to be.

Stepping into the lounge's thick air, the band strumming too loudly on a small stage in a crowded space, Faye could still feel the sensation of Wyatt's cool cheek on her lips from their good-bye kiss. By seven o'clock, all three children were fed, clean, and settled under blankets in front of the television. She left Wyatt cuddled up with Louisa, his body upside-down in an inverted spoon against his sister's back. Little children, she had learned, lie and lounge and sprawl in every kind of pretzeled position, their bodies stretching and contracting like newborns unfettered by any sense of personal space or decorum. Oh how she loved to see them this way, a heap of bodies so smooth and soft she wanted to soothe her adult worries against the salve of their flesh. Such moments without argument or tears had been appearing less frequently as Teague and Louisa ramped up their pre-teen competition for attention and space inside the home. The image of their combined contentment—staring absently, lips agape at the glowing tv, tossing popcorn and gummy candies into their mouths at odd intervals—spread behind Faye's glimpse of the adults around her now, their voices shouting over each other, their martinis sloshing and beers dwindling to a foamy residue. Here with Daniel, she settled into the cushy seat and into herself. She liked loud bars because it meant sitting side by side in the booth and holding hands under the table. As Faye's ears adjusted to the crowded room's pulsing din, the melody and insistent drumbeat eased into her consciousness. She released the day's work and strife from where they had burrowed into her mind. Daniel kept his jacket on. Faye pushed her slight frame up against his shoulder to feel close to him. Not often did they find themselves out of the house together and so completely unfettered. Daniel's jacket smelled warm and lived in. For twenty years, Faye had breathed in Daniel's comforting scent and tried to capture it. They had moved between cities and through the Midwest and now across the country to southern California. They had changed detergents and soaps and seasons and regions and age groups, but always Daniel retained his Danielness. Faye nuzzled her nose up against his neck, a quick open-mouthed kiss to the smooth spot just below his ear.

Faye and Daniel did not talk, and that was just fine for both of them. Daniel preferred music to chatter because the week had been long and the meetings had been plenty. A night out with his wife was best enjoyed this way, she cozied up beside him, their hands entwined and their drinks slipping away. He enjoyed hearing about Faye's work, but just as well he liked to lose himself in the music, to enjoy the warm looseness spreading through his bloodstream from the whiskey on his lips to its tingling residue at the tips of his fingers. They could catch up on the week's developments, run through the kids' theater, sports, and preschool schedules, and worry about the world at the breakfast table tomorrow. For now, Daniel released Faye's fingers and ran his hand along the curve of her thigh beneath her dress, suddenly eager to get his wife home to bed.

Aquinas Prep was back in the news. Daniel saw it first and passed it to Faye, pushing his tablet toward her as she set an open carton of yogurt in front of four-year-old baby Wyatt. Dinner, drinks, and lovemaking with Daniel had left good vibes coursing through Faye's limbs through a restful night and into the start of a joyful morning. With a glance at the tablet, Faye's placidity broke, a ripple of anxiety taking its place.

Aquinas Prep Teens Reveal a Culture of Harassment, the headline blared.

With a tap-click, Faye devoured the article, soaking up the information as she did all things Aquinas Prep, her nose pressed against the glass of an institution she no longer revered but still exoticized. A gaggle of teen-aged soccer players from the boys' team had posted a video of themselves chanting misogynistic and homophobic slurs against the girls' soccer team. The night had ended with piss-drunk boys shaving each other's uniform numbers into their crew cuts and breaking some lamps and other décor in the hotel where their tournament was being held. To make matters worse, visible half out of the frame was the team's assistant coach, an AP graduate and all-around good guy, who clearly made no effort to deter or punish the boys. The coach appeared to be holding an open bottle of beer.

"This just became a working breakfast," Faye said with a sigh, reaching back to grab her laptop. Title IX breaches at any local high school eventually spilled over to her workload at Sunset Bluffs.

"Is this Title IX territory?" Daniel asked.

"It certainly is." Faye spoke with command.

"It's not as if they were saying these things to the girls," Daniel noted.

Faye took an instructive tone in her retort.

"Title IX is about school culture and environment," she began. "If these boys—and especially the coaches—are not punished appropriately, girls in the hallways get the idea that no one cares if they are denigrated and disrespected. If you don't feel like anyone cares about you just because you're a girl, you can't focus as well or perform as well as your male classmates, and your education is being inhibited because of your sex. That's Title IX."

Daniel scanned the article now. "I'm surprised not to see a quote from Donovan," he said.

"That is strange," Faye agreed. "*The Sun Times* generally has Donovan on speed dial for these matters. I suppose they are probably less likely to reach out when dealing with something other than direct teacher-student abuse. I'm having lunch with him tomorrow. We'll see what he knows."

Lunch with Donovan was long overdue, but both he and Faye had barely been keeping heads above water this spring. Donovan had been embroiled in a complicated personal injury trial that ran a full nine days despite his hope that Oceanside Suites would settle with his client to avoid public coverage of its negligence. At home, his twin babies were just beginning to walk, a wrinkle that significantly complicated bedtime, bath time, and every time they weren't strapped into a car seat or highchair. Alongside his day job, Donovan jetted north, south, midwest, and across the ocean as often as he could to give lectures and trainings related to the sexual abuse of children by priests, religious, and other adults who could gain the trust of unsuspecting kids. His story was a memorized script, now. Donovan told the story of Fr. Mick's attention and his kindness, of the slow-creeping intimacy, of the grooming of his teen-aged ego, and of Fr. Mick's determination to attach Donovan so deeply to the priest's heart that he could not bear to disappoint him. His advocacy empowered him and, Donovan knew, saved lives.

The sanitized script was incomplete, of course. Very few people knew the unredacted version of what had happened to Donovan in that darkened Aquinas Prep chapel all those years ago. When he was alone, Donovan turned the details over in his mind. He swore that one day he would figure out what had happened and why. Until then, the media-friendly version had wormed its way in and set up shop. Donovan was comfortable with that story. He could tell it in his sleep. He wasn't really trying to prevent child abuse. That order would have been much too tall. His own abuse had rolled over him like an unstoppable train, and even now, as a man and a father, he saw predatory priests and sexual abusers as almost too cunning to thwart. Donovan spoke because he knew there were victims in the crowd. There were men and women who had already been groomed and betrayed and assaulted. They wore shame and carried guilt. They hated sex or craved it all day long. Their marriages caused anxiety, and they lived in constant fear of their abusers or with a deep longing for the love the abuser now withheld. Donovan spoke so that these survivors would feel less alone. Since the first afternoon that Fr. Mick had stroked his hair and whispered such beautiful blessings into his ear, feeling less alone was all Donovan had wanted. And so he told his story and accepted calls from strangers seeking someone—anyone—who could know what it felt like to swallow like sweet poison the love and hate the abuse had birthed. In the fifteen or so years since the settlement of his very public lawsuit, Donovan had addressed hundreds of town halls, education boards, medical conferences, and gender studies courses. In all that time, never once had he been asked to speak at a Catholic parish.

In the three weeks since the assault report at Newport East, Faye had thought often of Donovan and of his abuse. She had met with the victim, a boy named Lewis who was a strong, square-jawed athlete whose pride was so wounded he could hardly look Faye in the face. Faye's experience proved that each victim differed from the one before and the one after. Still, they shared similarities that shone in each gut-wrenching interview she performed. The girls looked small. They shrank back in their chairs, awash in powerlessness. The boys were embarrassed. They scanned the floor tiles and fiddled with shoelaces or shirt cuffs to avoid eye contact with anyone in the room. Girls and boys, younger and older, Latino, Asian, white, black, gay, and straight came to her hesitant. However great their pain, each kid worried most about one thing. When she asked if they had questions, each victim asked the same one: *What's going to happen to the person who hurt me?* A chill ran through Faye each time. *Not enough*, she thought to herself.

The locker room assault had been picked up quickly by local media. A story so sensational was bound for extra press, a reality that made Faye's job more difficult. At just the same time, Daniel was traveling more on business, meaning extra babysitting shifts for Faye's parents and long, forlorn looks from the kids when Faye insisted on reading and typing through family dinners. Other than Teague, her sensitive twelve year old, the kids were too young to understand or care about Faye's work. They knew she worked in a school and that she worked to help kids, and, really, what else was there to know? Waiting for Donovan's bright smile to come bounding through the deli's door, Faye thought of her children and an abiding sense of joy spread through her. Precisely because they were young, because they were hopeful and silly and patient, Faye's children filled her. The intensity of parental love overwhelmed Faye even after twelve years of mothering. Those early days in which she had nursed and wiped and bathed and soothed each child, their mouths and eyes hot with tears, their skin dry with diaper rash or slick from bath bubbles, had so thoroughly bound Faye to the children that it was a great surprise to discover that they were, body and soul, their very own beings. As a girl and a young woman, Faye had not particularly wanted to have children. At thirty-eight, Faye held close the secret her children had revealed: they had been sent to save her. And save her, they had.

Donovan walked briskly from the deli's door to Faye's table and sat down with a huff. Though they'd been friends for a dozen years now, each time they met Faye's mind flashed on the indelible image of Donovan staring down the news cameras twenty years before, his jaw strong but his brow furrowed, a boy shrinking into a man's suit. The meekness Fr. Mick had exploited in Donovan had never quite left, but Donovan had learned to pack it away where almost no one could find it. In their time as colleagues and friends, Faye had never seen Donovan move slowly. He carried his anxiety as determination. He was good natured and friendly to a fault, but Donovan survived by controlling the space directly around him. He would shake a man's hand, but never, not ever, would Donovan allow other men to clasp their hands however jovially on his shoulder as business men and buddies were wont to do.

Donovan greeted Faye with a wide smile. "I'm famished," he said.

Another quirk—Donovan had an insatiable appetite and ate voraciously in public spaces. Faye wondered if Donovan ate through lunch meetings (when other colleagues mostly picked at small fare) to busy himself and to avoid sustained eye contact with his companions. Faye stopped mid-analysis. Surely, there had been a Donovan—there was a Donovan still—whose intricacies and attitudes did not stem from his abuse. Surely, not everything about Donovan Presley had been formed by Fr. Mick. Seeing Donovan in the flesh, nothing was sure. The experiences of victims all around Faye told a worse tale than those outside the victim community could fathom. In many cases, nothing, it seemed, existed beyond the reach of the abuser's influence.

Leaning toward him, Faye grasped both of Donovan's hands and smiled.

"It's been too long," she said. "You look good."

"Do I look busy?" Donovan asked. "I feel a little harried."

"Not unusually so. How are the babies?"

"My gosh—" Donovan pulled out his phone to show Faye a video. "Walking. Just like that, they are both walking."

Faye smiled at the video of pudgy Don Jr. unsteadily following his bright-eyed sister from couch to coffee table and back.

"I've been in court a lot, so Molly is just drowning at home with the kids. But, really, everyone has been healthy. Things are good. Things really are wonderful."

An hour later, Donovan was sopping up marinara with the end of a French roll while Faye asked for his insight. Sunset Bluffs United had begun a swift investigation after the initial complaint, but as media coverage had grown, so too had Lewis Miller's reticence to talk about the assault. She worried now that pursuing the complaint might be more psychologically straining than the boy could handle.

"Our main concern is support for the boy who was attacked. We'd like him to be more forthcoming, of course, so we can follow this trail further into the team culture. That isn't my main priority, though. I'm worried about this kid. He needs to feel that we see his trauma as more than just a Title IX breach."

Donovan thought a moment.

"What's the kid's story? Is he queer?"

"Does that matter?"

"It might matter to him. Listen, the assault just happened. He likely hasn't processed it. It's going to be awhile before that trauma really plays itself out, before he even admits that this assault is different from any other schoolyard scuffle. Right now, right after, he's probably dealing more with embarrassment and self-loathing than anything else."

Donovan continued eating as he talked. Faye had pushed her plate away and followed his words closely.

"He thinks something about him brought this on. If he's queer, he thinks he deserves it because he's queer. If he's not, he's worried everyone's going to think he is and that he'll never lose that label. Sounds ridiculous, right, in the twenty-first century?"

Faye nodded. "No, I see."

"In this community, in the homes of his peers, we have hardly moved on this issue. This assault isn't about sex or even about control. It's about a homophobic culture that still operates on the principle that branding someone else means escaping that scrutiny yourself. And that's what these kids want— they want to blend into the dominant group and ride that stability as long as they can."

"What did they expect him to do after the assault?"

"First, they don't see it as an assault. Second, now it's worse for him. They expected him to either go along with it to show that he was one of them, or to tell, which means not only that he is *not* one of them but that people like him are out to take away their freedom to do whatever they want. That's what they hate most of all. They and their parents can't stand that someone else would tell them what is and is not appropriate behavior."

"Okay, let's say he is coming from a place of embarrassment and fear about perception. How do we translate an understanding of all that into a kind of support that can offset that script in his head?"

"Don't cover it up. Don't cover any of it up. Get the students on board from the school and from other schools in the district. You need a celebration of vulnerability instead of a drive toward some kind of unilateral ideal. Students need a real sense that they are united in their awkward, teen-aged confusion."

Faye nodded in thought, not convinced her students had such capacity.

"That's a big culture change."

Donovan wiped a napkin across his mouth and looked at Faye squarely.

"First, though," he said firmly, "clear and absolute punishment for those attackers."

"Yes. Now, if I can just get Roland to call them *attackers*. That would be a great start for accountability."

"I take it Coach is dragging his feet. Let me guess—locker room talk. Boys will be boys. They were just having fun?"

Faye picked at a few straggling fries on her plate.

"Absolutely right. I don't imagine Coach Roland would find it fun to have someone else's jizz drizzled on *his* head."

"You've certainly put me off my pasta," Donovan said. "What a nightmare. And what a bunch of assholes in that athletic department." Donovan's eyes brightened with a sudden remembrance. "Speaking of athletic department assholes—"

Faye jumped in. "Aquinas Prep soccer," she said. "What do you know about it?"

"I know it has school culture written all over it, and that if AP isn't encouraging that kind of attitude, it certainly is not discouraging it either."

"I haven't seen a lot out there since the initial headline. Boys and beers are not likely to cause outrage in any climate, let alone when measured against the status of AP athletics."

Donovan nodded. "Well, who does the story really speak to? The problem with these group aggressions, these verbal group aggressions, is that there's no complaining party. Girls are too embarrassed to stand up for themselves, boys are too squeamish to defend the girls, and the parents just burrow their heads straight into that red and gray quicksand where all indiscretions go, forever lost to the public eye."

With Faye, Donovan could afford a flippant tone. Faye likewise enjoyed catching up with Donovan regarding victims, student services, trends in school culture, and the invisible net of misogyny and abuse that stretched over society, trapping the most vulnerable and choking into silence everyone who had any hope of reform. Because they had seen the effects first hand, Donovan and Faye felt the gravity in their marrow. The weight of their trauma and the sense of their desire—no, of their *duty*—to expose the predators and protect everyone else bound them in a mutual understanding that opened a space for levity. They had built a friendship on this shared passion. They would not be silenced by the angry din that diffused its way through Citrus County. Citrus County oozed money, power, and irresponsibility. So many Aquinas Prep parents and Sunset Bluffs boosters lived with their eyes on a prize so shapeless and far away that they knew only that it was shiny and coveted, and so they wanted it at any cost. As Title IX coordinator, Faye had faced pushback and backlash from surprising corners. Likewise, she had found support that was equally unexpected. She hated that so many of her colleagues lacked compassion and bravery in fighting for the students they were tasked with educating. She never lost sight, though, of one tiny solace. At least at Sunset Bluffs, the men and women abandoning their moral duty were mere mortals. They did not wear the cloth of the Church and purport to hold the pathway to salvation. That hypocrisy was reserved for the administrators at Aquinas Prep.

"The principal can't be happy after licking the Bishop's boots to get the job and then finding one PR nightmare after another cropping up," Faye added.

Donovan scoffed. "I'd say this is a slow day for PR at Aquinas Prep. No rape and no clergy involvement? Nothing to see here."

Just as Faye readied to leave, Donovan reached gently across the table and placed his hand on hers.

"Before we go," he said nervously, "I have something else to tell you. There's news about your old AP choral program."

They had swapped stories and given advice many times through the years. A hesitant glint in Donovan's eye told Faye that this news was personal. She tightened her shoulders in preparation.

"It's *him*?"

"Yes. It's Vogel."

Faye's mouth went dry at the sound of her high school choir director's name. *Vogel. Edward Vogel. Doctor Edward Vogel.* A confusing shame pulsed in the pit of Faye's stomach. She had not thought of Doctor Vogel in some time. Now, apprehension gathered, as if the vibrant memories of her youth were under threat of extinction. Images of Faye and her friends skipping through a European *piazza*, Doctor Vogel leading their tour, flashed to Faye's mind and then fizzled away.

"Last week I ran into a friend of a friend whose brother was in your Aquinas Prep class. He said Vogel is dying."

Faye's face whitened, as did the memory she had conjured. Friendships for life (hadn't they all promised?) had been short-lived, their loyalty brittle. Faye had not seen her AP friends in years; she had not seen Doctor Vogel in more than a decade. She had lost track of him as the consuming joy of motherhood had overtaken her. For so long, Faye had willed all those people away, painted over their faces in the mosaic of her life. Now, upon Donovan's words, terror flooded her brain. To survive, she had edged those years out of her consciousness. She grabbed hungrily with both hands, desperate to reclaim them.

II

FAYE REACHED BACK UNTIL SHE FOUND her first Aquinas Prep memory: the slushy machine. By Faye's first day of high school in September 1994, the cherry slush dispenser tucked between the gym and the multi-purpose room was inoperable. A rusted "Cool Treat" sign peaked out; a crack spread down the middle. Faye glimpsed a relic of her childhood, imagined the reverberating sound of a plastic cup being lowered down the chute, frozen red sweetness flooding in too fast and then stopping suddenly right at the cup's flimsy rim. That was the Aquinas Prep of the mid-'80s, when Faye's brother had begun her family's trek through the prestigious Citrus County Catholic school. Faye remembered sneaking out for a treat from the hot, sweaty gym, two quarters jingling in her palm. Back inside, the roar of the crowd excited her, and she watched with little girl amazement as the Aquinas Prep cheerleaders swung their hips in unison, forming perfect shapes and thrusting the smallest teen-aged girl high into the air above them, her silver pom poms sparkling, red hair ribbons bobbing up and down as she flew toward the ceiling and collapsed back to her squad's waiting arms. To eight-year-old Faye, Aquinas Prep cheerleaders were superstars, and Aquinas Prep was heaven itself.

Superstars lived everywhere at Aquinas Prep. Fans exalted Aquinas Prep's renowned football program. The most intense AP rivalries drew bigger crowds than the Los Angeles Rams in the early '90s, and local newspapers ran full page stories lauding the future prospects of boys barely old enough to drive themselves to practice. AP basketball teams racked up state championships year after year, drawing crowds in the thousands who ooh-ed and ahh-ed at the muscular young boys with baby faces and huge basketball-dunking palms.

Because it was a private school, Aquinas Prep required a qualifying entrance exam (though Faye suspected anyone who could pay could gain admission). The *AP Red and Gray* released send-off stories each year about the ninety-nine percent of graduates who attended college after graduation. Critics loved to hate Aquinas Prep, and those talented, wealthy, or fortunate enough to belong there flaunted their attachment to it. Aquinas Prep could be insular. Its faculty was composed largely of AP alumni, and most students counted themselves third or fourth in their family if not second generation AP Eagles. Two elements comprised Aquinas Prep culture: tradition and rules. Faye loved following rules—a good thing because Aquinas Prep had more than enough of them.

The day's first warning bell rang at 7:25 for zero period's 7:30 start, but well before that early morning hour, deans and teachers prowled the grounds, watching for any hijinks within AP's ivy covered gates. The ivy was both decorative and protective. Aquinas Prep folded inward rather than extending outward to the local community. The ivy said something private was going on there; the gates kept out the undesirables who watched AP rush by out the oversized windows of the Citrus County bus lines. Aquinas Prep was prestigious but not defined by wealth. Sure, many students drove in from the oceanside mansions of Sunset Bluffs or the high hills of Vista View, but the public schools in those districts counted more greatly swollen budgets and a much larger share of spoiled, rich kids and even more spoiled, rich parents. The magnetic glow of Aquinas Prep came from a solidly middle-class Catholic community that was on the move. Most Aquinas Prep families were upwardly mobile. They paid hefty tuition but racked up debt in order to do it. It was worth it, they told themselves, to secure their families a place in the AP tribe.

Despite its price tag, Aquinas Prep sat smack in the middle of Padre Diego, an arguably run-down city at the heart of Citrus County. *Dangerous* did not exactly describe the area, but, still, the primarily white AP parent boosters were nervous. The local population had increasingly turned immigrant and poor in the preceding decade. Aquinas Prep in fact bisected Padre Diego, its surrounding neighborhoods getting more dingy and dry, the people there less white and more poor, as one moved north from AP; the houses got more lavish, the entertainment and people more eclectic and rich as one moved south toward the sprawling Shoreline Plaza Mall and the Pacific Ocean. Administrators, deans, teachers, guards, and AP's strongest, most lauded students walked the halls and the grounds with a sense of confidence. Each strict rule and rigorous academic standard, each unbeatable athletic squad and award-winning drama troupe, each Bishop-led Mass and service trip across the ocean said attending Aquinas Prep was a *privilege*. And, dearest students, *don't ever forget that*.

Detentions abounded for tardiness, talking, back talking, disrespect, gum chewing, and, most common of all, untucked shirts and other breaches of uniform policy. Less frequent infractions included unremoved facial hair, earrings that fell below the earlobe, socks that showed the ankle, sweatshirts with any but Aquinas Prep or university logos, skirts rolled at the waist, and shorts rolled at the thigh cuff. By Faye's sophomore year, Aquinas Prep had instituted random drug testing, and the presence of deans, guards, and overly vigilant teachers ensured that Aquinas Prep students engaged in very little illicit activity on campus. Naturally, Aquinas Prep students from every high school caste hosted boozed-up parties with the occasional marijuana joint and an endless supply of cigarettes, both tobacco and clove. Hook-up culture and friend group in-fighting won the day as in all high school societies, and AP's two thousand students stratified themselves into the familiar social cliques that had been ordering adolescent friendships for as long as anyone could remember.

Officially, Catholicism was the heart of Aquinas Prep. Prayer began each class: prayer not only before Fr. Jerry's Religious Studies but before Mrs. Gauthier's Algebra II and Señor Parker's Honors Spanish and before Life Science and World History and Mrs. Chastain's American Literature after 1850. Mandatory service hour commitments and all-school Masses evinced the steadfast belief that Aquinas Prep was growing souls, not just students. And yet, something else seemed at the core of AP values. Aquinas Prep promised and delivered superior education and athletics, superior resources and opportunities. Students and parents coveted this high school experience because it emphasized Catholicism and community, because it spread strength and spirit, and because it forged connections. Most of all, Aquinas Prep Eagles—administrators, faculty, students, parents, alumni, and fans—sustained themselves off a single core belief: their affiliation with Aquinas Prep made them better than everyone else.

By sixteen, Faye was busy yet unbound. She was a smart kid who studied into the night, waited tables at Cal's on the weekends, swam AP swim team, and was tennis team captain, but she bounced between tennis friends, weekend co-workers, and honors project partners in her spare time. Until, that is, Faye met Bryn and their world began to take shape. By the end of junior year, Faye had found her purpose via the elite Chamber Singer Choir of the Aquinas Prep choral program. In the warmth of the after-school sun, Faye and Bryn lay on a small, grassy hill in the Aquinas Prep grotto; down one side, the great concrete Aquinas Prep eagle stood guard. A brick-lined path fanned out from the other slope, snaking its way to the grotto's center and a flower-crowned statue of the Virgin Mary. Faye loved these afternoons. Her friends' excited voices floated above Faye's closed eyes, each encapsulating the personalities that so overjoyed her—the musical lilt in Bryn's voice, Leah's monotonous practicality, Ian's always too-loud sarcasm. A spirit of friendship moved among them, melodies jumping out here and there as they rehearsed, replayed, and drank in the music pulsing through their teen-aged hearts. These were her people, and she was theirs.

From her spot on the hill, sixteen-year-old Faye could see the half-hidden entrance to Aquinas Prep's modest chapel, serious, quiet, enshrouded by stained glass. Neither Faye nor her friends thought about Donovan Presley.

Freshman year, Faye had seen Donovan's picture in the newspaper and had wondered about the shy young man who seemed so scared and scarred by the soil she now clenched as if it fed her very soul. Back then, Faye had not yet met any of the people with whom she now spent every day. Back then, Faye had sung in the Freshman Women's Chorus, taking Doctor Vogel's music theory exams in stride, quietly learning her music, and trying to blend with a community she felt a bit ill-suited for. Back then, Faye had attended communion service at lunch in the Aquinas Prep chapel by herself, always sitting against the side so she could exit quickly and never be expected to share a reflection on the day's Gospel.

Now, as junior year came to a close, Faye felt empowered and strong, less swallowed up by Aquinas Prep culture and more like she had carved a platform and climbed upon it to take in the view. She loved Aquinas Prep. Her friends and teachers and her choir director Doctor Vogel and her tennis coach Ms. Spinner and her swim coach Ms. Berta all loved her back. Faye had fought freshman year alienation and sophomore year confusion and had found, junior year, her first big time crush. A tiny spark of joy at the sight of Stuart Mendelsen had grown to a flame so intense it had consumed junior year for Faye and for all of her friends. That Stuart didn't like her back saddened Faye to say the least, but she felt in this adolescent crush the first seeds of love. For that, her days of crushing on Stu had been wonderful and exciting. A part of her was tired of moping. Every part of Bryn was tired of hearing Faye cry about Stuart. But Stuart was a senior and would graduate soon. Both he and his rejection of Faye would fade as she and her friends embarked on their senior year and grabbed hold of every dazzling adventure that was finally in their sights. Yes, Faye told herself, senior year would unfold quite nicely.

The grotto grass wavered in a breeze so slight Faye barely sensed it. The chapel's stained-glass windows fractured the spring light into tiny shards of color that bounced off the mahogany pews. Donovan Presley had met his fate in that chapel, had been caressed, cunningly groomed, and violated by Fr. Mick in that sacred space, its air teeming with the warm smoke of extinguished incense. But ten years' worth of the Good News and the consecrated body, of loyal school girls in pressed plaid skirts and Fr. Jerry's wide, consoling smile had easily displaced Donovan's trembling hands and sweating palms. Aquinas Prep prestige and mystique had erased the quivering stomach that had lurched into his throat and tried to snuff out his breath. Time passed and everyone (but Donovan) moved on. The Aquinas Prep community and the Citrus County public took what Aquinas Prep offered. The archway of Mary's grotto, the chapel windows, the gym floor, the choir room risers, and the 300 building's heavy double doors were each inscribed with Aquinas Prep's revered precept: *To God Be The Glory*.

Officially, Aquinas Prep administrators and faculty followed strict, moral protocol, their personal lives no longer personal because they reflected AP culture and were thus subject to review and criticism. Unofficially, AP faculty knew to toe the line and under what circumstances those lines could be smudged. Gay teachers and unmarried cohabitating teachers did so discreetly. The alcoholics kept their coffee only slightly spiked. Smokers indulged during free periods in their cars off campus. Coaches sent surrogates up and down the state to secretly recruit top players while allowing Aquinas Prep to retain deniability. More than anything, AP teachers pledged allegiance to Aquinas Prep's reputation.

Teachers at Aquinas Prep came in several types. There were AP lifers, hard-core Catholic traditionalists, young upstarts, overgrown dumb jocks, and those with religious vocations (past or present). Most were southern California locals, though some had arrived at Aquinas Prep by way of Catholic high schools in the Midwest or as transplants who had come west following dreams or seeking futures that had ultimately unraveled. The girls chased Coach Jeff Martinez, and he chased them back. He was strong and coffee-colored with a wide, bright smile and thick, jet-black hair. At thirty, he seemed old to the students but incredibly young to the other AP faculty. Jeff had returned to Aquinas Prep to coach junior varsity basketball and teach typing just three months after concluding his stint playing college ball at Augusta University just north of Portland. Four years playing strong center had also earned him a Bachelor's degree in business, though Jeff Martinez had never planned to put that degree to use. Half-way through Jeff's senior year, famed AP head coach Greg McCaulley (nephew to the even more acclaimed Bishop Jim McCaulley) had promised Jeff a job coaching the Aquinas Prep boys JV basketball team as soon as he graduated and made his way back to Citrus County. In the six years since joining the faculty, Coach Martinez had led the boys JV team to six league titles and two Southern Region championships, had fathered for his wife two sweet-cheeked children (one more was on the way when Faye first saw Coach Martinez in 1997), and had found the teen-aged girls of Aquinas Prep such a boon to his ego that he had finally started flirting back. At the Las Vegas High School Invitational Tournament the previous spring, Coach Martinez had cornered in his hotel room one of the team's stat girls, an Aquinas Prep sophomore, and asked her to undress for him while he masturbated.

Thirty some years prior, Betty Frances, now AP Vice Principal, had planned out of high school to enter the convent, had been planning a vocation to religious life for as long as her memory reached back. She remembered the religious fervor that had gripped her on the day of her First Communion, her hands trembling at the altar as the priest had placed the holy disk so gently on her tongue. When her vocation turned out not to be one, the disappointment in herself and, to be honest, in God Himself began to gnaw at something deep inside her. And so Aquinas Prep became work and family all in one. She never married, had never fallen for a man the way she had for Christ Himself. Her roles in Church and school were quite constrained now, merely that of arbiter, keeping the peace among troubled faculty and students whose everyday refusal of propriety threatened to unravel everything she revered.

Jaqueline DeGroot took the brunt of student abuse at Aquinas Prep. Students snickered behind her back because of her imposing, amorphous physique. Ms. DeGroot stood out because she was more abrasive and less polished than most AP faculty. She was unmarried, was not (and had never been) called to religious life, and did not court student acceptance. She did not care a stitch if the students liked her. She had not come to Aquinas Prep to be liked. She came as a theological scholar, and, as such, she delighted in passing knowledge to the kids and charting the future endeavors of her brightest students. Jaqueline was well-liked on the faculty but still found herself largely alone on school grounds. If she had to say, she would call Doctor Edward Vogel her closest colleague, and that certainly wasn't saying much. They had never socialized nor eaten lunch in the faculty lounge together. Edward had never been to her home and did not know her birthday. What's more, Jaqueline did not especially like Edward. She admired his talent and was proud, on AP's behalf, of the choral program Edward had built after the previous choir director had left under scandalous circumstances. (There were rumors that Edward's predecessor had been caught after hours schtupping a newly hired biology teacher on his office desk.) Because Edward so often traveled for choral competitions and took overnight concert trips with a bus full of impressionable young girls, he regularly needed a female faculty member to tag along as chaperone. From the start, Jaqueline was the only woman to volunteer for the spot. Traveling Europe and New York and up and down the California coast, Jaqueline had gotten to know Edward. She enjoyed his company, but something about him gave her pause. He was too impressed with himself to care much for the opinions of others. And yet, beneath his stern facade, Edward seemed to be courting the students. *Too close*, Jaqueline thought. She sensed something there that shouldn't be—a sense of intimacy, misplaced if not wholly inappropriate.

  The Aquinas Prep choir director was a midwestern transplant from Kansas by way of the University of Michigan and the only AP faculty member to hold a Doctorate degree. Edward Vogel stood out because he refused to blend in. Walking the Aquinas Prep quad in shiny leather Oxfords with a square cut cap toe, Edward held himself erect, balancing his weight in his heels, an idiosyncratic stance that indeed made him seem (despite his unimpressive five-foot-six-inch stature) to look down on the rest of the Aquinas Prep community. In eight years, Edward had not forged friendships with his colleagues. He thought them too frivolous; they thought him too arrogant. After a crushing break-up (a *betrayal* is what it was, an *abandonment* by the only woman he had ever loved), Edward had joined the AP faculty gladly at first, allowing the work to consume him because his other life plans had fallen apart. The longer he stayed at Aquinas Prep, the more his dreams had dwindled. Leaving the University of Michigan a heavily decorated composer, Edward had planned to travel the world and to conduct the most elite orchestras in the world's most grand concert halls. Neither of those things happened. Edward dove headfirst into building the AP choral program, and in a blink, Aquinas

Prep choir had become everything he had. He tried each year, amidst so much other work, to compose at least one choral piece for his choirs to perform. Really, though, composing became less central as Edward focused on a more challenging repertoire and a more expansive competition travel schedule. They started with small, local competitions and over the years had developed a reputation for winning top honors at choral festivals across the state and the nation. As his successes grew, so too did his allotted budget and the trust placed in him by Principal Murphy. Increased trust also meant less oversight.

By the late '90s, Edward made the long walk each morning from his mailbox in the faculty lounge to his choir room, a standalone bungalow on the far south side of campus, past the lunch benches and nearly to the outlying athletic fields, and stayed put for most of the day. He thought some days during free period or lunch that he might saunter back toward the faculty lounge and strike up a conversation with Jan Jacobi, who taught freshman life science, or Jenny Mitchell, a bit of an odd duck who taught ceramics and 2D design. On nearly every occasion, Edward thought better of it and stayed in his office, eating a lunch he packed at home and listening to the sounds of the kids who preferred to eat lunch clustered on the choir room's risers instead of out in the crowd. Technically, students were required to eat at the lunch benches and could not hang around in classrooms (or choir rooms) unless scheduled to be there. Edward liked having the students within earshot. Like Edward, most of the choir kids lived on the social margins and were happy to be there. He offered the choir room as a place they could claim, and they made him feel less alone. Certainly, his faculty interactions were polite, but in a culture so preoccupied with athletics, his position in the arts made him feel a bit outside. This outsider status, to Edward's mind, conveyed a kind of elitism. Still, it was lonely.

Because he cared little about sports and even less about looking hip to the other young teachers, Edward did not exactly fit the Aquinas Prep mold. On the other hand, because he demanded excellence from his students, turned out award-winning choirs, taught college-level curricula, and was a stickler for crisply ironed shirts, solemn prayer, and self-discipline, Edward personified the Aquinas Prep mission. For everyone, life at Aquinas Prep meant a series of trade-offs and misdirection. Personal affairs and mild infractions of the AP moral code among the faculty were swept quietly under the rug as long as teachers hushed up AP's secrets and brought acclaim for excellent performance in any given sector. Edward may have been a bit brusque and, it was whispered, a bit too *friendly* with his students, but his résumé gleamed and his choral program soared. When rumors of his mild intoxication at a choir banquet or his inappropriate comments about the revealing curve of a student's blouse floated to Vice Principal Frances's office, she shut the door and buried her head in a stack of travel brochures: the AP choir had once again been invited to perform at an audience for the Holy Father in Rome. That was all the information about Doctor Edward Vogel the AP administration cared to record.

By June of 1997, more than four hundred students had sung their way through Edward's choirs. A number of them had gone on to professional careers in theater and vocal performance; others had slunk by with minimal effort and treated choir class like a social club. Edward had noticed Faye right from the start because she was demure and perfectly behaved. Edward placed a premium on respect and propriety, and so Faye endeared herself to him with her discipline and general maturity. The Aquinas Prep choir operated on a hierarchical system in which one gained power through any number of vaguely-defined channels. Outsiders assumed that vocal talent topped that list, but it did not. What was it? A certain combination of talent, attitude, and some kind of undefined gravitas ruled the day. The students knew this. Strictly speaking, the most important honor was not earned. Doctor Vogel bestowed a certain privilege on the students he most favored. He saw in them exactly what all students needed—a sense of devotion to his program and the desire never to let him down. As their senior year began, Faye and her friends were perfecting that allegiance.

So in the summer of 1997, the Aquinas Prep Choir readied to tour Europe. Peter's Way Travel Agency took care of the planning. They set tour dates and arranged accommodations and connected Doctor Vogel to the who's who of liturgical choirs along the pilgrimage's planned path from Paris to Rome. Now what remained were six weeks of daily rehearsals and nightly anticipation. By the start of senior year, Faye and her friends would be *bona fide* world travelers. Europe rehearsals began promptly each June morning at 9:00, breaking for snack at 11, for lunch at 1, and for closing prayer at 2:30. In the first few days of summer, Faye felt a shift in her position. Stuart, Lauren, Joachim, and all the seniors had graduated. Faye and her friends were top of the class, now. The privilege of Doctor Vogel's most coveted attention could be theirs. And immediately, it was. Doctor Vogel sidled up to the spots where Faye and her friends were clustered together whispering and giggling. He crouched beside them on the hill or leaned against the riser behind them as Faye and her friends ran through the previous night's adventures or made evening plans. He pointed to her more often during rehearsal—*Does everyone see how Faye is standing at attention, eyes on me?* He needled her, lightly, jokingly—*Everyone take care of their voices this weekend. No yelling and NO SMOKING,* he would say, raising his eyebrows and pointing two fingers playfully toward Faye. He moved in when he sensed she was reeling—*Are you okay?* He had mouthed the words silently between songs one Thursday morning, responding to Faye's tear-brimmed eyes. (She and Bryn had been bickering all morning about a secret Leah had let slip. Teen-aged emotions were running high but the scuffle would quickly pass.) A new sense of importance descended on Faye. She felt Doctor Vogel watching and entrusting her. As she took this mantle of leadership, she dug ever deeper into the ground beneath her. She felt tiny tendrils of life climbing up through her insides, flowering around and within her. Yes, she was happy here. She and her best friends, their senior year upcoming, had grabbed hold with fearless and uninhibited wonder.

Faye stood second alto between Bryn and Leah; their friends Ian, Tommy, and James hovered from the tenor riser behind them. The whole group learned swiftly and joyfully, their young bodies swaying this way and that as four- and six-part harmonies blended, swelling and diminishing at Edward's direction. They ate potato chips and picked apart squashed peanut butter sandwiches at lunch amidst raucous laughter. Once, Leah dared Faye to sneak past the guard to smoke a cigarette on break, and she did, squatting behind an old Volkswagen Bug and ducking her head further each time a car passed. Doctor Vogel made jokes when rehearsals were going well and spoke with derision when the kids disappointed him. Mornings at Aquinas Prep were gloomy; by the time they emerged from rehearsal, the metal door clanging as they burst through, the coastal marine layer had burned away to reveal bright blue sky and a day unfolding with possibility.

Summer nights in '97 brought blazing bonfires and sweeping sunsets. Faye's group went to the beach only at night, she and her friends bundled in thick red and white Aquinas Prep Choir sweatshirts, the corded hoods pulled tightly over ponytailed hair leaving exposed the ovals of their expectant adolescent faces. Faye's older sister Bridget was a daytime beachgoer and sunbather whose friends lathered on tanning oil and sizzled in the sun, nonchalantly tracking the boys who gawked at their ballerina physique and soaked up sexual tension with the sun. Faye's crowd was of a different sort, turning inward to find themselves, always talking and listening, planning futures and pondering philosophies. They drove through Citrus County's maze of freeways blasting classical music with cracked windows, smoking cigarettes with gold-tipped filters, and eating tortilla chips dunked in bright orange liquid cheese, always walking the line between childhood and adulthood. They talked about their crushes and their families, and, of course, they talked about sex. Faye knew a few kids who, like her sister, had done the deed in high school. The girl who sat next to her in Life Science had been caught giving a blow job in the AP gym parking lot during a basketball game the first week of freshman year. When the rumors finally died down, Faye had hesitantly worked up the courage to ask the girl what it had been like. "It's just like sucking on your skin," the girl had said, modeling on her own index finger while Faye's stomach flipped.

Three years later, Faye's knowledge of sex had grown only slightly. She and her friends whispered in shivering huddles at the beach, asking each other silly questions. The boys told lurid stories about masturbating with household items. Faye gasped and scoffed and felt better because they were all so lovably young and had no idea what they were doing. Faye never felt alone at sixteen. She and her friends harmonized and rehearsed, they laughed at funny lyrics, and they felt a fire of inspiration running through them. Even at night, counting stars on Bryn's driveway high up in the hills or roasting marshmallows at the beach, Aquinas Prep choir was never far from their minds. Always, even away from the Aquinas Prep campus, Doctor Vogel, because he was their director, held their center.

Each of Faye's friends was each one's best friend, but Bryn and Faye had been the first. Bryn and Faye's friendship had blossomed quickly when they joined Chamber Singers junior year. Shared nervousness became shared disappointment as each girl nursed an unrequited crush—Faye's on Stuart Mendelsen and Bryn's on Santino Reddleman. At sixteen, the two young girls were just that. They were *girls*. They circled around Stuart's oceanside neighborhood some nights in Faye's blue Mustang and scoped out his scene. They left anonymous love notes on Santino's beat-up green pick up truck under cover of dark and ran away laughing. They joked and blew bubbles with chewing gum and lay in the grass picking flower stems and spinning romantic fantasies that made them blush. They were both small in stature. Faye's athleticism and regular workouts made her strong though she was petite. Faye gathered her naturally curly hair into a messy ponytail or wore it pulled tightly into braids. Always the braids began the day neat and striking, but as the school day wore on, frizzy strands worked their way out, wanting so desperately to escape and curl away. Bryn's wide smile and bright teeth filled her narrow face, her eyes deep set, her eyebrows arched as if in surprise. Around Aquinas Prep and across the gear shift in her Mustang, Faye slipped her hand in Bryn's whenever she could. Bryn's empathy and warmth were contagious. She battled for the underdog, soothed the humiliated, and always buoyed Faye's brokenheartedness or self-consciousness. Her compassion came with a biting disdain for all those who perpetrated unfairness or made others feel small. Bryn's parents—Rudra and Bess Appammaraffil—had emigrated to California from India in the early '70s and fallen in love instantly upon meeting in a microbiology seminar at Stanford. Rudra and Bess were conservative, stern, and unyielding. Despite Bess's advanced degrees and progressive education, she demanded propriety, traditional values, and modesty for her three daughters. Bryn was especially thin, her legs like deep brown roots effortlessly carrying her slight, wispy figure. Her hair stretched dark, straight, and long down her back to the tops of her thighs. In sixteen years, Bryn's hair had never been cut.

And so, Bryn's haircut started all the trouble.

Bryn watched a bit wistfully as Faye's sister Bridget trimmed and styled Faye's hair for their impending flight to Europe. By morning, they would be Paris-bound. A sweet, exotic aroma floated in the air above Bryn's seat. It was the scent of fancy shampoo, of glamour, of the kind of beauty she had never allowed herself to want.

Bridget locked eyes with Bryn's mirrored image as Bryn sat waiting on a cushy divan behind the stylist's chair.

"What about you?"

"My parents won't let me cut my hair," she said with a snark. "My mom would kill me."

"How long is it?" Bridget asked.

Bryn turned profile and unfurled the thick coil of hair she had mounted in a figure eight on the back of her head. The hair cascaded down, dry and crimped from being fastened.

"You need to condition your hair," Bridget said not quite kindly. "And you really need to cut it. It will grow back so much healthier if you get rid of a lot of that weight."

Faye and Bryn beheld Bridget with a mix of admiration and skepticism. She was all make-up and confidence and popularity. She was the kind of woman these girls would never be. She had been an Aquinas Prep cheerleader, a girl who considered choir kids uncool. Now, while Faye and Bryn took summer study classes for college prep exams and set their sights on choral concerts across Europe, Bridget was out of cosmetology school and working as a professional stylist. Bryn eyed Faye in the mirror.

"I think you should do it," Faye said. "It will grow back. I mean, how bad can your parents' reaction possibly be?"

Bryn knew exactly how bad. Rudra and Bess had kicked her oldest sister out of the house after discovering a marijuana pipe in her pajama drawer. But, Bryn thought, her sister had thrived since then. She kept a neat apartment all to herself, worked full time as receptionist at a law office, and could stretch her arms wide to a future free of her parents' demands. Bryn dreamt of that freedom, too. Why not start now? Bridget threw a pitying look toward Bryn. The look challenged and prodded her.

"Let's do it," she said firmly.

Faye paced the hallway frantically. By the front door, her flowered suitcase bulged at the zippered seams. She called Ian.

"Bryn's parents are so mad," she said. "I don't think they are going to let her go to Europe. They won't even let me talk to her."

"Why the hell did your sister cut Bryn's hair the day before the trip?"

"I didn't think it mattered that much. Bryn said she wanted to do it."

"Well, we're screwed now. What can we do? What time did you last call her?"

Faye stopped walking and flexed her leg. She stretched her neck side to side and breathed deeply. What a mess. Bryn and Faye had plans. They would room together and explore together and sneak cigarettes at night and have two weeks away from parents to stay up talking as late as they wanted. Their plans were crumbling fast, now. Bryn's dad had berated Faye the last time she called. Faye's own father had never even yelled at her like that. In a house like Faye's, it was strange to imagine an adult being so impulsive or so unreasonable, but Rudra meant business. He was irate.

"Do not call here again," he had said resolutely. "Bryn cannot talk to you and she cannot go on a trip because we cannot trust her. Good-bye."

"I do not want to talk to her parents again," Faye said. "I suppose there is one other thing we can do."

Ian hesitated, eager to push the problem onto Faye and away from himself.

"You should call Doctor," he said. "That way he can call Bryn's parents and work it out."

The thought of calling Doctor Vogel at home unnerved and excited Faye. The kids had his home phone number. Doctor was like that. But she had never called him, had not imagined why she would ever need to. Once before a concert at Cal State Fulton, Doctor had invited the entire Chamber choir over for a barbecue. Faye remembered seeing Doctor standing apart from the group in his kitchen, leaning against the sink like a new kid that didn't know how to blend in. His eyes had locked on hers, then, the moment feeling awkward and intimate, like he was asking something of her that she did not understand.

"It's really late," Faye said. "It's almost eleven, and we need to be at the airport at six tomorrow morning. I'm sure he's asleep."

"Just call until he answers," Ian said, unbothered. "It's our only chance."

Edward answered on the first ring, his voice groggy from a long day. A cigar burned in the ashtray on his piano, a glass of whiskey beside it. The ice had melted down and a pool of sweat oozed out from all sides.

"Oh, hi," Faye said nervously. "This is Faye."

Faye. Edward's tired mind snapped to attention.

"Well hello, Faye," he said. "What's going on? Is everything okay?"

"No, everything is not okay. It's kind of a long story, but Bryn got in trouble and her parents are threatening to not let her go to Europe."

Edward ran a hand through his hair and took a drink. Eight years had conditioned him to student drama. He assumed the situation was not actually so dire. Yet, parental involvement presented a wrinkle he could not ignore.

Edward laughed lightly. "Tell me what you two did to get her in trouble."

"My sister cut Bryn's hair."

Faye felt how ridiculous she sounded. She knew the perfectly condescending grimace on Doctor's face at this moment. Would it be condescension or exasperation? She had grown accustomed to seeing both from him toward the students over the years.

"Your sister cut Bryn's hair."

"Right."

"And now Bryn cannot go to Europe."

"Right," Faye said, as if she were making sense. "But," she continued, "her hair looks amazing."

Edward dropped down into the swivel chair at his desk and chuckled at Faye's remark.

"That's hardly relevant."

Faye's voice turned soft and pleading. "This is a disaster. Can't you do something to fix it?"

The plaintive lilt in Faye's voice enticed Edward. He drained his glass and began scanning AP choir files looking for Bryn's contact info. Almost immediately, he closed the document and emitted a deep sigh.

"I really would like to help you, Faye, but I cannot go calling a parent in the middle of the night and getting involved in their decisions."

Silence stretched across the line.

"I thought for sure you could help us."

The pause grew. The air thickened. Edward sensed an intimacy he could not describe. Faye asked this of him and expected him to win the day.

"I really cannot get involved," he began. "I'm sure it will be alright. Bryn's parents are not going to forfeit the three thousand dollars they have put into this trip. It'll blow over by morning."

Faye had not thought about the money. She knew, now, that Doctor was right. Everything would be alright in the morning. The crisis averted, Edward and Faye held to the phone line, the moment's awkwardness keeping them in place. Faye had not wanted to call. Now, she wanted to keep him talking. Something slightly different in his voice intrigued her. Who is Doctor Vogel, she suddenly thought, alone in his house, answering her call, wearing (she imagined) something other than his school clothes? For his part, Edward drank in Faye's honeyed, entreating tone. He could not conjure an image of her house, what it must be like, and so he matched her voice to the picture of sweet obedience he had of her in the choir room at Aquinas Prep, her hair a mess of curls, her eyes so sympathetic they seemed almost tearful. He wished he could see her right now.

"Well, I guess I better go now," Faye stammered.

"Yes, better get some sleep," Edward returned. "I will see you in the morning."

Edward held the phone aloft after the decisive click of Faye's disconnection. A buzzing energy coursed through his limbs. Suddenly, the morning felt too far away. Edward took a drink of whiskey and felt his blood warming, a sexual energy stirring between his thighs. He willed the sensation away.

Edward couldn't help noticing his female students. The changes in some girls forced themselves into his consciousness. Sometimes he pushed the images away; at other times, he stoked them. Adolescent girls just opening to the world had flirted with him through the years. They spoke suggestively and flipped their long ponytails, their Oxford shirts buttoned too tightly across their growing breasts. They did these things, Edward understood, not because they were attracted to him. His freshman girls became women right before his eyes. They tilted their heads and batted their eyes and tried on womanhood because it was time for it. His job, he knew, demanded decorum and avoidance. He should take these insinuations and flirtations like he suffered their sweaty hormonal bodies filling the choir room with rank smells during fall heat waves, like he trudged through the voice changes that came to many of his Men's Ensemble at exactly the wrong time. They came to him as kids and left as adults. Over the years, Edward had attached himself emotionally to far too many of them. He was unmarried and childless. His brother, two sisters, and several nieces he saw on rare visits to the Midwest. Other than sex, an uncommon treat on a smattering of blind dates and set-ups, Edward derived his most intense feelings—glory in a performance, pride in a student accepted to a prestigious university or renowned chorale—from his students. He poured his energy and his heart back into them. Each year, he lost another group of nearly matured young adults heading blissfully into the unknown with a sense of expectant joy. Each year, dozens of fresh new faces arrived, and Edward felt the process begin anew.

Edward had noticed Faye's development over the previous two school years. He could spot a good student on a crowded riser from across the room, and Faye had impressed him immediately with her rapt attention to his instructions and her desire to please. During her first placement sequence, he had strained to hear her voice over the reverberating clang of the piano in the tiny audition room. Unlike most of his students, Faye did not like to hear herself sing and never wanted to sing alone. But Edward could hear Faye sing whenever he listened for her. Faye's voice was steady, strong, and dependable, blending and fortifying. She had seemed disinterested for the first few months and unassuming after that. After her second summer away, Faye came back to Aquinas Prep changed in stature and confidence. Already a junior and almost sixteen, Faye had finally gained a few pounds and a few inches. Edward's eyes occasionally rested on the hardly noticeable curves developing beneath her blouse and around her hips. Her body enticed him less, though, than what flowed out from beneath this previously detached exterior.

Increasingly, the problem these days was that kids didn't care about anything. Edward cared about everything being just right. And so did Faye. Faye devoted herself to Chamber Singers and to Edward. She helped him organize and grade papers, she made encouragement baskets for all the kids before concerts, and she let down whatever walls had been keeping her apart from the group's emotional center. What's more, Faye always included Edward like he was one of the group. Edward saw in Faye a leader who could craft and cajole and gather his choirs toward him and toward each other. Faye seemed to know, like Edward did, that a choir can be the voice of God, ushering forth a divine spirit only when its members enjoy consummate unity. Edward would win Faye's heart and, with it, a love that would perfect them all.

They arrived! Golden angels stood guard atop the Paris Opera House as Edward corralled his students to the steps for a photo. Edward soaked in the history, acting as stand in tour guide until the meet-up with their Peter's Way official chaperone. The students soaked in the love and independence and hormonal chaos that sprang organically from their loud, young bodies. The balmy, thick summer air sweated their *Aquinas Prep European Tour* tee shirts to their backs, but the heat wasn't bothersome. Jet lag was for the old. Faye and her friends, straight off the ten hour flight and ten hour time change, sang and called out to each other as they roamed the streets in search of breakfast.

"Stay with the group," Edward called out. "There are pickpockets in these streets and they are looking for people who are not paying attention to their surroundings."

Faye and a few others instinctively checked their book bag zippers and darted their eyes left and right. Most of the students carried on as before.

"Keep your packs in front of you!" Edward said this repeatedly as his group of teen-aged travelers moved, some quickly and some not so quickly, through Parisian crosswalks.

The horns of yellow taxis blared as locals bobbed and weaved around astonished tourists the likes of the Aquinas Prep choir.

At the hotel restaurant, Faye eyed the buffet of cold meats, thick sauces, and soft eggs suspiciously. Bryn heaped roasted vegetables and crisp toast points onto her plate while Faye picked carefully through a fresh fruit melange looking for strawberries. Tiny wisps of hair tensed at the base of Faye's neck when Edward walked up close behind her in line.

"You don't seem impressed with this spread." Faye detected a kind of condescending tenderness. "There's pastries at the other end of the table," he said.

Faye felt the warmth off Edward as he leaned over her shoulder and eyed her nearly empty plate. She hid her embarrassment, not wanting to appear too juvenile. She had not thought about how foreign the food in Europe would be. She looked toward the distant end of a long stretch of white-clothed tables. A puffy pile of croissants and breads teetered on several raised platters. She breathed a small sigh of relief but tried not to react.

"Thanks for the tip," she said quietly. "I love croissants."

Faye's eyes met Bryn's across the room. She smiled at Faye, a tiny coffee cup suspended in mid-air as she watched her friend. Faye chose a large, flaky croissant off the pile. She sensed Edward's gaze still upon her, but when she looked back, his attention was focused down on what Faye thought a putrid-looking plate of smoked salmon and herbs.

Leah's hand brushed the back of Faye's as their bodies caught and surrendered to the *Ave Maria*'s rhythm. Aquinas Prep sang many renditions of the Hail Mary in Latin, French, Russian, and English. Faye adored the Victoria's austere version the most because its harmonies each stood their ground. The soprano line did not dominate the rest as so often soprano voices did. Leah, Bryn, and Faye were all altos. Altos fortified. They grounded. Sopranos dramatized. They alarmed and ran shrill, jumping schizophrenically along the scale. Altos held deep emotion. They never let go.

Each voice tensed and quivered as the song closed. At the long, crescendoing *Amen*, everyone relaxed. An audible release of held breath ushered out as Edward gently touched together the soft pads at the tips of his thumbs and fingers. Each set of teen-aged eyes stared at Edward's hands as he quieted them. Immediately after, whispers and shouts rolled through the group. The teens were raucous and rollicking, wide awake with adrenaline and glee as they climbed the stairs from the basement rehearsal space to the richly decorated lobby of the *Hotel Regina Louvre*. Happiness and exhaustion descended upon Edward. The kids' energy enlivened him. Though their constant need of attention tired him, Edward loved to be in their midst. Night had fallen during their evening rehearsal. When they emerged from the basement, the hotel's multi-paned windows showed a darkened city.

"Straight to your rooms and straight to sleep," Edward told them all. "We have two morning concerts and a very long bus ride tomorrow."

Faye lingered behind the rest. Edward turned his attention to her when he saw she was waiting.

"Is it okay if Leah and Bryn switch rooms tonight? Leah wants to room with me instead of her roommate."

Though disruption to any plan rankled Edward, he wanted to give Faye what she wanted. Chaperoning teenagers meant saying *no* more often than they wanted him to. Playing favorites could invite even more problems.

"Our rooms are right next to each other anyway," Faye continued. "It'll be an easy switch."

Edward smiled with his lips closed.

"Yes, Leah can room with you tonight. But I do not want any horsing around or causing trouble."

Faye returned Edward's smile. "You know I never cause trouble."

"Everyone goes straight to sleep," Edward cautioned.

As Faye turned to leave, he called her back.

"Faye," Edward said in a low voice. "Don't tell anyone else that I let you girls trade. We can't have all of these kids room hopping. This is just for you."

Creaks and groans rose from the worn stairs as Faye climbed upward to her room. Doctor's voice echoed in her head. *Just for you*, she heard him saying. The feeling of such affection thrilled her. She could not name this sensation that squeezed her insides. Both Bryn and Leah waited expectantly in the hall. Faye smiled wide.

"He said *yes*."

Long after Doctor Vogel called lights out, Faye sat languidly in her hotel room's window seat. The end of her cigarette blazed red with each puff. The girls felt too excited to sleep but too exhausted to stay awake. As the AP choir went to bed, the streets of Paris awoke. Faye and Leah felt the noise level slowly rising from a moderate din to an intense cacophony of shouts and scuffles. Carousing Parisian crowds sang songs and clinked pints. Bastille Day celebrations spilled out from pubs and cafes to the maze of streets that stretched out from their hotel. Bright bursts of fire exploded in the sky, the red, white, and blue of revolutionary France lighting up trash-strewn alleys and brooding gargoyles. A palpable energy wafted up to the window where Faye sat smoking and thinking about the year ahead.

"The fireworks are so magical," Faye said. "What a night to be in Paris."

"Call Bryn," Leah suggested. "If she isn't awake, she's missing out."

"We're not supposed to be using the phone," Faye cautioned. "Doctor will go ballistic if we get caught being up or making calls this late."

Leah brushed off Faye's concerns.

"There's literally no way to get caught using the phone. You can blame me if we get in trouble."

The bedside phone buzzed red just as Edward stepped out of the shower. A terse, French-accented English came across the line.

"Pardon, Doctor Vogel. This is the front desk. You asked that I inform you of any telephone use in your collection of rooms. I'm sorry to report that there are phone calls being made from room 602 and room 604, repeatedly."

The reverberating boom of fireworks sounded as Edward descended a flight of stairs and walked the long hallway to Faye's room. He knocked firmly and heard a frantic scurrying on the other side of the door. He knocked again. Faye allowed a sliver of entry to the room. She squinted her eyes and pretended to have been sleeping. Edward looked down his nose at her.

"Did I wake you?" he asked with false concern.

Faye feigned confusion. "Yes. We've been asleep a long time."

Edward nodded as if he believed her. "I'm sorry," he said. "I just wanted to make sure you were not using the telephone in your room. It's far too late for that."

Surprise registered in Faye's eyes.

"Of course not. Good night, Doctor."

Leah laughed into her pillow as Faye closed the door.

"I stand corrected," she said incredulously. "How could he have known we were on the phone?"

Faye spoke with much less amusement than Leah.

"We better get to sleep."

Leah whispered over her shoulder as she dialed Bryn through the hotel switchboard.

"Why would we sleep now? Doctor has already been here and has gone back to his room."

On the first two treks from his room to Faye's, Edward had walked light-heartedly and amused. He would have some fun with these girls tonight. When Faye lied to him a third time, annoyance and real irritation crept into his voice.

"Enough of this, Faye," he said. "The switchboard tells me when you use the phone. Stop lying to me. Nothing angers me more than a person who lies. I'm disappointed in you girls."

Faye felt too small to speak. Edward's mouth turned down with disappointment and disaffection.

"Especially you," he said right to Faye's quivering lips. "Now go to sleep."

Edward turned on his heels and walked briskly down the hall. Faye dropped to the floor and started crying. To fail Doctor Vogel was unbearable. In the scolding tone of his voice, Faye felt her status as Doctor's most prized student slipping away. Against her will, against all reason, panic overcame her.

"I have to go fix this," she said to Leah.

Faye moved hurriedly down the hall without forethought. A trance-like desperation pushed her forward with such determination that she hardly heard Leah calling out to her.

Leah half-shouted in a raised whisper to Faye's retreating figure.

"Faye, come back. There's nothing to fix. We're not even in trouble."

Faye knocked hard, too loudly, on Edward's hotel room door. In the seconds before he opened it, words flooded her mind. Tears pricked at the back of her eyes. Edward pulled the door open with authority. Faye's words spewed forth in a tear-choked voice.

"I'm sorry I lied to you. I didn't want to get Bryn in trouble. I thought that it would be okay if we were talking on the phone as long as we were quiet. We only called Bryn's room. I need you to know that I don't lie and I always do what you want and I don't want you to be mad at me. I don't want you to be mad at me—"

Edward held a toothbrush in one hand and looked confused by her presence in his doorway. His expression sobered then embarrassed her. He seemed disinterested by this perplexing emotional outburst. His eyes registered no anger nor compassion. The knowledge of her own smallness washed over Faye. She wore the blue knit pajamas her mom had bought especially for this trip. They could not hide her shame.

Clearly, thought Faye, *he doesn't even care if I'm upset*. The revelation humiliated her. As quickly as she had come, before Edward uttered a word, Faye disappeared back down the hall.

Rain as from buckets had dumped on the city and then off again all day. Through most of the storm, Edward, the choir, and the chaperones had watched the rain pelting against the windows of their tour bus. The drive across the Franco-German border from Paris to Freiburg stretched eight hours instead of six as heavy traffic, silt-covered roads, and slow-moving teen rest stops slowed the trip. While Edward talked disinterestedly with Jaqueline DeGroot about her time teaching catechism at his old parish up north, Faye leaned her forehead against the cold window and watched rain drops race each other from side to side, surprised each time a rogue drop turned sharply off its path and headed straight for the edge of the pane. She replayed the night's embarrassment in a bird's eye view, seeing herself a tiny supplicant cowering at Doctor Vogel's hotel room door. Each time the image flashed before her,

Faye's flowery knit pajamas made her look more childlike and insignificant. She was close to tears now as she had been last night. Doctor had ignored her at breakfast (or so she thought), and now the rain made the day dreary and precluded her and Leah from sneaking a cigarette behind the restrooms on their infrequent stop-offs. The only remaining solace was the landscape, so Faye watched it slide by and waited to arrive in Germany. Between cities, Europe seemed a never-ending sprawl of countryside and livestock. Even in the rain, clusters of sheep dotted the hillsides, each group reviving Faye's wonder. *To whom did all these sheep belong?* She had seen no ranches or ranchers or living structures for hundreds of miles. Through the rain-soaked windows, the country was an impressionist masterpiece. Its blurred edges reminded Faye of Mary Poppins and the wet erasure of chalk drawings, their magical promise swirling to the sewer in a dirty mix of color.

Before he reached her row of seats, Faye could sense Doctor Vogel moving about the bus. Leah poked Faye's rib and jerked her thumb toward the aisle as he began his slow walk from behind the driver to the bus's mid-point where Faye and Leah had been whiling away the day. He glanced this way and that as he walked, curiously cataloguing her classmates' activities and saying a word now and then. She could tell by his short responses that most had asked how long until they could get off this damn bus. The raucous singing and jovial word games had died down in the last hour. Almost everyone was listless and bored now, reading silently, sleeping, or staring, as Faye was, out the windows. To steady himself as the bus slowly rocked, Doctor Vogel held with each hand to the rails that ran the length of the bus above the seats. Faye found herself sizing him up. For a man who was not very tall, Doctor Vogel's strong posture always commanded attention. He walked sure-footedly and with purpose even when there was nowhere to go. In his eyes, though, Faye discerned tiny pin pricks of vulnerability. She sensed, as he approached, that all his presence was a knowing act, carefully constructed to hide a kind of loneliness. As he reached to grip the bars, Faye noticed his short shirt sleeves creeping up to reveal dark hairs poking out from under his arms. She blushed and looked away until he was standing in the aisle next to Leah. Because he was standing and she was slouching in her seat, Faye felt inappropriately close to Doctor Vogel's body. She could hear the air conditioning whooshing out from the vents, yet her ears grew warm and her throat dried up.

Leah threw her arms up, exasperated. "Doctor, this bus ride is *forever*!"

"Vanda tells me we have an hour, tops. We will get off this bus. I promise you that."

Edward spoke directly to Leah. He lowered his chin, then, and looked past her.

"It's okay," he mouthed at Faye, giving a half smile, his mouth closed beneath a slightly fuzzy upper lip.

Leah's cool fingers laced into Faye's as she turned back to the window. The rain drops still chased each other, as chaotic and unpredictable as Faye's racing heartbeat.

Large patches of black, cloudless sky opened up over the streets of Freiburg that night. So, yes, Edward agreed, they could all go out walking after dinner. Some water stood and some trickled through the cobblestone streets of the darkened *Altstadt*. Here and there, natives strolled slowly, taking in the air after a day retreating from the violent storms. Faye huddled amidst Tommy, Leah, and James as she walked; Bryn held hands with Ian not far behind them; the choir broke apart in densely knitted groups and far flung pairings. Everyone was glad to be out of doors and breathing the earthy scent of fresh rain upon dusty streets. Jacqueline DeGroot and a smattering of adult chaperones brought up the rear. Edward, as always, took the lead. He walked among them and apart, never too far from their sight nor privy to their whisperings. As he walked, Edward marveled at the city's discordant, atemporal clash. Here, a centuries-old city gate stood strong, warning those who would dare flee to the untamed forest; there, the word *McDonald's* stretched across an archway connecting a bustling fast-food restaurant to the site of a 16th-century lynching.

The kids were sprawling more widely now. Edward called to his flock and waved his arms toward his chest.

"Let's stay closer together so we don't lose anyone."

The kids moved ever slightly towards a center point and continued as they were.

Edward deepened the timbre of his voice to get their attention.

"See this archway here," he began, easily taking the reins as teacher, father, friend, and tour guide. "This part is obviously new," he said, making a rounding gesture toward the familiar American restaurant logo. "The other side, though, connects directly to the city gate that dates to the 13th century. That's *seven hundred* years ago."

The kids responded less enthusiastically than he hoped they would.

"This plaque says that in 1599 three women were burned at the stake right here."

Everyone moved in closer now, gathering at the gate and giving quick glances toward the plaque Edward had indicated.

"That's awful," Jacqueline DeGroot chimed in. Clearly, she was here for the history.

"Why were they killed?" one boy asked. "What did they do?"

Bryn set him straight.

"In 1599," she said sharply, "they were probably killed for being women in 1599."

Faye admired Bryn's confidence. Feminism guided Bryn long before Faye had ever heard the word and buoyed her spirit in a way Faye would never quite be able to replicate. Too many *others*, always some boy or other, occupied Faye's thoughts. Her desire to please them crowded out the self she might have been without them.

Few kids were paying attention. Some girls laughed lightly. *Witches get what witches deserve*, Edward almost joked. He thought better of it, chuckled to himself, and waved the kids on to their next landmark.

Cathedrals rise up from European squares much like American skyscrapers in New York City. Both shock and impress by sheer magnitude, forcing the eyes skyward and daring tourists to confront the reality that they are, in comparison, so very inconsequential. But sky-high American steel calls the viewer ever outward to a world teeming with capital and greed. Grandiosity evinces success. The inner Rockefeller is spurred to accomplishment and the accumulation of riches that will make him as powerful as these massive buildings that stand before him. The cathedral inverts this tumultuous movement, turning the most stubborn soul inward. Its grandeur silences the world. Unanswered prayers hang hauntingly in each crevice. The cornerstone holds firm as visitors leave the Earth to its watch. *You will pass quietly out of this world*, the stone-still angels seem to say, *but a blip in the divine plan. The Spirit's work goes on.*

Generations built Freiburg Münster Cathedral. From three hundred years of labor—a spirit breathed mouth to mouth, heart to heart from one decade to the next—an open spire rises toward the Heavens in menacing Gothic fortitude. Even in darkness, the cathedral cuts the square, a presence weighty and expectant. This summer night of restless walking, each AP tourist found his way there, the giggling and talking and merriment subsiding in a reverse ripple from agitation to stillness. Without forethought, Edward and his students gathered beneath the Münster clock tower, their necks too inflexible and the night too cloudy to glimpse any high point beyond shadowed glass and stone. Rising wind brought the summer warmth under heel. Fat, gray clouds lightened the darkness now, encroaching on the open skies and threatening to turn them back indoors.

Santino Reddleman, an incoming senior like Faye and the wide smiling boy who had been Bryn's junior year crush, walked stoically toward Edward, his hands clasped behind his back. They leaned toward each other against the growing wind.

"Let's sing," Santino suggested. "Before it starts raining."

"Do you have your pipe?" Edward asked.

"Do I? Come on, Doc." Santino raised his hand gleefully, a silver pitch pipe glinting between his thumb and finger. "Always."

Edward smiled. "Go. Gather them."

Santino, keeper of the pitch and jovial leader of antics and singalongs, ushered Faye and her friends to the cathedral's entrance.

"Line up," he called with a broad grin.

Three lines of singers shuttled and shimmied, each looking for his place. Ready, arms to their sides, the choir stood shaped in a rainbow of rows. Edward stood apart; the rows curved ever so slightly toward his place at the center. Edward raised his hands and threw them outward with fingers spread as if pushing an invisible wall.

"Back up under the eave a bit," he said. "Rain is coming."

The rows shifted backward two steps, moving in unison to keep their shape. Edward held his hands aloft.

"*Lord, How Lovely,*" he said.

Santino blew a *D* on the pipe. Edward focused his gaze on each section before lifting then striking the first beat. Music flooded Münster square. Harmonies rose through the cavernous tower and through each aperture of the closed-off cathedral, its entrances locked but not sealed. As they swelled and quelled, bases dropping and tenors softening—*Lord, how lovely* (here the music stretched and soared) *is your dwelling place*—Freiburg residents lighted their living rooms and opened their windows. The sound rushed in with the wind. Jacqueline DeGroot and Annie Pickford's mom and Nicki Spirito's grandparents looked upward and awe-struck as the apartments around them alighted one by one and strong Aquinas Prep voices floated through Freiburg. Whoops and hollers drifted down from above once their voices broke off and their movement stilled. The people of Freiburg called for more, and Edward exhorted his choir anew.

"*My God Is a Rock*," Edward announced.

The unseen crowds above distracted his singers. He could sense excitement carrying their attention away. He touched his finger lightly beneath his eye, concert speak for *Look Here. Focus.* The choir parted without invitation; Elizabeth and Joseph stepped forward in preparation for their solos. Edward waited until all had quieted and turned their attention to him. When he could see each one—among them Ian's wide, shiny forehead; Leah, her face expectant and proud; James and Tommy, serious and determined; Faye and Bryn, eager and joyed—he nodded to Santino. A muted *Ab* sounded, and the music roared forth.

Lightning struck first, pulling singers and spectators from their reverie. Or, rather, lightning flashed above, illuminating them and expanding young hearts already so captivated by darkness and music and the quaint perfection of this impromptu, communal praise. Thunder followed too quickly, and without a slow-dripping warning, fat raindrops began striking Edward and the stones beneath his feet. Faye felt a confusing euphoria: spiritual ardor and teen-aged rebellion; the excitement of unexpected adventure; the sight of God billowing out from above and sinking deep into her soul; the sense that something wondrous and singular was happening now, in this moment. Windows shuttered and locked as the storm raged, but still the music wafted skyward. The music did not falter, but Faye felt the kids around her turn their heads away from Doctor Vogel's gesturing. She did not. She watched him cautiously at first. Then, her eyes bored into him. Away from the protection of the cathedral's archway, Doctor Vogel stood unsheltered. With each bright burst, a glow encircled him. Faye felt a numbness in her hands, at once both clammy and hot. She felt exposed as she stared at him.

The singers swayed in time, the meter urgent then mournful. Joseph strained against the wind, forcing his voice to a bellow. "*Stop, let me tell you 'bout chapter twelve. God sent Satan straight to Hell.*"

A spiritual reckoning transformed the ordinary night. Faye's friends receded to the blurry edges of her vision. She realized, then, that tears had formed at the corners of her eyes. Through the mist, she kept watching. Rain pelted Doctor as he moved undisturbed, his conducting swift and strong as it ever was. Wind whipped and drops fell loudly and hard, running together through the cracked streets and pooling around them. Rain matted Doctor's shirt close against his skin. From her front row view, Faye could see his hair getting heavy against the sides of his head. Above his eyes, though, wet strands hung loosely apart from each other. Every few measures, his right hand keeping the beat, Doctor ran his left hand swiftly through these errant hairs. Never did his hands fall. The unwavering passion mesmerized Faye. She could not look away.

Parents, chaperones, teachers, and kids all scampered to a covered outdoor passageway at the final coda. Tommy and Ian draped their arms over each other's shoulders; Jacqueline DeGroot stared wonderingly toward the sky; thunder and lightning relented only slightly. Unbridled laughter spread through the group. Here and there someone darted back out into the storm and ran circles around the open plaza. It was an all-out frolic now. Leah tackled Faye in a burst of joy and enthusiasm. While her friends talked, Faye momentarily lost sight of Doctor Vogel. She and Bryn and Leah laughed and huddled away from a passing burst of wind. She saw him, then, walking toward them. Faye peeled away from the girls and met him at the open space halfway between. They both smiled.

"That was really amazing," she said.

Edward looked up to the clouds with eyebrows arched. "I didn't expect that."

It seemed, Faye thought, like he was searching the sky for an answer. A thick drop trailed down from Edward's temple. Faye watched it slide across his pores and felt a sudden urge to touch it, to lift it from his skin.

"You're still dripping," she said, unwinding the sweatshirt from around her waist and holding it out toward Edward. "Here. Use this as a towel."

She offered and he took in one fell swoop, reacting before thinking it through. Edward wiped the sides of his face and back of his neck awkwardly with the cuffed, bright green sleeve. An odd sense of regret spread uncomfortably through him. He felt a breach, then, like he had done something untoward. He should have refused the sweatshirt, but that chance had passed. Now, he held Faye's sweatshirt awkwardly in his grasp. It felt too intimate. Just as she sensed his discomfort, Edward snapped back to the moment and handed the sweatshirt to her.

"Thanks," he said casually to Faye. He spoke loudly, then, projecting out to the scattered AP masses as he walked away from her. "Let's move, everyone. We better get back during this light let-up."

Faye glanced surreptitiously left and right and instinctively—without forethought!—buried her face in the fabric. It smelled only of musky rain and of raspberries from her own skin cream. Still, it had touched the bead of water upon his cheek and touched hers now. An odd sensation, at first exhilarating then immediately sour, fluttered at the back of Faye's stomach.

Bryn and Faye huddled close in their hotel bed, swapping funny stories and reliving the night's triumphs. Their laughing trailed off slowly, a few chuckles popping up every few seconds. The girls held hands beneath the coverlet.

Faye spoke hesitantly. "Can I tell you something?"

"Tell me everything," Bryn whispered.

She could hear Bryn's smile even in the dim room. Faye was glad for the darkness.

"I think I'm falling in love," Faye began, letting the phrase linger, "with Doctor."

A slight sigh escaped Bryn's lips.

"I know you are."

"I think I might be attracted to him," Faye continued. "I want to put his hand against my cheek and hold it there."

Both girls were silent for a few moments. Thunder still rumbled outside, but it seemed subdued and far away at this time.

"That's gross, right? Do you think something is wrong with me?"

Bryn squeezed Faye's hand.

"You are perfect," she whispered earnestly. "All you can feel is what you feel."

A burden lifted from Faye (even as this new, terrifying thought descended to take its place). Twenty years later, just when Faye felt an absence of compassion, Bryn would save her again. Across hundreds of miles, each woman balancing a baby on her hip, Bryn stirring stew with a wooden spoon and Faye sifting powdered sugar over a plate of French toast, Bryn's text would sooth her. *There's no wrong way to feel about what happened,* Bryn would counsel. Her words would hover over Faye, appearing like a shiny ribbon curling down from Heaven to pull her up from the depths of Hell.

European tours with his choirs brought Edward unparalleled joy. Lurking behind that elation, fatigue accosted him differently than it did the kids. Up half the night and for early morning rehearsals, sitting awkwardly through eight-hour bus rides, and eating and using the restroom only at precisely prescribed times bred absolute exhaustion that crippled Edward a few days into the trip. A night at the opera was exactly the respite he needed. Edward quite enjoyed the diversions during which he could feel more a part of his students than apart from them. And so, everyone spruced up and lined up to attend the *Bayerische Staatsoper's Don Giovanni* at Munich's National Theater. Edward counted six tickets for Faye and her friends. He pocketed the next for himself so his seat would be next to theirs.

In the dark, the days' exhaustion grabbed hold of Faye. Sitting between Doctor Vogel and Bryn, Faye succumbed gently to heavy eyes as the opening oboes sounded. She lay her cheek awkwardly on her hand for comfort, carefully avoiding contact with Doctor Vogel as she commandeered the arm rest between them. Well before the murder of Don Pedro the *Commendatore*, Faye's breathing slowed to a deep, pulsing rhythm, and she fell asleep.

Edward flinched involuntarily when he felt Faye pressing against his arm. *What exactly*, he wondered, *was she trying to do?* He glanced instinctively left and right to see if anyone else had noticed her touching him. His lips slightly parted, Edward prepared to rebuff her. He noticed, then, that she was asleep. The panic subsided, and relief rushed through Edward's body. Faye's arm was still folded awkwardly on the arm rest between them. Her hand, having slipped off her cheek, now rested beneath her chin. Edward shook off the strange fear that had gripped him. He had thought she was touching him purposely, sensually. Faye's flirtation had intensified these few days on tour. Already, Edward's initial thrill at her pursuit was tinged with anxiety. Heat rose from her skin as she slept against him now. Lighting in the theater illuminated their seats often enough that Edward could watch her and seldom enough that he would not be caught looking. Edward keenly felt Faye knitting herself to him on the trip, courting in him an intimacy he found wonderful and dangerous. Faye, so petite and tender—he wanted to wrap his arm around her now and to cuddle her against his chest like the child he never had. This nurturing impulse disturbed Edward, for he also wanted to put his hand on her thigh and between her legs. He imagined her body would feel hot and damp as her temple did now pressed against his shoulder.

Loud applause roused Faye. Not yet moving, she blinked away the blurriness and tried to re-orient herself. Still sleepy, she fought the urge to cozy herself up to the warmth she felt against her head. She realized, then, that she was leaning on Doctor Vogel. She remembered now. They were at the opera in Germany. Embarrassed, she sat upright and straightened her shoulders a bit sheepishly. As their bodies, hers and Doctor's, cleaved, Faye felt him readjust, too, as if he had been waiting for her to wake, holding still so as not to disturb her. Without looking at him, Faye leaned instead toward Bryn and rested languidly against her friend's willing shoulder. The music and the moment filled her. Edward glanced askance at Faye as she reposed peacefully in her seat. The feel of her body against his, at first so startling, had been soothing and satisfying. Now, her absence discomforted him.

Assisi delivered, literally, greener pastures. The lush gardens of Assisi rollick the complacent consciousness, enforcing quietude as a calm that moves in after a violent storm. Growing up in Citrus County, which is often steeped in drought and always steeped in concrete, most Aquinas Prep students experienced nature in small snippets or as passageways that almost but not entirely filled the space from town to town. Even the open expanses between suburbs reeked of city life, utility poles and advertisements heralding the quick return of commerce. Through four countries now, from France through Germany and Austria to Italy, Faye had watched intently, her forehead pressed against the cool pane of her bus window, as the countryside rushed by between major European cities. Here, though, was the first they had de-bussed and immersed themselves in a locale so pristinely rural. Leah and Faye linked arms as they bounded down grated steel steps and over the threshold from clammy bus to bright white sunshine.

Walking uphill into the walled city toward its namesake basilica, the AP tour group, a dense cluster at the start, fanned out as more rambunctious and athletic kids ran ahead and aging chaperones stalled behind. The climb was steep, deceptively arduous. That the Basilica of Saint Francis awaited them at the top gave the misleading impression that any prayerful supplicant was capable of scaling the switchbacks that carried them up the mountain. Faye and her friends stayed in roughly the middle of the pack with Edward. Santino and his crew had sprinted ahead but were falling back toward Faye's group now, exhausted from over-exertion and surprised to still be so far from the church.

A thin glimmer of sweat developed along Leah's hairline. The climb tired but enthralled her. Anticipation grew with each step; she could not wait to see the basilica and to look out over the vista that awaited them. Faye never saw Bryn's small frame perspire. Bryn seemed less tired and more bored by the constant exertion. Bryn's thin physique appeared strong, but she looked with disdain, almost disgust, on physical activity. Her mind always active, her heart always full, Bryn was an artist through and through. She doodled and wrote odes and composed hymns silently in her head. She dried flowers and covered her bedroom in exotic fabrics and canvases she had stretched, primed, and painted herself. Faye thought of Bryn as more spirit than body. Faye, the only athlete among her friends, strode unbothered, watching the others as she padded leisurely along. Edward stayed near them, trying, Faye thought, to seem unattached without wandering too far. He called out occasionally to the kids far ahead or trailing behind to *wait for the group!* or *stop giggling and catch up!*

When Edward waved his arm to the stragglers, Faye glimpsed beneath Edward's collar a piece of green string or fabric, as if he were wearing some kind of necklace. She could not remember having noticed it before, not even in Paris when she had found him—the humiliating scene flashed in her mind now—wearing only an undershirt, holding his toothbrush so innocently, so unaware of her!

She questioned him the next time he appeared beside her, their strides in sync.

"Are you wearing a necklace?"

At first the question confused him. Amid worries about the trek from bus to basilica, Edward had forgotten the scapular. He was conscious of it now, its scratchy fabric lightly brushing his chest and back as he moved. He reached into his shirt and pulled the small wooly square out to show Faye. They leaned toward each other. She extended her fingers toward the fabric but pulled them back without touching the woven image. The relic was wonderful and strange, like nothing she had ever seen. The square panel was embroidered with a tiny image of St. Francis. Even tinier Latin words were inscribed beneath the icon.

"That's beautiful," she said. "I've never seen something like that. Do you always wear it?"

"No," Edward answered, quickly tucking the square into his shirt. "It belongs to my father. He sort of adopted Francis as a patron saint. He asked that I wear it to Mass in the crypt here."

"Your father's name is Francis?"

"My father's name is Elias. Francis was my grandfather's name. Maybe that's why my dad has such a devotion to Francis. My dad has always been interested in ecology and animal life. Maybe the animals are the connection."

Faye hummed a quiet assent, taking in this bit of Edward's history and storing it away for later thought.

"That's lovely," she said. "What a nice thing to do for your dad."

New knowledge of Edward's life invigorated Faye. She wanted to turn this new word over in her mouth, so she said it out loud.

"Elias," she said. "What is your mom's name?"

Edward smiled. "Mary," he answered. "My mother's name is Mary."

They continued walking in silence. Ian came astride and blurted exasperation.

"I'm sweating bullets here, Doctor," he joked. "I don't remember this from the brochure."

Edward chuckled. "The view will be worth the climb. This is honestly a touch more strenuous than I had expected, though. I'm a bit worried about Nicki's grandparents," he said, turning around and walking backward up the hill as he peered down at the adults who brought up the rear.

"Keep heading up the hill. I'm going down to check on the others."

Faye watched a few paces as Edward left them. His shoes were too new. They gleamed too white, like he had bought them just before the trip. She tried to picture him buying tennis shoes, standing gingerly, wiggling his toes, taking and retracing steps along the thin carpet of a shoe store. She strained to imagine him doing something so ordinary.

At the summit, triumph extinguished exhaustion. Faye pulled the fresh air in with deep, full breaths and watched her classmates frolicking on the basilica's manicured front lawn. Carefully trimmed hedges spelled *Pax*, and, indeed, Faye felt blanketed with peace. James gathered them, Faye and their other most special friends, for a picture in front of the sanctuary's heavy double doors.

Faye and Bryn stood at center. The others pressed in around them.

"Leah, come on!" James yelled with a wave. "We're waiting for you. Grab Doctor, too!"

Faye watched Leah bound up the stairs, motioning for Edward to follow.

"Stand here," Faye said, stepping aside.

Edward smiled gratefully and took his place between the girls. Bryn reached her hand into the space behind Edward's back. Faye clasped it in hers.

Edward groaned loudly that night as he sank into his hotel bed and removed his shoes. They were, in fact, brand new. *Bad idea*, Edward said aloud to the empty room. Haltingly, he touched his foot, tending a blister forming there from the day's walking. He wondered whether by morning it would bubble and shift, or pop and smart, or heal itself into an almost flat crease like budding blisters sometimes did. He hoped it would be the last of these.

Thrilling. Rome thrilled them. The pizza, and the thick, chewy spaghetti, and the real Coca Cola in tiny glass bottles, and the pink strawberry gelato studded with bright, fresh berries, and the ornate bridges, and the massive columns, and the gold fleck of the Sistine Chapel—Michelangelo's fingerprints embedded unseen on the very walls—and, my God, the tomb of Saint Peter himself. They stared, eyes and mouths wide open, and struggled to absorb so much Heaven right there on that patch of Earth.

On the street, peddlers held pin-up calendars of sultry-looking priests. They cried out to the girls. "For you! *Sacerdoti Più Sexy!* The most beautiful priests of Rome! For you, American girls!"

Faye and Leah blushed; Ian scoffed; Bryn looked to the tops of her sneakers and shook her head fiercely.

Not since Paris had they found Europe so crowded and bustlingly urban. The chaos, Faye could tell, unnerved Edward. Vespas darted, flocks of pigeons picked at the flesh of discarded peach pits, and competing vendors yelled out to milling crowds. Edward's head swiveled as they walked, always counting and corralling his charges, all of them too young to foresee danger or know where they needed to go. Faye enjoyed afternoons most, when their larger company broke into smaller pods and left group by group to take in Rome at their own pace. As chaperones plotted and planned with a half dozen kids huddled around them, Faye and her friends fell back, waiting. When the others had disappeared, their Aquinas Prep tee shirts becoming a crowd of white specs in the busy foot traffic, Edward looked expectantly to the small group of loyalists that waited for him.

"Okay," he would say brightly, the stress of having fifty teen-aged dependents lifting from his shoulders, "let's see the city."

On this particular day, Edward leaned with his chest against the wide concrete banister of the St. Angelo Bridge, his eyes searching the Tiber below and his mind wandering away from the kids. Out of the corner of his eye, he could see Ian boosting Faye with hands clasped beneath her foot. She clambered atop and sat with her back to the watery abyss below. The railing was three times the width of Faye's seated form, but, still, Edward was startled by a sense of precariousness. The kids laughed, their eyes sparkling, and took photos of each other from different angles to catch the towering cement archangel statues, the distant church, the river rushing below, then just their own smooshed together faces. Edward's pulse quickened as he stepped closer and extended his arm behind Faye.

"Come on," he said as evenly as he could, "that's much too dangerous. Ian, James—please help her down."

Faye felt the presence of Edward's hand but not its touch. Without turning to see, she imagined his hand outstretched and fingers curved protectively toward her body, lest she tumble back. Leaning back would press his fingers to her shirt and against her skin. In the moment's joy, her best friends gathered on an Italian bridge and Edward's friendship all theirs, she sensed that he was too cautious to touch her.

"He's right," Faye said without argument and scooted toward the front edge.

James and Leah both leaned awkwardly toward Faye and supported her weight as she alighted. A hot breeze blew across the bridge and rippled through the thick green foliage that lined the river's banks.

Bryn chimed in. "Strawberry gelato is calling my name, Doc. Let's find a café."

Edward knew just where he wanted to lead them.

While the kids laughed with a hearty lack of reserve, Edward sipped his beer pensively, the taste at once bitter and comforting. Faye ordered sparkling peach juice, leaving it mostly untouched as she and Leah crunched thin wheat wafers with thick slices of soft cheese. Bryn ate an oversized scoop of gelato with the tiniest spoon she had ever seen. Ian and James ordered yet another *Margherita* pizza, a staple among the kids. Edward preferred his pizza the Italian way, dotted with thick slices of pancetta and a runny fried egg. In this afternoon heat, though, he simply nursed a *Nastro Azzurro* and absorbed the energy of his students enfolding him. From where they sat, Edward could see straight down the *Via della Conciliazione* to St. Peter's Square. From this café, it must have been twelve or thirteen years ago now, he and his fiancé had people-watched and dreamt of their future happiness, neither suspecting how close they were to letting go and building new, divergent lives. If he had known then, Edward mused, he might have stayed in Italy to chase accolades in the world of orchestral composition and to embrace a life of rich artistry. Instead, he and Jane had returned to Michigan and then headed west, chasing Jane's dream of medical school in California, a persistent desire that quickly edged out any plans to settle down in Edward's shadow. Without her intending to hurt him (Edward finally understood her lack of malice), Jane's promise had sidelined his opportunities. Just as much (this he *never* understood, would never admit), Edward's anger had pushed Jane out of his life.

Jane. Her name cast a warm glow from Edward's nostalgic center. He felt her memory like a vibration moving through him. All these years later, Edward thought of Jane often. She did not merely pop into his head unannounced. He summoned her. He conjured her. Then, when his Jane appeared, he turned her image over with great nostalgia and tenderness. In his mind's eye, Jane was still twenty-two. He never considered that she was almost forty years old now. When their time together stopped, they stopped with it. Their younger selves were forever entwined. He thought about Jane because he missed her. He missed Jane because he thought, now, that with her he had been happy. Edward embraced this vision and felt her long ago love breathing life into him. But when the reverie passed, he felt empty. Worse, he felt the crushing weight of a failure that could not be undone.

Edward told himself stories about those years with Jane. The stories were romantic and tragic and so lovely they made his heart ache to hold her again. Somewhere so deep they could not intrude on these stories lay the very real memories of his frustration with her. Their time in California had been peppered with bitter quarrels. He loathed the inartistic '80s pop music she played. Jane blasted it through the apartment even though she knew it bothered him. Almost, it seemed by the end, she did it *because* it bothered him. He resented the long-distance phone calls to her mother and her girlfriends, frivolous chatter that took her away from him and left him feeling distanced and uncentered. She had given him no choice, really, by insisting on the move to Southern California. She owed him at least a centrality in her life, the satisfaction of her attention any time she wasn't studying or taking exams. Almost immediately, though, she began to scatter her thoughts and her time. He found the neighborhoods crowded and dirty; the culture was uncouth and pedestrian. No one they met in Los Angeles appreciated Edward's experimental marimba compositions or his love of aged liquors or classical architecture.

Jane had opened her arms wide to the urban grittiness of Los Angeles. A young twenty-two, out to the coast for the first time from small-town Kansas via even-smaller-town Kansas, Jane readied for adventure and thrill, the trying on of masks before the real responsibilities of adulthood stabilized her. At twenty-seven, Edward knew who he was. He had sewn his oats and indulged his fantasies. Edward's college years had necessitated no trying on of personas, no forging of a new identity. Edward had always felt his Edward-ness, controlled his temperament, and followed his instincts. After the move, he felt himself an ill fit for Southern California, and, in reciprocal discomfort, the people and spaces there squeezed him too tightly or refused to make a place for him. Likewise, Jane announced only a few months into their engagement that she and Edward just did not fit.

The failed engagement haunted Edward. He felt rejected and wronged, equal parts humiliated and searingly angry. The years slipped by slowly at first. In those early days, the anger nearly consumed him. He courted Jane and followed her and called and sent flowers and begged her to take him back. She rebuffed him. Four years later, Jane was starting residency at Kansas Heart Hospital near Wichita and had just married a cardiologist there. Edward blamed her for this life of curtailed promise in which he had given up prized fellowships and great acclaim for a woman who then abandoned him. The wasted years, he called them in his mind. Those years had brought several small teaching and conducting gigs at a local community college and at several Catholic parishes, for which he had moved from Los Angeles to Citrus County and had started over. He met women through choral festivals and professional development committees. Some delighted and some repelled him. None captivated him. He made love to each one, envisioning Jane's flat white belly and the strong but soft embrace of her thighs as he did. At night, he tried to compose. His doctoral thesis, published years prior as *Expansions: a Concerto for Marimba and Band*, mocked him as a one-time composer relegated to small-time Church choir director. A different kind of man might have felt shame. Edward's confidence did not waver. The smartest man in every room, the most charming suitor for every woman, Edward withdrew from the world not to hide his shame but because he deserved so much better than the world would give him.

When he took over as music director at St. Crispina, he bought a house on Bonita Vista Drive in Fulton and began remodeling it slowly to his liking. Jane, his life's great love, was lost, but he resolved, finally, to redirect his passions. Love of the music set him straight. If small-time choirs were his medium, he would compose choral music for them to sing and would mold and perfect the intrepid singers who came to him unaccustomed to rigorous material. Alone on this edge of the country, its ridiculously mild winters and unending expanse of cold, gray concrete stretching before him, Edward would go it alone if he must. The music would fill his soul. Anger left quietly as Edward revived himself. Adoration of Jane, of their time together and the pining that followed, settled in its place, growing lush and beautiful, sprawling wide and reaching deep to cover the resentment that threatened to hold him back. Six months later, Aquinas Prep came calling with its promises of prestige, faith, and family.

Back in the very square where he and Jane had shared their last vacation and, he realized belatedly, their final moments of unmarred enjoyment, Edward had to admit that Aquinas Prep had generally delivered on its promises. He was used by now to the repeating reel of his own complaints— his knowledge too sophisticated for high school choirs, his aloof demeanor misunderstood by the common folk who prized high school athletics—but still he recognized that Aquinas Prep had done him well. Through the years, Edward had steered AP's choral program to the top of its field and elevated the program in ways that enabled his students to go on to strong careers in performance, teaching, and composition. Yes, his run at AP had been a good one. And yet he felt, the cold beer sliding down his throat, a touch of the bubbly liquid just kissing his upper lip, a wistfulness when he thought about what might have been. The students mostly liked him, and the parents, especially of the choir's best phenoms, mostly kowtowed to him, even courted his admiration. The sense of belonging, though, of real connection to these kids and their families was short-lived at best. *Four-year families*, he called them in his mind. Eight years' worth now of fresh-faced teens and budding divas and overzealous parent boosters had lavished musical-themed gifts upon him, dedicated their time to the success of his program, and even invited him to holiday dinners because his real family was in Kansas. In the end, though, the students graduated and moved on. They moved on from Aquinas Prep. They moved on from Edward.

His gaze half-focused down the cobbled avenue toward St. Peter's, half-focused down the tunnel of his past, Edward was rocked back to the present by Ian's boisterous laughter. The kids, Edward noticed, were watching Ian's antics: Bryn (generally serious) with a bit of skepticism, Leah (more brazen) in loud accompaniment, James and Tommy (always followers) with aloof approval. Eight years teaching high school had taught Edward to read the kids and their cliques. His favorite seniors had (inevitably) graduated. Stuart and Katarina and Genevieve and Garrett were headed off to college and not looking back. Faye had swooped in quickly though almost silently. Friendships were still shifting, but Edward could see the rest of them turning their eyes to Faye, letting her take the lead. She wasn't the prettiest. She wasn't a highly trained soloist. She was unassuming. Still, they gravitated to her. Edward had been studying Faye since summer's start. Soon, he would name top honors for the new choral year. He would bestow the grand titles of King and Queen of this year's Renaissance Pageant. The students coveted these roles, Edward knew, not because they signaled vocal prestige but because they brought with them his trust. Often, King and Queen were vocal superstars. Always, King and Queen were leaders. Edward chose his favorites. Everybody knew it. Since summer's start, Edward had been testing Faye. He felt her growing closer to him. Ian, Edward noticed, was also courting his favor.

No, Edward suddenly decided. *Ian is not the one.*

Ian easily had the best voice in his class. Ian, the voice, was strong and well-trained. But Ian, the boy, was rich and spoiled. Many of the AP kids had this in common, but Ian carried his privilege arrogantly like a sheltered, coddled child. Ian believed he deserved whatever he wanted. There was something *conditional* about Ian's loyalty, Edward surmised. Edward was determined not to indulge him.

At the table's head, Faye looked toward Ian but seemed to look *through* him. She watched Edward, his eyes focused at an unseen point in the distance. For just a moment, he seemed gone from them, and she wanted him back. Edward turned slightly, his beer bottle suspended between the table and his mouth, his lips just starting to pucker in anticipation of a drink. Faye narrowed her eyes a bit and smiled without showing her teeth. A surge of excitement rose in Edward. It had been years, he realized, since last he had felt desired. Something in Faye had shifted during this trip. Edward did not know in what way or to what end, but he felt that Faye desired him now.

The Peter's Way photographers clicked furiously as the Pope walked gingerly toward the Aquinas Prep choir and cupped each child's hands in his. Back in the States, Faye's parents would purchase this most perfect relic of their daughter's pilgrimage. Here was their youngest child, touched by a man who would reach actual sainthood. The meeting of Faye's and the Pope's hands dramatized an iconic replaying of Michelangelo's Adam. Godly perfection met imperfect mortality. Faye's parents cropped the photo for framing. Just where the glass met the gilded exterior, the starched tail of Edward's concert tuxedo splashed a dark blotch across the bottom corner. Each time she saw the picture, Faye trained her eyes on this shadowy stain. The fall of man, the mercy of God, and the power of the Church converged in this one enduring snapshot. Faye's mom had tried to cut Edward out. A darkened sliver remained.

III

SENIOR YEAR IN 1997 STARTED HOT. Bubbling rage spread from Ian's cheeks down through his toes when Edward announced that Faye would be Queen and that Merton Caceres would be King, King of Ian's senior year Renaissance Pageant when no one but Edward had even heard of Merton until now. Okay, of course Ian had heard of Merton, but he was new to Chambers this year (King had *always* gone to a two-year Chamber Singer), he had never sung in Men's Ensemble (King had *always* gone to a four-year choir member), and he just wasn't part of the right group. Ian was livid. He had given three years of his life to Edward's choirs and thanks to Faye had spent all summer kissing Edward's ass and pretending he was impressed with that arrogant fuck. Chamber Singer Summer Prep Week dragged on with Ian in a haze of outrage. Merton had come into Chamber Singers from the handbell choir, a special brand of nerds (from what Ian could tell) whom everyone forgot were even part of the choral program. When Prep Week ended, Ian's simmering fury continued, abating slightly when Edward awarded him the lead solo in the Pageant's enormously difficult finale. Ian was, after all, the choir's best male vocalist. By a few weeks into school, Ian pieced it all together. King was an honorary title for kids like Merton who stroked Doctor's ego (and maybe wanted to stroke the rest of him as well). Merton was just like Faye, all moony eyes and hop-to-it deference whenever Doctor was around.

Ian's parents bought him a brand new sports car to smooth over his disappointment about not getting King, and he rode high with Faye and the whole gang speeding around town and throwing their heads back in the ocean wind. Like all Citrus County Septembers, the fall of 1997 brought eighty degree days with Padre Diego winds that whipped into sixty degree nights at the beach. Wednesdays were Ian's favorite day because Chamber Singers was first on the rotating schedule, so Ian could enjoy the rest of the day without Edward's nasally laugh and stupid face trying to win back his favor. Ian planted his feet on the risers with perfect posture and clenched fists. *Doctor started this*, Ian thought, *not me*. Ian would sing and Ian would perform, but he would push back just a little. If they ever came to a crisis, Ian would not be on Doctor's side.

Mrs. Caceres called toward the stairs in a too-loud voice, her excitement carrying up to Merton's bedroom.
"*Ven rápido, hijo. Hay una chica al teléfono.*"
Merton's shoes bounded down the stairs two at a time. He shook the dark strands of hair away from his face as he put the phone to his ear.
"Yah, hello?"
The voice hesitated.
"Hey there. It's Faye."
Merton's heart froze in his chest. He shooed his mother away and sat down. The kitchen barstool skidded more loudly than he expected, and he almost jumped at the sound. He hoped Faye hadn't heard it through the phone. He needed to be cool.
"Well, hello Queen Faye," he responded steadily. "To what do I owe this great honor?"
Faye giggled. She had only really known Merton a few weeks, but in those few dozen days she had come to enjoy the corny manner in which he spoke to her. Merton was off beat in an endearing way.
"Now that we are an official couple," she said with a laugh in her voice, "I mean, we are King and Queen after all, I thought maybe we should get to know each other. Why don't we go for dinner this weekend?"
Merton flexed his fingers and wiped a clammy hand on the thigh of his jeans. He saw stars while Faye talked.
"Yes, I can do that." Merton tried to sound confident. "Are you sure you're up for it though? How do Ian and the rest of your group feel about it?"
Her friends' pettiness preceded them. It embarrassed Faye that Merton would think her so shallow and cliquish.
"I wouldn't have asked if I didn't want to go," she said slowly. "I'm not worried about them. But," she hesitated further, "what about Tiffany?"
Merton had been dating Tiffany Murray for more than a year. Tiffany was sweet and unassuming with alabaster skin and hair so bright blonde it was white. Merton found her cute and sexy. He told her often that he loved her because he was pretty sure he did. They were devoted to each other, which everyone in the choir world knew. They also were having everything-but-sex sex, which no one in the choir knew. The intimate secret bound Merton and Tiff in an even more special coupling. For high school, their relationship was pretty serious.

Merton waved at Faye's concern. "Tiff's a great girl. It's no problem."

Truthfully, Merton didn't care whether going out with Faye posed a problem or not. For three years, Merton had been watching Faye from afar and waiting for the chance to know her.

Oh, was it lovely to spend an evening away from the usual drama of her usual friends. Faye and Merton cruised down Pacific Coast Highway, the wind whipping Faye's hair back as she looked over the barrier to the waves cresting and crashing. The two swapped choir histories first. Merton came to Chamber Singers by way of handbells, the bastard child of AP choir: unglamorous, unromantic, and mostly hidden. Handbells practiced sixth period (the only AP block that didn't rotate and thus always fell last in the school day) so they had extra time to set up and tear down the handbell tables. The bell ringers were geeky, close-knit, hardworking, and usually played for all four of their high school years. The handbell choir was small, even smaller than Chamber Singers, and so its members had a special, nearly intimate relationship with Edward. From the jump, Edward and Merton connected. By senior year, Merton saw Edward as both a surrogate father and a friend. Merton was dependable, steadfast, and always there. When Edward stepped away to answer the phone or take care of choral business, Merton fell in as director and the bell ringers followed his lead without a missed measure. The day would come soon, Merton thought, when he and Edward would sip beers and listen to records. He could hardly wait.

Merton paid for pizza slices at TJ's on the beach. He smoked a cigarette at Faye's prodding even though he'd never smoked one before. Tiff certainly wouldn't approve of this, Merton thought. But he wanted to do as Faye did. The stars rose high in the sky when the two left the beach.

"Where now?" Faye asked expectantly.

"I know a place," Merton responded. "It's special. You'll like it."

Merton's favorite sculpture garden was little more than an office park, but it boasted giant modern art sculptures like a Japanese zen garden turned life-sized. At night the open space was nearly abandoned. Faye and Merton climbed atop then shimmied down the front side of a giant marble pyramid, scooting awkwardly while balancing paper bowls of frozen yogurt in their hands.

They sat at the base and talked.

"Were you surprised Doctor gave you King?"

"Yes," Merton said strongly. "Yes, except no, I wasn't."

Faye laughed out loud. "I know what you mean. It's surreal, right? But it makes sense."

Merton concurred. "It makes perfect sense."

He reached over and thumbed Faye's nose. The movement was sudden and surprising but not unwelcome. She felt comfortable with Merton. Her heart did not race; her hairline did not sweat. Faye was uncommonly calm, and it felt good.

"I knew you would be Queen," Merton continued. "You can tell how much Doctor Vogel likes you. He talks about you all the time when you're not around."

Merton noticed a glint in Faye's eye. She liked hearing Edward's praise of her. Now that the door was open, the two talked about Edward a lot. They traded stories and compared notes. The discussion animated Faye. She laughed at Merton's handbell stories, like the time Edward had conducted an entire performance with an errant lock of hair standing straight up above his eyes, and wanted to know everything Merton knew (which wasn't much) about Edward's private life outside of Aquinas Prep. The two guys had talked women on a few occasions. Edward thought Merton was too young to be tied down to Tiffany. Merton wasn't worried. He knew it would run its course in the end. Edward had alluded to some kind of heartbreak in his own past, but Merton had not pushed for more of the story. Faye and Merton realized how much they were talking about Edward. They changed topics, only to find their way back.

Faye had planned to spend half the night with Merton before meeting Bryn and the gang at James's house across town, but the hours piled up quickly and curfew approached while Faye still sat smoking with Merton at the sculpture garden. She leaned her head on his shoulder. The slight touch sent a current of life buzzing through Merton's nervous system. From afar he had watched her all these years. And now, so easily, he began loving the real Faye, the real girl twining her fingers through his at this very moment. In just these hours, Faye was already beginning to enjoy the way Merton loved her. Something about his deliberate and gentle movements, the way his eyes seemed to really see her without pretense or judgment, told Faye that Merton adored her. She leaned into it easily, peacefully.

"I think we will be great friends," Faye said brightly. "You're different. I really like that about you."

At home, Merton found his mom waiting in the entryway. She questioned him.

"*¿Tu cita no fue con Tiffany?*"

"No, mama," Merton said dreamily. "My date was not with Tiffany tonight."

She pushed. "*¿Quién era ese?*"

Apple blossom and cigarette smoke rose up to meet Merton as he removed his sweatshirt.

He sighed. "*El amor de mi vida, mamá.*" A deeper sigh, then: "*Pero ella no es para mí. Ella ya ama a alguien.*"

Merton knew the truth of his words. Faye might just be the love of his life, but she already loved someone else.

The three cousins who had been tasked for fifteen years with maintaining the Aquinas Prep campus hedged and weed whacked carefully, but at the top of the grotto's only hill sat a slight dip that refused absolutely perfect grooming. The awkwardly sloping angle required special by-hand attention that was given only about every three mowings, and so the patch grew unsteadily and at odds with the rest of the hill. Higher blades of grass stuck up here and there. Into this uneven spot, Faye tossed her bookbag. In short order, she threw herself upon the hill's cool grass, rested her head against the coarse canvas of her bag, and stared up at the deep blue sky. What a joy and a slog senior year had been so far and it only now heading toward October and Faye's seventeenth birthday.

Managing school, choir, swim, tennis, and work at Cal's made Faye's daily life a whirlwind of responsibility and fervor. She didn't know yet that life would always feel this way, that busyness would save her. The more Faye did, the better she felt. Edward's eyes followed her as she moved between groups of friends. Sometimes too noticeably, he turned his head at the sound of Faye's voice. He thought of her on his drive into work, the absolute vibrancy of Faye pulling him along to a life that suddenly held joy. On the days he doubted himself, when the loneliness came creeping in, Faye's calm presence filled him like a warm major chord settling down into a long decrescendo.

Faye never seemed to tire. She walked wide-eyed and ready into Monday night Chamber rehearsal, fuzzy wisps of her curly hair falling out of a ponytail, her slender torso swimming under a red Aquinas Prep tennis sweatshirt. Edward knew that Faye waited tables at Cal's on the weekends and a few weeknights too if they needed the help. But Faye was always on time and always ready. Yes, that was it. Faye's focus set her apart. Edward wanted some of that energy for himself. Faye carried herself with an egotism and confidence that Edward admired. Her intelligence and maturity were obvious. In that way, she was like he had been as a young person. But something about her seemed almost selfless in a way Edward knew he, himself, was not. She did for the others, he noticed, so that an infectious joy could carry them all. She made homemade treats and wrote poems and gave encouragement. The Aquinas Prep choir was made up mostly of kids who had never been on sports teams, had never been hoisted on their teammates' shoulders, and had never been superstars to the rest of their classmates. Faye filled them all with a wild need to reach out and grab the life around them. With Faye, Edward felt that, too.

A burnt out bulb in the overhead light of his office had darkened the papers on his desk, and so Edward was straining to see an order for new Chamber portfolios when Faye approached. She stood with a sheepishness that was uncommon for her. Edward cocked his head and expressed curiosity at her stance.

Faye smiled only slightly, her lips still closed around her teeth.

"This is for you," she said, her eyes on the object she held instead of on Edward.

She offered it to him.

"It's just a little photo collage. I made them for everyone," she continued, motioning toward the bustling choir room of students. "I didn't want you to feel left out."

The innocence of the gesture touched him. He took it from her as fathers would take macaroni crafts and silly tie clips from their children. Faye's inclusion of Edward pleased him. The childishness of the gift confused him. He was sure Faye had begun flirting with him. Some days, when their eyes met, she tugged at Edward, seemed to be bonding herself to him with steady, determined stares. Those looks had begun to stir something in Edward. But now this, a too-sweet handmade child's note with loopy, rainbow-colored writing and gold star stickers—the woman before him was only a girl.

"This is very nice." Edward laid a fatherly pat on Faye's shoulder. "You must never sleep," he said admiringly. "You're like Super Girl, taking care of everything and everyone."

The glug glug sound of water being guzzled down Faye's throat pounded in her ears. She was almost half way through what had turned out to be a rather difficult tennis match against a feisty Freshman counterpuncher from St. Therese Lisieux Girls Academy. When Coach Spinner approached on the changeover, her flushed cheeks momentarily alarmed Faye. She thought a teammate might have lost a set AP expected to win.

Coach Spinner spoke in a hurried whisper. "Did you see who's here?" Her eyes widened.

Faye looked nonchalantly across the courts to the sloped and darkened grass. The sun was starting to drop. Most spectators, like Faye's father, sat with jacketed arms crossed against the cold and settled their weight back in the folding chairs they had carried slung across their shoulders from the parking lot. But there, a few feet away from the usual fans, Edward crouched awkwardly in the grass, still donning his professional dress clothes though his collar buttons were undone. Faye noticed how small he looked from this far away.

Coach Spinner maintained her scandalized tone. "Isn't that Doctor Vogel? I can't believe he's here."

The ice water Faye had greedily drunk was so cold it numbed her mouth and brought a slight headache to the bridge of her nose.

"I didn't think he'd actually come," Faye said with forced equanimity. "I'm always telling him to check out a match."

Across a wide expanse, Edward and Faye stared toward each other. They were too far apart to read each other's expressions, but had they been closer, Faye might have felt the warmth spreading across Edward's chest like a tight hug. To watch her in this new milieu was delicious. Faye walked away from the spectators and planted her feet for return of serve. She twirled her racket against the court, a superstitious habit, and pretended nothing was amiss. Inside Faye's core, a glowing speck of excitement pulsed. Something was happening here.

Salad dressing spilled onto the table as Krystal dunked her fries in the tangy white sauce and shouted incredulously.

"But why did he come to the match, Faye? That's really weird."

Faye pushed a soggy tortilla strip around in her chicken soup. *For a best friend,* Faye thought, *Krystal sure has a way of shitting all over everything.*

Best friend was too strong. At the end of junior year, Krystal and Faye had been tennis friends on the court but had rarely socialized beyond scheduled AP tennis events. Now, in the first two months of senior year, Krystal had been calling Faye just to chat, inviting her to play tennis and have lunch at the country club, and had started sticking her nose into the drama of Faye's AP Chamber Singer life, her *real* life, as Faye thought of it. Bryn and Leah didn't like Krystal hanging around. She wasn't their kind of people. Krystal had professionally manicured nails and wore designer perfume. Her hair was blond and perfectly smooth; in summer she lifeguarded at Vista View pool in the exclusive gated community where she lived. Krystal spoke too loudly, a confidence born of wealth and teen-aged sexiness. In short, Krystal was too cool for Faye's friends. Bryn and Leah feared Krystal's popularity would pull Faye away from them. So at first, Faye saw Krystal apart from her choir friends.

"He came because I asked him to come."

Krystal's big, unbelieving smile got bigger, exuded more mockery.

"That's even more weird, Faye. How can you not see that?"

Faye giggled nervously. "You don't get it. You don't know him like I do."

"Why do you like him so much?" Krystal sucked down the last gulps of a diet soda. "He seems like kind of a prick."

"I didn't say he wasn't." Faye paused. She wanted to say that Doctor Vogel had been consuming her thoughts, that she felt popular and joyful these days and that all of it had come from him. The more she got to know Doctor Vogel, the more lonely and disappointed he seemed. She wanted to save him.

But she couldn't say those things to Krystal. Not yet. Talking to Krystal wasn't like talking to Bryn and Leah or even to Ian. Krystal was too far outside.

Faye settled instead. "It's hard to explain."

"Speaking of explaining hard things," Krystal began with a mischievous smile.

Faye blushed and shook her head vigorously from side to side.

"Oh God, I do not want to hear this," she said. "Seriously. I do not want to hear it."

Krystal raised one eyebrow and tapped her bright pink fingernails on the table.

"Except maybe I do," Faye laughed. "What did you do now?"

"The important thing," Krystal said emphatically, "is not what I did but to whom I did it."

Krystal specialized in gross details. Sure, Faye had been French kissing boys since the sixth grade, but nothing new had transpired since then. To a novice like Faye, Krystal's stories weren't just outlandish. They were downright unimaginable. Questions swirled in Faye's head, but even as she and Krystal were fast becoming friends, she couldn't bring herself to ask them out loud. How did Krystal know what to do? What did all these things feel like and taste like and how would a person know when it was time to do the next thing? The average Catholic school girl, Faye imagined, hovered somewhere between Krystal's flagrant, unbridled sexuality and her own bright white virginity. Krystal had transferred to Aquinas Prep from public high school at fifteen after her parents caught her having sex with the nineteen-year-old family friend they hadn't known was Krystal's boyfriend. *My dad would have pressed charges,* Krystal had said, flippantly, *if he hadn't been afraid that Zach's parents would get him kicked out of VVCC.* Faye quickly learned what an important role Vista View Country Club played in the lives of Citrus County's elites.

"Who even is this guy?"

"I told you about Darren. He's in my chemistry class, and he lives in Vista View. We know a lot of the same people from middle school."

"You didn't..." Faye let her question trail off. Should she say *have sex with him?*

"Not yet," Krystal said dismissively, "but I did give him a blow job in the parking lot after the football game."

Faye's eyes darted left and right to see if the people nearby were listening. Faye knew what a blow job was. Because she and Bridget had found a porn film in their parents' dresser drawer, she even sort of knew what it entailed. Still, blow jobs weren't for girls like Faye. She felt nervous and a little scared just knowing that Krystal was doing it. She shuddered. Friendship with Krystal meant voyeurism into a world of heavy boozing and *bona fide* sex and the kind of generally unrestrained acting out that Faye and her friends were not quite capable of. Faye's choir friends had crushes and made out at the movies and drank a few wine coolers and smoked a joint here or there, but all seemed a watered down version of adulthood. Faye and her ilk practiced mild curiosity under safely contrived circumstances. Something about her brashness gave Krystal a more mature quality. Faye felt caught somewhere between judging Krystal and admiring her, jealous and relieved to be free of all that sex stuff. It hardly mattered. Faye wouldn't have sex until marriage. That was the plan.

"I thought you still liked Tom," Faye offered, lifting a cherry by its stem from under the frosty surface of her chocolate shake. "Is Darren your boyfriend now?"

Krystal fluttered her eyes at Faye's naivete.

"He's not my boyfriend," she said with emphasis. "We just hooked up after the game and that was that. I mean, he might like me, but I don't really want to be exclusive with a guy like him. He's pretty boring."

Shaking her head, Faye raised her voice in disbelief. "Then why would you—" she looked left and right again and then hushed her voice. "Why would you give him a blow job?"

Tap, tap, tap went Krystal's nails on the table. Everything about Krystal vibrated with energy and flippancy. Everything was a grand adventure; nothing was sacred.

"Because it's *fun*," she said. "It's kind of a rush, you know, because they love it so much."

Faye did not know. She tried to imagine it, but the words could not form a coherent picture.

"Well, it doesn't sound fun to do it at all, but especially not in a parking lot with a guy who is too boring to date."

"You would have done it if Stuart had liked you back," Krystal said almost defensively.

Faye considered the suggestion.

"Maybe," Faye capitulated. "But those days are gone, now."

"So what's going on with this Doctor guy? Does he like you or what?"

The fabric beneath Faye's armpits felt suddenly uncomfortable. She wanted to brush off Krystal's suggestion and to believe it, too.

"I don't know what's going on," Faye said.

She wanted to tell Krystal that she felt grateful to Doctor Vogel and drawn to him, that his brusque outer shell was in fact fractured, that he needed love and she felt compelled to love him. But she didn't.

"It's hard to explain," Faye repeated. "But he's lonely, you know? I feel like I want to help him, make him happy, or something."

"Oh I bet he wants you to make him happy, too," Krystal said with a lascivious lilt.

A tightness spread through Faye's chest.

"That's not what I meant," she said, chuckling with embarrassment.

Since Europe, a burgeoning sexuality had awakened in Faye. An excitement rose up in her when she thought about Edward and in those moments each day that their eyes would meet. She followed his hands while he conducted, welcoming an indescribable urge to press his palm against her cheek, to twine his fingers through hers, to touch the puckered skin between his nose and his upper lip. In the choir room earlier that week, Edward's slightly billowed shirt had brushed against Faye's arm. Faye's body had responded with a swirling rush of desire so sharp she had almost collapsed.

The hairspray-filled air left a chemical taste on Faye's tongue.

"Hold still," Bridget barked, pulling Faye's head back with ever greater force as she teased Faye's hair out into a voluminous and uncontrolled afro.

"Now for a little dirt," Bridget continued.

She smudged dark eyeshadow first under Faye's eyes then across her neck and her exposed shoulders. Bridget swiveled Faye around in her seat and stepped back for a full look.

"There," she said proudly. "Now you look like a cavewoman."

Kids came to the AP choir Halloween party dressed as ghosts and mummies, ballerinas and pirates, Disney princesses, nerds, old ladies, ghouls, and other common and not-so-common festive phantoms. James, a Disney lover who promised to one day be its CEO, showed up as a Mouseketeer. Merton was a vampire; Tiffany a vampire-bitten victim covered in white makeup with drops of deep red blood. Bryn and Tommy took on a confusing brand of Lucy and Desi, Bryn's bright orange wig clashing against the deep brown of her skin.

Faye made the rounds at first, saying hellos and snapping photos. Every few minutes she scanned the crowd, waiting for Edward. She had to catch his attention. When Edward arrived, costume-less in his regular work slacks and Oxford shirt (though without a tie), Faye kept her distance and watched. In the corner of the room, out of the way of buffet tables stacked with sandwiches, potato chips, caramel apples, popcorn, and sodas, Faye lowered herself as seductively as she could into a plush armchair. Each time Edward looked at her, Faye cast her eyes down with a sheepish grin. Students and parents flitted around him, but Edward spoke to them with distraction. The vision of Faye in the corner, her hair a mess of frayed curls, her skin smudged and eyes darkened, pulled his attention away. This was Faye like he had never seen her. As the party started breaking up, Faye stared squarely at Edward until he looked her way. When Edward saw the glimmer in Faye's eyes, the sparkling lights and deep, rhythmic music slowed and stretched. The edges of his consciousness blurred. Hot desire surged out from Edward's heart to his thighs.

Once home, as he flipped on the piano room light, Edward grabbed the cordless phone and dialed Diane's number. By the third ring, he was pouring a shot of Dewar's to the back of his throat. Edward skipped the pleasantries when Diane answered.

"I'm just home from a school function," he said, "and bumming around bored. Can I come by for a night cap?"

Diane wasn't Edward's type. She was mousy and a bit overweight and, more importantly, not very imaginative or bright. They had met at a choral directors' conference a few years earlier, and she fit the bill for the kind of on-again-off-again relationship that provided company when he felt most alone.

The front door pushed open, unlocked. Edward slipped in quietly. Diane drank down a glass and a half of sauvignon blanc before leading him into her bedroom. In nearly complete darkness, Edward and Diane moved swiftly to a desperate love making characteristic of those who for too long have not been intimate with each other. The warmth and pleasure overwhelmed Edward. He wanted to draw the feeling out. He stilled himself before orgasm and turned Diane over, waiting a beat so he could start again. Edward steadied Diane on her hands and knees this time. He pumped himself harder and harder into her, thinking of Faye's wild cavewoman curls.

Wax dribbled onto the flimsy paper shield at the base of Faye's candle. She readjusted the angle with some difficulty while keeping arms locked with Sister Catherine on her right and a pudgy, glasses-wearing teen-aged boy on her left. The November evening was chilly by Southern California standards, but this Wednesday night was the only for which Sister Catherine and AP Campus Ministry could engineer a permit to gather. The permit had been quite unnecessary. Only a handful of Mrs. Crawford's 70 Advanced Placement Government students had shown up, and thus they fit neatly on the public sidewalk running along the east side of the Her Choice clinic. Citrus County numbered dozens of abortion clinics. *They call them women's health centers*, Mrs. Crawford, Faye's snooty, judgmental history teacher would say, looking down her nose.

"They say they're providing healthcare for women," Mrs. Crawford had said in class the day before. "They are murdering babies is what they are doing."

The staunch rhetoric and the equally strident passion of Faye's classmate, a boy named Brian who studied Latin and planned to be the US President one day, riled Faye up and landed her at the Her Choice Rite to Life protest. Mrs. Crawford counted the protest as extra credit for a class in US government that over the years had focused ever more importance on religious liberty, the overturning of *Roe v Wade*, and the need for a national prohibition of abortion. Curiosity and a false sense of civic maturity drove Faye's attendance at the vigil. Sure, as a young Catholic she favored life and reviled abortion, but of the latter she knew very little. Getting pregnant meant having sex first, and Faye had found sex very easy to avoid. The kids at Aquinas Prep swallowed Mrs. Crawford's inflammatory narrative. It was hard to stomach the thought that girls all over Citrus County were having sex with people they hardly knew then throwing away the unwanted children that resulted. Abortion and carelessness went hand in hand. Women got abortions because they were careless, and, Mrs. Crawford stressed, they were careless because they were selfish.

Few women entered the clinic that evening. Those who did glanced only briefly toward the smug group of teens, nuns, and middle-aged women, a cohort of protesters all white, safe, well-fed, and well-protected. A tired woman with scraggly brown hair pulled back to the base of her neck met Faye's eyes as she approached. The woman struggled to open the clinic's door with one hand while using the other to push a stroller through the narrow doorway. Shame hung over this quiet moment. Catholic teachers and parents and Sister Catherine and the wider Church never withheld forgiveness, but neither had they withheld judgment. A chill passed through Faye. It was she, not this woman, who felt suddenly embarrassed and vulnerable. *I feel sorry for you*, the woman's exhausted, gray pupils seemed to say, *because you have nothing better to do than stare at my wounds*.

By winter's approach, the days shortened. Faye's anxiety intensified. Her fascination with Edward moved resolutely in where once only a passing curiosity had been. When Edward trained his attention on Faye, sweat broke out in a thin sheen at the back of her knees and she felt her blood rushing.

A rainy Monday, Bryn pushed a tightly folded note into Faye's palm as they clasped hands for morning prayer. When Edward turned his back, Faye opened the note, hiding it in the folds of Vaughan Williams' *O Mistress Mine*.

Remember Scripture, Bryn had written. *"If your right hand causes you to sin, cut it off and throw it away."* Bryn's loopy handwriting continued: *And if your _____ causes you to sin…?!*

Edward turned his head abruptly when he heard Faye's stifled laugh. She blushed.

It's not just me, Faye thought. Leah was fascinated by Edward; Merton talked about Edward like they were best friends. They all wanted Edward to choose them. They wanted solos and prestige and friendship and the spotlight of Edward's praise. It wasn't enough that they had each other. They wanted to have him. They wanted to *give themselves* to him.

But my God what were they thinking? Edward was a grown-up with a capital *G*. He spent weekends remodeling his house. He had his own house to remodel. He had a Doctorate degree and had lived all around the country. He made sex jokes Faye and her friends didn't even understand. Edward controlled the room and the parents and all the kids, but Faye thought too that he *wanted* something. He leaned in to the kids, Faye thought, and when he did, a flicker of vulnerability appeared then quickly vanished.

Faye woke each morning wanting to see Edward. She searched for him along the brick-lined diagonals of Aquinas Prep's quad. She stayed after school to chit chat about his life and talk about her college plans. The day that Edward gave Ian and Faye detentions for tardiness, despite their good excuse, she was humiliated and angry. On days when he refused to look at her, Faye thought she might go insane, thought she *was* going insane, that she had imagined a flirtation that just maybe had been all in her head. Some days Edward seemed to look right through her, a glint in his eye like he was seeing a different Faye than the one standing before him. She lay in bed at night and thought about him. She imagined him sitting in his black leather office chair and pulling her onto his lap, his mouth hanging open with wet desire.

"Is it thick or thin?" Faye spit the question into Edward's office phone, brimming with excitement.

At home, Faye's sister Bridget cradled the phone in the crook of her neck as she poked through her mom's pencil holder in search of a letter opener. Moments before Faye's lunchtime call, Bridget had plucked from their parents' mailbox a manilla envelope embossed with the Sacred Heart University seal.

"I'd say it's pretty hefty," she said, slicing open the top.

As Bridget pulled a thick university catalogue from the envelope, its cover gleaming with glossy photos of the Sacred Heart campus, Edward leaned against his office door frame with arms crossed and eyed Faye.

It came, Faye mouthed in Edward's direction. *Sacred Heart admission.*

"Dear Ms. Stoneman," Bridget read, "we are pleased to offer you admission to Sacred Heart University. Acceptance of this offer grants admission to an elite and prestigious scholarly community and formally confers your membership in the class of 2002 at Sacred Heart University, Potato Creek, Indiana. Congratulations!"

Edward watched Faye buckle in his office chair, her mouth agape, her eyes welling with tears that didn't fall. She swallowed hard and beamed, shouting over Edward's shoulder to the choir room behind him.

"I got into Sacred Heart!"

Before Edward could speak, Ian rushed into the office, grazing Edward's shoulder as he hopped around the desk and bear hugged Faye right out of the chair. The news trickled out to the risers. Leah and Bryn then James and Merton followed Ian. The teens crowded Edward out of his own office. A moment later, Edward lost sight of Faye amid the gleeful commotion.

Senior year was half complete. Bryn and Faye stretched and made room in their friendship, their lunch dates further apart, Faye's weepy looks toward Edward causing great distress as Bryn watched from the risers. Her friend was in love, and Bryn knew it couldn't end well. Tommy warned Faye to pull back from Edward. (School rumors about Edward's lustful eye scared and disgusted him.) Krystal wedged herself into Faye's life, and Leah slowly backed herself out. Merton and Edward swapped stories and traded music recommendations. Edward wished he could take Merton for a beer. He needed a new fishing buddy. Edward and Ian shared a tenuous peace, the rage still lodged close to Ian's vest.

Faye was confused. It was too embarrassing, wasn't it, to think Edward handsome? *How could a forty-year-old man be handsome?* Besides, he had that nasally laugh and was always pulling his pants up awkwardly around his belly because he was maybe twenty pounds overweight. And *my God*, how her friends never let her forget that. But oh! How Faye adored him and loved him and wanted to touch his face and put his fingers in her mouth. She could not bear to part from him.

IV

SPRING OF 1998 BROUGHT WITH IT the promise of great change in Faye's relationships. She and Krystal were best girlfriends now. Leah's hurt feelings alternately peeked out then took cover. Ian, James, Bryn—all the seniors made college plans and prepared to wind down their Aquinas Prep legacy. It seemed to Faye that she and Doctor Vogel were changing, too.

The traffic on University Boulevard moved more quickly than Faye expected. The taillights were few. She crossed Edward's intersection too soon. Nerves were getting the best of her, so Faye turned right instead of left and took the long way around three blocks instead of driving directly to Edward's house. Anyway, she ought to call before arriving. Smoke curled up from Faye's burning cigarette as she clinked each coin into the payphone. A busy signal resounded. *He must be on the computer*, she thought. For a moment, she reconsidered the visit. He had invited her, hadn't he? She replayed their conversation, exchanged congenially if not flirtatiously, as she had sat on Edward's office floor the previous afternoon.

"What's going on with you this weekend?" he had asked.

"Saturday night I'm going to a play for extra credit points in Sullivan's Advanced Spanish IV. The play is at Cal State Fulton."

She had dropped the university name casually but with a knowing emphasis. Edward neatly arranged some stray papers on his desk. He had stared down the papers, not Faye, as he responded.

"The play is at Cal State Fulton, is it?" he had said with nonchalance. "You should stop by my house since you'll be so close."

And so now here she was, at the gas station on the corner of Edward's crossroads, a quivering cigarette in her hand. Faye felt in over her head. This hesitation was silly. *Just go,* she told herself. *Just do it.*

Before exiting the car, she covered the cigarette smoke with a splash of raspberry perfume. Her hair was freshly washed. Her curls stuck out a bit wildly. A light clicked on over Edward's back steps as she approached. She smoothed the satin front of her dress and knocked. From her few visits (a Chamber Singer barbecue and two special rehearsals), Faye knew Edward never used the front entrance.

The door swung open and Edward stood before her, his eyebrows raised in unknowing expectation. He wore jeans and a faded tee shirt advertising *Bye Bye Birdie,* an Aquinas Prep senior musical from the days when Faye was still in elementary school. Already, there seemed something improper about seeing Edward this way. She could sense his indecisiveness. He looked unsure, even vulnerable.

"Faye," he said with surprise in his voice. As he spoke, Edward pushed open the screen door. "Come in. What are you doing here?"

A tightness seized Faye's insides. Warmth spread across her cheeks.

"Oh, I'm sorry to interrupt," she stammered. "I'm sorry if you didn't want me to come. I just thought, because you said I should stop by."

Edward relaxed in visible relief.

"The play at Fulton. That's right. I'm sorry I forgot. Come on in, really. I was just tooling around at the computer. You are not interrupting."

The house was as Faye remembered it. As on other occasions, the chaotic messiness of Edward's home struck her. At school, Edward meticulously demanded perfection and attention to detail. Everything had its time, and everything had to be done just right. The house gave just the opposite vibe. The house was not dirty, but everything seemed slightly undone. Haphazard stacks of paperwork and the lack of living room furniture suggested a house in transition, like the occupants were still moving in.

The scent of raspberries and vanilla rushed at Edward as Faye entered his home. Intense desire—unwanted, uninvited—swirled through Edward's core. He pushed it back.

"You smell good," Edward said. The words poured out before he could stop them.

"Thanks." Faye sounded more shy than usual. She stepped lightly, looked around with inquisitive, doe-like eyes.

Spending time with Faye was generally easy. Edward knew from experience that teenagers liked to talk about themselves. Faye talked about troubles in her high school friendships. She told him who had spurned whose crush and who got rejected from their university of choice. Ian had been denied admission at UCLA, Bryn and James had dated briefly only to break up in dramatic fashion amid rumors that James in fact favored Leah. New rumors followed that Leah was gay and therefore quite uninterested in James from the start. Faye carefully skirted her own thoughts, so Edward asked about them.

"And how are *you*?" he prodded. "Have you settled on Sacred Heart?"

Since Faye's acceptance the previous December, she and Edward had not often talked about her future. The inevitability of separation crept around them.

"Yes," she said softly, "but I can't imagine going. I don't think I'll be okay there."

Seriousness and steadiness were Faye's signature traits. She was not the bubbly co-ed Edward imagined when he thought back to his days starting college. Still, Faye was a striking young woman on the cusp of a brilliant future. Admiration, jealousy, and sadness fought within him.

"You have such an amazing life ahead of you, Faye. I hope you know that. You cannot even imagine how wonderful things can be. Sacred Heart is perfect for you."

She offered a weak smile. Faye loved Edward's praise of her. She loved more, though, the sense that he wanted her to stay.

"I know," she countered, "but I'm just not ready to go. There are," she paused, drawing her words out dramatically. "There are *people* here that I cannot bear to leave."

A wave of nausea swept across Edward's middle. He wanted to take her hand. He wanted to caress her, to feel the warmth of her skin against his. *Don't touch her*, his angry, frustrated inner voice scolded. He was wrong to have even let this vulnerable, loving girl, all of seventeen, into his house alone. Edward pressed his body more firmly against the back of his chair, forbidding himself to move.

"Life figures itself out as you go," he said with a resignation that surprised him. "I never thought I'd end up where I am now."

Talk of Edward's past roused Faye from her own reflections. The kids all knew Edward's Doctorate was from the University of Michigan. From their previous discussions in Edward's office after school or on late nights on the steps of the choir room, the fog rolling in after evening Chamber Singer rehearsal, Faye knew that Edward had grown up on a farm in Kansas, that he had come to Aquinas Prep in the shadow of some heartache, that he wanted more than his life was giving. Faye reached greedily for more knowledge.

"How did you come to be here?" she asked. "Why California after Michigan?"

The precious lift in Faye's voice enticed Edward. Her interest thrilled him.

"I can't tell you the whole story," Edward began. Jane's ghost presented itself. "I had a fiancé in Michigan. Her name was Jane."

The word *fiancé* hung in the air between them.

"I had planned after my Doctorate to study in Europe and tour the world, but," he laughed awkwardly, "I followed my heart instead. Jane wanted to come to California for medical school, so I agreed."

"What happened?" Faye asked, leaning into the saga. "Did you plan the wedding and everything?"

With a brusque head shake, Edward tried to lighten the mood.

"No, nothing like that," he said. "We broke up about three or four months after I moved out to Los Angeles. She was deep in medical school and just had her sights on something different, I guess. I honestly don't really know what happened. She left me."

An emotional heaviness persisted despite Edward's efforts to sound unaffected.

"That was a long time ago." Edward thought for a moment. "1984."

The date startled Faye. For most of 1984, Faye had been three years old.

Faye grimaced.

"I'm so sorry," she said. "That sounds awful. I suppose without it, though, you wouldn't be here. We wouldn't have you. Aquinas Prep would not have you."

A spring breeze wafted through an open window in the front room of Edward's house. A nearly imperceptible shiver cycled down from the roots of Faye's curls to her calves. Tension had suddenly supplanted their easy banter. Faye wanted a cigarette, but she did not want to leave. Edward wondered how to redirect their conversation. He disliked self pity, but he loved Faye's sweet concern. The moment soothed him.

"What shall we do?" he asked. "I have a recording from the Concordia Concert if you're interested."

"No," Faye began. Here, in Edward's house, Faye wanted more of him. "Do you have recordings of anything you've written? Can I hear something you wrote in your Doctoral program?"

Pleasant surprise spread across Edward's face.

"Of course I do," he said, walking toward the back of the house. "Let me find some tapes. It'll just be a minute."

Faye tapped her fingertips together lightly while she waited. Her eyes scanned Edward's house. She liked the feel of it. The hardwood floors seemed wonderfully strange. Her parents' whole house was carpeted, except of course for the geometrically-patterned linoleum that floored the kitchen and bathrooms. Edward's unstructured environment felt mature without being fatherly. He lived alone. Everything about Edward suggested the freedom of adulthood. He could and would do whatever he wanted. Still, Faye thought, *something is missing.* Alone with her, Edward projected a sense of loss, a suggestion that what he truly desired had somehow eluded his grasp. Instinctively, Faye wanted to fill that space.

"This is the score," Edward said, placing a Xeroxed mix of notes and staves in Faye's lap. Seating was scarce in Edward's living room, a space so filled with crates, books, and boxes that it seemed more a workroom than a place where two people might sit and chat. Faye sat on a folding chair against a low wall separating the front room from its other half, Edward's real workspace that housed his computer, paper-cluttered desk, and piano. As the music began, Edward set a glass of water on the storage crates that comprised a makeshift end table within reach of Faye's chair. He retired a few steps back to the kitchen table and spread his copy of the composition out before him.

"You can follow along if you want," he said. "It might be tough since you aren't used to all the orchestral lines, but the violin and oboe carry a pretty clear lead."

The first notes sounded so deep and so slowly that Faye could hardly decipher them over the crackling of the old recording. Faye's eyes drifted up from the score to the glass of water, the few ice cubes reduced already to flat disks dissolving in the tap-warm liquid. She had not asked for a drink and almost never drank water. She wondered if it would seem strange to ask if he had a soda. *Better not*, she thought. *That might make me seem like a kid.* She was glad of that water glass now. The music sounded ominous and queer and made her feel like she was invading Edward's space. She needed a place to put her hand, so she picked up the glass and took a tiny sip. The water lightly touched her lips. Across the room, Edward sat pensively, his eyes on the composition.

Faye felt a richness circulating through her limbs and pulling her toward Edward. Her hands felt hot and clammy. She stole a glance at Edward and took in his calm stillness. She imagined beneath this placidity that his hands would feel twitchy and impatient, the music begging him to conduct the way the beat of a pop song causes a dance floor crowd to bop their heads and bend at the knees. As the music intensified, Faye began to feel nervous, afraid to look up or to look around or to otherwise spoil the feeling that she and Edward were sharing something private. Faye stopped following the score and closed her eyes. The darkness of the rising notes made the room feel small. She imagined herself and Edward standing opposite each other in a shrouded space, the insistent pull of the violin pulsing in bursts of light around Edward's smoothly shaven face and bright blue eyes. Something fluttered between her thighs as a flurry of trumpets started and stopped, started and stopped, each wave climbing a bit higher, each ending in unfinished frustration. Discordant melodies kept coming, the intensity so violent and dramatic that Faye leaned forward on the edge of her seat, waiting for the melody to crest and resolve. In the absence that followed the final crescendo, Faye opened her eyes and found Edward watching her, his chin resting gently on his curved palm.

"It's called *Loon Shadow*," he said. "The loon is a symbol of freedom and," he hesitated, "exploration. Some people," he continued, a mysterious lilt in his voice, "consider the loon a sign of sexual adventure."

Faye's stomach dropped to her knees. *Sexual*, a word so forbidden and terrifying, sounded lovely in Edward's deep, gravelly voice. Edward registered the moment of intrigue and fear in Faye's eyes. He tried not to react. He chided himself. *Slow down.*

"I guess for me it was only a symbol of a false start," he said in a much lighter voice, trying to laugh away his failed career and the too forceful attempt at flirting with this young girl.

Stability took hold in Faye at Edward's self deprecation.

"I think it's amazing." Faye spoke with genuine emotion. "The piece is so beautiful. I can feel it right here" she said, touching the flustered space between her breasts.

A swell of emotion washed over Edward. Had he been watching from outside, he might have judged himself pathetic and small, his ego stoked by a child's appreciation of his talent. Here, in the room with Faye, the tape player still crackling, the spring breeze countering the thick air that hung between them, Edward felt that Faye might be the one to save him from his despair. Jane was gone, and with her, Edward's youth. For years, the weight of loss and disappointment had tainted his many accomplishments. *No more*, he thought. Faye could make him young again. So much seemed possible now.

Two whiskeys turned to three then four as Edward replayed Faye's visit. Lust and panic flooded him. He did not touch the girl. He knew better. Now that she was gone, he paced the house. Everything felt untethered. Edward wanted to imagine Faye's soft, curly hair falling down over her bare shoulders and to touch himself. A vibration ran from his thighs all through his middle and even up through his chest and throat to his mouth. He needed the explosive release of an orgasm in which he could envision the full possession of this girl, imagining his hot mouth devouring all her sweetness and her supple, unspoiled youth. In fact he had started to do just that, leaning back in the chair where she had sat and watching the bulge in his briefs stir as he smelled the remnant of her perfume on the air in his house. He thought about her knees on his hardwood floor, her expectant brows and shy eyes looking up at him as he thrust his hips toward her mouth and felt her take away the painful isolation that followed him like a persistent odor. He had stopped, though, before finishing this fantasy. He forced himself out into the night air and smoked a cigar. He walked in the dewy grass as midnight became morning, picking some overripe plums and checking the chickens in their coop. Fantasizing about students was a kind of hazard of the trade. But there was something about Faye that he did not want to sully. The fierceness of his desire for Faye had increased so quickly it threatened to undo him. He feared the seeds of this lust would take hold inside him and grow into thorny tendrils that could choke his usually stoic nature.

As daylight dawned, Edward dug in the back closet for a stash of cocaine he had buried there a few months before. He was not a habitual user these days. Edward reserved cocaine for emergency sobriety or to push through a night of productive composing. Two lines sobered Edward for the day. He had been awake all night. In three hours, he would need to arrive clear headed and composed to direct the St. Crispina church choir. Easter was only a few weeks away. Between now and then, Edward would unfold the Lord's Passion before pliant congregants, his own soul battling the Evil One that stared out through Faye's wide, pleading eyes.

"You're quite gussied up for a father and daughter dance," Faye's mom said, beaming. "Gee, you sure do look beautiful."

Faye tried for the second time to apply lipstick and, for the second time, wiped it off brusquely with a tissue. Make-up and hairstyles and feminine glamour were her sister's area. Faye did not have the pretty girl gene that guided cheerleaders like Bridget and girls like Krystal who had perfectly painted nails and the tendency to give blow jobs on the second date to any number of high school crushes. Faye answered the ringing telephone and waved her mom away at the sound of Ian's voice.

"What are you and Krystal doing tonight?" she asked.

Since February, Krystal and Ian had been dating. Krystal was deep in the fold now, her frequent presence pushing Bryn and Leah outside the circle just as they'd feared.

"I think we'll just go for a drive down the coast," Ian said casually. "We might go out to the tower. Nothing as exciting as your big date," he laughed. "What are you wearing?"

Faye sized herself up in the bedroom mirror.

"I'm recycling my dress from last year's winter formal, the lavender one with sequins. Bridget did my hair but didn't have time for make-up. I'm trying to do it myself, but I'm failing. At least it's just a father and daughter dance."

Ian scoffed. Ordinarily Faye found his irreverence funny. Tonight, she was too nervous to laugh.

"Father and daughter dance my ass," he said with emphasis. "I know who you're really getting dressed up for. Doctor Vogel is your real date."

Faye's stomach dipped. She felt suddenly aware of the scratchy sequined fabric cutting into her skin across the back of her neck. Faye hoped Bridget's up-do made her look just sophisticated enough to entice Doctor Vogel. The anticipation of seeing him felt delicious and warm.

"You're disgusting," she said caustically to Ian. "I've got to go."

In bed after midnight, Faye replayed memories from the AP Choir's Annual Father-Daughter Dance in her mind. In the half darkness, she watched the lighted wick of a candle bobbing back and forth as it cast shadows over the contents of her room. She saw again the gleam on Edward's lips as he had looked her up and down, his eyes meeting hers briefly, his smile so slight that only she could see it. When he touched her waist and asked her to dance, Faye had felt her insides shaking so hard she thought she might faint.

Now, in her bed, she could conjure the feeling again, the manic energy, the wetness seeping out between her legs. Her body hummed with excitement; Faye, the rest of Faye, was terrified. *I cannot leave him*, she thought. *Please*—she whispered an errant prayer that could not possibly be answered—*don't make me go away from him.*

Thank God Annie Pickford's dad had saved Edward, had touched him gently on the elbow and said, *I'm going your way, Doc. Let me just drop you at home.* The ride to Edward's from the dance venue was only a few blocks. Hell, he could have walked it instead of accepting the lift. Maybe next year he would walk rather than leaving his car abandoned in the parking lot overnight, its lone presence a sign that he couldn't control his drinking. The screen door banged shut as Edward slipped backward across the threshold. He stumbled, more drunk than he had thought. The night air touched Edward now through the screen. He felt cool where damp circles of sweat had formed beneath his arms. Memories of the night's events assaulted him.

Edward thought of many of his girls as adopted daughters; others had been the objects of his fantasies. This night, all of them had glittered and twirled on the dance floor, their fathers mostly watching from the sidelines, their pride bursting out from beneath rented tuxedos and wilting boutonnieres. Each year, the Father-Daughter Dance stirred in Edward a mix of excitement, regret, and sadness. Always, the night's end was a lonely one. The lights turned up and the confetti settled, all the other men ushered their vibrant daughters, adrenaline pumping, curls coming unfurled from picture-perfect hairstyles, a sweet sheen of sweat across their foreheads, to waiting sedans and carted them away to the homes their fathers had built. Edward returned to an empty house. Most years he had kept himself in check with a shot of whiskey before the dance and only a beer or two during it. Tonight, though, something had undone him. It was Faye, he realized now. Edward had tried to avoid her for most of the night. He took do-si-do direction from Leah, danced an awkwardly formal waltz with Bryn, and swung Tiff across the dance floor to the bopping tune of *Sing! Sing! Sing!* All night he had kept one eye on Faye.

Light from the mirror ball danced off Faye's sequined dress and pulled his attention her way. She seemed especially happy this night, and, Edward could tell, she was performing this happiness so that he would notice her. She laughed more loudly and readily than usual, sipped a soda with perfectly pursed lips, and, resting from so much high-heeled dancing, let one shoe dangle off the edge of her slender, white foot. After dancing with so many others, Edward could avoid Faye no longer. And so, they danced and they laughed, and when the song ended, Edward held Faye's hands in his. A second too long, he held them. In her high-heeled shoes, Faye stood almost exactly Edward's height. His whiskeyed breath fell hot at the base of her neck. For a second only, Edward rested his hand on Faye's waist. Struck by his own impertinence, he moved quickly away to the bar for another whiskey. He had several others after that. His initial exhilaration turned sour; Edward was moving too quickly from pleasantly drunk to the arid and distasteful sense of being hungover before the night's end. Faye's behavior had become bolder since the night they had listened to *Loon Shadow* together. During school and at rehearsals the two were talking less, studying each other more. He wanted her. Here, drunk at a dance celebrating teen-aged kids and their fathers, Edward wanted this young, girlish thing to be his.

Edward walked unsteadily past his piano, its dark wood tinted blue from the lighted computer screen opposite it. Down the short hallway he stumbled to the bathroom, a brief pause there for a long, satisfying piss and a gargle of mouthwash. *What a debacle!* So many whiskeys at AP Choir Father-Daughter. He hoped he had not made too much a fool of himself dancing with those girls. He clucked his tongue. *Impossible!* Everyone in that program fawned over Edward. Through the years, without nuance, he had instructed the girls and their parents alike. *Always ask yourself*, he would tell them with a half-joking smile, *what would Doctor want?*

The whiskey still felt hot in his veins. A light buzzing fluttered through his limbs. Replaying the night, he felt too energized to sleep but too drunk to pick at his guitar or have another drink. *Loon Shadow* still sat in the tape player. He keyed it on and fell into bed thinking of Faye. He smiled broadly. *What would Doctor want?* Sober, Edward controlled his urges. Now, sleepy and drunk, remembering the delicate touch of Faye's fingers enclosed in his cupped palms, Edward allowed himself to indulge the fantasy. *What would Doctor want?* He wanted to feel Faye's bouncy, sweet-smelling curls brushing against his skin, to bury his face between her perfectly young breasts and burrow his mouth into the wet folds between her thighs. There was no denying his desire, now. Edward splayed one leg out across the bed and tightened his grip around the base of his cock. Behind closed lids he imagined Faye riding on top of him, her nipples hard and bright, her mouth open and wet, her eyes sweet and almost afraid.

Nathan Pickford phoned his wife from his office at the hospital.

"Did Annie get home alright from the dance?"

"Yes. She said everything was just magnificent. Did you end up getting called away early?"

"No," Nathan began, hesitantly, "and thank God I didn't." He nearly whispered the next part, genuine embarrassment in his voice. "I found Doctor Vogel in the parking lot. He was absolutely falling down drunk. He was about to get into his car."

Helen Pickford breathed in sharply, her mouth open slightly in an *o* shape.

"Did any of the girls see?"

"Thank Heavens, no," her husband confirmed. "Doctor and I were just about the last to leave. I had been helping a few of the mothers load some camera equipment into their vans. He seemed a bit embarrassed. He hopped in my car eagerly, and I got him home alright. Still, though..."

Nathan Pickford's voice trailed off, a mixture of sadness and a kind of relief.

"It must be difficult for Doctor Vogel," Helen began, "to see all of you, the fathers, so happy and proud with your daughters. That poor man does so much for the girls at Aquinas Prep and has no wife or child of his own." Helen shook her head with the *tsk tsk* of a woman secure in the rightness of her own family, concerned for a lonesome soul like Doctor Vogel. She spoke empathetically. "That poor man. God bless him."

A bit tired, to be honest, of spending his birthday alone, Edward said sure, he would let Merton and Faye take him out for a celebratory dinner. It was unusual that Edward's best friends were teenagers. *Was it pathetic?* Edward wondered. *Certainly not*, he concluded. *Pathetic* was much too harsh. Edward had acquaintances and colleagues. He dated Diane and a few other women when time permitted. Gary's move to Arizona (a bad divorce) couldn't be helped. It was just that his colleagues at Aquinas Prep didn't have the same interests that Edward did. He and Matt Brown, a science teacher, talked home renovations on occasion, but Edward cared about little else than his choirs and their successes. Talking with Merton stabilized him, made Edward feel like he had a real friend. Faye, on the other hand, made his head swim. It terrified him, sometimes, how much he desired her. He readied eagerly, listening for Faye's wheels on his driveway. The kids had asked him to choose, and Edward had chosen a small but exquisite sushi bar in downtown Fulton. Edward patted some aftershave on his cheeks and checked his reflection in the bathroom mirror. Merton would offer a welcome distraction. Edward needed a safe place to focus his gaze so that he would not find himself searching for the smooth curve of Faye's earlobe or the delicate slenderness of her wrist. He wondered how Faye would be dressed. So often when he expected a womanly performance, Faye turned up in jeans and little girl tee shirts. Her flirtations confused him. *One of us is doing this wrong*, he thought with a chuckle.

Faye lit one more cigarette as Merton signaled an exit from the freeway.

"I'm starting to regret this already," Faye said glumly.

"Don't do that yet," Merton said with characteristic optimism. "The night is still young."

The triteness brought out Faye's smile. Merton was a walking repository of aphorisms.

"I would not have let him choose," Faye complained, "if I would have known he would choose sushi. What am I even going to eat?"

"Why don't you try some sushi? You might like it, girl."

Merton always called Faye *girl*. She loved it. At an age when every girl wants to be a woman, Faye felt the title not as a derision but as an elevation. Tiff might have been his girlfriend, but Faye was Merton's *girl*.

"It hardly matters," Faye said. "I can't imagine I'll be able to eat anything. I'm too anxious. I just don't want Doctor to think I'm juvenile and picky."

Merton reached across and gently tweaked Faye's nose. "You *are* juvenile and picky."

Faye rolled her eyes and flicked her half-finished cigarette out the window as University Boulevard came into view.

"Thanks."

"You are quite welcome," Merton responded. "Your picky immaturity is endearing. Besides, I don't think Doctor will be focused on what you are eating."

Merton regretted the comment immediately and was glad that Faye ignored it. The unspoken rules required that no one acknowledge the strange goings on between Faye and Doctor. Merton cupped Faye's hand where it rested on her thigh.

"Well, you look beautiful, girl. Dinner will be great."

From the backseat of her own car, Faye listened as Edward and Merton talked sushi-rolling technique and newly released compositions for six-part handbell choirs. Her cheek leaning against the cool window, Faye wished she could smoke but didn't dare. Regardless of her unique position, some lines remained intact, bright white, *do not pass go.*

Dinner conversation came easy and continued through each course of sushi to each of Doctor's miniature tea cups of sake and through the flat smears of pistachio ice cream they took turns stripping from tiny scoops set in a porcelain dish at center table.

"I don't mind talking to you two about these things," Edward said, holding his mouth half open to counter the sudden coldness of the ice cream against his teeth. "People at Aquinas Prep would get all worked up if they thought I was job searching. Truth be told, I need to move up into university conducting before I've been away from it too long."

Faye and Merton both nodded, lapsing into student mode as they did when Edward talked about adult stuff. His rich tone seemed instructive, even when he did not intend it as such.

Faye stammered. "Would you really leave Aquinas Prep?"

Edward understood her attachment but was unmoved by it. He had let Aquinas Prep choirs hold him back for too many years already. Two years before, he had turned down a college job in West Virginia for the sake of finishing out the high school years of the talented band of seniors who comprised Chamber Choir that year. When no job offers came the next year, Edward vowed not to let his devotion to his students overwhelm him any longer.

To Faye's precious concern, Edward responded flirtatiously.

"With you gone," he began, "there won't be anything left for me there."

Edward met eyes briefly with Merton to gauge his reaction.

Then, he backed away.

"The two of you are much more mature than the rest of those kids you hang around with," Edward continued. "Don't worry about my future. We can still see each other no matter what happens with Aquinas Prep."

Faye smiled shyly, her insides beaming.

"Have you ever done that?" she asked, unsure of her own direction.

"Done what?" Edward answered, a spoon suspended before his closed mouth.

Faye had heard the rumors. Merton had, too. Waiting for Faye to continue, Merton involuntarily clenched his jaw. She wouldn't dare.

"Have you ever gone out with a former student?"

Edward repeated her phrasing. "Gone out with?"

"Have you ever dated one of your former students?" she asked.

A lump rose in Edward's throat. Faye's hands trembled beneath the table. Merton's face flushed with embarrassment on Faye's behalf.

Edward trod carefully. He thought immediately of Marielle Winterson from '89 and Juliet Carbone of '92. Had he *wanted* to date those girls? Yes. Had he *wanted* to teach them about adult love and carry them from teen-aged innocence to sublime sexual pleasure? Yes. He had *wanted* to, but he had not.

"No," he said evenly, appearing neither surprised nor offended. "I have never dated a student."

Faye and Edward shared a fleeting glimmer of understanding. Clear as day, with Merton looking on and sushi chefs plating orders, Edward sensed Faye's true confession. *I want to be the first. You can date me.*

Edward dipped another bite of ice cream. Faye watched his lips close gently around the silver spoon and his eyes flutter in enjoyment of the cool sweetness. Her head buzzed; the muscles in her thighs tightened then contracted. The moment assaulted Faye, and she thought she might faint. Faye grabbed Merton's knee beneath the table and dug her fingers into the coarse fabric of his jeans. He leaned toward her.

"Are you okay?" Merton whispered. "Do we need to go?"

From across the table, Edward could sense the spreading wide of Merton's fingers across the top of Faye's back. He watched with interest and—*was it envy?*—as a few floppy strands of Merton's hair fell across Faye's cheek while Merton spoke into her ear. *They don't need me,* Edward thought. Unless he could insert himself further, they would maintain a separate world he was too old and too outside to understand.

Faye pushed herself lightly away from the table.

"I'm sorry," she said quietly. "I just need to use the restroom."

In the night air outside the restaurant, Faye smoked to calm her nerves. Back in there, at the table, Merton and Edward were talking with animated gestures about something. All of this—the swirl of desire at the soft wetness of Doctor's mouth on a spoon, the urge to hold his eyes with her gaze, to re-order her life so she would not have to leave him—was becoming too real. When they were alone these days, a new desire pushed up into her throat. She wanted to tell him.

Merton half stood when Faye took her seat at the table.

"Everything okay?"

"Oh sure," she said nonchalantly. "I just needed a quick break."

Edward could smell the cigarette smoke from across the table, its acridness merging with Faye's sweet perfume and the restaurant's rich, oily aroma. She seemed nervous, and with good reason. Two cups of sake tempered Edward's anxiety about this experiment. He was happy, now, to be here with these two young people who loved him. He felt their compassion for him like a warm blanket draped across his shoulders. Lately, he had been wanting for physical intimacy. He knew he could not touch Faye, and so he looked forward with longing to the end of the night when he would shake Merton's hand and feel the clap of this strong, young man's palm on his back.

Bargain hunters at the Aquinas Prep Choir Rummage Sale sifted through boxes of cheap dining sets and flipped uselessly through old books, their covers crunchy and unyielding from age and lack of use. Many of the kids searched for hidden treasures; other students hung listlessly around without bothering to look busy or be helpful. The chance to see Edward under the bright morning sun caused Faye to bound from her car and jump into the fray. Before reaching the spot where Edward stood, Faye heard his muted, almost jeering laughter and stopped to smooth out her wrinkled shirt and take a breath deep into her stomach. The students weren't required to work or even to attend the event, but Faye was Choir President and she felt a sense of duty to represent her board. More, Faye coveted any chance to see Edward outside of school hours. This Saturday morning her hair was freshly washed and still wet. A touch of apple blossom fought the smokiness that clung mightily to her clothes from the drive over.

Shoppers, students, and parents obscured Faye's view of Edward as she wove her way among the tables. She had slept poorly in anticipation of this morning's event and struggled to find her friends in the day's bright sunlight. She spotted Leah's mother immediately. That bossy woman unnerved Faye. Mrs. Fallon fawned over Edward (though most of the mothers did) and pushed Leah shamelessly to the front of every pack. Worse, her nose seemed always to be in Leah's business. Sure, mothers watched out for their daughters, but while Faye's mom knew only the bare basics of Faye's teen-aged circle, Mrs. Fallon inserted herself everywhere she wasn't wanted. As every phone call crept toward midnight, there was Mrs. Fallon picking up the line. *Leah, honey, it's time to hang up.* When Faye tried to leave the Fallon house past dark for a sleepover at Krystal's, Mrs. Fallon's church lady prohibition: *I'm sorry, dear, but I can't have you driving around town so late when your parents expect that you are here.*

Faye pasted on her most conciliatory smile.

"Good morning, Mrs. Fallon. Is Leah around?"

Leah's mother raised her eyes only slightly from the box of merchandise at her fingertips.

"Hello, Faye. I was just wondering the same thing. You kids shouldn't be just loitering and lollygagging. Be a dear. Find Leah and tell her to run over here to help sort these records."

Faye fluttered her lids hard as she walked away. That Mrs. Fallon always kept character.

Faye released a long breath and looked side to side among the aisles. Then, between a large box of ski goggles and a neat array of tennis rackets (some old, made of graphite; some older, made of wood), Edward stepped into Faye's path and smiled. In her mind, Faye had dubbed this look Edward's *spring smile*. Something about his greetings had changed since Christmas. She couldn't quite explain it. This spring Edward seemed to almost look through Faye when he encountered her. She and Edward seemed to be speaking a language no one else understood, their movements like a secret handshake though to the others, everything appeared as it always had been. Edward drew a slow breath in before speaking. His voice sounded new for the day. Faye felt his rich tones pulsing between her ears.

"I thought maybe you weren't coming," he said.

Faye's stomach quivered. She and Edward had always talked easily, like friends. Lately, talking to Edward made her nervous. She found herself choosing words carefully instead of freely.

"I'm sorry I'm late. I didn't sleep well. I haven't been sleeping well."

Edward tilted his chin toward his chest but kept his eyes trained on Faye's. He hadn't slept so well either since his birthday. The nearness of Faye's graduation hung heavy between them. So too, more so, did the inevitability of Faye's leaving for university.

"You're counting the days," he asked. "Is that it?"

Faye shrugged. The brightness of the day seemed unbefitting. A few graying hairs peeked out from the collar of Edward's tee shirt. Faye wanted to fold herself against his chest and close her eyes.

"It will be alright," Edward said with fatherly assurance. Then, cryptically, "We'll figure it all out."

Morning turned to afternoon and the curious crowds dissipated. Parents began to clear tables, collapse sun-blocking canopies, and encourage the kids to help out already or just go home.

"Okay, friends," Faye said with confidence. "I must get to Cal's."

Leah frowned disapprovingly. "I thought you were off today. Didn't we talk about hanging out at my house after this?"

After the interaction with Leah's mom, work looked more appealing to Faye than usual.

"I didn't think so. Anyway, I have no choice. I was able to trade my morning shift for a 3 to 7 swing, but I still have to work. See what James and Tommy are doing. You should come visit me at work. I'll buy everyone dessert."

Leah smiled and thought maybe she would do just that. A piece of pie and a hot coffee at Cal's would be nice. If customers were few, she could chat with Faye without the others overshadowing her. Leah's friendship with Faye had been fading since Christmas, but they tried now and then to revive it. This spring, Krystal and Ian had consumed most of Faye's time. And, too, there was this unnerving infatuation with Doctor Vogel. Faye whispered about it with Ian and Krystal but brushed it off as a joke whenever Leah brought it up. As the only juniors in their group, Leah and Tommy thought they'd better stay out of it. Soon the seniors would graduate and move off to universities across the country. She and Tommy had their own senior year adventures to start planning.

Faye tried looking nonchalant as she sought Edward's whereabouts for a good-bye. On a table of odds and ends, she spied a stuffed lamb. Its wool looked like the real thing: soft, haphazardly puffed, not quite clean. A 10¢ sticker clung to its nose. The miniature figure felt heavier in her hand than she expected. Faye and the lamb stared at each other, the lamb's eyes impossibly tiny pinpricks of knotted black thread.

Edward found her before she could find him. He walked up beside her and announced his presence. "Cute."

Faye turned the lamb's face toward him. "It is, right?" Faye tried a coy, flirtatious smile. "Do you have a dime?"

Edward reached into his pocket. A few coins jingled there.

"I do," Edward flirted back (Faye thought), "but if I pay for it, the lamb becomes half mine." He leaned toward her the slightest bit and took the animal from her hand. "We would have to share it."

She would feel a fool thinking back on this great excitement. So juvenile and inconsequential yet so glorifying. The promise of something *together* with this man! Yes, they would share the lamb.

Faye blushed. "What should we name it?"

Edward thought a moment and then straightened back into his familiar, instructive posture.

"Worthy," he said emphatically.

Faye repeated the name warily, unimpressed. "Worthy?"

Edward pressed the lamb back into Faye's hand, letting his fingertips linger on her palm for only a moment.

"Yes," he said, starting his retreat. "Worthy is the Lamb."

Faye would be middle-aged, a mother shepherding her four young children into Good Friday service, when she realized Edward had been quoting the title of a Church hymn: *Worthy Is the Lamb*. Edward, by then, would be gone. Entirely. Fully. Amidst soaring voices, hot tears would sting Faye's cheeks. She would envision the long lost Worthy and his threaded eyes, would feel her heart fold down on top of her stomach, and would squeeze her son Wyatt's hand to keep from physically collapsing.

But now, as Edward walked away from her on a bright spring morning at the Aquinas Prep Choir Rummage Sale, Faye could only laugh and think one thought: *My God, he is so old!*

Parking across the street made Edward feel so ridiculous that he moved his car closer instead. He inched slowly into a slot in the Cal's parking lot and turned off the engine. He sat at a great enough distance from the restaurant's large front windows to be inconspicuous. He made sure not to slouch, or duck, or look otherwise strange. Sitting in a parked car in his Church clothes on a Sunday morning, he could have been waiting to meet a friend. He had even rolled down the driver's side window so he would appear relaxed to people that might pass by. Faye reminded him often that she waited tables at Cal's on weekend mornings. *You should stop by for coffee*, she always said, *after Church*. Edward had not considered her invitation in earnest until Christmas break when two weeks off school had meant two weeks without Faye. He had thought about it nearly every Sunday afternoon this spring. The longer he sat without seeing Faye, the more nervous he became. The stuffed lamb rested in the plastic divot between the front panel and the gear shift, its bed a mess of coins, paperclips, and half crumpled receipts. Edward rolled up his window and turned the car back on so the air conditioner could blow cold air in his face. Waiting, watching, straining for a glimpse of this girl thrilled him at first. After a few minutes, the wait felt interminable and the whole escapade humiliating. Worthy eyed Edward with pity.

Edward cast his gaze down to shift into gear, and when his eyes focused for a last glance at the restaurant, Faye was there at the window. She smiled broadly and touched the table lightly with her fingertips. This was Faye's way, her way of putting people at ease with her chatter. Edward watched as she spun away from the table and reappeared with a full pot of coffee. Everything in Cal's moved chaotically on a busy Sunday morning. Other food servers darted by. Crowds of Churchgoing women in big hats and families with small children milled about in the lobby, and middle schoolers climbed on the railings just outside Cal's wide front doors. Faye wove herself in and out amongst the people. She chatted, took orders, delivered food, wiped tables, and laughed. She laughed with the customers and with her co-workers. A customer told a long story (so it seemed from Faye's attentive stillness at the booth). Then, Faye laughed heartily, gently clutching her chest. Faye nearly crashed into another server, a full tray of drinks in hand. Then, she laughed nervously, a crisis averted. So much laughter.

A longing stirred in Edward at Faye's unabashed glow. He envied her unbounded energy, the zeal with which she approached so many tasks. He had been that way, too, at her age. Back then, the world had held much possibility and much time. Then, he hadn't been often alone or felt uncertain. Edward hated looking backward and held no respect for people who constantly wallowed. He was doing both these days more often, and so he loathed himself for such banality. As he drove away, Edward saw Faye walking briskly to another seating area. Her ponytail bounced as she moved, a bright green bow moving in time along with it. *I must see more of her*, he thought. Then, with a sardonic chuckle: *Yes, I must see MORE of her.*

"Delivering reports on dead composers?" Ian fumed over chili fries as he straddled the lunch benches. "What a terrible fucking way to spend our last week in class."

Edward had assigned composer projects for the final days of spring. They all agreed it was a bullshit move (though Leah only whispered the word in case one of the lunch supervisors was near).

"You have to do something," Bryn demanded, glaring at Faye. "Get him to change his mind."

Faye thought on it. "Okay," she said. "I'll talk to him."

Ian suggested the email. In her seventeen years, Faye had only sent one email, a request to the financial aid department at Sacred Heart. Her mother had shown her how to dial up to the internet and send the message from her parents' account. The mysterious technology had begun snaking its way into everyday life. Email and the internet were new to Faye and to her parents; Edward spent much of his alone time online; Ian talked in computer chat rooms with boys from other countries that he had met during tours with The American Children's Chorale.

Faye worded the plea carefully and pressed *Send*. Off it went through the ether to Edward's email address.

Here and there, a student emailed Edward or sent him an instant message. Often the messages came from the quiet, nerdy kids because they showed the most interest in the new technology. Shooting into his inbox after an almost interminable buzz of attempted connection, these notes relieved a bit of Edward's loneliness. The email from Faye surprised him. (The email originated, in fact, from a Robert Stoneman, a man Edward surmised must be Faye's father. Edward's stomach had flipped and frozen at first. Contact from Faye's parents worried him.) His luck was in. Faye's email presented exactly the opportunity Edward needed. The computer's glow illuminated a pensive Edward as he typed. The school year was waning. In Edward's life, Memorial Day brought inexorable loss. The students graduated; he was left behind.

Edward closed his eyes and recalled the curve of Faye's breast beneath her sequined dress at the dance. His pulse quickened; his cock stirred. Faye's desire for Edward had become more brazen, he thought, since that night. Her flirtations were less hidden; her need for his companionship more desperate. Moving Faye from student to lover would not be easy. Acting now would help attach Faye to him before the tide of graduation activities and the lure of Sacred Heart pulled her away. He needed Faye to see him as *Edward*, not as an Aquinas Prep teacher.

He leaned back in his chair, revisiting the repertoire of fantasies that had been building that spring: Faye on top of him in his bed, her hair cascading over her breasts; Faye touching herself in the choir room, her plaid skirt hiked up above her thighs, the buttons of her crisp, Oxford shirt undone just enough to reveal a silky red bra; Edward sitting in the plush leather of his AP office chair, Faye on her knees pleasuring him, her head bobbing up and down. In more than a decade, since Jane, in fact, he had not felt such wild sexual energy coursing through him. He would show Faye, Edward thought to himself, the joy of a lover who wanted to devour her absolutely, body and soul.

What sign could he send with this message?

Edward's response appeared the next morning:

> *For you, Faye, I would do almost anything. I'm sure you know that by now. But sometimes I have to make decisions as a teacher. This is one of those times. The other kids have been ignoring the rules for too long. They must have consequences. Try not to worry so much. Nothing will ever be the same after you leave Aquinas Prep and go out into the world. Enjoy it here while you can.*
> *Edward*

Edward. The word leapt off the page. Not Doctor Vogel, or Doctor, or Doc. *Edward.* Dryness squeezed Faye's throat as she read his response. The new word paralyzed her. Worthy looked up at Faye from her nightstand. She squeezed the tiny lamb into her fist and breathed in the scent of Doctor Vogel's briefcase. He had returned the lamb in sixth period the day before after keeping it a few days at his home. The scent pulled a whirlwind of feeling straight down from her breasts to her thighs. It was intoxicating.

I knew it, she thought. *Doctor* likes *me.* She swallowed deliberately, moistening her throat and calming her pulse.

Later, she and Merton talked alone.

"What can I do?" she asked Merton. "I can't just ask what's going on with us." She paused. "Can I?"

Merton studied the ground. As he thought, his eyes downcast, curtains of jet black hair concealed his face. Faye could see only the glowing tip of a cigarette pulsing with his breath.

"Really," she prodded. "What do you think is going on here?"

"It doesn't matter much what I think." He hesitated. "What do you want? What are you going to do in two weeks when he asks you to date him? You control what happens and what doesn't."

Faye reached for Merton's cigarette and took a long, slow drag. She knew one thing with certainty. None of this felt within her control.

In one week, Faye would graduate. She would deliver a valedictorian speech and accept family praise. She would drink wine coolers and smoke dozens of cigarettes on the beach with her classmates. Then, Aquinas Prep would dump her out of its bosom into the shadows, her spot being readied for a new student to take her place. The thought panicked her. And what of Doctor Vogel? Even alone in her room, with no judgment, no watchful eyes, Faye blushed when Doctor criss-crossed her thoughts. In her darkened bedroom, she lay awake and remembered every word he had said to her that day. She replayed the night she had visited his house alone, conjured memories of his birthday dinner, his lips closing sweetly over the ice cream. *Loon Shadow* boomed through her stereo with crescendoing trumpet blasts. When he gave her the recording, she wondered, had he thought she would listen to it at night in her bed? A chorus of oboes filled the room. She listened with closed eyes, her fingertips exploring the tingling folds between her thighs and drawing circles around her nipples as she thought of him.

Because she was valedictorian, Faye walked beside class president Chaewon Lee and the salutatorian Analisa Morganson. As the class of '98 paraded in under *Pomp and Circumstance*, Faye looked for Edward among the faculty. The fast-moving line would not slow enough for her to find him. By graduation night, she could not remember the feeling of delivering that speech. She delivered each word perfectly to thunderous applause, but it felt to Faye like she wasn't quite *there*. Like her five hundred classmates, Faye existed in suspension between Aquinas Prep and a future that was breathing down her neck. There was no denying it now. Graduation day meant the end of the life she knew.

Edward found her among the throng. He hugged Faye gently, spoke quietly while her parents looked on.

"The speech was perfect," he said curtly. "Absolute perfection."

Faye smiled, and a curl fell from behind her ear to the corner of her mouth. Edward leaned in and added, more quietly, "just like you."

Before Faye could respond, he disappeared toward the mass of students. They reached for Edward with boisterous enthusiasm. In her white high-heeled shoes and flowing purple dress, Faye felt like a Victorian maiden. She nearly fainted as she watched Edward walk away into the crowd.

The graduation ceremony was still fresh, her diploma case still empty. The official certificate would arrive by mail. Nothing had changed, yet. Grad Nite commenced at nine. *Class of '98* proclaimed itself from banners and novelty eyeglasses and glittery table toppers across Aquinas Prep's sprawling gymnasium. Faye searched the dark dance floor for her friends, her classmates' familiar faces distorted by mirror ball splashes and black light glow. Santino spotted Faye wandering alone and scooped her up in an enormous bear hug.

"We did it, Faye! We. Did. It." His warm smile infected Faye and brought down on her the striking magnitude of the moment. Yes, they had graduated. It was over.

Faye hugged back and then released with a nervous sigh.

"Yes, we did," she confirmed. "I can't believe it all went by so fast. What a rush!"

The glass always looked half full to Santino. His smile beamed wide and proud. A few drops of sweat gathered at his temples. His fluorescent orange shirt glowed vibrantly in the purple haze. He bopped his head to the music.

"I have to hit the dance floor, Faye. You know it's calling me."

"Of course," Faye yelled in response, the music an ever louder encroachment on their conversation.

"I'm not much for dancing. Have you seen Merton? Or Ian? Or anyone I'd be looking for?"

Santino's eyes darted quickly from corner to corner and he put a hand to the top of his head.

"Yes," he stammered. "Yes, I have. But I don't remember who or where."

Faye laughed.

"Yes I do!" He concluded. "I saw Bryn getting her hair braided at some kind of a glitter and spray paint hairdo booth. I think the last time I saw Merton was outside when I first got here." Santino's hands jerked at his sudden remembrance. "Yes, he was outside. He was talking to Doctor Vogel. Doctor was outside with Merton."

Faye's heart leapt into her throat. "Doctor was outside with Merton?" She repeated Santino's statement as a question. "Why was Doctor here?"

Santino shrugged and jumped aside to make room for a passing conga line. The big smile returned and rounded out his cheeks.

"I'm off. Catch up with you later!"

Moments later, Santino spun around with a sudden memory, stuck his head up over the crowd, and yelled: "Great speech, Faye!"

Leaving the gym as a group of kids entered, Faye crashed directly into Merton. The collision turned into a jostling, rollicking embrace. Merton kissed the side of her head, Platonically, comfortably. He pulled back after the hug, his big eyes calling forth the feelings Faye had spent all day suppressing.

"How are you, girl?"

Faye smirked first. A long exhale followed.

"I am doing okay, I think." Faye drew each word out with exaggerated hesitation.

"I knew you would be." Merton smiled toward the floor.

He had a habit, Faye once noticed, of drawing back when they spoke. Sometimes Merton struck an almost deferential posture with her. He had secured her trust easily, was wise and open in a way her other friends were not. Merton could handle her—she thought this now—but he didn't. He let Faye be herself, especially where Doctor Vogel was concerned. At the thought, she looked past Merton to the foggy parking lot.

"Is he here?" Faye rarely mentioned Edward by name. Merton always knew whom she meant. "Santino said you two were outside talking when he got here."

Merton nodded without comment at first.

"I'd check the choir room if you want to see him. He said he might hang around a bit longer. Let's plan a time to meet inside," Merton offered, "later."

Faye checked her watch. It was almost half past nine. Aquinas Prep administrators required every attending graduate to be inside the gym and accounted for by ten o'clock. Barring prior parental arrangements, Aquinas Prep would keep the kids under lock and key through the night.

"I saw a popcorn machine in the back corner where the risers are usually set for school Masses. Let's meet there at eleven to compare notes on the evening so far."

Merton squeezed Faye's waist playfully. "I can't wait." He stepped aside and, with a chivalrous wave of his hand, ushered Faye out into the summer night. "Go do what you need to do," he said. "I'll see you in a couple hours."

The choir door clanged at every use. The metal door and metal frame clanged open and clanged shut. On occasion they closed unevenly, the clang and clash of a mismatched puzzle. Through the years, the clang wound its way into the fabric of choral activity. During the height of a school day, student voices drowned out and overpowered the clang. At the close of late night Chamber rehearsal, the clang sounded tired as were the kids. Edward pulled the door closed those nights with a stern finality, telling the door he was done for the day.

Fog hung like smoke in the orange rays that spotlit the choir room where it sat on the east side of campus, a few hundred feet from the gym's official Grad Nite festivities. At his desk, Edward dozed as he sat waiting for the clang to rouse him. Merton would find Faye, he thought, and Faye would find him. He need only wait for her to appear.

And so now, with the expected metallic clang, Faye arrived with an unexpected degree of luminescence. Faye was girlish and aglow. Body glitter was sprayed across her skin. She wore too much blue eyeshadow and bright blue ribbons were braided through her hair. Her presence overwhelmed him. A pang like hunger gripped Edward deep in the belly.

The chair squeaked as Edward rose. He met Faye behind the risers. "I had just about given up on you."

These days, conversations with Edward eked their way out. Long silences interrupted their speech. Neither knew what to say. After months of chatter, four *years* of talking, Edward and Faye had grown silent. Words faltered. And so they raised eyebrows, smiled shyly, turned their eyes away, or stared a moment too long. What they needed to say was unspeakable.

Unexceptional words came. She asked obvious questions. "What are you doing here so late?"

A boring retort followed. "Just doing some work," Edward said. "Waiting to see who might stop by."

His caginess endeared her. *He was waiting for me*, she thought. Tears welled up from the back of Faye's throat. She swallowed hard. Faye wanted him to speak of it first, but she couldn't wait. What if he just let her leave? Her eyes found the tops of his black leather shoes. She watched the skinny corded laces as she spoke to him.

"When will I see you again?"

"Oh, we'll see each other here and there. You can be sure of that. You can come around any time."

Faye nodded. The lightness of his tone confused her. Old doubts came creeping. Maybe, after all, he didn't like her *that* way.

As he continued, Edward tilted his head ever so slightly. He measured his words carefully, like they were being surveilled.

"When do you leave for Sacred Heart?"

Faye curled her fingers around the riser's rail and moved her hand back and forth in a soothing motion. The steel felt cold and strong against her skin. She pictured the airline tickets, LAX to Chicago Midway. They stared out at her each morning from the hutch above her dresser.

"I move in the last week of August."

After a longer pause this time, Edward lowered his voice. His tone shifted. Something glimmered behind his eyes. He picked up mid-sentence, pulling Faye into a cipher he expected she would understand.

"—And when is your birthday?"

Fear seized Faye's body. Her braids felt too tight and her grip on the metal railing felt tenuous and sweaty. The room wobbled a bit, like she was about to vomit. Her brain refused a quick answer.

She spoke glumly, like she had done something wrong.

"October. My birthday is not until October."

I'm seventeen, she thought. *And I will stay seventeen until I go.*

The phrase flitted from her thoughts to his.

She's seventeen, Edward knew. *She will stay seventeen all summer.*

The clang of the choir room door exploded into the cold silence of the room. Ian and Krystal burst through in stage entrance theatrics, sugar drunk on the swirling tornado of cotton candy Krystal held aloft as they walked arm in arm. Krystal herself was all sugar crystals and sparkles. Her voice bounced off the mirrored walls and empty risers.

"Hey valedictorian," she teased. "Come with us. School is over. School is *over* now. You are needed at the party!"

Rattled by their sudden intrusion, Faye overreacted.

"My God, you guys," she panted, spinning around with a hand to her heart. "You scared the *shit* out of me." Faye mouthed the curse word inaudibly. It was still *school*, after all. Doctor Vogel was still a *teacher*.

Ian picked up Krystal's train. "Sorry, Doctor," he boomed. "Faye needs to go with us. I've got a crazy game of Twister with her name on it."

Warm, wet air whooshed in as Krystal and Ian rushed through the door to rejoin the graduates. Voices echoed back in their wake.

"Come now, Faye! The doors close in five minutes!"

A great despair cemented Faye's feet to the tile. She wanted to stay with Edward, but she knew her place. She belonged with the other kids. Edward did not want Faye to go. If he were being honest with himself, he wanted to go with her. He was too old for Twister and hair dye and glow sticks, but those were the currency of teenagers, and he wanted to share everything that touched Faye's life. Edward saw the fate that awaited him. He thought of the dark path to his back door, a great expanse of quiet stretching through the house, and an ache snaked its way through his middle.

Edward looked to the empty space past Faye's shoulders and then glanced back briefly over his own. Alone. He brushed Faye's cheek with the back of his hand.

"You better go," he said.

Faye spoke to the tops of her shoes. "I wish you could come."

"I'll be okay," he confirmed. "We'll talk soon."

A loud din, interlaced with squeals and shouts, reached Faye from across campus as soon as she cleared the last of the choir room steps. Her friends awaited, and she would join them.

Time had run out for Faye and Edward at Aquinas Prep.

Mist rose off the freeway as Edward drove home. Murky air lurked outside and a fog clouded his thoughts. Capturing Faye would take some planning, some finesse. He had to act soon, even if she was only seventeen. If he waited, she would leave him behind. The world would overshadow him. Life had intoxicated and assaulted Edward for twenty-four years longer than Faye had been alive. He knew life's allures and fluidity. He needed to take Faye now before the joy and the newness of university life swept this girl up.

V

TWELVE-YEAR OLD TEAGUE WAS USUALLY the last kid to pull the covers over his head. But tonight, the end of the day could not come quickly enough. He was tired from so much thinking about this business with Maya's birth mother. Nothing in Maya's family was easy; everything in Teague's house was. Whenever Maya talked about her troubles, Teague felt a strange guilt. Why did he have it good while Maya was so often sad? He wanted to do something nice for her, but he couldn't figure out what that would be. *Better sleep on it*, he thought. He'd ask his mom in the morning.

Across the hall, Faye fought a heaviness as well. Her eyes were rimmed red from crying. She flashed on the crumpled napkin left on the luncheon table. When Donovan said *Vogel is dying*, Faye's gaze had fixated on that flimsy, discarded napkin. She had stayed standing and breathing but had burrowed her mind into the folds of that soiled paper so that she would not float away from firm ground. *Vogel is dying*, Donovan had said, and Faye had nearly lost her mind.

A burning at the crease of her eyelids reminded Faye how visceral her earlier hysteria had been. After lunch with Donovan, Faye had taken the afternoon off and driven out to Fulton to go running in Edward's old neighborhood. She should have gone home for a therapeutic swim, but when life concerned Edward, like a swallow she returned to the place he had lived. Each pass in front of his house, Faye craned her neck to see over the gate that now blocked access to the garage and back gardens (if indeed Edward's fruit trees still grew). As she ran north, parallel to the row of houses, Faye glimpsed first the living room shades and the small kitchen window that looked down on the sink. (Edward had turned his back on her there, washing dishes with a childish petulance after a fight about Ian phoning Edward's house.) Running south, Faye counted each window along the side yard: guest room, bedroom, bathroom. (She could still feel the counter's smooth tiles, wetted by the splashing faucet as she washed her face and dripped tears from her mouth into the basin).

Two doors down, a yellow tabebuia tree bloomed in full, filling Faye's lungs with a heady scent each time she passed. The bursting of its golden trumpets was enough to make Faye's heart weep, their unabashed brightness the absolute proof of resurrection. Louisa had loved flower picking and tree climbing as a toddler. Faye saw her toothy grin and sweet child fleshiness in the falling flowers. Really, this life had been so full of blessing. A mysterious joy jogged in sync with Faye's solemn sense of doom. She knew, then, it was time to go home. Her children's love awaited.

Daniel didn't ask about her distracted countenance at dinner, but he looked her way a few times with expressive concern. *Better to just come clean*, Faye told herself. She could not keep Donovan's news to herself for long.

"How much time does he have?" Daniel chose his words carefully, coating them with soft pity.

Faye ran a hand through her hair and arched her back to relieve a stress ache building near her hips. "I don't know. All Donovan said was that Vogel is dying."

Daniel tip-toed with his voice. "That's too bad."

"I suppose it is," Faye answered with listless hesitancy.

What else could Daniel say? He felt no compassion for this man, would rather the subject was not broached again for the rest of their days. No one would blame him, Daniel thought, for wishing this monster of a man would just go ahead and die already. Aquinas Prep had sucked so much air out of the start of Daniel and Faye's marriage. Even their Italian honeymoon had been peppered with emails from the law offices of Hamilton, Shane, and Dupree about legal forms Faye needed to sign.

Daniel had been swallowing raw hatred of that bastard for all nineteen years he had known Faye. Staying quiet was usually Daniel's strong suit, but with this Vogel business, not speaking up caused a constant internal battle. For nineteen years, Faye's invocation of that man's name (rare though it had been) sent an acidic rush lurching into Daniel's throat. The humiliation he felt on Faye's behalf wasn't the worst of it. He could tell in Faye's voice that she not only forgave Vogel but felt sorry for him. He wanted to be proud of his wife's empathy. Truthfully, Faye's allegiance to that man was as disgusting as it was confusing. Everything about Faye's response to Vogel confirmed what Daniel had surmised from the start. That asshole had brainwashed his wife so thoroughly that she would never escape him. By proxy, Daniel would never be rid of him either.

The fastidiousness of Faye's routines meant that evenings brought counter wiping, quick vacuum sweeps, and sometimes a few late-night laps in the pool, the rhythmic spreading of the water a balm at the end of a long day. Tonight she could not summon the energy for evening chores. She needed wordless comfort. Daniel's face stretched long with the uncertain look of a bystander who didn't know how to help. Faye reached fingertips down to toes then straightened up, her limbs tight and unforgiving.

"Just lie down," Daniel offered. "I'll finish up in the kitchen and be back to rub out those knots."

When Daniel returned, she was nearly asleep. His wife could not rouse herself enough for the glass of creamy liqueur he had brought. Approaching quietly, Daniel pushed aside a curl to kiss Faye's shiny temple, already damp with sleepy sweat. She stirred.

"Was I asleep?"

Daniel *shushed* gently and lay down next to his wife. With small movements, Faye rocked her body sideways and laid her head on Daniel's breastbone, one hand falling against the softness of his stomach. Faye's eyes fluttered with the effort of re-waking. She breathed in the familiar ordinariness of their bedroom. For nineteen years, she had assumed this pose, settling herself onto Daniel's stable frame, her knees pulled like an infant's into her middle. The anxiety did not go away, but some sense of equilibrium crept in. Before long, Faye breathed heavily. The milky cocktail spread a ring of sweat around the glass.

The ding of the microwave made Maya giggle and so Teague laughed, too.

"You did it way too long!" she chided. "Look how the cheese is flat on the chips like they're burnt."

Heat from the plate radiated out and stopped Teague before he touched it.

"Let me get a hot pad," he said with confidence. "It's way too hot to grab."

A few minutes later, the sun-happy tweens were scraping the final few nachos from their plate and contemplating another dip in the pool.

"Let's go back inside before my sister gets home," Teague suggested. "When Louisa sees us, she's going to bother us."

"Okay." Maya smiled wide. "I'll race you to the other end," she offered. "I'll even let you choose the stroke."

Teague looked toward the sun in contemplation.

"Obviously not butterfly," he laughed, "since I'm the worst at butterfly. Let's just do freestyle."

Maya gulped the last drink of root beer from her can and headed toward the edge of the pool. Teague repositioned his goggles, shouting to Maya as he did.

"You forgot your swim cap!" he yelled.

Maya's sigh reverberated across the pool.

"I don't need it just for playing around. Don't wear yours so we'll be equal."

Teague hated the swim cap, too. He didn't mind it while he was swimming, but he looked stupid putting it on. He usually turned aside so Maya wouldn't see him struggling to stuff his fluffy curls under the impossibly tight spandex seal.

"What about your hair, though? Your mom will freak out if your braids get ruined."

This time Maya's sigh was deep like a groan.

"You're always looking out for my mom," she said with a careless laugh.

Teague felt a little nervous. "I just don't want you to get in trouble," he said, "because your mom might not let you swim here anymore."

"My hair will be fine. My mom doesn't know anything about box braids 'cause she's white." Maya continued bitterly. "She's just worried about the money."

Teague suddenly thought of his own mom. Sometimes he still missed her during the day while she was at work. As far back as Teague could remember, he felt something inseparable about him and his mom. Even as he walked around school and ate fries with William and swapped jokes with Maya, he felt as if his mom was with him, like he could just crawl back into her and hide himself from the world. The other kids, especially Maya, didn't seem to feel that way. Maya had been grumbling about her mom as long as Teague had known her. Teague thought Maya's mom was alright. She cared a lot. She bought Maya horseback riding lessons and let her keep a family of guinea pigs in her room. Still, they didn't seem close. Teague never saw Maya and her mom hug. Maya's family didn't cuddle on the couch during movies like Teague's did. *Maya's mom isn't really her real mom. That's probably why*, Teague thought. Better to change the subject.

Teague kicked his swim cap aside and ran to meet Maya on the pool's brick border.

"What do I get if I win?" he asked.

Maya punched Teague in the arm. "We'll worry about that if it ever happens," she scoffed.

Teague felt in slow motion the warm imprint of Maya's fist on his skin. His heart flapped wildly in his chest, the feeling of joy almost dizzying.

When Louisa arrived home from school and clamored for her brother's attention, Teague and Maya were toweling off and heading down the hall.

"Teague, make me some nachos before you go to your room. Can you? Please?"

Teague folded his towel over at the waist.

"Go ahead and start playing without me," he said to Maya. "The console should already be signed in and ready to go."

The buzz of her phone interrupted Maya's plans. Teague found her bent over the screen in frustration. His television was off, the game not queued up. Something was wrong, and he didn't know whether to ask about it or ignore it.

Just listen to her, his mom had said. *All anybody wants is to tell their story, to feel like someone else hears them.*

"Is it your mom?" Teague asked.

Maya touched a hand to her brow and spoke without looking up.

"My birth family wants to video chat again tonight," she said flatly. "I hate seeing them. I mean, I love seeing my mom, but it just makes me sad. Why would she give me away and then have all those other kids?"

Teague had wondered this, too. Maya's birth mom had only recently gotten back in touch with Maya and the California parents who had raised her. The foster care system had removed Maya from her birth mom's Colorado home when Maya was just six months old. The parents Teague knew had been the only parents Maya had ever known, too. Now, twelve years later, Maya found that her birth parents had gone on to build an entire family without her. She had two sisters and a brother, three little kids who lived in a clean house and ate takeout around the tv and played in the sprinklers during the hottest part of Colorado summers.

"You don't know what it's like to see the three kids your parents kept after they threw you away," Maya said earnestly. "They gave me away but they kept those kids."

"That's awful," Teague said hesitantly. "Did you ask your birth mom why she didn't keep you?"

"Yes. My mom told me not to, but I asked anyway."

"What did your birth mom say?"

"She said she was in a bad *circumstance* when I was born." Maya emphasized the word to show how foolish it sounded. "She said it was the circumstances. She couldn't afford to take care of me. So she gave me up."

Teague had heard from his own mother that Maya had been *severely neglected*, his mother called it, as a baby. Her birth mom hadn't just given her away. The state had taken Maya because her mom was addicted to drugs and had been leaving Maya alone in a filthy apartment. Maya's piercing cries had alerted neighbors that a baby was starving. It seemed like Maya didn't know about these circumstances. They hadn't talked about her birth family very much. Every time they did, it was like a cloud settled over Maya's sunniness. Teague felt relieved each time she returned to her regular self. It wasn't just that he didn't like her to be sad. He felt nervous when she got that way because he didn't know how to help her.

"I was thinking," Teague spoke quietly, "that your mom gave you up because she really loved you."

Maya raised an eyebrow with skepticism.

"How do you figure?"

"Like, she didn't keep you just to have something to do. Some people have babies and then keep them around to show them off. But she was thinking she wanted you to be happy and have all the best stuff, and she couldn't take care of you."

Maya had never thought about it that way before.

"Maybe it was like she really loved you and that's why she didn't keep you."

Teague felt the clouds beginning to part, sensed Maya letting this comforting thought settle in.

"Besides, your birth mom wouldn't be talking to you now if she didn't love you. It's not like she needs more kids. She already has three kids at home."

Maya grabbed a cream-filled cookie off a stack piled high on Teague's desk. She twisted the top off and licked a bite of sweet icing into her mouth.

"That makes sense," she said, starting to smile.

Teague's confidence bloomed. He kept going. "I bet she's missed you all these years. She wants to get to know you like a friend even though you already have a mom and dad now."

The weight of her mom's text rose like steam off Maya's warm skin. Teague *got* her, and that made everything alright.

Teague felt a shift in the room. Late afternoon light streamed through his window. The rays reflected off his colorful collection of Rubik's cubes and set a glow on Maya's perfectly smooth skin. He felt so close to her now, so proud that he had said the right thing to make her happy. For a few weeks they had been bouncing around the idea of trying a first kiss. Lots of kids at school had already kissed. Those kids had been boyfriend and girlfriend less time than Teague and Maya. Teague was hesitant, though. He knew Maya didn't really like people too close to her. She liked her space.

He laughed a little and blushed.

"What's going on?" she asked.

Teague's ears felt hot, like they were starting to sweat. He looked over his shoulder to make sure Louisa wasn't eavesdropping in the hall.

Teague folded his hands and spoke to his thumbs as he twiddled them around. "Do you think you would like it if I kissed you?" The room was starting to wobble. "On the cheek," he added. "Would you like it if I kissed you on the cheek?"

The cookie Maya held stayed suspended halfway to her mouth. Her hands remained steady, but blood whooshed quickly between her ears.

"I think I might," she said shyly. "But I'm not sure."

Teague felt disappointed and relieved all at once. It was like having a sore throat and so getting to stay home from school. He spoke right away so Maya wouldn't feel weird.

"Let's just wait for another time, then," he said with forced nonchalance. Then he laughed. "You wouldn't want your first kiss to be when you're sad, anyway," he said. "That would be kind of dumb."

"Well, I'm not sad anymore, but still, let's wait. Maybe soon we can hold hands or something," she offered.

"I would really like that," Teague said. "Let's try it next time we hang out."

Television voices floated down the hall from Louisa's room. Everyone and everything else felt far away. Teague and Maya studied each other, their lips turned up in soothing smiles.

Maya's tongue swiped the last dab of icing from the chocolate cookie base.

"Eat these chocolate parts," she said with an easy tone. "I only like the middle."

Oh, how comforting were the sounds of his mother! Wyatt dug his body into his mattress but lifted his head high to hear the bumping closed of the kitchen cupboards. His mom pushed in the top rack of the dishwasher, the glasses tinkling against each other as she did. *Thunk* went the oven light as she pushed the bright metallic button above the stove. A rushing of water sounded as she filled the plastic reservoir for the next morning's coffee. There were shadows from the hall light against his closet and the sad news that tomorrow was Wednesday and so his mother would leave extra early for a department meeting and he would sleep through her good-bye kiss and wake up with an ache at the lingering scent of her lotion on the bathroom towel. Tonight, though, the soft padding of her slippered feet and the efficient *on-off-on-off*, the *open-close-open-close* of his mother's chores, covered Wyatt like a protective shield and sent him off to sleep.

As Faye packaged leftovers and bleached counters with the efficiency of a domestic automaton, the Loyola Institute pumped the Catholic Saints podcast through her headphones. Down the long tunnel of Fr. Ambrose McMillian's soothing voice, Faye followed the story of Ireland's St. Dymphna, one of several young women whom the Church revered precisely because she had evaded her would-be rapist and therefore kept her purity. Keeping a rapist off one's trail was noble for sure, but concern that sexual assault—the fact of having been assaulted, not the threat of it—was worse than literal death demonstrated the timeless belief in both Church and secular society that a woman swallowed the shame of whatever merciless torture a man thrust upon her. And so, all over Ireland, lifeless and nearly colorless brick buildings rose from the turf. St. Dymphna's Asylum for the Insane was spelled out on their imposing iron gates. Many were now called St. Dymphna's Hospital for Mental Wellbeing. By whatever name, they housed generations of women driven mad by a society intent on exploiting their bodies and throwing them away. Martyrdom probably looked pretty good to some of those women.

Since the birth of her babies, Faye had gotten old in all the good ways. The body she had shielded from lovers in her late teens and early twenties because it seemed foreign and ugly felt strong now, each muscle a reminder that she had housed and birthed and carried three children into the world.

Bright silver hairs were showing up more often as she neared forty, but she saw in them a buoying sense of accomplishment. Faye had earned smile lines and brow creases while nurturing young, intellectual women at St. Anne's and sheltering the voiceless teens facing abuse that could destroy a child from the inside out.

Faye's Catholicism had matured, too. As the 1990s became a new century, the Church had failed so many Catholics in the most important ways. But scandal and abuse had not affected most Catholics in the manner Faye expected those traumas would. Most Catholics went on with eyes down and shook their heads in the face of the few stories that hit the press. In fact, as victim after victim came forward, the public got tired. The faithful got tired. Faye remembered thinking it was like watching endless B-roll of destroyed towns after tornadoes. After the initial shock, one flattened house looked just like the others. There was nothing new to see and no way to undo the damage. And so, viewers flipped the channel and the powers that be carried on without apology or accountability. *Now hear this*, the Church proclaimed: *We're building a new cathedral; we're choosing a new Pope; we're sending missionaries to fight disease in Africa.*

But Faye did not look away. Just the opposite was true. She followed the news down into the darkness, reading with bated breath the harrowing stories. She and Daniel shed tears for the children. Most who had suffered the horrific assaults had been young boys like Teague at the time of the abuse. The landscape was soon dotted with grainy home movies and polished, artsy documentaries that featured live interviews with the grown men, some well into their sixties, who woke up screaming after meeting their vile predators again in their nightmares. Many of the abusive priests had died, but plenty lived on, looking feeble and harmless though the world now knew the truth of their two-faced piety. Accused priests came in all forms: obstinate, contrite, sympathetic. The victims shared remarkable similarities. Whether old, young, balding, bushy-haired, blue-eyed, or dark-skinned, the victims wore weariness like an old, pilled Catholic school uniform. They were exhausted. They were burdened.

Faye wept for the survivors just as she had wept after first meeting Donovan. To Faye's mind, the gruesome debauchery wasn't the worst of it. The facade of tenderness cut deeper than the depravity itself. *I knew how much he loved me*, Donovan had told Faye. *I never doubted it. Even through the worst pain,* Donovan said, *even through the most abject humiliation, I believed that no one else loved me like Fr. Mick did.* Donovan had dusted away the moment's earnestness with a quick flip of his floppy brown hair. *That's why these guys are pros*, he said casually. *They know just how to get you.* Faye sat with Donovan's pain, could almost smell the rising incense, feel the smooth satin of Fr. Mick's stole. That Donovan had survived the abuse and the suicide attempts and the recklessness that followed was a miracle. Donovan's survival—the onward marching of all those wounded victims—was more improbable than Incarnation itself.

Because Faye had looked those devils in the face, because she advocated for the victims and walked the picket line outside Fulton's diocesan offices, the resurgence of her faith came in the twenty-teens like a long awaited surprise. She and Daniel had not left the Church nor the faith, but their hardened hearts had turned askew, searching for a Catholic way forward. And then, as she rocked Teague to sleep in the dim light of his Illinois nursery, Faye had begun to sing. The hymns of her childhood (*Here I am, Lord*) became the lively exhortations of the Aquinas Prep Chamber Singers (*Fare thee well! I am going home!*). Teague's perfectly smooth nose, his big eyes, his too-tiny-to-clip fingernails, and his mischievous laugh brought God right into Faye's arms. Yes! She was going home to feast in the Church.

Faye's matured faith was grounded differently than her childhood faith had been. She knew now that monsters were real. She did not suffer hypocritical fools. She spoke up and spoke out. Master deceivers had sullied her Church, but they would not destroy the Church that was building inside her. And as the breaking of a fever brings insurmountable joy, this incarnation of God in her own child felt more fragile and sweet than it would have in a world without demons. Faye had begun then, when her children were babies, to read the lives of the saints, especially the scores of mothers, like Saint Elizabeth Ann Seton, whose journeys evinced sacrifice and absolute fearlessness. Many women of the Church were revered for having given their lives to God, a code that meant they had been religiously consecrated and so spared themselves the real struggles of life: men, sex, parenting. As a mother, Faye had given her life to God, too. It sounded kind of silly, but it was true. Because she loved them and they loved her, Faye's children would redeem the world. They had already saved her.

The sudden touch of Daniel's warm hands caused Faye to jump. Dishwater splashed against her blouse. When her alarm subsided, Faye leaned her head back lovingly into the crook of Daniel's neck and breathed in the sweet residue of a long day. Daniel lowered Faye's headphones then raked his hands therapeutically across her scalp.

"Are you working at all before bed?" he asked.

Work often crept into evening hours during the week. At each new year they resolved to shelve the late night emailing and report writing in favor of more time for pleasure reading or prayer or even watching television together. By March, March being a generous estimate, the overwhelming needs of students and clients indeed overwhelmed the Collins home. Faye and Daniel found themselves again needing to hit the reset on a balanced life.

"I should," Faye said wanly, "but I won't. Let's just get in bed."

At nine o'clock, *get in bed* meant the promise of cuddling in the glowing tv light and the great likelihood of sex. And so, Daniel squeezed his wife at her hips and walked happily to the bedroom. Stripped down to his boxer shorts and a worn tee, Daniel moved his legs loosely against the sheets and imagined the pleasure of his wife's body in anticipation of her joining him. The house lights went dark as Faye made her way toward her waiting husband. The joy of stretching out her tired limbs pushed Faye down the hallway. The little kids slept soundly, their breathing loud and rhythmic. Faye opened Teague's door, hoping he was already asleep. Light burst through the crack. Teague met his mom's eyes reflected in the mirror above his desk.

"Oh, hi mom."

Faye put a hand on Teague's shoulder and a kiss on the top of his head.

"Time for lights out, baby."

Teague groaned. "Just give me a minute," he said.

Teague smeared a bright white paint marker across the electric blue body of a cartoonish figure at the center of his drawing. He sat back, then, and gave the paper a satisfied nod. His voice called out to Faye just as she disappeared into the hallway.

"Mom?" he asked hesitantly.

Faye pushed the bedroom door fully open and leaned against the frame.

"Does Maya know about what her birth mom did to her when she was a baby?"

A deep breath filled Faye's lungs. Teague was old enough to know life's difficulties but not savvy enough to process them.

"I don't know what she knows, so you probably shouldn't say anything to her about it," Faye sighed. "What makes you ask? Has she been talking about her birth mom?"

"She's upset that her birth mom has all those other kids. It makes her feel like she's bad or something because they gave her away."

The weight of the world sat heavily on teen-aged shoulders. How many times had Faye heard the same? Bullied students and sexual assault victims and teens tossed out by angry parents came to her nearly dragging with the heaviness of adult disappointment. These kids were God on earth and evinced undeniable human dignity. Faye wanted to hold each of them and whisper into their souls the great truth: you are enough.

"Poor Maya," Faye said.

The sympathy in Teague's eyes moved her. How in a world of darkness did this beautiful child exist, his wants so pure, his heart so open?

"She's going to need good friends to carry her through," Faye urged with a resigned head shake.

Teague blushed. "I think I helped her the other day," he began. "We talked about her birth mom and she felt better after she talked it out with me. Maya's a really cool girl. She's kind of special, like, she's more honest than other kids. She doesn't fake anything."

"That does sound special," Faye said. "I can see why you two found each other."

"I like her a lot," Teague said proudly.

Love for her first-born surged in Faye. So quickly twelve years had gone. How quickly another six would fly, and out into the world her heart would walk. What mattered was to send all this love out there with him.

Faye smiled. "Get to bed."

"I am pretty tired," her son said sheepishly. "Good night, mom. Love you."

In the bathroom, Faye dipped her fingers into a tin of silky pink cream and massaged it into her flushed skin. Daniel waited in the bed. Faye needed a beat to prepare, to redirect her energies. The sadness and sweetness of two pre-teen friends swirled through Faye's head. Like she had, Teague would live a life of love and heartbreak. Love and heartbreak would chase each other like tumbleweeds whipped up in a tornado's winds. Faye had known love chaotic and compulsive and explosive. She had loved so hard it pained her. Only her children—only the two seedlings who had never grown (she had lost two pregnancies) and her three improbably perfect babies—filled her body and soul without reservation or consideration. She had suspected for some time that the only true love was between parent and child. The children were always part of her, so indescribably so that she would find herself thinking of their bodies as part of her own even four, nine, or twelve years into their independent lives outside her womb. Their orbit, mother and child's, had seemed small for so long, but the world had come creeping in. Faye felt acutely this night that so much brightness would soon vie for Teague's attention. She would not, indeed *could* not, keep him hers much longer.

And so, like a prayer, a whisper rose in Faye. She wanted another baby.

Warmth off Daniel's skin and a cool breeze through the bedroom window stirred and soothed Faye all at once. She traced Daniel's brow with her fingers, kissing his eyes and the hot skin of his temple as she spread her hands across his back. The weight of Daniel's body pushed her fingers into the bedsheets. Faye enjoyed this anticipatory part of lovemaking. She loved Daniel with gentle caress, luxuriating in the sensuality of her husband's still, quieted body. But then, when Daniel's mouth met hers, Faye's stomach dipped. As he reached for her breast, Faye's body folded and cocooned. Her mind drifted and counted, finding faces in the popcorn ceiling overhead. She pulled Daniel's body over hers like a shield, trying to release her breath, offering space inside for her husband to fill. She rushed him toward orgasm. Then, with unparalleled relief, their lovemaking ended. Life resumed.

Hot water raced in streams along the curve of Faye's breast and poured down, gently seeking the crevices between her thighs. Always, Faye showered after sex. She couldn't remember when this routine had taken hold, though she knew the trend had been recent. Some days during college, she and Daniel had laid for hours in bed, making love several times in between television shows, thunderstorms raging or snow faintly falling outside Daniel's apartment window. Weekends in Tolono, Faye's grad school colleagues had taken her and Daniel on rounds through college town bars late into the night. Sex those nights finished in such chaotic intensity that Faye fell immediately asleep, surprised the next morning by the sloppy bedsheets and her dry, scratchy-feeling skin. Faye soaped herself gently, stroking in solace the sore spot between her legs. An imprint of Daniel's desire had left itself there, her body a repository of the men she had loved and those she had merely satisfied. The tender feeling of openness, her postcoital body like a draining wound, reminded her that sex had left its mark. Faye remembered that first tug of pain when her virginity had been taken. (*Yes, taken!* She admitted this only to herself.) What she had discovered then still held true now. The lasting aches of sex were persistent and expected, bringing with them the hope that if she were hurting, her lover, thank God, was satisfied.

A grin greeted Faye as she slipped clean and fresh back into her husband's arms. She flipped and scooched in their familiar pattern, her calves laced through Daniel's, his hand on the small of her back, his kiss against the side of her ear.

"The kids are getting too old," she said.

"I know."

A warm silence engulfed them.

"Wyatt," Daniel continued, "told me he's worried about where he's going to college."

Faye chuckled in the dark.

"That's ridiculous," she said flatly. "He's four years old. He should know he's going to Sacred Heart like I did."

"In that case," Daniel said with a lilt, "he should be worrying about how he's going to pay for it."

These moments redeemed Faye. She squeezed Daniel's hand in the dark and felt the strength of their union.

Faye spoke softly, just above a whisper. "I think we should have another baby."

Please say yes! A silent prayer formed quickly on Faye's lips.

But how could he agree to another child? Oh how greatly he loved their children, but to Faye's waves, he was unbothered water. Daniel's feet lay always on firm ground. How *measured* he was. Alone in her thoughts, Faye seemed no more than a collection of wants. Daniel, she remembered thinking once, seemed not to want for anything. He excelled as Director of Sales but did not dream of a promotion to VP. In the old college days, Daniel had smoked casually. Faye had lit cigarettes one from the next, unable to get enough of anything that filled her. When they went out, Daniel sipped Manhattans. Faye tossed back too many sweet martinis and waltzed unevenly down the hall when they got home. Daniel was one scoop in a paper cup to Faye's double ice cream dip in a fresh-baked waffle cone. He was the same way, really, about sex. Faye preferred quantity to quality. She had learned early from her brother's teen-aged friends and from tv and movies and novels and boyfriends that boys wanted as much sex as they could get, and that if she wanted to keep the boy, she had better give it to him. But not with Daniel. The *quality* of their intimacy and of all things lured Daniel. Give me all the life there is, Faye pleaded. Daniel loved all that he had. Though his own family was large and Catholic and always wanted more of itself, Daniel had wanted as few kids as he could get away with. It was Teague and Louisa, really, who had convinced their father that they needed a baby when Faye and Daniel had called it quits on babymaking. With glee, she remembered how seven-year-old Teague would beg in his sweet girlish voice. *I want a baby so I can rock him in the rocking chair, Dadda. He can be my baby.* Well before birth, as soon as Wyatt's unfurling form had softened Faye's slender waistline, the whole family had fallen in love with him.

Her voice came even more softly this time. "Did you hear me?"

She could feel a smile in Daniel's kiss against her neck.

"We'll talk about it later," he said, drifting off to a contented love-drunk sleep.

At any assembly, Faye could spot the troubled kids. Quite simply, they were the only ones paying attention. The others popped their gum and stared indiscreetly at their phones, trouble-free and thus absolutely uncaring about social issues and community resources. Kids who needed help followed Faye with their eyes, too embarrassed to copy the emergency hotline numbers off the big screen behind her, too frantic under their quiet facades to consider ignoring the problem. Trina Hendricks pulled a glittery red phone case from her pocket and checked the time. The phone mocked her. She did not feel glittery at all. In fact, the gym felt hot like summer though it was only spring. Pungent waves of oniony sweat, musty deodorant spray, and grape bubble gum wafted toward and then away from her. Trina's nails dug crescent marks into her exposed thigh as her cheeks began to salivate at the odd mix of odors. The nausea that had abated in third period geometry threatened to return. Trina squeezed her eyes closed and pictured herself paddling into the harbor. She heard water lapping lightly against her board and felt a cool breeze teasing her skin. She wished she were on the water now, wished she were still the Trina Hendricks she had been two weeks earlier.

The positive pregnancy test was still wrapped in toilet paper and shoved in the bottom of her book bag. The ink lines started fading on day six. Trina knew this because she checked it secretly each morning after her parents left for work, each time hoping the thick plastic stick had disappeared and that the whole ordeal had been only a vivid nightmare. No such luck. Each morning, the stick greeted her. Trina dreaded seeing the stick and dreaded not seeing the stick. She felt a twinge of something, almost comfort, each time she found it there. Beneath fear and absolute panic lay a certain pleasantness borne of keeping this secret. With her eyes closed, she could see the stick now, tucked in the thin fold of her backpack where the red canvas met the protective faux suede bottom. She had a sudden urge to hold the stick and run her finger over its bumpy plastic cap. Trina imagined her insides as deep red folds of tissue. She imagined a baby floating there, its head a large, alien mass like the Developing Fetus pictures from her Life Science textbook. Of course the baby would not look like that yet (*or would it?* Trina couldn't remember when a girl went from a missed period to an actual growing baby).

The plan to tell her mom about the pregnancy had stalled, then rebooted, then stalled again. Because Trina was a late bloomer, as her mother always said, by sixteen her periods had numbered maybe seven or eight. She couldn't even remember because they were so sporadic and often unmemorable. Only when Laly had reminded her—*you were on your period last time we swam at Joshua's, remember? You took my last tampon*—did Trina realize that six weeks had passed and that maybe she was pregnant. Thirteen more excruciating days had dragged by with the double-lined test buried in Trina's bag. Now she listened intently as Doctor Collins from the School Culture and Equity Office lectured the kids on sexual harassment, victim blaming, medical services, and the school's new peer counseling program. Trina didn't much believe in fate (and sometimes not even in God), but she sensed that this woman with big curls and a sympathetic smile had come to help her.

Lugging the projector back to her office, its heavy weight bumping against her thighs, Faye thought about Lewis Miller's noticeable absence from the aptly titled assembly *Just Joking: Harmless Prank or Sexual Harassment?*

"It's a timely topic," Marilyn had said.

Faye had swallowed her cynicism until Marilyn was gone.

"Methinks," she whispered to Paul, "Lewis Miller would have found it much more timely *before* he was assaulted."

Lewis had not yet returned to school. A few weeks of homeschooling at his family's Aspen lodge would be just the remedy, his parents were sure. *Some fresh air and distance will make you forget all about this unpleasantness*, Lewis's mom had cooed at him. Faye knew the opposite to be true. Lewis needed immersion and support, not isolation.

"Seclusion will feed the shame," she had told his parents. "It's likely that being surrounded by friends will be more helpful."

His mother, a heavily perfumed woman named Margeaux, had turned her nose up indignantly at Faye's suggestion.

"You don't really know my son, though, do you?" she had asked. "If you had taken the time to know him, this probably would not have happened."

Back at the Title IX office, Faye noticed a shy, wide-eyed student milling about the hallway. She recognized the girl's cropped black hair and dark-rimmed glasses immediately from the assembly. She had locked eyes once with Faye and then looked quickly away. Rolled up in her hand, the girl clutched a PAL flier she had grabbed from one of the Title IX resource buckets. Faye and Paul had designed it together:

Need to Talk?
Try a PAL!
The Newport East
Peer Assistance Leadership Program
is HERE for YOU

Trina flashed a noncommittal smile, still deciding whether to approach Doctor Collins or to pretend she had merely been cutting through the office on her way back to class.

"Hi there," Faye said brightly with a welcoming grin. She immediately offered an escape. "Just passing through, or did you have some questions about PAL?"

Sweat broke out along Trina's collar. Queasiness bounced quickly into her throat. Her mind flashed on the stick wedged beneath her geometry book.

"I guess maybe I have some questions," Trina said. "I should probably get to my next class, though."

The girl's telltale hesitancy gave her away. Though Faye wasn't a counselor *per se*, being able to read teen angst was critical to the success of her office. The *guesses* and *maybes* and *probablys* of this student's response told Faye that the girl needed her help.

"I can write you a note so you won't be marked tardy," Faye proposed. "Maybe just come grab a snack and see if you feel like talking."

Faye pushed open her heavy office door and extended her arm as if to say *you go in first*. She spoke to Trina's back as the girl brushed past her.

"I guess you know from the assembly that I'm Doctor Collins. I'm sorry I didn't catch your name."

Trina sank awkwardly into one of the cushioned chairs. She wasn't in trouble, not really. But being in a grown-up's office made her feel like she was.

"Trina," she mumbled. "I'm Trina Hendricks."

Faye made small talk while Trina settled into the unfamiliar environment.

"I'm sorry it's so dismal in here," Faye said with a shiver in her voice. "There's not much light on a drizzly day like this one."

"I love the smell of rain," Trina said softly. "Other people say rain makes them feel gloomy, but I love cloudy skies."

This sudden burst of feeling delighted Faye. She liked Trina's openness, liked that she was polite, that she was trying to act like nothing was bothering her. Faye's heart swelled toward this incredibly young girl who would not have been clutching a purple PAL flier if today were an ordinary rainy day with earthy-smelling skies.

Trina scanned Faye's office, its walls heavy and dark with thick leather-bound books. Her eyes rested on a photo of three kids. All three smiled so big Trina could see their pale pink gums. They were the smiles of real happiness, not the phony *cheese* smiles that kids sometimes wore in photos. Doctor Collins would be a good mother, Trina supposed. She knew a lot about kids and how to keep them safe. For a moment, the picture transported Trina to the warm space of her childhood, her mother dressing Trina and her two sisters alike and braiding their hair in matching patterns. Trina could not tell if the baby was a boy or a girl. The three kids in the photo wore matching pajamas that seemed boyish but not overly so, the cuffs a vibrant yellow, the bodies covered with multicolored train engines, some with puffs of white smoke trailing behind them. Trina looked more closely at the baby with its big, curling eyelashes. She needed to tell someone. Why not Doctor Collins?

Sitting sheepishly, Trina picked at the edges of the PAL flier, unsure how to start. Faye spoke first to break the ice.

"What did you think of the assembly? I'm not sure whether that kind of presentation really goes over well with the students."

"I think it does okay," Trina said. "A lot of kids don't pay attention but that happens in class, too. I think the people who really need it are listening."

Faye felt Trina's response as a sweetness given her. Scared as she was, this girl was trying to appease Faye.

"I see you've got a PAL flier," Faye said, pointing to the paper that was slightly unfurling in Trina's weak grasp.

"Yes, I was wondering if maybe I needed to get involved."

"Tell me, do you want to volunteer as a mentor? Or," Faye said this carefully and warmly, "were you thinking that you might want a PAL to chat with about something?"

"I think I need—" a lump rose in Trina's throat. She was afraid she might vomit here in Doctor Collins's crisp, clean office. "Oh, I'm sorry." Trina interrupted herself and moved to stand and go. "I'm not feeling too well."

"Close your eyes and take a big breath in through your nose," Faye said reassuringly. "There's no rush." Trina sat back into her seat.

Many students quaked at the start of these talks. Most gnawed their nails or fiddled with keys or paper or anything else that would distract them. All spoke with their eyes on their laps. Faye jumped up and pushed open a west-facing window. A cold breeze shot through the blinds to Faye's desk.

"There," she said with refreshment. "I always get warm when I'm anxious about something. I notice that cold air can resettle a person when they're feeling sickly." Faye spoke patiently. "I'm here. I will hear you."

A long pause stretched before them.

"Have you been hurt?" Faye asked. "Do you feel in danger from someone at school?" She continued with even more sincerity. "Or from someone at home? Even someone you love?"

The girl's startled intake of breath told Faye she was on the wrong track.

Trina thought of Cash, then, how gentle and patient he had been with her. She remembered how cool she had been with Cash. They had slipped off to his bedroom during a house party Cash was hosting while his parents were traveling in Mexico. Trina had seen the nervousness trickling through her boyfriend's limbs. He had knocked over a soda on his nightstand climbing onto the bed and had asked if they could turn out the lights before he took off his boxers. After it was over, they lay unmoving while the party's thumping beats vibrated through the rest of the house. Cash had traced his fingers along the birthmark that spread out across her shoulder. *It's cool that you have this mark*, he had said. *No matter what else changes, you'll always know you're still you.*

Trina knew girls who had been assaulted, even raped. Everywhere she looked, boys harassed girls who said *no* (and shamed girls who said *yes*). There were boys who kept lists of conquests and boys who kept tallies for Best Blow Job, Tightest Pussy, and Firmest Tits. Not Cash. Cash had asked Trina not to tell her friends that they had *done it*. He didn't want them getting the wrong idea about him. She had felt so lucky that a boy like Cash had liked her back. But now, this.

Tears welled in the corners of Trina's eyes as she blinked them open. She looked directly at the kids in the photo. She was almost sure now that the littlest one with the super long eyelashes was a boy like the oldest. Their faces like cherubim spoke to her. Trina looked at Faye, a woman and mother who stood before her with cheeks plump from a budding smile. Trina could be a mother, too.

"I'm pregnant." Trina spoke the phrase in three distinct syllables.

Then, again: "I'm pregnant."

Trina relaxed visibly once she had spoken. Trina felt, indeed she looked to Faye, as if she had just vomited a poisonous secret. Faye raised her arms out in a show of support.

"Okay," she said, moving toward Trina then crouching down beside her. "Okay."

Trina nodded. "I'm pregnant," she said again. All these weeks she had feared it and thought it and even once had written it (and had quickly flushed the sticky yellow paper square down the toilet). Saying it was another thing altogether. The sound of it intoxicated her.

Faye spoke softly but with confidence. "May I take your hand?"

Trina smiled her assent.

"Okay," Faye said again. "We can handle this."

Color pooled back into Trina's cheeks. Her breathing shallowed. *How?* She wondered. *How will anything be okay after this?* Adulthood spread before Trina a mysterious landscape she must traverse too soon with too few tools.

A spark of delight pricked Faye's heart at the thought of a baby. She did not let it show. Joy was a sign of privilege. Unlike Trina, Faye had long ago survived the tumult and violence of youth. She was through the abyss, out of the fire, on the other side of paradise lost.

VI

A SHOCKING THING HAPPENED IN EARLY summer of 1998 after Faye graduated from Aquinas Prep. This thing always stayed with Faye. Her father's best friend Duane died suddenly of a heart attack at fifty-three years old. Faye's father, a Sheriff's Deputy familiar with death of all kinds, told her the news with a long, yellow face. The pallor on her father's strong jaw frightened Faye in a way that made her feel like a child. But Duane's death stayed with Faye not because he died young. His death haunted Faye because it flashed in each of their faces the reality that we cannot imagine the awful trauma that is breathing down our necks. An optimism and faith and an infectious joy push us forward even as death stalks us from behind. On his drive home, Duane pulled to a pay phone at the first critical pangs. His hand clutched at his chest; panic flooded his brain and body. He called an ambulance, but the paramedics found an empty lot when they arrived. Duane had changed his mind and driven off, believing he would be safe, believing the end could not be here just yet. Minutes later, death moved swiftly in, leaving him cold and lifeless in the driver's seat.

The morning of July 6, 1998, Faye smoked a surreptitious cigarette in her parents' backyard while the house was still asleep. She studied the air for a sign of things to come. The stillness around her felt sharp, not an oppressive heat but the feel of a day that was going to be hot. Now, at six am, nothing new was happening, but the sun was rising on the everything possible.

In a phone call one week prior, Edward and Faye had set the terms. Actually, it should be said, Edward thought they had set the terms. Faye wasn't quite sure what she had agreed to. But there they were, a few weeks after graduation, speaking quietly and carefully into their cordless phones, pacing back and forth in their respective Citrus County residences. Faye paced awkwardly from her gingham-sheeted bed to the full-length mirror tacked on her closed bedroom door. Three dozen times, Faye walked to and fro, cradling the phone as they talked. She peeked occasionally out the drapes to the front walk to ensure neither her parents nor her sister would arrive home and catch her talking sex with her teacher. Every so often, she would lay across the bed, the slight weight of her torso wrinkling the light summer blanket. She would kick her feet a few times up in the air and pick at the plastic glow-in-the-dark stars stuck to her headboard with removable putty. Just as suddenly, she would stand up and start pacing again.

Edward had started the phone call sitting at his computer, whiskey glass in hand, but he too had begun to pace. He charted a path between the Bechstein and the bathroom door, the hardwood floors creaking. Edward felt outside himself as he heard his voice questioning Faye. Faye sensed a foreignness in her own voice as well. Listening to Faye describe her desire for him, Edward felt himself teetering on a moral precipice. It was as if he had found a wad of money on the ground. A flood of instant astonishment at his good fortune rushed in astride the immediate knowledge that he should not take it for himself. As a young man, Edward's high cheekbones and trim physique had easily attracted women looking for adventurous sex with no strings attached. His flair for the romantic had made him a good catch for those looking further down the road, and Edward had in those days rarely been without a woman if he had wanted one. But that was decades ago. Edward could not believe Faye desired him as he was now, overweight and tired and scrubbed of his youthful vibrancy. His cheeks had taken on a ruddiness when he approached forty. He was embarrassed now by the extra weight that had collected around his middle and of the softness of his upper arms.

Faye thought certainly an adult man could not find her attractive. Her hair was an uncontrollable mess of curls and her face was still studded now and then with pimples. Unlike some girls her age, Faye did not know how to shape her eyebrows or apply mascara. Boys outside the choir had paid her little attention at school. Faye thought disparagingly of her own body, was ashamed of her too-small breasts, and planned never to let anyone see the horribly bushy pubic hair that had finally filled out in the last year. Edward asked if Faye thought of him when she touched herself (she did) and if she knew how to have an orgasm (she did, though she had only this year discovered a reliable method).

The silences between them got longer as the questions and answers got more uncomfortable. Edward admitted that he had been fantasizing about Faye for months and that he worried about Faye leaving so soon for college. Edward insisted that she tell no one they were speaking of these unspeakable desires. Faye told Edward she could not bear to be separated from him. Faye insisted that she was saving herself for marriage. Her virginity was not negotiable, she had said, *no matter what*. Faye was afraid of looking foolish;

Edward was afraid of getting caught. Faye needed Edward to love her; Edward wanted to bury his face in Faye's soft, fragrant curls and cup her perfectly curved breast in his hand. More than anything, Faye wanted to make Edward happy; Edward wanted this, too.

"We really can't be seen by anyone," he had said.

Edward had paused, then, thinking of a diplomatic way to ask Faye to spend the summer giving him blow jobs and letting him finger her. "This relationship would have to be an in-house relationship. And we'd be doing in-house things."

Silence had spread across the cities between them, the line so quiet the phone seemed to have gone dead. Faye stared straight ahead at the painted wall of her bedroom—she suddenly remembered the hue on the paint store's color wheel. *Buttermilk Batter.* Edward ran a hand through his hair, leaving an errant wisp hovering over his forehead. He sank back into his chair and awaited her response.

Finally, Faye spoke. "Okay. Dinner at your house, then?"

"Yes. Dinner at seven next Monday."

Edward woke up late (after drinking too much the night before) and was behind schedule all day. He vaguely remembered the dating rituals of his younger days, and so he set to cleaning the house and preparing the dinner that would usher him and Faye across the bridge between their past affiliation and the intimacy that lay ahead. He swept the floors and untangled cobwebs from corners. He washed whiskey glasses that had accumulated in the sink and neatly filed dozens of papers that had gathered between finals week and the start of summer. He washed, dried, and re-tucked the stale-smelling sheets he'd been sleeping on repeatedly for weeks, recoiling at the visible flecks of sloughed off skin on his pillow and the stains lower down from nights he had fallen into bed after too much booze and masturbated before falling asleep. He threw open the windows early in the day. Especially to a Midwesterner like Edward, July in Southern California was not particularly stifling. But the air was somewhat more still than in spring. He hoped a greater cross breeze would dissipate the cigar-tinged air that hung through the middle of the house.

The cleaning continued methodically from one room to the next, Edward's living room pulsing with a recording of Rutter's *Gloria I*. And thus the day passed so full of chores that Edward managed to keep in the periphery the clouds alternately forming and receding at the edges of his consciousness. Edward wanted a partner. He worked tirelessly to produce award-winning choirs, the music transforming their young lives and moving them toward the divine experience of community and spirit. And for it all, he went home alone, forgotten while they caroused and celebrated a youth he could never retrieve. He did not want recognition. He did not want gratitude. He wanted to belong, to feel the exhilarating rush of possibility he witnessed every day in his students. For years now, students had been Edward's most reliable companions. His hot and cold relationship with Diane had fizzled out months before and his fishing buddy living now in Arizona visited only rarely. Beyond the Slater and Sons grocery clerk and the tellers at West Coast Bank, Edward hardly interacted with anyone. Tonight, Edward would write his own daring script. Edward would play house with the only person who seemed to see him as he wanted to be seen.

"You should wear a skirt," Krystal said with a laugh when Faye modeled the pre-planned date night outfit. "Easy access."
Before leaving her house, Faye tied a thin purple sweater around her waist, imagining it a cotton chastity belt that could buy her time if Edward tried to touch her *down there* (but of course he wouldn't; they were just having dinner). She carried a lunchbox in lieu of a purse (like most Aquinas Prep girls did in the late '90s), enjoying the aesthetic mismatch of the Sesame Street puppets on the outside and the cigarettes and car keys tucked inside. Faye felt, even then, the tug of her liminal state, adulthood calling even as she held tightly to the comfort objects of adolescence. She and her friends still toilet-papered houses, watched cartoons, and wove friendship bracelets. They ate steak with ketchup, loaded their coffees with sugar to hide the bitterness, and mixed their vodka with Kool-Aid. Tonight, though, Faye would play grown-up with the only grown-up who seemed to understand her.
That Monday evening at 6:45, the frenetic stop and start blinking of taillights on the 57 freeway to Fulton signaled that rush hour was near its end. The adult world, exhausted from a full day of meetings, errands, caretaking, and worry, shuttled itself home or to second shifts; Faye was headed to Edward's house on a drive she had made several times before with far less trepidation than she felt now. Her stomach flipped, and she felt a buzzing nervousness running through her limbs. As the smoke from her second cigarette curled inward toward the driver's seat, Faye dropped her wrist to send the smoke hurtling back outside the car. She felt a strong breeze rushing by as the traffic began to move more swiftly.
Edward seemed confused when he opened the door and found Faye standing on his back porch. It was almost, she thought, like he wasn't expecting her. Edward's surprised expression stayed with Faye for years after that night. Looking back after everything had fallen apart, she wondered if Edward had hoped she would not come, that she, seventeen-year-old Faye, would avert this disaster. Faye wore navy blue corduroy pants and a new white top patterned with bright turquoise flowers and dragonflies etched in raised white ink that shimmered against the less vibrant white of the background. Only the closest attention revealed the white-on-white details.
Edward told Faye to relax while he quickly showered and changed clothes. The usually cluttered house had always given off an air of spontaneity. She could tell this night that he had been getting ready for her. She lay on the living room couch—*Make yourself at home*, he had said—and closed her eyes just as orchestral music floated out from the sitting room. Faye's journey had been like an arduous trek toward an unseen apex, each uncertain step bringing her

closer to the triumph of Doctor Vogel's affection. The year seemed a whirlwind of progress and stumbles, her footing more secure as she neared this final height, the stakes higher, the fall greater should she trust the wrong patch of earth. For months, Doctor Vogel had led her along this mysterious climb. Now, she lay waiting for the revelation of the promised land. Faye held then released a deep breath. *This is what you've been waiting for*, she thought. She couldn't imagine thinking of Doctor Vogel as her boyfriend or her partner and certainly not a *lover* (what an adult word!). She wanted Doctor to be *hers*, and it felt already in this space that he finally was.

Showering now meant an uncomfortable dampness that would encourage Edward's chest to start sweating when the cool air of his bedroom met his warm post-shower skin. Usually so deliberate and calculating, Edward's mind pinged between exhilaration and dread as he lathered up under the hot water. He felt energized by Faye's desire but nervous about her age. So much about her was too young—he had hoped she would wear a tight skirt for easier access to her legs or a revealing top that would shape her breasts, but she was, as usual, dressed like a teenager. *At least*, he thought, *she's not wearing overalls*. Faye and the other girls, for reasons Edward could not fathom, often wore those clunky shape-refusing garments, and he chuckled for a moment envisioning himself trying to unclip the stiff metal buckles to touch Faye's body hidden beneath the bib. But Faye's youth turned him on. He hoped Faye's willing submission in the classroom would cross over to the bedroom. He had always been attracted to Faye's nonchalance. She wore almost no makeup and spoke to him demurely with tiny eye-smiles and a pursing of her lips. Tonight required no regulations and no subtlety. Tonight, he would push past their Aquinas Prep boundaries and drink in the sweetness he had for so long been able to smell without tasting it.

Over dinner, they talked about friends and family, about Faye's impending move to Sacred Heart and Edward's college years at Kansas State and the University of Michigan. Faye pushed gnocchi around on her plate as she talked about the summer's quick cycling of emotions. Her parents still enforced a midnight curfew, but Faye and her friends had all felt a shift in their homes, the adults suddenly aware how soon their children's own consciences and instincts would determine their movements. Though they played hard and soaked up the joy of teen-aged life, Faye and her friends also had been rigorous students, all of them making grades and accepting entrance to top tier universities. The summer sun in SoCal after graduation came with an enormous sense of relief for the Aquinas Prep standouts who had suffered through months of physics cram sessions, advanced placement exams, final class projects, and precisely prepared admissions essays. Faye's effusive words flowed easily out. Edward watched closely as she spoke. So many days at Aquinas Prep, Faye had been his only joy. He felt comfortable and relieved to have her here in a house that had so often been empty but for the music he played to cover the quiet.

As Edward cleared the dishes and poured himself another glass of wine, Faye moved from the small dining table to the couch. She wanted to step outside for a smoke, but she was too nervous to move from her spot. She crossed then uncrossed her legs, tried tucking them under her, and eventually straightened her back against the paisley-stitched pillow and stretched out. Edward returned with one dish of ice cream, and thinking better of her position, Faye let her legs drop to the floor so he could sidle up next to her. He sat so close she could feel the heat off his skin. Her face had never been so deliberately close to his, and though she wanted to sink into his gaze, shyness overcame her. Edward fed her a tiny bite of the ice cream, a gesture so romantic it was embarrassing and almost off-putting. He was nervous, too, and he needed a way to get close to her. With the next bite, Edward left a thin trail of ice cream on Faye's bottom lip. A nervous giggle rose in her throat as Edward leaned forward and kissed her mouth.

Without pulling back to meet her eyes, Edward set the bowl aside and began to kiss her with more force, his tongue pushing into hers. The smell of his cologne—a scent she had so craved—felt aggressively invasive.

This can't be happening. He is kissing me. Doctor *is kissing me.*

Faye froze. Edward backed away, creating a rush of air that steadied Faye's head. He raised her hand to his mouth and gently kissed the backs of her fingers. Suddenly, Faye felt young to him again. He wanted to give her room to change her mind, but he was afraid she would run away.

He nearly whispered. "Is this the kind of closeness you want with me?"

Faye's eyes seemed beseeching and scared.

She quickly said yes. Faye wanted Edward near. She wanted to recline against the softness of his middle and the strength of his chest, to tell him she loved him and run her hands through his hair after a long day at work. She wanted to give him gifts that would make him feel loved and to snuggle her head up into the crook of his neck when she was tired. This closeness she wanted. She had not thought about what extra expectations these intimacies carried.

After it all happened, Faye hardly remembered the move to the bedroom. By the time Edward carried her there, he had already taken off her clothing. For months, Faye had dreamed about a date with Doctor Vogel. It had appeared in her mind's eye like a movie reel, a rollicking frenzied chaos of eagerly clashing bodies, the romantic strains of Barry Manilow or Lionel Richie blasting a backdrop to the passion. She thought Edward would look into her eyes and hold her face in his hands. She would feel complete and happy. Instead, she was paralyzed.

Faye desperately wanted to cover her body and to be gone from this place. She was silent, unable to utter a word. She could feel herself responding to his touch, the wetness seeping out of her as he moved swiftly over her body with his hands and his mouth. He kept saying her name. *You're so beautiful, Faye.* Each time, it panicked and embarrassed her. *You're so wet, Faye.* (*What, on Earth, could that mean?*) Faye's voice was trapped in her throat. *What should I say? How can I tell him to stop? Do I say Doctor Vogel? Or Doc? Or* Edward? The bedroom was dark but for a hovering residue of light that filtered in from the kitchen and sitting room. How easy and free the conversation out there in the light had been! She was desperate to be back there before any of this had begun. Faye closed her eyes as Edward continued touching her. When she tightened her lashes against her face, an aura of light revealed a replicated image of Edward's bedroom. Reverberating shadows pulsed out from the glowing outline of his light fixtures and the dresser opposite the bed.

Edward had thought the drumbeat of their lovemaking would be like a symphony that started slowly and rose to a climax. The line that had seemed so bright at Aquinas Prep had begun to blur in the preceding weeks. Now, on closer inspection, he saw that it was made of chalk and that he could simply erase it. He had wanted sex with Faye to be sweaty, chaotic, and explosive, a sense of final release given the months he had spent swallowing his desire or trying to reject it. Instead, the silence was deafening. He thought about stopping but knew acknowledging her silence might worsen things. It was too horrible to think that Faye wasn't enjoying this, that she hadn't even wanted this after all.

Crouching back toward the floor, his eyes now accustomed to the bedroom's darkness, Edward grabbed Faye gently by her ankles and pulled her body to the edge of the bed. He lifted her legs over his shoulders and slid his arms up under her torso, spreading her legs apart and thrusting his tongue against the insides of her thighs.

A thin layer of sweat pasted Edward's dress shirt to his back. The adrenaline pushed him forward. Warring forces tore at each other violently. He feared that he was disappointing and upsetting her, but the untouched perfection of her breasts and the supple whiteness of her belly overcame him. He could not stop trying to devour her. The uncomfortable ache of his cock against his jeans frustrated Edward. So, finally, he spoke to her.

"Will it scare you too much if I just unbutton my pants?"

"Yes," she answered quickly. "Don't. Please."

He stopped, then, and crawled up beside her, cradling Faye up against him. Only then did he notice the warm tears coursing down her face. When he pulled back from Faye's body, she reached for the sheet and tried to cover herself.

"Why are you trying to hide? You're so beautiful."

Relief poured through Faye when she realized it was over. She couldn't figure out what had happened. She had wanted to love him, to memorize every curve of his body and to fold herself inside his embrace. Instead, she couldn't even look at him. The paralyzing fear had taken over. *Paralyzed. Overcome.* These words ran through her brain on a confusing loop. She remembered almost no sensations from that night: not the thickness of his fingers as they entered her, or the hot heaviness of his breathing, or the wet sheen above his lip from where he had put his mouth up against her. Panic overcame them all. Panic and the desire for it all to pass. She wanted it to end, so she could have him back as he had been before. She did not yet know that sex would always be like this, the desire to be done with it always outweighing even the most pleasant sensation.

The numbness fell away as Faye lay unmoving atop the sheets. Edward felt his desire waning and was no longer aware of his breathing. Everything had stopped. Rutter's *Requiem*, pumping through the house since before dinner, suddenly burst upon their consciousness. Joyful voices proclaimed the *Sanctus* while Faye and Edward pondered what they had done. Rutter had released the renowned piece just as Edward had started the doctoral program at the University of Michigan's school of music. Its beautiful cacophony had burrowed immediately into Edward's consciousness and taken root there with his deepest visions of man's quest for the divine. Edward considered himself faithful, if not pious, and as he lay beside Faye, he knew he had done something awful. He had thought she might flinch, or pull back, or ask him to stop—all of which she had done at some point that night—but he had never thought she might cry so much. She didn't seem angry or hurt. Meekness, shyness came to his mind, and he felt a rush of empathy.

He ran the side of his hand down Faye's still damp cheek. "Am I ever going to see you again?"

The answer came so softly he couldn't tell if she had said *no* or *I don't know*. He didn't want to push her by asking again. Instead, he caressed her and wrapped his arm over her waist. She responded warmly, moving her naked body against his entirely clothed one, comforted by the familiar and safe feel of the closed up buttons on his shirt. For Edward's part, lying fully clothed on his own bed disoriented him. He held her then, quietly, and focused on the music. The glorious strains of the *Sanctus* gave way to the *Lux Aeternam* and the long, slow pulling of a violin's bow. Faye came back into herself and sat up, suddenly aware that her curfew was approaching.

Sleeping in was not a thing Faye did. Faye always rose with the sun. On Saturdays in her childhood, she awoke just before seven, enough time to wipe the sleep from her eyes and pull on shorts and tennis shoes before her father arrived home from his graveyard shift at the Sheriff's Department. Her father would arrive promptly at 7:15, and the two would head to the local courts for an hour of rallying and match play before grabbing a donut and returning home—all before Faye's mom and three siblings had even stirred from their sleep. Sundays brought 10:30 Mass at St. Cecilia, but first, Faye woke naturally around dawn and tooled away the morning watching cartoons alone in the quiet house. Despite the media's consistent showing of sleepy teens still snoozing at noon, teen hormones hadn't swayed Faye's sleep patterns. She loved the feeling of starting a new day, her daily checklist ready to be run through and conquered.

That summer of '98, the change in her father's work schedule meant that both her parents left the house before rush hour. Her oldest brother had been five years out of the house, renting an apartment on the outskirts of Citrus County and coming home sporadically for family dinner or to pick up straggling mail. Bridget still lived at home but spent most of her time working or carousing with friends and a boyfriend; the next in line was two years gone at Cal Berkeley on a softball scholarship. Faye and her grandmother spent mornings and afternoons at home while her father worked, Faye stepping outside now and then for a quick half cigarette whose stench she quickly covered with perfume and starlight spearmints.

The morning after her date with Edward, Faye woke slowly. The order of Faye's world felt upended. Who was Edward now? She could think of him only as Doctor Vogel, Aquinas Prep choir director, the man whose conducting had been conducting her movements since at thirteen she had joined his Freshman Women's Ensemble. As her eyes adjusted to a bright new day—she had slept well past her usual waking hour—the tiny blue flowers painted on her dresser came into focus. Faye scanned the hutch above her desk, fixing her eyes on a picture.

The photo showed Faye and her closest high school friends in Assisi, their arms draped around each other's shoulders, their faces beaming, their AP European Tour tee shirts gleaming white in the bright sun. She remembered Doctor Vogel standing at the center, his arms folded across his chest, touching neither Faye nor Bryn, who stood on either side of him. Faye could still feel herself holding Bryn's hand behind Doctor's back. In the lush hills of Assisi, Faye had wanted so badly to lean her body against Doctor Vogel's, to wrap him in their collective embrace. She remembered the heat rising off his freshly cut hairline. His cologne had smelled sharp that day. It was tinged with the slight sourness of sweat from their hike up the hills to the Basilica.

As she looked at the picture this summer morning, Faye thought about her absent friends. Bryn babysat her niece most days and cruised around with a boyfriend most evenings. She would leave soon for a gap year traveling India. Faye wanted Bryn's advice just now but thought better of inviting her criticism. *Later*, Faye thought. She would go to Bryn if things got too out of control. Senior year, Krystal had stepped into Faye's choir world and Ian's arms and generally into Leah's place in Faye's life. For months, Faye had been blaming Leah for withholding friendship. Remorse churned Faye's stomach, now. It was she who had abandoned Leah first.

Faye let her gaze focus on the photo of Edward. A surge of joy stunned her. Shock and nervousness fought in the pit of her stomach. *Incarnation*, she thought. *Coming into being*. She and Edward had been born anew. Edward's exhilarating and terrifying pursuit of her the night before came back in chaotic flashes. Something blossomed in Faye as she remembered that he had kissed her, his mouth opening and closing so forcefully over her lips and her nipples and between her thighs. It was unbelievable. She, quite literally, could not believe it had all happened, and she had no idea what to do next. Like solving only the red side of a Rubik's cube, Faye saw that with one puzzle solved, she had created a dozen more complications.

By midday, Faye had fully woken, smoked three cigarettes, paced a thousand steps, and revealed to her closest friends just how passionately

Edward loved her. She called Krystal first. Krystal conferenced in Ian, who later called James. Faye could not bring herself to say the words.

"You won't believe it." Faye cradled the cordless phone against her shoulder as her quick light of a cigarette brought a pungent rush of heat into her chest.

Krystal sat up, alert. She had been waiting all morning for Faye's call.

"It happened so fast. Everything. Everything happened so fast."

"Oh my God, did you sleep with him?"

A bolt of fear shook Faye. She shirked off the idea. "Of course not. Don't be ridiculous."

"But you guys did other things? Come on, just tell me."

Faye's emotions had not yet crystallized around this new song developing in her soul. She tried to examine it, to reach the tenderness she felt for Edward. She felt instead a discomfort about her feelings for him. How could she tell of this thing? How could she describe how happy and terrified and accomplished and ashamed she felt? This morning, the morning after, she was all of those vibrating chords, her heart and mind an orchestra rising and falling, one movement serene and the next so dramatic and haunting that she sucked in her breath and felt strangled. She didn't mention the crying, did not tell Krystal about the lump that sprang to her throat when she thought Edward might remove his pants and position his body even closer to hers. Sex was Krystal's territory. Better to let Krystal say those awful things.

"I can't say it. It's too embarrassing. We did everything else."

"Oh my fucking God, Faye! Did you suck that old man's dick?"

Faye's cheeks grew hot at the word. "No! He had all his clothes on. God, no. I didn't do anything. I just let him do stuff."

"Holy shit, Faye. You let him go down on you?"

Faye nodded inaudibly as Krystal spoke. *You let him*, she heard Krystal say. Yes, she had let Edward touch her in those terribly adult ways. She didn't think he would do that. She didn't ask him for that. Yet she had not stopped him. The night stretched before her as one long act, a scene in which she lay weeping, immobilized by disbelief and unaware of her options. She had felt Edward's tongue probing the tightly clenched parts of her that no one else had seen. Her body had alternately opened to him and recoiled in fear, and through it all, she had waited patiently for it to end, her mind drifting away to memories of Edward that were much more pleasant. She took refuge in those memories—the way Edward's eyes would come alive each school day when he first saw her, the pride that would pour forth when Edward fisted his hands and quieted a crescendo at the end of a commanding Chamber Singers performance. Faye loved *that* Edward. She loved Doctor Vogel, and she would go back for more touching from Edward if it meant knowing that Doctor Vogel loved her back.

"Faye? Hello? Did he? Did he go down on you?"

"Yes." Faye's triumphant tone surprised herself. Krystal often had lurid stories and scandalous news to share. Now, Faye had bigger news than any of them ever would.

"Oh. My. God. Holy shit, Faye. Just, *oh my God*. I don't even know what to say. He's, like, forty years old. He's, like, dad age. In fact, he IS my dad's age."

"I know. He's different, though. I talk to him just like I talk to Ian and James. He's just one of us, really. He and Merton are basically best friends."

"Well, Merton's weird, too." Faye flinched a bit at Krystal's judgment. A year earlier, all of them had been Faye's friends. Now, the kids who still came around—namely Ian and James—were *our friends*, meaning hers and Krystal's. Krystal had inserted herself right in the core of Faye's friends, but she didn't know them like Faye did. She certainly did not know Doctor Vogel, would never understand why this man, whom Krystal thought was too old and too fat and too arrogant and too *uncool*, was Faye's whole world.

"How was it? Are you going to go back there?"

Faye picked at the torn cellophane wrapping on the cigarette box she held. She pushed down the hot surge in her throat and forced away the image of herself naked and sobbing in Edward's bed, so quiet after years of talking to him, so confused after years feeling sure and safe.

"I have to go back."

Driving the 57 freeway became habit as Faye went back to Edward's every few days over the next two weeks. Each drive brought new excitement at Edward's steady gaze, his slow creeping smile, the way he seemed to both drink her in and look right through her. Once, Faye brought chicken sandwiches from the corner drive-thru. They ate on the back porch, sharing ketchup awkwardly like new friends at summer camp. She had never imagined Edward doing something so ordinary as eating French fries, the excess grease soaking through the waxy yellow wrapping. When a day at the beach or outlet shopping with Krystal delayed Faye's drive to Fulton, the glowing sunset followed Faye in the rearview mirror. On those evenings, she sat smoking and flipping through magazines on a stool at the mouth of the garage while Edward worked on household projects. In the living room, Faye would relax as Edward pulled her against him and dipped his tongue lightly into her mouth. She liked the way Edward kissed in the living room. Living room kissing felt like kissing a boy. Edward's bedroom kissing felt threatening, his mouth trying to swallow hers up as his breath got hotter and his grip on her got more forceful. She liked quick visits when she knew Edward could not take off her clothes or pull her hand toward that *thing* she could not name and did not want to think about.

Some evenings, Faye slipped her sandals off at the back door and headed straight to the couch where Edward sat, leaning her head against his shoulder and pulling at her curls while he spoke to his mom long distance from Kansas. When everything else had fallen apart, Faye would fondly remember this tableau: the sound of Edward's rich, gravelly voice filled the air as he talked of daily nothings to his mom. Faye snuggled against him and pretended they had made a life together. For his part, Edward enjoyed this fantasy, too. He lusted after Faye's perfectly taut youth and wellspring of sexual arousal. And he cherished the thought, like she did, that in another world they could be normal, two people who had once been Doctor Vogel and his Aquinas Prep student now transformed into real lovers.

While Faye and her friends lounged on the sand and played skee ball at the Peninsula Pier, Edward was building a medicine cabinet and laying wood flooring in his newly remodeled bathroom. He almost never went out; there was no one to go with. Edward felt the accustomed isolation of a man living alone for many years. Faye's youthfulness unnerved him, but for a man like Edward, the idea justified the act. As long as Faye came to him, parking casually in his driveway and choosing how late she would stay, it didn't matter that he had been having sex since the day in 1972 that he had turned fifteen, a full *eight* years before Faye had even been *born*. Because Faye made him dizzy with desire and wistful with longing, it didn't matter that she was so obviously terrified of his body and felt more helpless and less willing with each encounter.

Alone in bed each night, Faye's thoughts raced and she feared she was losing her mind. She could not think too long about any of the things Edward was doing to her or how they made her body feel. The past felt sealed away and safe; Faye tried to stay there in her mind, to play like a tape on repeat her memories of the Father-Daughter dance and the storm in Freiburg, memories of Renaissance Pageant rehearsals and touring Roman ruins. Daily affection from her grandmother—the feel of her paper thin skin, watching her eyes alight with excitement over card games and word puzzles—soothed Faye and brought her to the only present that felt stable. Faye's world was changing around her. Aquinas Prep was closing itself off. Old friends like Tommy and Leah had become suspicious of Faye and had detached from her; Krystal, Ian, and James were buying extra-long sheets and packing away childhood memories. They were college-bound co-eds opening to a world beyond Citrus County. Finally, there was the strange case of Doctor Vogel, a man Faye so admired but who was concealing a sexually insatiable Mr. Hyde. Doctor Vogel talked freely of sex but of little else these days, cutting Faye with dismissive remarks and becoming a persistent and condescending man she was supposed to call *Edward*. (She never could.)

As her departure to Potato Creek loomed, Faye cut her hours at Cal's until she worked only Tuesday mornings and one afternoon-evening split. Tips meant extra money for churros and cheese fries, the magnanimous feeling of treating her friends to dinner and renting canoes to paddle across the bay at Peninsula Pier. Faye yawned with boredom and leaned on her hands during the slow 2:00 to 4:00 stretch between the Cal's lunch and dinner rush. She called Edward to pass the time and check in.

"I'm meeting Krystal for a late movie. I'll stop by for a quick visit and to change after work."

"Make sure you don't make it too quick," Edward quipped. "I can't stand when you tease me and take off."

Faye's stomach flipped and she chewed her bottom lip. "I should probably have an hour or two. What's your workload like today? Will you be ready for me around 6:00?"

"Hearing your voice, I'm ready for you now."

"Well I'm at work for at least another hour or two. I thought you were working in the garage, anyway."

"That's not the kind of ready I mean." Edward laughed his always jeering laugh. Faye felt embarrassed and small. "Talking to you is making me hard."

"I bet it is." Faye spoke with a sultry lilt to her voice. It was easy to impersonate a grown woman on the phone. It wasn't so easy at Edward's house.

"Maybe this evening you can do something about that."

She twirled the springy plastic phone cord around her finger and felt her stomach tremble.

"We'll just have to see, won't we?"

"With that in mind, I'll get all my projects done this afternoon. Can't wait to see you. Get here as soon as you can."

"Great. I'll bring pie from work."

Summer nights in Citrus County were more mild than visitors expected, even in the parts, like Fulton, that were twenty miles from the ocean. The cool evening air stilled Faye's nerves, and she settled into the sense of familiarity she and Edward had shared at Aquinas Prep. Sugary peach glaze burst upon Faye's taste buds as she and Edward scooped pie from the Styrofoam Cal's container.

Edward took the bite Faye offered from her fork. "This is really good."

"Peach pie is my absolute favorite. A few summers ago, I broke out in these terrible hives, and the doctor determined I had eaten too many peaches. In the summer at Cal's we literally stand in the prep kitchen dipping slices in whipped cream while the baker makes the pies. It's amazing."

"I've never had it."

"You've never had peach pie?"

"Not like this. My mom used to can peaches when I was growing up. We ate peach pie that was baked in the oven, not fresh. Not cold."

Literary visions of a warm farmhouse kitchen sprang to Faye's mind. She soaked in every detail of the past lives that Edward revealed. For children and teens alike, adults seem to fall fully formed from the sky, always grown, always in charge, always existing only in their role as parent, uncle, teacher. As Faye had become interested in Edward, he too had become interesting to her. She wanted to know all of him: where he came from, what he had seen, whom he had loved. She had learned already that he was the oldest of four children, the youngest a boy as well, their two sisters sandwiched in between. Beginning their family in Nebraska with Edward's birth, his parents had moved back upon his grandfather's death to the family wheat farm in Kansas on which Edward's father had been raised. Because Edward was so old, or so it seemed to Faye, and because he was native to farm country rather than the suburban sprawl of Southern California, Edward's childhood unfolded for Faye in romantic, sepia-tinged images.

"Is it difficult being away from your mom?"

The question seemed ridiculous as soon as she had spoken it. Edward was forty-one, had left his parents' farm for university life, graduate school, the mid-Atlantic, and then California before Faye had even been born. The simplicity of her question touched him, though, and suddenly he too envisioned the rustic glow of their family home, he and his brother playing piano by the fire, Millie at the clarinet, Anna setting the family table, his mother in a flowery or paisley-printed dress always covered by her pale yellow apron. What had seemed stifling when he was a teenager in the early '70s had since crystallized into an idyllic pastoral.

"Sometimes. Yes," he said as if in a revelation. "Sometimes I miss my mom. I left a long time ago. All of their lives go on without me."

"Is everyone else still there?"

"More or less. My brother and one sister are still in Kansas. Anna's in Nebraska."

"Will you ever go back?"

Faye knew Edward hated California, that he had moved west in pursuit of a fiancé who had broken his heart and left him to a disappointing life in the shadow of their breakup.

"I like the environment there so much better. I like the openness. The landscape here feels buried."

Edward's musings crept into Faye's consciousness in melodramatic visions, his childhood the warm bloodiness of *The Red Pony*, his remaining family the generational dystopia of the Trask family farm east of Eden.

"You want the Steinbeck life?"

"It's not really like that. Well, it's not *only* like that. I have no grand illusions about life on the land. I never had any plans to follow my father into agricultural work. My father was an expert in irrigation systems and ecosystem restoration. He worked the land as a kid and then became an academic in his later years, always approaching the farm more as utility than nature. I hated all the work. I let Glen do the dirty stuff. He hated me for that. And my mom always let me get away easy. I was the oldest. Her favorite."

Edward chuckled, then paused. Surprised by the rush of emotion, he set his palm on Faye's knee. "In summer I would lie on my back for hours listening to the cicadas and trying to count the stars. Out there, alone, even as a little boy, I could feel the music. The swaying wheat like cello notes on the breeze. I miss the earthiness of Kansas and the wetness of Ann Arbor. Everything in Ann Arbor and further up in the U.P. is so lush. Everything here is manufactured."

A sense of loss seemed to come over Edward as he described these bygone moments of his youth. This version of Edward was Faye's favorite. Faye wished he would talk to her like this more often. Listening to his compositions—to *Loonshadow*'s intensity, both piercing and tender—had told her. Beneath Edward's calloused exterior was a gaping wound that needed healing. That was what Faye wanted. She wanted to heal him.

"I can see what you mean," Faye said, though she really couldn't. She was from a different place and a different time than Edward, born in the 1980s when even in the Midwest most family farms and many small family businesses were going the way of glass milk bottles while corporate restaurants and discount stores restructured the American experience.

The conversation halted. Faye almost said that work had been dead and that she'd hardly made any money; Edward thought about asking Faye to help him hang the new medicine cabinet. But the moment was still and serene. They let the silence unfold and enjoyed their treat. They sat in the backyard grass, Faye's legs tucked beneath her and Edward's stretched out in front of him. Faye had never seen Edward act so casually, without preparation or purpose. She was still not able to call him *Edward* when she spoke to him, had never seen him just being Edward. Every encounter with Edward brought something she had never imagined: Doctor Vogel washing dishes at the sink; Doctor Vogel ironing a shirt; Doctor Vogel blowing his nose; Doctor Vogel eating peach pie out of Styrofoam on the back lawn.

To be fair, Edward had not yet gotten used to the out-of-school Faye, either. He disliked Faye's smoking (he smoked cigars but loathed the smell of cigarettes), and he flinched each time he lifted Faye's skirt or seductively slipped down her jeans to find her childish butterfly-printed panties. What had at first caused an incongruous excitement had begun to feel shameful. He couldn't understand why she didn't try to look older or to be more seductive in her appearance. They were supposed to be different, now. But Faye kept being Faye. She in fact seemed to flaunt her youth. Her friends often called his house when she was visiting, intruding on his time with her and never letting him forget how carefully he must tread with this underage girl. Only a few days in, Edward felt he could not trust her to keep quiet but knew he could not afford to alienate her from the other kids or to anger her. Walking this tightrope was exhausting, but Edward's loneliness and Faye's persistence kept him balancing over the abyss below. Sitting in the grass with her now, a shiny dot of sticky syrup clinging to her lip, Edward felt such peace that he let these worries go. He moved in to kiss her sweet mouth and felt her lean into him.

"Let's go inside," he said between kisses.

"I have to leave soon."

"Your friends can wait." He kissed her ear and whispered hotly, "tell them *Doctor* made you late."

They both laughed lightly.

She stood without answer and let him scoop her like a hurt child, her arms wrapped around him, her face buried in his neck. Always at Edward's,

Faye faced this liminal journey between spaces, Edward either carrying her bodily or leading her by the hand. From the kitchen to the bedroom; from the piano room to the bedroom; from the backyard to the bedroom. At Edward's, nearly all days and all activities ended there, the lights off, the blue sheets turned down, Faye's clothing dropped piece by piece to the wood floor as Edward removed it and her body went still. Edward's probing and pawing became more persistent and more urgent each time. Rolling onto his back, Edward positioned Faye's naked body on top of his clothed one, sitting her up so that she straddled him on her knees. She sat back rather shyly, leaning forward enough so that her hair would cover her breasts. Daylight saved, the summer sun had not yet set, and Faye was embarrassed to see her own body, especially the awful tuft of curly hair between her legs.

Edward breathed deeply, and she saw a glint in his blue eyes. "Sit back. Let me look at you."

Edward reached up and squeezed her breasts. The cool air sent a shiver across her skin. Goosebumps appeared around her nipples and made them seem to protrude and darken unnaturally. She looked down at her navel and tried not to meet Edward's eyes. He licked his fingers and rubbed them across her nipples. Faye dropped her arms to her side and rested her weight back onto Edward's hips. She laughed a little, though she didn't know why. It felt wonderful and strange.

"This will be one of your favorite lovemaking positions," Edward said wistfully, imagining Faye the grown woman she would someday become.

Faye laughed again when Edward said *lovemaking*, such an embarrassingly romantic word. She tried to imagine it, too. Edward moved his hands down from her breasts and slid his fingers inside her. She wanted him to move his hands back up, to run his fingers along her ribs or to cup her face in his hands. When he pushed them into her down there, his fingers met an instinctive resistance from somewhere inside. Panic set in whenever Edward crossed that barrier. She was afraid he would go too far, and she didn't know how she would stop him. Edward gripped Faye's hips and grinded her down against the stiffness inside his jeans. She pulled away from the abrasive material and the shock of feeling his body that way. He laid her down and faced her.

"Please touch me, Faye. I'll keep my clothes on. I promise I won't scare you. Just do this for me."

Pleasing Edward was all that Faye had wanted for as many months as she could remember. But she couldn't do it. Not this.

"I can't."

Edward pulled Faye's hand below his waist, letting go when he felt how strongly she was resisting. He turned away from her and stared blankly at the ceiling, the rush of blood beginning to recede.

"I spend all my time trying to please you," he said, standing up and turning his back like an aggrieved child. "I'm going to make a drink. Maybe you should just go. Your friends are waiting."

Edward left the bedroom. Faye began to dress.

The ringing phone brought them both to the middle of the house. Edward let the machine pick up.

You've reached 992-6882. Thanks for calling. Please leave a message.

Faye reached for the phone as she heard Ian's voice. "Hi Doctor, this is Ian, just looking for Faye and thought she might be there."

"It's me. I'm here," Faye said breathlessly as she picked up the receiver.

Edward drained his glass as he walked back toward the kitchen. He set the glass down too firmly on the counter so Faye could hear his annoyance.

"I'm leaving here in a few minutes. I'll see you there."

Faye disconnected the call but continued to cradle the phone against her chest. She spoke to Edward's back as he labored unnecessarily over a leak at the kitchen faucet.

"I'm sorry. I told them not to call me here."

Edward turned around contemptuously. "You better not be telling them what goes on here. I'm serious about this."

"I'm not," she lied. "They think we're just hanging out, which we are."

"Well, maybe we shouldn't be. It doesn't seem like you really want to be doing this."

Hot tears welled up in Faye's eyes.

"That's not true. Of course I want to be here. I'm just scared."

Here it is again, thought Faye. *Another lecture and another apology.*

Thus continued the predictable cadence of their time together. Delighted companionship begetting unrequited desire, then bitterness, disappointment, and a persistent sense of misunderstanding. So many nights had ended this way. Edward's frustration was palpable; so too was Faye's panic at being separated from him. She told herself not to cry, but the tears fell anyway.

"Shit. I'm sorry. I'm sorry," she said urgently.

Faye rushed to gather her things. Edward's anger drifted away. He stopped her at the door. *Here we are again,* he thought. *More tears and more appeasement.*

He kissed her hard on her mouth then pulled her head to his chest.

"I'm sorry," he said with conviction. "Don't be mad at me."

"I don't know why it's like this."

Faye wished her stupid fear would go away. She wanted to want what he wanted. She couldn't understand why her mind and her body wouldn't agree, why she couldn't just act out the fantasy she had played on repeat all through senior year.

"You just need more experience," Edward said with authority.

"Are you saying I need a teacher?"

Edward kissed her again, this time wrapping his arms around her waist and pulling her body against his.

"Yes." Again, Edward's sardonic laugh. "And I'm just the person to teach you."

Krystal called just before curfew.

"I never got the chance to ask. How was tonight at his house?"

Faye could still hear Edward's irritation. *Maybe you should just go*, he had said.

Faye answered without hesitation. "Amazing."

"Sleeping at his house is a terrible idea," Krystal whispered fiercely at Faye, the two huddled together suspiciously in Ian's backseat.

"Why? I want to *sleep* with him—"

Faye noticed Krystal's obvious revulsion.

"Not to have sex with him," Faye clarified. "Just to *sleep* with him."

"But what if he sleeps *naked*? What if you get into bed and then he takes all his clothes off? What are you going to do then? Get out and run away?" Krystal was half laughing but with exasperation. No one understood the stakes or what might actually happen.

"He wouldn't do that," Faye insisted. "He knows I don't want that."

"Yes, but how long is he going to go slow for you? Faye, he's an adult. He's a *man*. He's going to start wanting more. How many weeks have you been going over there?"

"Almost three."

"It feels too risky to me."

Momentarily, Faye reconsidered. Krystal was experienced, non-virginal, unafraid of sex, and a self-professed expert at blow jobs. Even she faltered at the thought that Edward might ask Faye to do sexual things she wasn't ready for.

"Nothing will happen. Don't be so dramatic."

Away from Edward, Faye never feared him. She received each terrifying sexual advance as a momentary panic, as fleeting as the suggestion itself and immediately subsumed by the vision of Doctor Vogel that was much more familiar than the Edward she came to know that summer. The Doctorness of Doctor was fixed in Faye's mind. Years before, Faye had decided who he was. *That* Edward stayed intact deep in Faye's soul, a burst of light so vibrant and beautiful that Faye could only feel warmed when she imagined it. When the new Edward acted out, Faye retreated to this idol and took comfort there until the threat passed.

"Besides, he can't do *anything* to me tonight." Faye gave a side glance to the front seat. Ian and James talked about upcoming tryouts for their college choirs.

Faye pointed toward her lap. "I'm on my period," she mouthed.

All four friends rushed to meet curfew at the night's end, each whizzing down a different freeway, replaying in their minds the night's jokes and emotional highs. The days of their final summer were fast disappearing and college loomed, but for now, every night felt like a triumph of teen-aged freedom. They had extra late curfews, time-tested friendships, their own cars, pocket money, college roommates waiting in the wings, and as much love and everything-but-sex as any of them wanted. Faye didn't know yet that never again would summer nights feel so light, her heart so open.

A natural night owl, Edward stoked his creative energy by drinking whiskey and plucking at his guitar. Faye's headlights in the driveway brought him to the back door, the familiar cadence of her step immediately enticing him.

"No curfew tonight?"

"My parents think I'm spending the night at Krystal's. What do you say? Ready for a private slumber party?"

Edward didn't know from where she had gathered her courage, but he knew she wouldn't have come like this, in the middle of the night, unless she were finally ready to reciprocate his advances. He could hardly believe his good fortune. Faye was offering herself up. He had Faye all to himself, no clock to watch, no curfew to meet, no friends calling to interrupt, and presumably no fear holding her back.

"You know I'm always ready," Edward said coyly.

Emerging from the bathroom, Faye found Edward waiting in his bedroom's doorway, a candle flickering, Bach's *Mass in b Minor* dramatizing his slow walk toward her. She wore red Aquinas Prep tennis team sweats.

"Is this your sexiest lingerie?"

That knowing smile followed, the flirtatious grin Faye had loved at school but had become leery of this summer. The smile spelled growing desire, the transition from romance to sex and a long tug of war that would leave Edward angry and Faye humiliated. *Not tonight*, she thought. *Not when we have all night to be together.*

Suddenly, Faye felt conscious of the thick menstrual pad between her legs. She got nervous and almost shouted.

"I'm on my period. So, I don't want you trying to do anything to me tonight."

Disappointment didn't describe it. Edward was angry. He wanted to understand, but *really*, he thought. *Not tonight?* Edward remembered the breathless yelps Faye emitted when he touched her with his tongue. Her tiny moans sent a euphoric buzz through his head. He needed more of her. *Not tonight*, he thought incredulously, *when I have all night to do with you whatever I want?*

"Well, I don't know what you expect when you come over here," he said with annoyance, turning his back and disappearing down the hall toward the kitchen.

Stunned by his change of tone, Faye climbed into bed alone and waited for him to return. The unpredictability drove her mad. Edward's mood swings befuddled her, forcing her to question everything she knew she had heard, to wonder whether she was victim or aggressor, deceiving Edward or being manipulated by him. In the past three weeks, Edward had begun speaking indifferently or even harshly to her at times. In all the years they had known each other, Edward had never criticized Faye. She couldn't believe how quickly everything had changed. Sometimes they seemed like their old selves, but Edward had found new things to love about Faye. He talked most often about her body and everything he said seemed to have a sexual undertone. Also, Faye now realized, there were things Edward didn't like about her. It made her feel awful. And—oh God she hated thinking this—there were things she didn't like about him. Only a month ago, she never would have thought it possible to be angry at Edward or to pull away from him.

Edward returned in better spirits. He slipped off his jeans and cozied up as close to her as he could get. He kissed her roughly, her face pressed unnaturally against his by a hand at the back of her head. Angry no longer, with Faye in his bed, Edward was aroused and determined.

"You kiss me like I'm going off to work in the morning," he said flatly. "You need to open your mouth more." Edward's famous chuckle followed. "You never opened your mouth wide enough when you sang, either."

Always the past sat between them. *How far away those Aquinas Prep choir days seemed! But only weeks ago!*

Faye tried to comply, kissing Edward back but finding herself absorbed by his powerful sucking. She thought she would love this part, but she didn't. She knew some adage about insanity and doing the same thing but expecting different results. But here she was, again. She loved Edward, which was supposed to mean she would love being kissed by him, but it was too physical and awkward and wet and uncomfortable. She couldn't squirm away or find her own rhythm, so she let her body relax and took her mind away. Soon this part would end, and Faye would have what she really needed. She would be asleep in Edward's bed and Edward's embrace.

When Edward grabbed between Faye's legs, she bolted up and pushed his hand away. Hot panic swept over her. She wondered if he had already felt the enormous bulge stuck like a diaper in her underwear. She didn't wear tampons like Krystal did. She had tried, spending a humiliating afternoon in the bathroom while her older sister—beautiful, glamorous, sexually active by her early teens—coached from outside the door. *If you can still feel it,* Bridget had said, *you did it wrong.* Eventually Faye gave up. *I couldn't wear tampons until I started having sex, until after I was married,* her mother had said. This did not console Faye. It made her inadequacy somehow more embarrassing. Bryn and Leah said the same. They just couldn't figure out how to put it in. Faye felt normal, then. Faye remembered she and her girlfriends talking about sex as they sat up late in their European hotel rooms. *Thank God we're not boys,* she remembered Leah saying. *I just hope my husband knows how to get it in there! Because I sure don't.* This made them laugh hysterically, too young to realize how much agency they planned to relinquish. Sex was something a boy did *to you*, not with you.

"Remember, I'm on my period."

"I know. It doesn't bother me. It's okay."

It was not okay. No, it was not okay with Faye. Everything about her period was intrusive. She hated the feel and the smell of those pads, the crippling cramps, and the all-day fear that blood had leaked onto the scratchy polyester plaid of her Aquinas Prep skirt. She hated sitting on the side of Ian's pool at that time of the month, unable to join in. Krystal wore tampons like a real woman. She could swim any day she wanted. Faye's period was heavy and hurtful. But most of all, it was *private*. Somehow, Edward's nonchalance made everything worse. He was so grown up and so *gross*, she thought. *No.* She would not let him remove her sweats. She could not even bear the thought of Edward seeing her panties on a night like this, the plastic wings of the maxi-pad only half sticking, catching a few pubic hairs in their adhesive and rubbing against her in a consistently formed line of irritated skin. They fought about it some more.

"Stop."

"Don't worry."

"Stop."

Edward crouched down toward the end of the bed and grabbed Faye's waistband on each side by her hip bones, intending, she could tell, to pull them down and put his *mouth* down there.

"*Doctor.* Stop." She didn't mean to yell, but she just could not let it happen.

He released the cloth. It slapped back lightly against Faye's tender, pale skin. They waited, in silence.

Finally, without emotion, he spoke. "The name is Edward."

"I'm sorry."

"It's after one o'clock. Let's just go to sleep. I have church choir in the morning at seven."

As Edward stretched to blow out the candle, Faye glimpsed the outline of his erection against his briefs. She looked away quickly, settling into the pillow as the extinguished flame, smelling sharp and warm, filled the room. A minute later, Edward pressed ever so gently up against Faye's back, his legs and arms enveloping her with a tenderness that felt lovely and redeeming.

Edward could not remember the last time he had slept in bed with a woman. Certainly, it had been more than a year.

"Your body fits right into mine," he said sweetly, feeling romantic, grateful, and no longer angry.

Because I'm a kid, Faye thought sarcastically. *And you are a grown-up.* Always, this stark reality stayed with her.

She answered quietly. "I guess so."

Some time later, abrupt movement awakened Faye. Disorienting darkness followed. She had moved in her sleep and was now facing Edward. After a moment, she realized he was holding her in place. His arm was wrapped beneath her back and up around her torso. She tried to make sense of what was happening, but her mind would just not work. Something was happening, and she was in the middle of it. When she tried to sit up, Edward intensified his grip and would not let her go. She became aware, then, that he was moving his other hand, rhythmically, steadily, stroking his penis while he clutched her up against him. Faye could not take her mind away this time. There was no time to flee or to spin illusions. She stayed still. She stayed there, in the moment, feeling shamed. Oh! Such great embarrassment she felt. She did not speak. She could not cry. She did not move. A bead of sweat rolled from Edward's temple across to hers and slid down toward her mouth. She waited and wondered if there was anything more humiliating than this: if *ever* in her life there would be something more humiliating than this.

The end came with Edward's low, exhausted groan. Faye thought of a person sinking with great relief into a soft, cushy chair. Her body rolled back slightly onto the sheet when Edward relaxed the arm that held her. Immediately, Faye was out of bed and out of the bedroom. The lights were still off. Faye's reflection was barely visible in the bathroom mirror. An unfamiliar and pungent smell rushed into the back of her throat. Edward's semen had soaked into her tee shirt. She could feel the dampness against her skin. She removed her shirt, rinsed it in the sink, and put it back on while it was still wet. The fabric clung to her skin and sent a forceful chill down her body.

"Faye?"

She froze at the sound of Edward's voice.

"Come back to bed."

Faye waited. She didn't know what time it was, but the house was too dark for the sun to be up. She could not go back to Krystal's so late. She could not go home at this hour and risk waking her parents. Faye stepped outside to the back steps. She shivered in her wet shirt and dragged desperately on a cigarette. Going back inside was her only option.

Before she reached the bedroom, she could hear Edward snoring violently. Faye set herself as close as she could to the edge of the bed. Edward slept deeply enough that he did not feel her return. She lay still and watched the room come into focus. She had never noticed the crystal doorknob on Edward's closet, but she saw it now. It was out of place. It looked like something out of her grandmother's house in old Los Angeles. The morning lightened slowly while Faye watched Edward's room. What she had thought was a striped belt hanging from a hook became a necktie she recognized from her school days. It was red. A few sets of piano keys splashed across it in a zigzag pattern. On the floor against his dresser leaned a framed poster advertising the AP choir's concert in Rome. As Choir President, Faye had arranged the gift for Edward. She had found the framing company, taken the poster in, picked it up, and wrapped it in thick red paper with a glittery silver bow. The clocks in his house were not digital because they were old (*like him*). By 5:30, Faye could finally read the time on the novelty clock that sat at Edward's bedside. A porcelain orchestral conductor stood atop the actual timepiece, his hands poised for a downbeat. Faye laughed at it the first time she saw Edward's bedroom. He said it had been a gift from his first class of students. The little man looked a menacing mess of protruding limbs in the dark, but as the morning sun rose, he only looked goofy and playful. The alarm,

Edward had told her, played the famously dramatic da-da-da-DAAAA of Beethoven's *Fifth Symphony*.

It was over now. Faye had slept in Edward's bed. She had dreamed of waking up beside him, of reading the Sunday paper and wondering together which priest would say Mass and whether the homily would be instructive or boring. They had spent their first night together, but they did not go to the diner around the corner for strawberry pancakes or read the *Citrus County Sun Times* over coffee. They did not wake slowly in each other's arms, Edward's blue eyes twinkling with happiness, Faye feeling serene and finally grown up. No, that was not how it was. This is how it was. Faye left quickly and quietly. On the drive home, she sobbed so ferociously that the sound of her own wailing scared her. She screamed at the windshield and swerved dangerously as she balanced a cigarette in her left hand and pounded her right fist fiercely into her thigh. The burst of pain helped but was not strong enough. Faye clenched her hand and pumped it hard against her heart, right where her hand would rest for the pledge. Her fist's contact with the firm surface made a satisfying thump.

She pictured Doctor Vogel in his concert tuxedo, the tails starched, his posture dignified. Oh, how she adored him. He had shown her Bronzino in the Louvre, the resurrected Jesus twisting away from Mary Magdalene's grasp. They had toured castles in Germany and lit candles in a hidden alcove off St. Peter's Square. Every minute, then, she had wanted to be near him, to enjoy the terrifying thrill of falling in love with him and with the world he opened to her. Across the continent he guided the inspired and chaotic and sweaty mess of high schoolers, each performance bringing a more consuming joy than the last. Always he stood before them, his eyes piercing and serious, his expression open and inviting. As he conducted he *exhorted*. He *beckoned* them, and Faye rushed after him to the brink of that spiritual perfection. They all loved him, but none loved him more than Faye did.

It cannot be like this, she thought. *I must fix it.*

No one could know that Edward had so humiliated her. She could tell no one.

Prayer was not possible that morning. Mass moved over Faye in slow motion. On this morning, Mass at St. Cecilia grated when it should have soothed. Fr. Joe's green stole hung too unevenly and the lector spoke with forced enthusiasm. The priest's humble *Kyrie* dripped such authenticity it became disingenuous. The jubilant cadence of the *Gloria* mocked her. Faye needed to focus, and not on the disappointment and embarrassment she could feel bubbling up beneath her placid exterior. She sat between her parents, a strange reminder of her youth. Faye was the last to grow up and the child that her father was most proud of. He sat there now, beside her, in a pressed blue Oxford and a Sacred Heart tie. Congratulations on Faye's selection as Aquinas Prep valedictorian and her acceptance to Sacred Heart still poured in from fellow parishioners. Faye noticed her father's genuine serenity as she tried valiantly to avoid the images crowding her own head. He beamed throughout Mass, occasionally squeezing Faye's fingers into his warm, inviting palm. The pride emanating from her parents was almost unbearable.

Across the county, Edward donned a shiny blue robe and conducted the St. Crispina Catholic Church choir. Like Faye, he chased away the images of their night together. In such a holy space, Edward tried not to replay the feel of Faye's body against his and the explosive orgasm that had sent the room spinning in circles. Uneasiness had filled the house after Faye's departure so quickly and early that morning. Edward suspected she was put off by his persistence, but he considered her discomfort an inevitable part of the learning process. He did not want her to stop visiting him, moony-eyed, fresh, and in love as she was. He wanted her more malleable and more trusting. And so he pressed forward, certain that pushing Faye the slightest bit would unfold a world of pleasure for them both.

The ground jumped upward toward Merton, signaling an end to a cramped, balmy 12-hour flight from Munich to Los Angeles. He couldn't wait to stretch his legs and shake off the indecipherable odors he felt clinging to his hair and to the sweatshirt he had kept draped over his lap the whole long flight. He stood slowly when the captain announced their final arrival, working a kink out of his knee and brushing crumbs out of the creases in his shorts. He thought about a giant, messy cheeseburger. He loved traveling but missed the greasy familiarity of American fast food. He thought also of Tiffany's bright fair skin and perfect red lips, his own Snow White waiting patiently for his return.

Meeting Faye for coffee was last on Merton's list of official homecoming activities. After a grasping and groping *Welcome Home* session in the backseat of Tiffany's car, the couple disengaged for the night, and Merton drove toward Faye with great anticipation. He found her sitting prettily at a wrought iron table in front of the mega-bookstore that doubled as a hip new coffee shop, its singing siren logo only then in 1998 starting its rise to the top tier of cultural import. She was smoking (Faye was always smoking) and seemed to be reading. As he watched her turn a page, he noticed a sense of boredom or preoccupation in her movement. Faye appeared to be reading a novel, but Merton knew she in fact examined her own story. She hurtled a plume of gray smoke obliquely to her left as she furrowed her brow. Faye's smaller intricacies never escaped Merton's observation.

"The King returns!" Merton called.

Faye lifted her hands and let the novel snap close of its own momentum. She spoke with fervor, though not with joy.

"Yes, my King has come back."

Their embrace was deep, a long, wordless hug.

By closing time, the conversation had turned from Merton's travels to the happenings in his absence. They cradled coffees and smoked cigarettes as the darkened sky succumbed to a full blackout and a low hanging fog rolled in.

The bookstore latched its doors and baristas shooed Merton and Faye from their table, but the night had not yet ended. Banished from the coffee shop patio, the two leaned against their cars in the deserted lot. Faye talked around her secret.

"I have something to tell you," she began.

"Do I want to know?"

Faye did not look down, as she often did when talking with Edward. Her eyes aligned directly with Merton's.

"No. You do not want to know. But you have to know. I need you to know this."

Merton stopped leaning back against his car. He stood straight, bearing his weight on both legs and preparing to receive Faye's revelation. He knew only that Doctor Vogel must be involved. Faye always came to Merton with her concerns about Doctor. It had been a consolation of sorts, all these months, that while Faye did not return Merton's affections, neither did she chase or indulge any of Merton's classmates. Doctor transfixed her, his existence a pull that drew her ever closer to him and away from a sense of her own well-being.

He hurt her, Merton thought immediately. *He turned her away.*

"What did he do?"

Faye's hesitation surprised her. She wanted Merton to know how much Edward loved her, to show Merton how special she was. She was so special, Edward could not let her go. Edward needed her. Edward was happy now, and everyone had Faye to thank. None of that sounded right, though, in the abandoned lot, the fog creeping in, Merton sizing her up with anticipatory pity. The truth seemed too sordid, too embarrassing, and too shameful.

"Doctor and I have been—" she stopped. "He and I have been hanging out. Together. At his house."

Merton's eyes widened. He repeated Faye's words.

"You've been hanging out," he said, "at his house."

"It started right after you left for Europe. Everything escalated so fast."

Faye paused and chewed her lip a moment.

"I spent the night there—I mean, I slept over at his house—on Saturday."

Merton maintained his calm exterior as waves of emotion toppled each other in his breast. Confusion, envy, and anger chased each other, each one drowning out the other momentarily before another overtook the first. He had been prepared to console Faye. He was not prepared to counsel her through this absolutely preposterous affair. Like the other kids, he had thought it would never actually come to this.

"What do you expect me to say?"

Faye looked down and crossed her ankles. She lit a new cigarette silently. They stood, unmoving.

"I need advice. I don't know what I want to do about this."

Merton chose his words carefully.

"You don't need me to tell you this is a bad idea. You *know* it can't end well. You're asking because you want me to tell you it's okay. But is it? Is it okay, Faye? Only you know that."

Anger was winning. Merton had begun raising his voice. Enjoying Faye's school yard flirtation was one thing. Taking advantage of Faye this way was quite another. Doctor knew Faye was younger than she seemed. She was impressionable, *virginal* in so many ways. Doctor knew Faye would do anything to make him happy.

Merton lowered his tone and reached toward Faye as if to lift her chin.

"Is it okay?" he asked again.

Faye shook her head slightly and crossed her arms more fiercely than before against the cold night air. Tears traced paths on her cheeks and gathered around the curve of her nose.

"It was okay at first. Sometimes it's okay still. It's confusing."

"I don't understand," Merton said flatly. "What are you guys doing? What's going on over there?"

"I'm not very experienced. It's more difficult than I expected. I didn't think I would feel this way."

Merton could tell that Faye was hiding details. The romantic in Faye would not say what needed to be said. Merton needed to know what the hell was going on.

Softening, Merton questioned her.

"What way is that? How do you feel?"

"Scared," she said quietly. "I didn't think I would be so scared."

The word triggered Merton's concern. He stepped toward Faye.

"You should not feel scared, Faye. Is he making you do things you don't want to do? Scared is not part of sex."

"Isn't it, though?" she said defensively. "This isn't like you and Tiff." Faye let go a frustrated sigh and out with it a thick stream of smoke.

"He's a *grown-up*, Merton. He's not like us. I can't ask him to just *cuddle* with me."

"Like hell you can't," Merton shouted forcefully.

Merton tried to suppress the rage that was building. Anger roiled in him at Doctor for manipulating Faye and at Faye for getting into this in the first place.

"That's what relationships are. You tell him exactly what you want, and he does not make you do anything else. That's common sense, and it's relationship 101. Why do you think Tiff and I aren't having sex? It's not because I don't want to. *She* doesn't want to. So I don't ask her to. That's how relationships are supposed to work. Plain and simple."

"You know it's not simple. I can't stop going there. It's *him*, Merton."

Faye paused, searching Merton's eyes for understanding. Merton wasn't like her other friends. That he trusted Doctor wasn't the point. Merton wanted for Doctor the way that Faye did. Chambers had given them everything. Somehow, without their asking, Doctor had fixed what felt wrong in all of them. They wanted *for* him, so that Doctor would feel whole.

"I can't stop going there," Faye said again. "It's *him*."

Three days had passed since the sleepover at Edward's house—three days of wishing she hadn't cried like that and three days of wondering if Edward was tired of her yet. She wondered if it was true that a girl's period stopped flowing when a man touched her down there, but she was too embarrassed to ask Krystal and hated even remembering that Edward had said that. For three days, Faye had played the night over in her mind. She and Edward had never fought before this summer. Since their first kiss, they had begun to fight quite a lot. Not to fight, exactly, but to quarrel. The bedroom was a quarrelsome place. He had grown disappointed in her, and it felt awful. Edward had never used that tired tone with her at school. He had used it for the kids who talked when he was talking and who forgot to spit out their gum before rehearsal. Faye had been a paragon of good behavior. Now, Edward seemed less to admire Faye for doing everything just right and more annoyed that she couldn't do what he wanted. Each day she planned to do things better next time so that he would believe she was grown up enough to do what he needed.

The summer heat was just starting to break as Faye grabbed her bag and ducked out of Krystal's house, her friends calling to her from the backyard pool.

"Stay here!" Ian yelled.

"I told my sister I'd be home early to hang out," she called, looking back at Krystal with a knowing eyebrow raise. "You will cover me, right?" Faye asked.

Krystal nearly sang her taunt in mock anger. "Fine! Leave me for a hairy old man even though I only have four more weeks before we're moving thousands of miles away from each other."

Krystal had a way of making everything seem fun and frivolous, even the reality that Faye was now messing around with her teacher. Krystal treated the whole thing like a prank. Faye wanted to be like Krystal, to talk about hard-ons and blow jobs like they were no big deal, but she just wouldn't have known where to start. In Edward's bedroom, things never went as planned. It was like there were two of her in that house. When Edward's hand brushed against hers, Faye felt her insides collapse on each other, an ache both thrilling and almost painful pulling straight down between her legs. She wanted Edward to soothe it. Yet, when he pressed his body against hers, a paralyzing fear rose into Faye's throat. Thinking of the real Edward's nakedness, of the possibility that he would force his real body with its guttural groans and its heavy warmth onto her mouth, was so terrifying it was too much to even consider. So she promised herself it wouldn't come to that. Of course Edward would never ask that of her, certainly not after the frenzy she had caused the night of the sleepover.

"You have Ian here anyway," Faye said. "Go do whatever it is you do when I'm not around. And remember—if my parents call, tell them I'm already on my way home. And then call me at Doctor's."

Faye pulled the car door closed with a loud thud and drove swiftly from Krystal's across three freeways into Edward's side of the county and down his street. Somewhere between Krystal's and Edward's, the sun finally finished its late summer sunset. Lamplight glowed around the shutters across the front window of Edward's house. Faye took a final puff and stomped out her cigarette as she walked the familiar path to the back steps. The automatic porch light clicked on as she reached for the screen that covered the open back door. Faye pulled the handle ever so slightly, shifting the screen door open toward her and peeking her head into the house.

"Hello?" she heard Edward call.

"It's me," Faye answered hesitantly.

Inside, she tried to act casually. She followed Edward's voice through the narrow passageway from the back door to the front room, finding Edward at the kitchen table in the slightly larger dining space that opened up off the galley kitchen. There was room enough only for a round table and two chairs. Because Edward was alone, the two chairs had often felt one too many. But now, Faye was here. Edward looked up with anticipation and pleasant surprise, his hands lightly brushing away greasy crumbs from a pair of microwaved taquitos.

"I'm just finishing a quick dinner. I lost track of time working on next year's Pageant script."

Faye crossed her hands at her waist and took a deep breath, unsure what to do next. Edward half stood, and Faye awkwardly leaned toward him, his lips almost brushing her cheek but instead landing on her ear as she tucked some curls behind it. The television blared in the background. Tom Brokaw was announcing the nightly news. Faye only then realized she had never seen the television playing. He noticed her noticing it.

"I just keep it on for company." Edward reached back with the remote to mute the reedy voice of a woman reporting on currency issues in the European Union.

Edward leaned back in his chair and looked at Faye. Each time she arrived he told himself to slow down so he wouldn't frighten her away. The sweet smell of raspberries wafted toward him as she sat. Already he began to feel a wave of energy pulsing through his thighs. He pushed the last of his makeshift dinner away to clear the space between them. He wondered why she kept coming back, especially after their last night together.

Faye, also, was taking stock of the situation, trying to figure out if they were okay or if they were still fighting. Three days ago, Edward had been so imposing, his annoyance with her causing a palpable anxiety. She had left his house in hysterics. Now, he seemed humbled, his microwaved meal an especially ill fit for a man who presented such curated elitism. She was beginning to sense that Edward lived a sort of suspended teen-aged existence because he had no one but himself to care for, no one with whom to share all this grown-up independence. Seeing the soggy, artificially steamed taquitos on his paper plate felt like a humiliating intrusion of his privacy. A tiny smudge of sour cream clung to the corner of Edward's mouth. This was Edward under the tuxedo-clad conductor that all the kids and their parents adored. He was a man who ate microwaved dinners at 9:00 on a Saturday night and sat with his back to the television in an otherwise quiet, lonely house. Something about the thought made Faye want to weep and made her love Edward so much she could hardly stand it.

Her unannounced visit had caught him off guard, and he looked, to Faye, unbearably casual in gray sweat shorts and a tee shirt that had been washed too many times. Before summer, when she had daydreamed a relationship with Edward, she had pictured dull moments like these and been thrilled by the thought of seeing Edward *unbuttoned*, as it were, out of his teacher's uniform of black slacks, dress shirt, and tie. But now, in real time, the sight unnerved her and she felt uncomfortable. Seeing the fleshy parts of Edward's body, the parts that had always been covered at school, made Faye feel that she was out of place or discovering a secret she shouldn't have unearthed. *Of course that's absurd*, Faye thought. Everyone wears shorts around the house in summer, even if they think their legs are too fat or untanned or don't like how much hair they have on their thighs. Of course he would do that like other people did.

"I'm glad you're here." Edward reached across the table and ran the back of his hand along her arm. "I didn't expect you tonight." Edward paused. "For various reasons."

Faye felt better immediately. It was good that Edward wanted her there.

"I missed you a lot," Faye said sheepishly. She felt embarrassed saying sappy things like *I miss you* and *I don't want to leave you*, but she couldn't stop herself. He must have missed her, too. He had touched her and kissed her and done all those grown-up things to her. Certainly he loved her. A man wouldn't do those things to just any girl. If he didn't need her as much as she needed him, he wouldn't have risked getting caught.

"Well, I always like to see you. But at least I got quite a lot of work done without you distracting me," he quipped with a smirk. "I think this Pageant should be my big swan song. It's going to be really huge. A lot of new stuff like a side theater, a play within a play. There will be a lot happening."

"That sounds really cool. Have you decided who will be King and Queen yet?"

"I think so," Edward replied. "It's going to be a big surprise. But I can't tell you."

"Why not?"

"Because you're still one of them," he answered with a chuckle. "I don't believe my secrets are safe with you."

Faye swallowed her guilt and tried to look placid.

"Where are you coming from tonight?" Edward asked.

"From Krystal's. Ian and James were swimming. Everyone's just hanging around eating burgers."

"You didn't tell them you were coming here, did you?"

"I had to tell Krystal. She's my alibi."

Edward gave Faye his standard look of annoyance, one hand on his hip, his head slightly tilted with irritation.

"I can't just go wherever I want without my parents knowing. I have to trust somebody."

"Well, I don't think you should trust them. You'll see after you all move away from each other. Those guys are not good enough for you and they probably wouldn't protect you if it came down to it."

"They don't know what's happening," Faye said quietly. "They think we're just hanging out."

"Apparently we are just hanging out," Edward said with annoyance. "You don't seem like you really want to do much more."

Faye frowned and an agitated warmth spread through her. In school she had been allured by his inappropriate innuendo, but now she tired of it and felt he was being unfair.

"I'm sorry," she mumbled under her breath. "I just get nervous. I'm new at this."

Faye paused, then turned on her heels.

"I'm going out for a smoke."

She grabbed her lunchbox from the front seat of her car and sat on Edward's curb, knowing what likely awaited her when she returned.

At his desk, Edward sipped some whiskey and scanned the house. He found and lit a cigar, puffing methodically. The alcohol loosened the day's tension and pulled a tingling sensation through his chest down to his feet. He felt his body stirring in anticipation. Tonight he would coax her further.

Edward moved them swiftly to the bedroom. He led her by the hand into the still-dark room and lifted her easily onto the bed. After just a few weeks together, their kissing had become routine but discordant. Faye held Edward's cheek tenderly with her right hand as she kissed him, keeping his face close to hers, opening her mouth the slightest bit, and shyly letting her tongue touch his lips as they closed around it. Edward's kissing was explosive. He grabbed and sucked and breathed his hot breath down her throat. Their disconnect reminded him of a time years before when the most gifted but uncooperative student in his choir had been singing too fast throughout a performance, persisting even as Edward glared at him and forcefully pushed his time-keeping hand directly toward the kid. "Why were you singing ahead of the beat?" Edward had asked him later. "I was trying to speed you up," the boy had answered.

Edward could feel Faye trying to slow him down, but he wanted so badly to engulf her and to feel all the parts of her against him. After Edward peeled away Faye's clothes and began putting his fingers inside her, she stopped kissing him and looked straight up at the light on his ceiling. Once her eyes adjusted to the dark, she could just make out the pentagon shape covering the light bulb. She kept her eyes there and went away in her mind, thinking of the thunderstorm in Freiburg, of how intensely she had loved him that night and of how wonderful it felt to know that he desired her this way. She heard herself release a soft cry when his palm pushed against her special spot, and she didn't know whether she wanted to roll away or open herself to him.

"My God Faye, you're so ready aren't you?" he said.

Faye didn't answer. *Ready for what?* she wondered. She wanted him to keep touching her, but she wanted more for it to be over so she could remember that he had done it.

In a sweeping, almost imperceptible motion, Edward pulled his shorts slightly down and untucked his penis from his briefs. Already he was moving her hand toward it. Faye felt her teeth clenching and she pushed her legs more tightly together to force his hand out. She pulled her hand back, but he was so strong that her arm hardly moved. Edward was holding her. She wanted him to hold her. But she wasn't ready to see that part, the part of him she kept telling herself could stay hidden. Faye did not yet know how quickly a man could take out his penis when he was ready to use it, when he decided it needed to be satisfied.

"Please, Faye," he said. "Just touch me here."

Edward wrapped her hand around him. The shift in Faye's mien was familiar by now. She was shutting down. He was losing her.

"It's okay," he whispered. "I'll show you what to do."

Edward curled his fist around Faye's hand.

"Just do it like this," he said, pulling her hand in an up and down motion, squeezing the top of his penis each time.

Faye tried to do as he said. She watched her own exposed navel and moved her hand loosely so that she was hardly touching his body. She pictured herself floating above and looking down on them, saw Edward facing her on his side, his hips turned out just enough for her to touch him without crushing her hand between them. Edward's worn shirt clung to him more tightly now, damp with a thin layer of perspiration, his briefs and shorts still pushed down, his penis jutting out from them awkwardly. Faye thought about her parents and family and about all the choir kids at Aquinas Prep who would never believe she had done this. It was impossible to believe that she was here, that she was touching a penis—*his* penis, *Doctor's* penis. Edward breathed slowly through his nose, savoring her touch. Faye kept touching, but she began to shake. At first a small tremor like a chill passed over her, but then she started trembling and tears stung the back of her eyes.

She tried to speak. At first only a squeak came out.

"Am I doing it right?" she asked. "Can you hold me?"

Edward cupped her face in his hands and kissed her, gently at first and then with more urgency. "Do it tighter," he said.

Faye tried to look into his eyes, to remember how bright they could be when he was proud or excited. He kept them closed, though, and she felt the distance between them growing.

"I can't," she whispered, a tear sliding down her cheek.

"I want you to do this for me," Edward said. "Put your mouth on me."

Panic lurched through Faye's body and up into her throat.

"I can't do that," she said more forcefully. "I'm not—I can't—I never—"

They had been at this impasse before.

"Okay. Fine," he said. "Just keep touching me. Do it like this."

Edward wrapped his hand around Faye's and squeezed her hand tightly over him. He buried his face in her neck and pulled her leg over the top of their hands and his body.

"Just like that," he said, his breath getting shorter and his grip tighter.

Edward stopped just short of finishing, and Faye thought it was over. He let her hand go and squeezed the underside of his cock toward the base, a trick he had long ago learned could stave off his orgasm so he could start building the momentum again. Faye leaned on her elbow and breathed out a long sigh. She needed a cigarette but knew she wasn't supposed to leave. She could see that Edward was slowing his breathing, almost counting his breaths. When the urge returned, Edward pulled Faye to him and pushed his body forcefully against her thigh. Hot tears bubbled in Faye's throat as the semen smeared across her skin.

Faye showered quickly in a daze. Edward was still lingering in the back doorway in his tee shirt and briefs when she pulled away from the house. The oncoming headlights blurred together through Faye's tears. She tried to smoke without dropping ash along the inside of her car door, but the no-traffic airflow was strong and she couldn't close the window. She needed to air that unwashable smell of semen and cigar off her. How did she keep ending up here? She had told Edward about her fantasies, admitted she had fantasized senior year about his soft lips and strong hands. She had asked for this, but she hadn't known it would feel so terrible.

At home in her bathroom, Faye stared blankly at the mirror. She looked plain because she did not know how to wear makeup like Krystal did and looked stupid because she was puffy-eyed from crying like a little kid would.

"Faye, are you home?" Faye's mom asked, rapping on the door.

Faye stuck her head out and smiled weakly.

"Yes, I'm home for the night," she said.

"Okay good. Good night, sweetie pie." Her mom hesitated and turned her head back to Faye. "Is everything okay?" she asked. "Why is your hair wet?"

"Oh," Faye said nonchalantly, stroking her wet ponytail. "We swam at Krystal's." She invented more detail for good measure: "I have chlorine eyes, too."

"I don't understand why you are crying," Edward said harshly.

He was incredulous. Irritation and confusion billowed through Edward's body, his initial surge of sympathy supplanted now by anger and frustration. Sobs ushered forth from Faye like Edward had never heard.

"I said you don't have to do it, so what's the big deal? Just let it go, Faye. Seriously," he said for emphasis. "I'm not mad. *Let. It. Go.*"

They were fighting, again, about Faye's refusal to reciprocate during sex. Faye's volume decreased momentarily to a whimper and then riled up again, her whole body tense as she clenched her fists and curled her knees to her chest. Sex was gross. Faye recoiled instinctively each time the thick, sticky semen landed without invitation on her skin. But that wasn't the worst of it. She feared losing Doctor Vogel.

I'm starting to doubt your sincerity. That's what Edward had said.

How could she make him see? What was it to love a person as they were, with faults and wounds and fleshy mortality, if your love was measured in orgasms? Edward was teaching Faye a love she was too young to understand.

Curfew loomed. Tears kept falling. Faye's chest heaved up and down as she pulled her blouse back on. Edward sat on the edge of the bed and tried to strike a conciliatory tone. She seemed not to see him, to resist his condolences instead of softening toward him. Edward's anger intensified in the face of her persistent crying. The satisfaction he derived from Faye's visits was becoming less worthy of the difficulty this relationship entailed. This tantrum was completely uncalled for, and Edward just had no earthly idea how to stop it.

Not again until he was a father would he feel this mixed sense of powerlessness and frustration in the face of emotional chaos. He would watch in astonishment, later, as Amy, his seven-year-old daughter, writhed on the floor of her perfect purple bedroom, pounding tiny balled fists into the floor and gushing wet tears despite the privilege that abounded all around her. In those later years, as now, he would watch perplexed from the outside, feeling only that something was wrong and that he lacked both the ability and the desire to fix it. He would remember Faye, then, haunted by the sublime agitation he had seen in her teary eyes.

Something about the wood floors and the broad windows stopped Edward's house from feeling claustrophobic to Faye, but indeed most surfaces in the front room, piano room, and mud room were generally stacked with papers, portfolios, cassette tapes, writing implements, sheet music, junk mail, and decorative trinkets (which Faye presumed had all been gifts). Faye got the feeling the chaos went unnoticed by Edward because he was always working.

Or maybe there was a method to the madness, as they say. In any case, that nothing was carefully placed made Faye feel much more at ease in Edward's house than she otherwise would have. She sat where she wanted (often on the floor as she had done in his choir room office at Aquinas Prep), she set her drink where she wanted (except on the piano), and, because each room was a veritable treasure trove of AP's past performances and Edward's musical interests, she could always occupy herself while he worked.

"Are you bored? I have to finish up these Bach packets for Chamber Prep Week." Edward put a hand on his hip for a momentary break and raked his fingers through his hair. "And by finish I mean I have to finish them *tonight*." He dragged the syllables out for emphasis. "They must be at the printer by tomorrow morning."

Faye smiled as she spoke. "I am not bored."

Faye loved watching Edward work. She liked sitting by his side as he flipped through catalogs of sheet music. She especially liked working in separate rooms, he sitting at the kitchen table and she writing poetry at the computer that was perched awkwardly on a small desk between the piano room and the more wide open front space. In those moments, Faye allowed herself to sink into the illusion that they really were sharing a life.

The summer heat drew Faye outside. She smoked a cigarette languidly on Edward's back stoop, closing her eyes and rolling her neck from side to side as the *Pie Jesu* of Rutter's *Requiem* floated out from the living room. The *Sanctus* would follow, bringing with it the remembrance of their first night together, the abstract triumph and the thick, hard tears. Here they came again, tears prying at the edges of her eyes. She shook them off and returned to the piano room.

Faye noticed a crate of albums wedged between the piano and the wall. "Can I look through this stuff?"

Edward nodded briefly in her direction. "Sure. You can't play them, though. My old turntable is buried in a closet somewhere."

Faye gingerly moved each album forward with her index finger, recording this knowledge of Edward's past. She recognized some bands (though not their album titles) but had never heard of many of them.

"Those are my brother's albums," Edward said without looking up from the papers he was arranging. "He lived with me for a little while back in Michigan, and somehow I ended up with a few of his boxes. One of these days, I'll get around to returning them. That's why I keep them out. Doesn't seem to help, though. They just sit in the corner collecting dust."

So it was a glimpse of Glen's life Faye had been gathering. It hardly mattered. Everything attached to Edward she wanted for herself.

Suddenly, there it was, in the middle of the closely pressed albums: a black and white portrait of Edward, aged about twenty-five. The portrait stunned her. The image staring back was, actually, stunning. He looked squarely at the camera and did not smile. Instead of their usual blue, his eyes were gray but still penetrating. Though he did not smile, he did not frown, either. She wanted, as she always did, to touch the divot of smooth skin just beneath his lips. His chest, muscular but lean, was bare. Curly dark hairs stood out against the contrasting paleness of his skin. On closer inspection, Faye noticed the slightest thread of a mustache across the handsome young Edward's upper lip, and she laughed. The intensity of the image somehow lifted, and Faye pulled it out of the stack with a casual flair.

"How old are you in this photo?"

Edward glanced her way absent-mindedly at first. Upon seeing the cardboard backing, remembering the hidden artifact, he chuckled and walked slowly to where Faye sat.

"I don't know. Probably early twenties. Jane shot that for a photography class she was taking at Wichita State."

"It's beautiful," Faye said quietly.

Edward took the photo from her hands and examined it.

"What happened with you and Jane? Why didn't you marry her?"

Faye suspected that their broken engagement was the cornerstone of his sorrow, of his inability to find true happiness despite the professional and personal adulation showered on him at Aquinas Prep.

"Jane and I had a rough relationship," he began carefully. "We were long distance for most of it. The sheer logistics of being apart, especially back then when travel and communication were more difficult, and the mental exertion of graduate school on top of all that were just too much. It was exhausting all the time. We would miss each other and be too busy to stay connected and then spend all our time in bed on the rare occasions we did get to see each other. There was never much time to take stock of the changes that we were both going through. And then, she decided to apply to medical school in Southern California, so decisions had to be made."

"And you decided to get married?"

"Yes. That was the plan."

Faye's mind unspooled images of a young Edward packing his bags during a Michigan winter, striking out across the plains to California to woo the woman he loved, certain she would return his affection.

"How did you propose?"

Edward sort of tousled his own hair, a nervous, adorable habit. "I knew the owner of this lounge we used to go to in Ann Arbor, kind of an old-fashioned tavern. And so, I set up with him that I wanted to propose, and he planted the ring under her chair that night at the bar."

Edward wandered toward the guest room as he talked, calling over his shoulder as the scene unfolded in Faye's imagination.

"A massive snowstorm came through that night, kind of unexpectedly. We still made it to Lou's, but because of the weather, the lounge was nearly empty. Jane had wanted to hear this local jazz band that we had seen often when she was in town. They were there, and because the crowd was so thin, it felt like they were playing just for us."

From the closed off second bedroom, Edward brought out a photo album, worn and cracked, the plastic film covers only barely clinging to the sticky pages. Inside, Faye saw fading Polaroids of the same Edward she had glimpsed in the portrait—trim, confident, sexy. She recognized her Edward, Doctor Vogel, in the shots, but this Edward was more at ease, more humble. Even in Europe or at the end of a triumphant performance, Faye rarely saw Edward look as vulnerable or as happy as he did in these pictures. The woman pictured with him had feathered brown hair, a modest yellow dress, and a shy smile. Faye liked her instantly.

"I ordered us each a glass of champagne for a toast, I told her I was ready to move to California, to follow her anywhere I could be with her, and so, I grabbed the ring and placed it in front of her."

The ring box was in front of Faye, now. Edward held it before her and opened it slowly. The diamond still gleamed, pear-shaped and crystalline. Two dark blue sapphires cradled it, all wrapped in a shiny gold band.

"And then I said, *Love of my life, will you marry me?*"

A strangeness and sadness permeated the room. Faye sat facing Edward, his arm awkwardly outstretched in the midst of a memory. Edward was far away, his brow heavy with regret. She caressed his hand and softened her gaze. For a moment, Faye saw Edward as he was rather than as the man he meant himself to be. He was indulging a long-lost grievance, nursing heartbreak, prodding a wound so old only he could find it hidden in the depth of his skin. She loved this Edward, and, Lord, she was afraid of him. This intimate outpouring shamed her with its grave intensity. Gently, Faye took the boxed ring from Edward's hand and set it beside her on the piano bench. She curled his fingers around hers and brought them to her lips, kissing each one slowly, licking away the wounded pride, the lost future.

Edward sighed deeply. "That was a long time ago."

A long time ago, Faye thought. But here, in this cluttered house, the ring was not lost nor hidden. Out it had come at a moment's thought and, roaring with it, the past.

Edward kissed Faye softly. "Your card came in the mail today," he said. "Thank you."

Faye felt Edward returning across the expanse of space and time to the Fulton orbit and the life he and Faye were pretending to live.

"Cards are my thing," Faye said cheerily. "I love getting them and giving them. Cards make everyone feel good. And with you," she said hesitantly, "it's much easier to write my feelings than to say them."

"Yes, I noticed you're still not saying my name."

"But I'm writing it," Faye said proudly. "That's progress."

Edward chuckled, prepared to let this oft-rehashed argument go in exchange for Faye's coy smile and her soft touch upon his arm.

"My mother would like you," he said after a moment. "She's always harping on me to write to her. You're much better at that kind of thing than I am."

Faye smiled but did not respond.

"She's desperate for me to get married and have a child."

It was Faye's turn now to leave the woodenness of the wooden floors and the sweet smokiness of Edward's cigar-scented home, to drift away from the realness of the space between them. That she would write cards to Doctor Vogel's mother seemed a preposterous fantasy.

"My grandmother's name was Natalie," Edward continued. "I've always thought the name delicate and elegant. What do you think? Do you like the name Natalie?"

"For a daughter?" she asked.

"For *our* daughter," Edward said, a warm sensation of embarrassment and desire spreading across his cheeks. Faye was prone to romantic musings and theatrics. At forty-one, Edward deserved a few delusions of his own.

Faye swallowed shallowly, almost choking on the scratchy dryness of her throat. She imagined bearing Edward's child as she would the two of them walking on Mars, an absolute physical impossibility. She had known one Natalie at Aquinas Prep, a plain-looking bookworm afraid of her own shadow, and one Natalia in grade school, a stuck-up rich girl from Seacliff whose mother, a Russian immigrant, complained incessantly about insufficient discipline in American schools.

"I like Natalie," she said softly. "It's pretty."

Edward gathered the album and the ring in his arms, preparing to put them away.

"The card surprised me when it arrived. It reminded me of what I first—*noticed* about you." Edward almost said *loved*, but he pulled back. "When you were in school, it amazed me that you had so much time to do all these little things for other people when you were so busy with swim and your grades and working."

Edward looked at Faye tenderly, and she felt again that they were back where they had started before all the sex and the fighting. Sometimes, he did see her, and being seen by him felt better than anything else.

Toilet papering Edward's house was not Faye's idea, but she went along with it. The favored escapade of middle- and high-schoolers alike, toilet papering a person's house had always involved a mix of admiration and stick-it-to-you. This time was no different. Krystal, Ian, and James were obsessed with Faye's obsession. They hated and blamed Doctor for what he was doing to Faye. Three mischievous teens sat watch this night, waiting for Edward's kitchen to darken and for him to disappear with their friend from the front room that faced the street to his bedroom at the back of the house. The actual toilet papering of Edward's house was a bore. There were no large trees, gates, or other appendages in the front yard on which to drape the annoying décor. They scattered the white squares across the lawn and around some shrubs and rose bushes, moving quietly and trying to look inconspicuous though it was far too early in the night to not be seen. Giving Doctor a mess to clean up wasn't the point. *The thrill of it*, Ian thought. The thrill of asserting themselves any way they could.

Since Doctor had slighted Ian at the beginning of his senior year, had given *his* Renaissance Pageant lead to Merton (that ass-kisser), Ian had been nursing a slowly burning rage. It culminated now with Doctor's abuse of Faye. *Yes, he was abusing her*, Ian thought, *even though Faye wanted it*. He abused them all by expecting them to stay silent because he was a grown up and a teacher. Ian still had not figured out how he would punish Doctor for this, but he knew, in the end, he would not let Doctor get away with whatever he was doing to Faye. Ian and James wanted Doctor to know he was being watched. Telling the right people would be too hard. Faye would hate them. Sending smoke signals was all they could think to do—look at this man's house! There's something wrong inside! Faye thought Edward would laugh it off. She knew her friends' smug sense of pride in what they had done would buy her more weeks without anyone telling.

Inside the house, Edward escorted Faye to his bedroom and laid her on top of the blankets. Faye knew what was coming as he slinked backward toward the edge of the bed.

"I don't want you to do that. I don't want you going away from me," she said. "I like you to stay close to me."

She wanted to look into his eyes so she could remember him the way he had been at Aquinas Prep, to keep her face and his close.

Whatever position Edward chose, Faye felt uncomfortable. The weight of Edward's body felt too heavy when he lay fully on top of her; when he rolled to the side, she feared he would ask her to touch him down there or would begin touching himself, ending in the deep groan and the sickening smell of semen wafting up toward her. Every time he took off his clothes, she resisted his pleading to put her mouth on his penis. Faye willed the fear away, but it did not budge. Edward's hope remained high. A little experience would go a long way, he assured her. Soon, she would get used to the feel and the smell of a man, and their desires would align. Two things surprised Edward every time he tried to make love to her: Faye's body gushed and opened to him more readily than any woman he had ever touched. Also, Faye was petrified.

The toilet papering infuriated Edward. Pieces were tacked along the rose bushes that lined his driveway. As they walked toward her car, Faye plucked a couple white squares from the tangled thorns.

"It isn't a big deal," she said. "They're just messing with you."

Edward bent with annoyance at the end of the drive, gathering his arms full and refusing to look at Faye.

She hurried to him and wrapped her arms around his waist from behind. "Relax," she said.

Edward pulled away so violently that Faye nearly toppled back into the flower bed.

"What are you *doing?*" he hissed. "Somebody could *see* us."

Just then, they saw the message, spelled out in shaving cream on the lawn.

Edward clenched his teeth.

"Get out of here."

A heady nausea passed over Faye. She took one step toward him.

"Go home."

She would not forget the look on his face, both desperate and stern.

"Now."

Faye looked back at the lawn as she stepped into the car. Ian's shaving cream message was clumsy but unmistakable.

She's 17.

A busy signal buzzed all day, the up and down cadence drumming like an ambulance siren in Faye's ear. Edward was browsing the internet or had taken the phone off the hook. Whatever the reason, Faye wasn't getting through. She called every fifteen minutes until the line opened. By late afternoon, she had left ten or twelve messages—she had lost count after the first few, her mind dizzy with anxiety, her stomach knotted with the thought that Edward would not see her again.

The line rang and the machine blasted his voice again.

You've reached 992-6882. Thanks for calling. Please leave a message.

"It's me again. Please pick up—"

"What do you *want*, Faye?" Edward sounded exhausted and annoyed. She answered with silence. "Really, what do you want me to say to you?"

"I just want to talk."

"I'm busy. I have things to take care of around the house. I have work to do. I don't have an hour every day to sit on the phone with you. I think you've gotten the wrong idea about us."

Quiet anger bounced back and forth between them. It was Faye's turn now. Edward had always had time for Faye, and she had made time for him. She had stayed after rehearsal to keep him company, had listened to his woes, and had been the only one to care about his feelings. She had listened to his pleadings all summer and had done so many of those sex things she did not want to do.

"That's strange," she said sarcastically. "You don't have time to *talk* to me, but you seem to have an hour every day for sex with me."

Courage grew in Faye as her fury increased. She had loved him so much, so openly, so joyfully. His belittling of her feelings was insulting.

"Obviously you don't give a damn about me," she continued. "I'm sure you could find an hour every day for me to suck your dick."

The words poured out of her like an exorcism. Saying them felt awful. She wished she could take them back, but it was too late.

Edward sounded incredulous. "Is that what you think? Because I don't want to lose my job, because I don't want to go to *jail*, I must not really care about you? This isn't a God-damned kid's game, Faye. This is my whole *life*. If you'd rather play these games with your friends, then go ahead."

A loud sob rushed forth from Faye.

"Leave me out of it," Edward said dismissively. "In fact, just go away and leave me alone."

Faye held the phone, the line still open, and cried painful, retching moans. She screamed into her pillow so that her grandma would not hear, soaking the blue gingham fabric until it appeared thin and translucent. A headache began behind her eyes and spread all over to the base of her neck. She wept and then stared, unmoving, at the phone in her hand. She was too furious to call Ian. Her very small world began to lose shape and close in on itself. Gone was the open expanse of summer, the thrill of Edward's affection, and the belief that she had finally found love. Edward was angry at Faye and Faye was angry at her friends—what was left? *Really*, she thought, *where can I go now?*

Talking to Krystal helped a little.

"I told Ian not to do the shaving cream," Krystal said flippantly with a pop of her chewing gum. "Doc will get over it. They always do. Promise me you will forget him for the night. It's date night, remember?"

Faye had forgotten.

"I've been crying for three hours," Faye said weakly. "I can't possibly go anywhere tonight. Tell Billy I'm sorry. I just can't."

"I will not tell him that. You'll feel better after a shower. This is exactly what you need. You need to forget about that fucking fat old man and have a normal relationship. Billy is perfect for you. He's smart, and he's Catholic, and he's a virgin, like you. And he's not fucking forty years old or your teacher. Right?"

Krystal had a way of talking to Faye that was so irreverent it was endearing. Krystal kept Faye's secrets and lied to cover her tracks and gave Faye blow job tips just in case. That Krystal didn't like Edward meant that Krystal obviously loved Faye.

"Alright K," she said. "But I'm doing it because you want me to, not because I want to start dating someone else."

"Well, it's not that serious anyway. He knows you're going away to Sacred Heart in a few weeks and he'll be back in Minnesota by then. It's summer, and it's fun, and you need it. Get ready. Ian and I will meet you guys at the club."

"Don't tell Ian about me and Doc," Faye said urgently.

"I never do," Krystal lied.

Billy arrived at 7:00 to pick Faye up for their double date. His real name was William Beardsley IV, but everyone called him Billy, and he was Krystal's neighbor in the exclusive Vista View Estates. Billy was a freshman home for the summer from St. John's, an elite Catholic university in Minnesota. When Billy rang Faye's doorbell, her headache still raged like an explosion inside her skull. They were headed to the Vista View Golf and Tennis Club, a swanky venue where only club kids like Krystal and Billy felt comfortable. Faye wore more eyeliner and face powder than usual to offset her tired tearfulness. Krystal was right. Billy was dapper and sweet and obviously interested in Faye. He talked a lot but not too much, asking questions about Sacred Heart and telling all about his freshman year at St. John's. Unlike Faye and her friends, Billy had attended public high school. The transition to St. John's had not been smooth. A men's college, St. John's proffered elite education with strict rules about Mass attendance, gender relations, and general decorum. Billy's stories fascinated Faye. His college seemed plucked from the pages of a nineteenth-century Irish novel.

"I had no idea colleges like that still existed. Sacred Heart has single-sex residences and chapels in every dorm, but there's no obligatory Mass attendance. Your school sounds extreme. It sounds like a seminary."

"I think that's it," Billy rejoined. "Traditionally, a lot of students go through St. John's on their way to seminary. That's the idea."

Faye sipped her coke, served elegantly in a water goblet with a maraschino cherry garnish.

"Why are you there? Will you be Father Billy one day?"

"I'm there for lacrosse," Billy said brightly. "I'm on a lacrosse scholarship."

"That's right." Faye suddenly remembered Krystal telling her as much. "I did know that."

"The rigor has been good, though," Billy continued. "It's tough, and I like that. The guys are friendly. There's a slowness to the school and, really, to Minnesota that I don't hate."

Billy cut a bite of steak and popped it into his mouth. An alluring confidence and maturity shone forth from this boy. He was at most eighteen months older than Faye, but he seemed much more settled and more certain. Faye wondered if a year at Sacred Heart would imbue her with such surety. She remembered Krystal saying that Billy was a virgin. He had classic good looks, though he was a bit short, and perfectly styled hair, though he wore glasses rather than contacts. The glasses themselves were clearly expensive and elegant like the rest of his clothing. Everything about Billy, inside and out, was attractive.

Dinner at the club led to drinks in the hot tub. The two couples sat opposite each other on concrete steps in the bubbling water, its froth leaving sprinkles on their chests as it spouted up from below. Krystal giggled as she leaned into Ian, her hands reaching for his trunks under the water. Booze dripped through Faye's veins. Her headache was gone and a lightheadedness had taken its place. She saw steam rising off Billy's bare shoulders. He was strong, his skin smooth and tender but taut. She moved her body a bit closer, allowing herself to relax and enjoy the moment. Billy wrapped his arm around her shoulders, pulling her even closer so that her head rested against his.

"I think they want to be alone," Billy whispered into Faye's ear. As he did, he kissed her there ever so lightly.

A jolt of sexual energy shot through her. The day's tension, the tears, the heavy dinner, and the exhausting hot tub heat converged all at once upon her body.

"I need some air anyway," Faye said. "It's getting too hot in here now."

Poolside, Faye and Billy talked about sports and books and family dynamics. Billy was the oldest; Faye the youngest. He had left a gaggle of Catholic kids behind in Vista View Estates. It was tough being the first for everything, he told her. First to take on responsibilities, first to make mistakes, and the first to go away.

"At school," Billy said between sips of his beer, "I missed my family way more than I thought I would."

Faye liked that Billy talked about his feelings. He was emotional and open in the same way that she was. Krystal and Ian were like that, too. They all liked to talk and hated pretense.

"That's such a sweet thing to say. You seem like a really sweet guy."

Billy smiled with his lips closed, demurring at the compliment.

"I'm glad you accepted this date," he said with a chuckle. "Krystal told me you were pretty hesitant."

"I was. But I'm glad I came."

Billy moved in closer, the heat rising off his damp skin in the cool outdoors. Faye let him kiss her mouth, tasted the remnant of his beer, both bitter and sweet, on his thin lips. The kiss was light and perfect. He pulled away and smiled, showing all his teeth this time.

"That was nice," she said.

He leaned back in and kissed her softly again, this time placing his hand on her cheek and parting his lips the slightest bit. She could tell that he was nervous, his kiss slightly timid. And, she thought, his touch felt just right. Because it was summer and because they were young, they made out by the pool, feeling each other's tongues and teeth. Billy held Faye's head with his hand or reached down to fold his fingers in hers. He draped a white VV Estates towel over her shoulders when the hot tub heat finally wore off their skin and the cold air began to chill them. Somewhere across the way, Krystal and Ian were doing Faye-didn't-know-what, but she knew it involved more sex than was on her mind. As curfew neared, Faye and Billy stopped kissing and squeezed themselves onto a single pool lounge, the plastic slats sticking awkwardly to their legs as they looked up at the hills.

"This has been a great day," Billy said. "With a perfect ending."

Faye thought back on her day, the hours spent reaching for Edward, the smoking and dialing and listening to the persistent busy signal that spelled Edward's disinterest in her. A fogginess had descended upon her in the hot tub and had not yet lifted. Her hand rested unmoving in Billy's. She could smell the chlorine and beer that lingered lightly on them both.

Edward's voice flooded into her head. *Just go away. Leave me alone.* Her throat felt suddenly dry as if caked with dust that would not let her swallow. Even as Billy still lay beside her, the distraction he offered scurried away. She needed to go home. She needed to call Edward. *He didn't mean it. He can't stay mad at me,* she thought.

"I need to find Krystal and I need to leave," Faye said, sitting up sluggishly and looking for her box of smokes.

She lit a cigarette as she walked around the pool to the hot tub deck. Deserted.

"They're probably up in the hiking trails. More *private.*"

"And more dirty. Gross," Faye laughed, blowing a stream of white smoke toward the sky. "Are you okay to drive me home?"

"Oh, sure. I only had two beers, and it's been awhile since the last one."

At Faye's porch, Billy kissed her good night and suggested they go out again the following week. Faye muttered a noncommittal response about packing and plans.

"Well, thanks again for a great night," Billy said with finality. "Ring me up if you have time before you leave for school."

Inside, Faye stood with her back against the door, feeling her eyes adjust to the darkness of the entryway. It would be her house for only another month. She heard the slow opening of her parents' bedroom door as she sat on her bed, the blanket still rumpled from her frantic tantrum earlier in the day.

Faye's mom checked the room across the hall. Faye's grandmother slept away in a newly installed hospital bed. The familiar blend of cherry almond lotion and Noxzema face cream wafted toward Faye. Her mom, fresh from a shower, was all sweetness and motherly warmth.

Faye's mom whispered. "How was your date?"

"Really good. He was nice."

Her mom gave an eyebrow raise and a tilt of the head. "Sounds exciting. I'm off to bed. Dad's already asleep." She leaned in for a kiss then disappeared down the hall.

Faye lay on her pillow and circled back to the day's beginning. She heard her parents' bedroom door close and then open again. Her mother reappeared in her bedroom doorway.

"Oh, this is strange. Doctor Vogel called here tonight looking for you."

Terror instantly consumed Faye. She could feel the blood pumping in her eardrums. Her hands went clammy.

"What did he say?"

"He just asked if you were here, and I said you were out for the night. He said not to bother calling back, that it was no big deal."

"That's weird." Faye tried to sound natural. "I'm sure he'll call back if he needs something."

Faye sat motionless on her bed. The overhead light burned brightly. Her digital clock read 12:37. The day had been an emotional marathon, and still it would not end. She needed badly to hear Edward's voice and to know that he still wanted her. She dialed and waited. In her quiet house, the persistent ringing sounded too loud in Faye's ear. No answer. She called again. No answer. Faye imagined Edward asleep in his room, his snores echoing through the otherwise noiseless house. Tears pricked the back of her eyes, slowly at first and then with more force. Agonizing panic ran through her. She was trapped in this room and this house. She needed to go to him, but she could not risk getting caught or raising suspicion. She had cried all morning, and now she was sobbing again. Her chest felt heavy and her afternoon headache came roaring back. The club and the kissing were distant now, as if they had never happened. *But*, she remembered, they *had*. Edward must have been desperate to have called her house, to have talked to her *mother* while Faye was leaning into another boy's hot skin, pressing her lips against his. Her dinner's rich cream sauce and the poolside beer lurched in her stomach. An hour later—1:45—she emerged from her room. Only darkness seeped out below her parents' bedroom door. They were asleep. Quietly, furtively, controlling her tears and her breathing, Faye picked her lunchbox up gingerly and opened the front door in one quick swoop to keep it from creaking. She smoked and sobbed, speeding across the freeways to Edward's house. After the toilet papering incident, she had hardly slept the night before. Crying increased the exhaustion, but adrenaline pushed her forward.

The back door was locked and her knocking did not rouse him. She walked in circles and whispered obscenities. She felt crazy, like this relationship or affair or whatever it was might make her insane. A new form of humiliation gripped her now. She was too embarrassed to make a loud scene but too frantic to go back home. She knocked on Edward's bedroom window, reaching awkwardly over a bed of bright purple flowers that looked black under the night sky. Finally, she heard the cracking of the back door. In the dark, Edward opened his house. Faye rushed in. Darkness shrouded the mudroom and kitchen. It was dream-like and dreamy and nightmarish all at once. The day's anguish had undone her. She collapsed submissively and eagerly in Edward's arms. He scooped her up and carried her to his bed. She could hardly see him in this light, but she could feel him and smell him. She was tired of fighting and of trying to stay afloat. Faye wanted to drown in his strength and his sweetness.

"Are you okay?" His voice, throaty and sleepy, washed the day away.
"I am now."

"Meet us at the Zipper," Krystal said forcefully. "It's at the back of the lot where the blacktop meets the baseball field. Be there by 7:00. James gets off work at 6:30, so *no later than 7*. I don't want him third-wheeling us without you there."

Because Aquinas Prep drew students from so many cities, AP teens filled their social calendars with Epiphany Carnivals, May Crownings, and Autumnfests at many local Catholic parishes spread throughout Citrus County. Ian's parish, Our Lady of Sorrows, which everyone called OLS, hosted the only Summerfest. Its early August scheduling meant competition with the much more grand Citrus County Fair, but because it was local, easier to navigate, and less expensive, the OLS Summerfest got top reviews and billing among Citrus County Catholics.

"What time are you and Ian going?"

"His parents want us to make an appearance in the afternoon while his cousins are there. Probably 3:00. Gosh, it's going to be unbearable, his aunties and cousins hanging all over me and asking us questions about everything. They're kind of fun, but they're just crazy. Over the top."

"Sounds awkward."

"It wouldn't be if you would come with me. Come on, Faye. Please? You owe me like a hundred times over this summer."

"K, I haven't seen him in two days. I like going in the afternoons better. So we can talk more instead of, you know, all that other stuff."

"How is the talking going? I mean, have you talked about what will happen when you leave?"

"We're talking around it. I told him about my roommate calling, about my mom taking me dorm shopping and all that. We talk about me coming home to visit at Christmas. We don't talk about our *relationship*. I don't think I'll like what he has to say if I bring it up. So, I don't."

"Do you think he loves you?"

Faye sighed and bit her lower lip. She needed a smoke, but the house was full and she couldn't get by her parents.

"Of course he does. That's the point. No man would risk his career just because he wanted to *get some*."

"You don't know men very well, Faye."

Krystal's experiences made her more confident and more cynical than Faye. She also was most often right about the things that boys and men wanted.

"He wants more than sex," Faye assured Krystal (and herself). "I'm sure he could find a woman to have sex with if that was all he wanted."

Krystal eyed Faye with skepticism.

"He wants someone to love him," Faye added. "And I love him."

"Did you tell him that?"

"Not in those words, but he knows. He must have known before all this started."

"Did you tell him about Billy?"

"Of course not. I mean, I could. I doubt he expects me not to go around with boys my own age."

"Go around with? I'd say he probably doesn't think you're making out with boys by the pool."

"I was out of my mind that night. It doesn't count."

Krystal sensed a heaviness in Faye's voice, a darkness that had emerged and receded almost imperceptibly since Faye had begun spending time at Edward's house. She brightened her tone and lightened the conversation.

"Okay. Go see your old man boyfriend instead of rescuing me from Ian's family. Meet us at 7 and we can get funnel cakes and sneak beers and go on Faye-approved non-upside-down rides."

"Thanks, K. I don't know how I'd be getting through this without you."

"I know. I'm the best, aren't I?"

"Hand me that sponge," Edward called over his shoulder. "It's in the bucket."

While Krystal and Ian ate pizza and binged on chocolate-dipped soft serve cones, Faye was learning about trowels and grout floats and the proper alignment of tile. She had dropped by Edward's unannounced, as she often did, to spend some time with him before meeting her friends at the festival. He was knee-deep in a bathroom remodel.

"What's next after this project?"

"Well, I'm not sure." Edward, kneeling with his arms outstretched toward the shower wall, sat back onto his heels and spread his grout-encrusted fingers out over his jeans. "Have you been in the other bedroom?"

Faye shook her head no.

"Without intending to, I've turned it into a kind of dumping ground for everything I haven't organized yet. Papers, compositions, boxes of old stuff from everywhere I've lived. It's just a big mess. And I haven't made any improvements to the room itself since I moved in. It has old wood paneling on two walls and really hideous plaid wallpaper on the other two. Green shag carpet. The works."

Edward grabbed his beer, sitting precariously among tools behind the half-installed sink, and drank from it.

"The whole room needs to be overhauled. I'd also like to add some overhead lighting in there. I keep pushing the project, though, since there's really no reason to even use that room. Except when my sister brings her kids out, but they haven't been to visit in years."

"How long have you lived here?"

"I've been in this house since 1988. Geez, that was fast. Ten years."

Faye touched Edward's arm and smiled.

"What?"

She shrugged. "Nothing. I just wanted to touch your arm."

Edward kissed her softly. Faye just could not believe it. She would never get over this feeling. How wonderful that she could touch Edward whenever she wanted.

Edward leaned in again, this time kissing her neck and brushing his hand across her breast.

"I said you could stay if you didn't distract me," he whispered coyly. "I'm starting to feel *distracted* by you."

"Don't stop working yet," Faye cautioned. "Your whole night will end up wasted and you'll wish you had gotten more done."

Edward turned his back to her and applied a layer of grout to another small section of the tile.

"My roommate called this morning from Chicago."

"Oh that's cool. What's her name again?"

"Peggy. Her name's Margaret, but she said everyone calls her Peggy. I'm pretty optimistic, though she doesn't seem very much like me."

"What does that mean? She's not dating an old man?"

"You're not that old," Faye began, though she knew that wasn't true. Edward had twenty-four years on her. "Nor can you really call this *dating*."

Edward turned his head to look at Faye, the grouting tool still balanced in his right hand. She thought, for a moment, that he looked hurt, but the notion seemed ridiculous and too romantic.

"What else would you call it?"

"I thought I wasn't supposed to call it anything. What's the point of giving it a name if I can't talk about it to anyone?"

Edward sighed. "You knew this would be difficult. I don't think either of us has any clue where we're going with this. All I know is that you are leaving me. So, what would you have me do? I fall in love with you and then what? You still leave."

In love with you—Faye heard only that, and it rang in her ears. Edward in love with her was too sad and too wonderful to imagine. Though he never said it, though he berated her for being afraid and inexperienced, and though he belittled her when she wouldn't please him, Edward must love her.

"I know. I won't be gone forever, though. I don't know what to say. I know I don't want to stop coming here. That's all I want. To be with you."

"Me, too." Edward sounded sad. Tired. "Okay, back to your roommate. You say she is not like you. She is not dating a forty-year-old man."

"I don't think she is," Faye said with a smirk, "but I don't think she would tell me if she were, right?"

Edward chuckled and shook his head. "You have a point. You know, I told my brother about you."

Faye's eyes bulged open in disbelief. "You did? Why? What did you tell him?"

"I know I told you not to tell anyone, but, I just—I don't know. He called the other day and we got to talking and I just told him I was seeing someone really young, a former student. I guess I wanted to brag about you. I told him you were going off to Sacred Heart in a couple weeks. That we were just feeling things out."

"This is Glen, right? What's he, thirty?"

"Yes, Glen. He's—born in '65, eight years after me, so—he'll be thirty-three next month. He's the baby."

"What did he say?"
Edward laughed. "*Be careful.* He said *just be careful.*"

The Tilt-a-Whirl twisted and turned, spinning and catapulting Krystal and Ian into a dizzying euphoria. They laughed and screamed, alternately thrown together and then apart as their buggy swept across the surface of the ride. Krystal wore jeans that were a half size too big so they would hide the slight bulge at her waist and a crop top a half size too small so it would accentuate her breasts. Her eye shadow was not just bright pink but glittery as well. She exuded sex and liberation, the kind of carefree confidence that comes from a life of money, attention, and opportunity. Everywhere she went, Krystal had the prettiest face and the brightest eyes. She was a little insecure about her weight, but, unlike Faye, she knew how to bury her self-doubt and compensate by drawing attention to the parts of herself she liked.

Ian was fascinated by her. The first time she led him into the hills behind her house, took down his pants, and went to her knees for him, he nearly fainted. Really, he had thought he might faint, his head breaking open on a rock and bleeding out along the trails while his pants were bunched awkwardly around his thighs. The whirling rides and sugar-scented air made Ian a bit light-headed this night, too, and he could not have been happier.

Krystal broke his reverie. "What time is it?"

Ian checked his watch, feeling, because she had asked, the change of late afternoon heat to cool evening breeze. OLS was much closer to the beach than Krystal's house was. Before the Tilt-a-Whirl, they had unwound the sweatshirts from their waists and zipped them up over their short-sleeves and Krystal's exposed navel.

"It's almost 7:00. Where is James meeting us?"

"They're both supposed to meet us at the Zipper at 7. Let's head that way."

"The three of us should ride it if James gets here first. Faye won't go on that, right?"

"We can't," Krystal said, taking a drink of Diet Coke in a plastic OLS Summerfest cup. "It's a two-person ride. They won't let one person go alone in the cage."

"That's dumb. Who cares if there's an empty seat?"

"It might have something to do with weight distribution or something. Anyway, I promised Faye we wouldn't make her do scary rides. I'll just stay off so you and James can go together."

"I swear to God," Ian said in his serious, combative voice, "if she is late because of that dirty old man, I'm telling her mom."

"Give her a break. She got in so much trouble with him because you wrote that *She's 17* on the lawn. Just let it go."

"Why are you taking her side on this, Krystal? He's *gross.* He's *old.* He's an asshole. And it's *illegal.* It's illegal for a reason. What if he *rapes* her? What if he is already doing that and she hasn't told us? What if he gets her *pregnant?*"

"Whoa. You are way out of control. What if he gets her pregnant? She told me they're hardly doing anything. Okay, that's not true, but *she's* hardly doing anything."

"Well, she doesn't need to do anything for him to get her pregnant. It's insane. It's absolutely insane that we are letting her do this."

"You just hate him, Ian. Admit it. You just hate him because he gave Merton that stupid King of the Pageant thing. If it were a different guy, you wouldn't be writing shaving cream messages and threatening to get her in trouble. If you tell, she will hate us. Hate. Us. No more Faye. Period. I know what's going on. I won't let her get hurt."

Ian looked skeptical.

"Besides, you thought it was hilarious a month ago."

"I never thought it was hilarious. I thought it was crazy and shocking, so I wanted to see if she would actually do it. If *Doctor* would actually do it. I didn't think it would turn into this."

"There's James. Let's stop talking about it. Faye loves that fat old fuck, so let's just let her have him for now."

"Okay, but we might as well head to the payphone next. We're calling Doctor's house at 7:01 if she isn't here."

Tile placed, grout inserted, excess wiped clean—by just past six, Edward was tracing his hand in a figure eight around Faye's breasts. As usual, her nervous laughter sat with them. She tried to cover herself beneath Edward's sheets because the room was not yet dark, but Edward insisted she leave her body exposed so he could admire her.

"Why don't you like me seeing you nude?"

The word *nude* seemed hilarious because Faye was immature and because no one had ever seen Faye naked, not even Krystal. And they were as close as two friends could be. They slept in the same bed at sleepovers, snuggling under the covers. They traded stories about sexual fantasies and experiences—Krystal had told her how to masturbate in a way that would actually cause an orgasm. But still, they turned away when changing into swimsuits or otherwise exposing their most private areas.

"It's embarrassing. I don't like the way I look. I look ugly. Down there."

Edward pushed the sheet back and cupped his hand over the dark patch of hair. Faye kept her eyes on his.

"Perfect," he said, softly touching her. "You are perfect. There's nothing ugly about your body."

Faye wanted to believe him. Falling in love with Doctor Vogel during school had awakened her sexuality, but everything since July 6 had taught her that sex was gross and awkward and scary and uncontrollable.

"I've never seen anyone naked," Faye said quietly.

"You've seen me." Edward spoke with such a gentle tone that Faye wanted to cry.

That wasn't really true. Most often, they did those things when the room was dark. And, too, anytime Edward took off his pants, Faye avoided looking at him. When he asked her to, she touched him *there*, but she always kept her eyes on his. Each time he begged her to put her mouth on him, she not only said no, she physically stiffened and pulled away. She had felt the loose skin of his exhausted penis shrinking away on her thigh after he orgasmed and had felt it hardening and pushing against her back or her panties. He had positioned her on all fours in front of him and rubbed it along the outside of her vagina, making her numb with panic that he might try to stick it in her. But still, she had not really seen it. She had chosen to look away and to simply *be away* while those things happened.

"I've never really looked. It's too weird for me." Her own words shamed her. She sounded small and stupid. "And you've never been naked with me anyway. You always keep your shirt on."

Edward laughed. "So, you noticed that. I'm a little self-conscious, that's all. About my weight. I'm a lot heavier than I was when I was your age. And when I was ten years older than you." His nasally laugh, again. "And twenty years older."

This admission humbled him, and Faye softened. She remembered all over again that she wanted to be the one who truly saw him. Loving Edward had gotten really difficult that summer. At school, there had been nothing about him she didn't love. She remembered the humiliation she had felt on his behalf the time his shirt button had slipped out of its closure and the class had seen a peek at the pale white skin of his navel. He moved his arms furiously when conducting, and, without his knowledge, the hairy skin of his belly poked out where the button had come undone. She knew she had to tell him, but she knew that telling him would feel too close, too familiar. She should have found a way to signal him or to take him aside and whisper so that no one would hear. But she didn't. Instead, ten minutes later, Spencer Sinclaire laughed a loud *Ha!* from the top riser and yelled, "Hey Doc. Your shirt is totally open down by your belt." Edward looked as if Spencer had punched him in the face. Never had Faye seen Edward not in control of the class, or of any room in which he stood. Edward had looked instinctively at Faye. She blushed so hard a line of sweat emerged at the top of her collar. She pretended to start coughing so she could cover at least part of her face.

Faye smiled, now. "You shouldn't be self-conscious either."

"Look at me," he said beseechingly. "See me."

Edward pulled down his briefs and put her hand on him. He asked again, but she closed her eyes. A tear slipped out.

"I'm sorry," she said. "I'm not ready."

Other days she had been angry at his persistence. Some nights, his purposely mean humiliation of her had been almost too much to stomach. But this, today, was her fault, and she knew it. She disappointed him. She failed him. She realized she wasn't enough. *He needs a grown-up*, she thought, *not a kid*.

Faye opened her eyes and took his hand in hers. She spoke with a lilt in her voice.

"Have I ever told you what my favorite part of your body is?"

He followed suit, dropping the heaviness of his tone.

"Well, we know what is not your favorite part." He snickered. "Okay, what is it?"

"This." Faye held one hand gently beneath his wrist and rubbed the other along his forearm. "In school it would drive me wild when you would roll your sleeves up and show your forearms. That's weird, right? They just look strong. I always wanted to touch you right here."

Faye brought his arm to her lips and kissed it seductively, nuzzling the soft hairs against her cheek and then licking the skin there. Edward closed his eyes and began touching her. This time, he laid her back upside-down, her head at the foot of the bed. He rubbed himself along her body, saying obscene things that mortified Faye. She responded with silence. She could not even speak his name.

When Edward moved further up and straddled her chest, Faye's mind shut down altogether. He kept going, standing over her and lowering himself toward her mouth. Time stood still. She really was paralyzed now, her head spinning, her limbs so heavy she could not lift them, could not move. The hotness of Edward's thighs crowded out the air around her. She saw his chest rising erratically and could tell by the furrow of his brow that he was concentrating. His mouth hung open in the shape of a moan. But she could not hear him. Someone had turned off the sound in Edward's room. Her tongue felt two sizes too big for her mouth. She didn't know where to put it or how to push Edward away without hurting or angering him. She lay still and tried to turn her head toward the open window.

The clang of the Aquinas Prep choir room doors came suddenly into Faye's mind. *She walks in beauty like the night.* Doctor had said this to her one spring afternoon as she burst through those loud metal doors. *She walks in beauty like the night,* he had said. Now, they were so disconnected, held together only by this thrusting beast that forced itself in and out of Faye's mouth while she lay unmoving and uncomfortable. Being upside-down disoriented her, and her exposed body felt suddenly cold. It was evening, now, and the heat coming in through Edward's back window had turned cool. Edward moved himself carefully back onto the bed. Faye's mind turned back on. *Oh thank you God,* she thought, relieved that Edward had stopped without finishing. He staved off the end and then started caressing her again, bringing her back to the present with gentle kisses and locking eyes with her. A few minutes later, Edward ejaculated on her chest. When the phone started ringing, he was straddling her torso. Faye's head hung off the foot of the bed. Edward held himself up on top of her. The machine clicked on. Faye was used to the greeting by now.

You've reached 992-6882. Thanks for calling. Please leave a message.

Ian's voice blasted through the speaker. "Doctor, it's Ian. If Faye is there, tell her she's *fucking* late. Let her go."

Ian slammed the phone down, rattling its metal box. His hands shook. He had never cursed at an adult before, but no adult had ever tried fucking his teen-aged friend.

The line cut out. Faye tried to sit up.

"Oh shit. They're going to kill me."

"Just stay here," Edward said flatly. "Stop letting them tell you what to do."

"I promised I'd be there by 7. I have to leave now."

Edward wiped the sticky fluid off her body with the corner of the bedsheet and brought her up to meet him face to face. He kissed her forehead and tucked an errant lock of hair behind her ear.

"That was amazing," he said. "You did really well for your first time. I hope you enjoyed it."

Faye squeezed his hand but did not respond.

"I better go."

High Mass in a European cathedral brings to Earth the very Incarnation of God. Like the Church itself, like the ringing of the bells at the consecration, the grandeur of High Mass beckons and pleads—*Look here!*—not because the beauty is so magnificent or the clanging so persistent, but because in the priest's very hands is the truth and the way. There is God Himself.

The previous summer, Faye and her friends had sung High Mass at *Santa Croce* in Florence, its Gothic arches rising high above the humbled Aquinas Prep choir. After mass, they had toured *Santa Croce*, Faye pausing to admire a Santi di Tito painting in a dimly lit alcove. She could smell Doctor Vogel's cologne and feel his strong stance planted behind her, but Faye did not turn to him. She continued examining *Supper at Emmaus*. Seeing God seemed both easier and more difficult than people thought. Faye could always find her love for Doctor Vogel in this memory, in the fleshy warmth emanating as he stood behind her in the north aisle and witnessed the revelation of Jesus to the men who served Him.

To God Be The Glory, Doctor had always said. *To God Be The Glory*. The phrase followed Aquinas Prep everywhere. It was emblazoned on their Chamber Singer sweatshirts and engraved into their choir pencils. Their music portfolios, their garment bags concealing dingy concert attire, and the leaflets announcing performance schedules all exclaimed it—*To God Be The Glory*. What glory was there in this? How, now, to reconcile the Doctor Vogel of *Santa Croce* with the Edward who had forced that unspeakable humiliation on her, who had turned her into someone she believed she was not? Faye replayed Edward's final look of contentment, the exhaustion and peace spreading across his face as she grimaced and willed herself to be gone from that bed. Hadn't she wanted for Doctor Vogel what he wanted for himself? Faye's love of him was sacrificial, perhaps even Godly. That, Faye supposed, could be glorious.

The lights at Summerfest flashed green, yellow, bright white, and purple. They flashed and ran and swirled, a chaotic mess of color and light punctuated by screams of terror and jubilation as Citrus County Catholics and their guests rocked and twisted high up in the air. The incongruous smells of syrupy cotton candy and coagulating garbage competed as the OLS blacktop transformed itself into a playground of joy and fellowship. Faye's eyes darted frantically as she searched for her friends, heading first to the gym's payphone—Ian must have called from there—and then to the Zipper where originally they had planned to meet. James was waiting there, alone. He extended his left wrist awkwardly in her direction, his elbow contorting to show the digital display—8:25.

"I know," Faye said, moving in for a hug. "Everything went wrong. I lost track of time, I left late, there was an accident at the 57-55 interchange, and there was traffic leading in here. Parking was a nightmare."

James stared stone-faced, unmoved by Faye's excuses.

"Krystal and Ian are pissed. Well, Ian is pissed, which means Krystal is annoyed. Ian almost called your parents."

Tensions did not diminish as the night continued. Ian seethed. Faye tried to make light. Krystal walked between the two, her arm linked through Faye's.

"You need to choose, Faye. I can't let you keep seeing him. This is fucking ridiculous. He's *forty years old*." Ian screamed, his voice so loud that Faye looked around frantically and shushed him despite the maddening din of the Summerfest crowd.

"Choose what? Choose you or him? That doesn't even make sense. Our friendship has nothing to do with whatever is going on with me and him."

"What is going on with you and him? Are you sleeping with him?"

The question—perfectly reasonable—shocked Faye. "Of course not. You know I wouldn't do that."

"No," Ian said haughtily. "I do not know you wouldn't do that. Apparently, I don't know anything about you."

"You know I can't stay away from him. I need him. He needs me."

"He *needs* you? He needs to be in *jail*. Leave me out of it, then. I'm not lying for him. I'm not standing by the Zipper for 70-fucking-minutes waiting for you when you would rather be with him."

Ian wasn't actually angry at Faye. Doctor Vogel was to blame. A frenzied chaos overwhelmed them all. Edward seemed to be tearing them apart when they were most confused and afraid to let go. Later, when Ian and James and Krystal were living real adult lives, when they were supervising employees and raising children, the moral quandary they evaded that summer would show itself in sudden night sweats, in uneasy attitudes toward their children's teachers, and in general discomfort during discussions of sexual consent. For now, they lashed out, yelled, threatened, and receded, leaving Faye to keep doing what she was doing—and, thus, Edward would keep doing what he was doing, too.

"Listen," Krystal interjected. "Why don't you boys go off and do some boy things or whatever and cool down."

"No way. We are going on the Zipper," Ian insisted. "*All* of us."

Faye's throat went dry. Her feet felt heavy, like they might hold her in place. "I can't," she stammered. "I just can't. I do not do upside-down rides."

Ian glared at her darkly. His usual humor was gone. She detected no sarcasm in his voice.

"Tonight, you go on everything we want. Or I call your parents."

Faye squeezed her eyes tight and dug her fingers into the thick foam padding of her lap belt. The Zipper zipped and flipped and disoriented her even behind closed eyes. The luminous sky, bursting with carnival light, seeped through the cage. Faye held her breath at the bottom of her throat and tensed her stomach muscles like a person doing sit-ups. The clanging vibrations were worse than the upside-down. In fact, she suddenly realized, she could not tell whether they were right side up or upside down, climbing the Zipper or falling down its opposite side. Faye heard James whooping with pleasure and grabbed his warm, smooth hand. She was riding the Zipper. She let out a yelp to match Ian's floating down from above her. Faye finally relaxed, but only when their cage lost momentum and settled into a steady rocking no worse than a playground swing.

Top Spin came next. Ian dragged Faye by the hand along the expansive stretch of seats, the ride a giant platform of rows, theater style, attached to a menacing metal arm. From behind her harness, Faye could see far out across the OLS parking lot. She saw small children riding a tiny coaster in dinosaur-shaped seats and people walking like zombies through a plastic-walled mirror maze, big bulbous lights bordering it like they would a cosmetics table. The Knights of Columbus beer booth and the OLS Girls Volleyball pizza tent backed up against each other, lines of hungry patrons snaking their way from the food aisle all the way to the carnival games. The Zipper had left Faye queasy but emboldened. As the rows of seats plunged forward and spun, Faye pulled in a deep breath and pushed away her fear. The wind against her face was exhilarating. Over and over the ride toppled, Faye and her friends spinning head over feet, higher and higher until each revolution began to move back toward solid ground. The fear was so real. But oh, the strength! The resilience! The ride was nearly over. She had ridden Top Spin and would survive. Riding in spite of the terror made it thrilling. But never, never, ever would she ride these rides again.

Faye sipped a soda in a daze after the rides, her body still lurching, her face flushed with excitement but getting rosy from the cool night air. She wandered away from the others, hoping to sneak a cigarette and gather her bearings. Summer was winding down—the summer forever spoken of as *that* summer, a time of punishments pretending to be antics and of risk passing itself off as sacrifice. That summer when a wolf in shepherd's clothes smothered Faye with desire masquerading as love.

Ian and James leaned lazily against a metal railing, deciding the group's next move. Krystal followed to where Faye stood smoking, trembling.

Krystal spoke compassionately, almost regretfully. "Are you okay?"

Faye's body convulsed suddenly. She vomited her stomach's pitiful contents and stayed bent over.

"Do you think it was the ride?"

"No."

Faye shook her head slowly and kept her eyes focused on the shreds of mucousy bile at her feet.

"I gave Doctor a blow job."

Having done it now, having done with her mouth that awful thing Edward had been begging for all summer (and having found it not playful, erotic, or loving and absolutely nothing like it seemed in a VC Andrews novel), Faye resolved to never do it again. Edward had surprised and cornered her the day of the OLS Summerfest. She would not let that happen again.

In classroom 405 at Aquinas Prep, Ms. DeGroot, who taught Freshman Catechism (Gospel Principles and the Apostolic Age) and Senior Religious Studies (Reformation and the Age of Enlightenment), proudly displayed an oath and, to the horror of her students, actually asked that they recite it out loud as a class every few weeks.

I will not have sex (again), they said in unison—some bored, some with mock enthusiasm or uncontrollable giggles, some half covering their mouths to hide their blushing—*until I am married in the Church and can, through my vocation as a married person, attain the complete fulfillment of my created purpose.*

The *again* shocked Faye and stayed with her. The first week of freshman year, the oath stunned her. Faye had looked sheepishly around the room. Sure, she was young for her class, just thirteen. But the oldest among them could not have been more than fifteen. *I will not have sex AGAIN? Who on Earth*, she wondered, *would have already had sex?* The older she got, even into the real adulthood of graduate school and married life, she never forgot Ms. DeGroot's poster, its faded tan edges pulling away from the wall, or the paradox of such a serious word like *sex* in twirly pastel lettering. Ms. DeGroot and the poster gave stark reminders of the mercy that awaited God's people. Always, the offer of reconciliation and transformation were there. In God, one could eternally start over, try again, and redefine oneself.

Nothing worked that way at Edward's house. Edward, it seemed, had other ideas. Faye's silent consent, that she did not bite or scratch or scream or just *leave* already and never come back, sentenced her to more of Edward's pleading, berating, huffing, puffing, and head-shaking. Try as she could to grab control, control eluded Faye. Edward decided when, again, she would do those awful things. So, a week after Summerfest, on an especially contentious afternoon, she took the reins, refused right then and there. Faye watched in horror as the bed and the walls and the light stayed the same, but Edward himself transfigured. Edward tore back the sheet and stormed out of the room, leaving Faye sitting up in his bed bewildered, her breathing shallow, her pulse racing.

Edward called back over his shoulder, his tone caustic: "You're always talking about love," he sniped. "This is how grown-ups love."

A knot twisted and tightened in Faye's stomach. Faye knew what he meant. If she *really* loved him, she would do what he wanted. And, by God, she did love him. He reappeared a minute later, sipping a can of juice and wanting, she could tell, to remedy the hurt feelings. Edward lowered his chin and raised his brows, looking, Faye thought, remorseful and exhausted.

"Okay," she said weakly. "Don't be mad. I'm sorry."

Another sleepover. With the first morning light, Edward's beside alarm clock—the wide-grinning conductor, white gloves perched in downbeat position—woke them both with the loud strains of Beethoven's *Fifth Symphony*. With a pat to the conductor's head, Edward snoozed the alarm and nuzzled Faye, sweetly at first then persistently, pushing and rubbing himself against her playfully until she agreed, again, to do as he directed. After the conductor's third reprise, Edward rolled out of bed and headed to the bathroom, calling back to Faye as he disappeared around the corner.

"Come shower with me."

Faye gathered the sheet in folds around her body and cut a path instead from the bedroom to the back door. Dragging a heap of sheet behind and around her, Faye smoked a cigarette slowly and watched the light rising off the dew on Edward's rose bushes. The sun peeked in scattered rays through the uneven rooftops of Edward's neighborhood, casting a not-yet-hot glow on her morning, beautiful and absurd as it was. From where she sat, Faye could see the raised blinds of the neighbor's bedroom window. Instinctively, she snuffed out her cigarette and snuck quietly back into Edward's house.

She found Edward leaning toward the bathroom mirror, his face half-covered with a puffy smear of shaving cream. Steam rose from the running shower, dampening and warming Edward's exposed body. Prickly goosebumps jumped out from his skin as Faye's protective sheet slipped down, propelling a burst of fresh air as it fell to the floor. Edward smiled as she appeared behind him in the mirror. He reached one arm back awkwardly around her torso as she locked her hands around his waist and looked out around his shoulder. Edward felt her breasts, cool and tender, flattened out against his back, the familiar scent of cigarette smoke caught in her messy morning curls. Locking her fingers together against the firmest part of Edward's middle, Faye looked past his body into the mirror's reflection of his eyes, those always captivating portals she had watched and been watched by all these months. Though they both were naked and the morning light was bright, Faye felt a sudden sense of comfort and security. She did not notice the fleshiness of his backside or the wrinkled penis slinking away in the shadow of his protruding stomach. Both, for a moment, watched the mirror in silence, its glass showing the ordinary couple they might have been at some other time, in some other unrestricted space.

Faye lay on the bed, freshly showered, in no hurry to head home. Saturday meant her parents at home to tend to her grandmother, no regular shift at Cal's, and no morning Mass. She thought perhaps that Merton could meet for pancakes or Krystal for coffee and a walk along the beach. She watched Edward start rushing as he checked the clock, pulling jeans on with some difficulty and smoothing out a gray AP Chamber Singer polo over his worn undershirt. He disappeared from the bedroom, reappearing with his briefcase and a travel mug of coffee.

"I have to get out of here," Edward said, appearing flustered as he tried to latch his wristwatch, his car keys dangling from his mouth.

"Where do you have to be on a Saturday morning?"

"Well," Edward began, "I'm running late for our first Renaissance Pageant prep meeting." Faye detected something playful in Edward's tone, a mischievous sense of having gotten away with something satisfying and secretive. "They'll be waiting for me," he continued, "at Leah's house."

"You better think of an alibi on your way there," Faye said coyly, crawling toward the foot of Edward's bed and raising her naked body up to meet him. She kissed him fully on the mouth and slipped her tongue between his lips. Edward grabbed her with both hands and kissed back.

"You certainly can't tell that prude Mrs. Fallon what made you late."

"And *you*," he said between kisses, his breath growing hotter, his hands and mouth moving down from Faye's face to her belly, "better not get me going again."

Edward released Faye reluctantly and moved to gather his things.

"Can you write me some quick directions to Leah's house?"

"Certainly."

Faye grabbed a crumpled tee shirt from Edward's floor and pulled it over her head. At the kitchen table, she hastily charted by memory the route to Leah's house. At the bottom, she left her signature marking, a lower-case cursive *f*, the sweeping tail flowing into a scribbled heart.

Edward kissed Faye quickly as he grabbed the directions from her raised arm.

"Be careful when you leave. Don't hang around out front."

Faye questioned him, a bit of mockery in her voice. "Are you ashamed of me?"

Edward let out an exasperated breath.

I'm ashamed of me, he thought.

Faye could feel his unspoken admission.

"I wish I could tell all of them about you," Edward said. "They would never believe it."

Faye's heart swelled. She never got enough of Edward's admiration. Every time they fought, every time his words cut her, every time he pushed and cajoled and coerced, Faye covered herself in the memories of their past.

Edward had loved her, she knew, before the blow jobs. He must have. He had loved her before the deep groans that came each time Edward needed to be satisfied.

Edward muttered discomposed apologies as he passed through the foyer at Leah's house. Twittering voices carried to him from the living room. The choir parents in attendance—all of them women—quieted and looked up as he, the meeting's presider, entered twenty minutes late. They held him in no contempt. This room full of volunteer coordinators, stage hands, and fundraisers waited, as much as any school girl, with bated breath for each word Edward uttered. In fact, like Faye and all her friends, the choir parents reverently called him *Doctor*.

"I apologize for my tardiness. I hope you've been enjoying yourselves at least," Edward began. "It looks like Mrs. Fallon has put together a wonderful spread for all of us."

Edward nodded in the direction of Leah's mom. "Thank you, Karen."

"Okay, let's get started."

Settling into an overstuffed chair, Edward realized his notes were not at hand. Scanning the room, he saw Leah lurking in the corner, carefully watching the adults but staying out of their way.

"Leah," he called. She caught his eye and moved at once to his side. "I think I set my briefcase down by the front door when I came in. Can you go grab the stack of yellow papers out of it? They should be clipped together, right on top."

From the entryway, Leah could hear the women's small talk revving up again. She clicked open Doctor's briefcase and grabbed the bright yellow sheets. As she did, a half sheet fluttered out. Even before she retrieved it, she recognized her friend's writing. There they were—hand-written directions from Doctor's house to her own. Beneath an unmistakable *xoxo*, Faye's whimsical and equally unmistakable signature heart. Leah heard Doctor's steps on the tiled floor behind her. She whirled around.

"Did you get lost?"

"Oh, sorry," she managed, suddenly short of breath and embarrassed for them both. "Here they are."

"Thanks. It's nice to see you today," he said warmly. "Summer's lonely without my students."

Leah smiled shyly, her heart pounding between her ears.

"I'm just off a bad break up," Merton spat. "I don't feel like going out."

Faye pleaded. "Come with me to Doc's tonight for a change of scenery."

Most of the night was remarkably unremarkable. When Faye and Merton arrived, Edward was relaxing rather than working. He sat on a stool in the cluttered garage, puffing a cigar and looking with unfocused attention toward the sky. The news ran low on a portable black and white television, its light casting a small glow around Edward's face. Merton approached first, and the two men shook hands in greeting. Faye and Edward did not embrace. Faye did not smoke, though she really needed a cigarette just then. Without forethought or discussion, they fell easily to old roles.

Inside, Edward spoke to Merton as both leaned against opposing kitchen counters.

"Are you around this Sunday? My church choir is doing the Biebl for Feast of the Assumption. They're pretty strong, but we can use another baritone if you're free. Just to kind of fill out the sound."

Merton's face brightened and he answered enthusiastically.

"I'd very much be interested in that. What's the details?"

"We do three Masses," Edward began, popping open a beer. "I'd prefer that you do all of them, but I'll take whatever I can get. Mass times are 8, 10, and 12. I'll even treat you to brunch after."

"Sounds amazing."

Merton then motioned with a half-full water glass toward Faye.

"What about you, girl? Want to sing?"

"I haven't been asked," Faye said coyly.

Edward smiled the same flirtatious grin he had perfected at Aquinas Prep. Standing here with Merton and Faye transported him to those days (*only weeks ago!*) that seemed from another life.

"We don't need you," Edward said irreverently.

Faye blushed. "But I can come?"

"Yes," Edward affirmed. "Of course you can come."

"I would like to come watch, but no, I am not going to sing unless you absolutely need me. And it seems you do not."

"Our regular liturgical work is fine. Because the Biebl is a men's piece, we just don't have as much richness there. That's really the only place I need you, Merton."

"Sounds good."

Merton wrapped his arm around Faye's shoulder. She took his hand instinctively in hers as she always did. Merton nudged her slightly, playfully, with his upper body.

"You want to sleep over on Saturday and we'll just go together?"

"A slumber party sounds good," Faye said approvingly. "Maybe I'll sneak a little lemonade and vodka into the Caceres homestead."

Edward took a shallow swallow of his beer as he watched Faye teasing Merton (as she had done all year). How, Edward wondered, could Merton wait so patiently for Faye to see him? How, he found himself thinking, could Merton hold back all these months while Faye flirted so flagrantly and dared him to take her? The humiliating answer, Edward suspected, was that Merton, at eighteen years old, was a more noble man than he. The thought burned him. Edward's nervous system felt flushed with irritation. He had the distinct impression that he had been forgotten.

"Why doesn't Faye stay here?" Edward addressed Merton instead of Faye. "You can pick me up for the early Masses and then she can meet us at the church for noon Mass and brunch."

Merton's mouth hung open in surprised discomfort. His answer came slowly.

"That sounds good."

Sunday morning, leaning sullenly against the driver's door, Merton smoked a cigarette and waited for Edward to emerge from the house. Merton kept his eyes down, seeing wisps of his own dark hair framing his vision and noticing steam wafting up from his mug. The smell of coffee rising, sharp and dark, soothed him.

"You, too, with the cigarettes?" Edward's voice broke his reverie. Edward seemed, Merton thought, to have a fresh and almost playful demeanor for such an early morning appointment.

Merton waved his hand half-heartedly, the salute led by a cigarette still balanced between two fingers.

"Those things will kill you," Edward sarcastically cautioned.

Merton shrugged off the comment.

"Something has to," he said dryly.

Merton stubbed out his cigarette even though they'd be driving his car. As Edward walked around to the passenger door, Merton glanced back toward the house, hoping to catch a glimpse of Faye.

"She's asleep," Edward said knowingly. He smiled a wolfish grin.

Though the drive to St. Crispina was mercifully short, Merton's discomfort grew and the air felt heavy on his shoulders. Not often were two grown men in the front seats of Merton's car—he mostly drove with Tiffany or Faye, both rather slight in build, or with his younger brother, only an elementary school kid. This morning, the space was too small. He and Doctor were too close. *Too close*, Merton thought. Then, immediately, he wondered why feeling close felt bad, wondered when he had developed this simmering anger toward a man he esteemed above everyone. He cracked a window to feel less confined and to let in some noise. He thought about the conversation with Faye at the coffee shop, the possibility that Doctor was forcing himself on her.

Merton spoke with caution, trying to inflect casualness, even flippancy, into his voice.

"How was last night?"

Edward tilted his head toward Merton at first and then looked away before speaking.

His familiar chuckle and then, "Wouldn't you like to know?"

Merton did want to know. He wanted to know why he returned from Europe—adrenaline high, endorphins pumping, ready to spring out of school and into adulthood—to find the world so gleefully upside fucking down. Faye wanted to be with Doctor Vogel, but that just did not matter. *Wrong*, Merton's inner voice kept repeating. Doctor wronged them all with his behavior.

Merton's words slid out more forcefully than he intended.

"She's just a kid."

Edward looked Merton full in the face, his expression so blank and blameless Merton feared momentarily that he had misinterpreted his and Faye's relationship. Doctor, he could tell, had no intention of being judged or berated. He would not admit fault and he would not have Merton challenge his right to do with Faye whatever he pleased.

"Don't give me that garbage," Edward said emphatically.

Merton fixed his eyes back on the road in front of him.

"I am not talking about this with *you*," Edward continued. "It is not your business."

The words hit Merton like a hot, heavy slap. In four years, Doctor had never spoken an unkind word to him.

A quivering in Merton's stomach spread out toward his hands. He clenched the wheel tightly to hide the tremor. Nausea pulsed at the base of his throat. He swallowed hard to push it down.

"Understood," Merton said matter-of-factly.

A minute of silence passed. St. Crispina's hallowed steeple came into view. Hatred crept into Merton's heart, and, because he felt such hate for a man he so admired, Merton hated himself a little bit, too.

"Mind-blowing," Edward said, snickering. "Last night with Faye was mind-blowing."

Faye slept so well that she actually overslept, sneaking through the side door of St. Crispina just as the *Kyrie* commenced. She genuflected quickly, her knee only grazing the floor, and blessed herself with an abbreviated motion as she slipped into the pew. The chorus moved in unison, their faces reverent, their mouths tiny ovals of perfectly harmonized sound. Merton looked less than comfortable draped in the choral gown's blue polyester. Yet, his focus on Edward's conducting, his furrowed brow and forward-leaning posture, reminded Faye how much Merton loved the music and, more, how much he loved Edward. Faye was aglow, her mind circling peacefully around memories of the night before. Edward had been satisfied and so joyful, running his fingers along her arm and kissing the back of her neck as they faded in and out of sleep. *This is my favorite part*, Faye had whispered aloud. *I love having you here with me*, he had said back. That was almost like saying he loved her.

Because Catholicism had created Aquinas Prep, Edward's authority, the morality of Faye's childhood, and, in fact, Faye's very being, it designed the patterns of her thought and wove the ornate borders of the adult world she was growing into. For some, Faye did not yet know, Catholicism was a life attachment like a club card stowed a dozen places back in a stack. Later on, when she became the age Edward was that summer, she would hear other people reference a distant Catholic past with indifference. *I was raised Catholic*, they would say, in the same way one might say *I visited the Grand Canyon one summer*, the story of an event begun and ended without much consequence.

Even at seventeen, Faye's engagement with Catholicism was pervasive, a *raison d'etre*.

Senior year at Aquinas Prep brought a semester's course in Christian Love and Marriage taught with an unintended irony by Fr. Jerry Schmidt. Fr. Jerry, a young Jesuit, was easily recognized by his extra wide smile, his unmistakable lisp, and his white cassock. Fr. Jerry imprinted himself in Faye's memory because—presumably without having had sexual intercourse himself—he planted in her an understanding of sex that was communal and connective. This new view of sex as love transformed the prohibitive culture she associated with Catholic moral teaching and opened to her an image of lovemaking as divine and glorious, a good rather than a disgrace.

Faye watched Edward's shoulder blades contracting and expanding now as he conducted, his feet planted firmly but his body swaying with the Biebl's *mortis nostrae*. She thought of Fr. Jerry's teachings. *Life and love*, he had written in bright white chalk. Sex was for *life and love*. God is love, Fr. Jerry had said, and in our acts of love, God is there. As Vatican II had trickled down into the lives of the everyday faithful, there had arisen a new generation of Catholics. *God is love*, the Church of Faye's youth proclaimed. As she grew into the heart of adolescence, she tried to square the circle of this great moral question. God was love and sex was love, but God was purity and sex was sinfulness. Faye knew that Edward was flawed and impure. But, oh, how loveable she found him! In loving Edward, Faye would find God and fix Edward's brokenness. For Faye, God was love, and love was Edward. At St. Crispina's and in every Aquinas Prep bumper sticker and in the darkened Fulton house and forever in the depths of Faye's consciousness, Edward was the face of God.

The choir room door clanged shut, a loud metallic bang announcing Faye's arrival. Edward kept his back to the door, crouching ever so slightly closer to the floor as he scrawled instructions on the portable blackboard. The door's sudden clicking open and swinging shut startled Edward, but he did not turn around. He focused on the chalk in his hand, trying to keep his writing consistent, level. Edward and Faye had not been together at Aquinas Prep in more than two months, certainly not since the July evening when the whole world had wobbled and lost focus and caught fire.

Edward finished his note—*Sing your part from start to measure 42*—settled the chalk in its wooden tray, clapped the chalk dust from his hands, and whirled around to look at Faye. He wore jeans and white tennis shoes, a mix of darker and grayer hairs peeking out from the open collar of a white AP Chamber Singers polo shirt. Faye looked first to his hands and then up to his mouth, smiling when she saw his anticipatory eagerness. His eyes smiled before he spoke to her. Edward kept his hair slightly less groomed during summer than the school year. His skin had darkened a bit from summer days working in the garden. As he stood in so ordinary a pose, one reminiscent of the Edward she had admired and had wanted to get close to all those high school days, she remembered with surprise that they had spent much of the summer arguing. Faye was overcome by how strong and beautiful Edward looked.

"You made it," he said to her. "What time is it?"

"I think almost 1. I'm sorry it took me a while to get away. I had to wait for my dad to relieve me. My grandma's regular nurse didn't come today."

Edward stood with one hand on his hip and the other on his head. He considered the blackboard's instructions and his next move. Faye thought he might greet her with a kiss like he always did. She had thought he might, but she was not surprised when he didn't. The walls could see and the walls might talk, and here, at Aquinas Prep, they were used to ignoring the urge to be anything but Doctor Vogel and his model student.

"I have errands to run for Prep Week," Edward said. "Should we go out and get some lunch while we're at it?"

And so, at 1:00 on that August day under a bright sunny sky, Edward and Faye emerged together from the choir room on the Aquinas Prep campus. They walked together, without touching, to Edward's green sedan parked at the base of the steps and climbed into the front seats. Edward waved without fanfare to the AP security guard as he and Faye drove through the ivy-covered gates and left the campus.

When Faye and Edward returned to the school, the clanging choir room door greeted them. This time when the door clanged shut behind them, Edward pulled it tightly. Faye heard it click with a finality that meant it was not just closed but latched. Edward looked over his shoulder toward the small rectangular window that faced outside. He turned back and began kissing Faye. As they kissed, he ushered her toward his office, closing that door behind them as well and pushing her up against his desk. A strange mix of nostalgia and desire descended on Faye.

Edward reached his hand into the wide gap between her overalls and her skin.

"I thought you would wear a skirt," he said through kisses. "In my fantasies you're always wearing a red plaid skirt and a white blouse."

"In mine," she offered, "you're always wearing black pants and your gray button-down shirt."

The conversation thrilled Edward. Faye did not often talk about sexual things.

Faye giggled. Her stomach tensed at the embarrassing conversation; she felt a tugging down between her legs each time Edward's tongue touched hers.

Edward put his fingers inside her and pressed his mouth up against her ear. "You know what would feel amazing right now?" he whispered.

Faye's jaw involuntarily tensed. She started to pull back, opening a small pocket of distance between them.

"Don't worry," he said with condescension. "We absolutely cannot get caught doing that here."

Saved by circumstance, Faye thought. Each muscle in her body slackened when Faye realized that Edward would not expose himself to her in the office. Edward lifted her onto the desk and wrapped her legs around his waist.

"Let's go to my house," he said breathlessly, "so I can get these clothes off you."

Edward's voice was scratchy and dry. She loved it and loved him, but sex talk summoned a barrage of bad memories—the overwhelming paralysis when Edward removed her clothes, the humiliation of him ejaculating on her body while she tried to twist out of his grasp, his disappointment that she could not please him as willingly as he wanted her to. Edward wanted to take her home. Faye wanted to stay here, in the office at Aquinas Prep where she had learned to love him and where she had always felt safe with him. She loved this intimacy, her arms around his neck, his familiar smell filling all her senses. Heat seeped from his skin through the thin fabric of his Chamber polo. The fleshiness of his body felt lovely and beautiful in her hands. Even as she felt his erection nuzzling against her, Faye was not afraid. At his house, where no one saw or constrained them, that pulsing, insistent part of Edward consumed their relationship. That persistent demand for gratification caused arguments and robbed Faye of that which she most desired: an intimacy with Edward that did not depend on his sexual satisfaction. Here, where he could not push her or make demands of her, even this part of Edward felt loveable, like a mere part of the whole person Faye adored.

"I can't," Faye said with feigned disappointment. "I'm going shopping with my mom."

Edward pulled her against him one more time. "I suppose I'll have to go take care of *this* myself," he said with a chuckle. He pulled back, then, straightened his clothes, and opened the office door.

Faye tucked her shirt down inside her overalls and headed out of the office. Before opening the choir room door, Edward looked suspiciously out the window.

"I'll be thinking about you in that plaid skirt," he said.

"I'll think about you tonight, too," she said back coyly. "In your gray shirt in the office chair."

It felt good to flirt with Doctor Vogel again.

Faye burst through the metal door onto the choir room steps, the summer sun flooding the room as Edward's eyes followed her out.

Edward and Faye had traveled the world together, first in small California bursts to San Diego and Fresno, then to nationals in Florida and Carnegie Hall in New York, and even across an ocean to France, Germany, and a full ten days in Italy. They had eaten gelato in the Piazza Santa Maria Novella, walked the hills of Assisi, toured the Neuschwanstein, and taken in a show on Broadway. Then, the kissing had sent them underground, Edward's half closed garage hiding all but their feet; touching and tasting in Edward's darkened bedroom. The night of their one dinner date, both Edward and Faye were nervous. Edward had suggested dinner out at a small Italian bistro by his house. He had dined out with Faye twice before, but always with Merton to buffer the unease and deflect attention. Edward's birthday dinner had been particularly uncomfortable, Faye staring at him with her big green-blue eyes, doing her best imitation of a grown woman flirting and forcing Edward to control the rising erection that both exhilarated and nauseated him. Edward had much more to lose than she did if they were discovered. It would only take a glimpse from someone he knew—an Aquinas Prep history teacher stopping in for a late night cocktail or a choir parent carefully eating spaghetti over business with a client—to unravel his career and his reputation. Edward's malaise was so deep that such an enormous risk hardly fazed him. He wanted so badly to feel normal again. If they discussed the latest movies over pasta like other couples did, he wouldn't feel so lost. He could tell himself, then, that sex with Faye was okay.

"Do you still want to go?" Edward asked. Faye had been aloof since her arrival. She seemed sullen instead of talkative. "Are you fighting with your friends again? You don't seem *in the mood.*" He said the phrase slowly, a playful tone reminding Faye that his favorite part of the evening always came at the end in the bedroom when the mood turned erotic.

"Of course I want to." More quietly, she added, "I spent all day packing."

"When do you leave? A week?"

"Yes. I go August 28, but a moving truck takes most of my things this weekend. They have a whole system in place. They take boxes and trunks going to Sacred Heart from all over the country."

"And you're getting sad about leaving?"

Edward drained the remaining whiskey from his glass and beckoned Faye to come sit beside him. His hand felt cool wrapped around her shoulder. His fingers felt slightly damp from touching the glass. She leaned into him.

"I don't want to go."

"Sure you do." Edward spoke casually, almost flippantly, about her departure. "You'll see when you get there. This is an exciting time for you."

"It doesn't seem like you're upset that I'm going." Faye leaned into the curve of Edward's side and looked straight toward the blank tv to avoid his expression.

"I'll miss you, but there's nothing I can do. Do you want me to be upset?"

"You just never talk about how you feel. I thought we were doing this because you really wanted to be with me. It doesn't seem like you want me around if we're not doing—" Faye hesitated—"all that other stuff."

Faye's accusation hung in the air.

"Do you love me?" she asked.

Edward sighed less with annoyance than with uncertainty.

"Oh, Faye. This is a big discussion. Let's go to dinner before it gets too late. Plenty of time to talk later."

Tears stung Faye's eyes but she blinked them at bay. His avoidance embarrassed her.

"I love doing *this*," Edward said, turning her face to his and kissing her fully on the mouth. His kissing turned quickly forceful like it always did, and she pulled back out of habit.

"We better go before I change my mind and carry you to bed."

Faye blushed. After these many weeks, her skin still grew warm and tense at the thought.

Fulton fluttered with muted enthusiasm. A few couples dotted the dining room of Il Ghiotto. Edward wore black slacks and his gray collared shirt because Faye had told him she liked it best. She had loved in school watching Edward almost visibly heat up a few songs into each rehearsal when the body warmth from so many singers made the air feel more heavy. Just when the students started peeling off their sweatshirts and cursing Aquinas Prep's lack of air conditioning, Edward would unbutton his shirt cuffs, folding his sleeves back just slightly and revealing the tender underside of his forearms.

Faye wore a burgundy dress that was too tight for her style but not nearly tight enough for 1998 nightlife. The dress fit, Faye supposed, but she was uncomfortable in it. She tied matching burgundy ribbons in her hair before leaving the house. There, in the loopy bows around her two long braids, Edward could see the Faye he knew.

Edward leaned in over his menu after the host had poured their waters and walked away. "Your shoes give away your age."

Faye hadn't thought of that. She shuffled her leather Mary Janes under the table and wondered if Edward was trying to embarrass her. Edward ordered a bottle of pinot noir and drank half of it before they had finished their entrees.

They arrived back at Edward's house relieved that they had not seen anyone they knew. Edward stretched out on the sofa, lifting his head and shoulders for Faye to slip in beneath him and cradle his head in her lap. Faye's question still lingered above the couch where they had left it before dinner.

He could hear it prodding him. *Do you love me?* she had asked.

Edward readjusted the pillow. He stood it on end, trying to lay his head only on the bottom third, wanting to settle more deeply into Faye's embrace as he began to feel drowsy from the pinot and from the heaviness of Faye's entreaties. At school, Faye's presence had been one of few things that could make Edward feel light and joyful. Now, every conversation pulled them toward an indefinite darkness that Edward did not know how to navigate. He wanted to love her as if she were a real woman that he could build a life with. But he knew she was leaving him soon.

He had made a mistake getting this involved, Edward knew, but no matter. Now, he woke in the mornings knowing that he might not end the day alone, that Faye wanted to be near him more than she wanted anything else.

He could not take Faye to the symphony and sip champagne with her during intermission. He could not tell his mother, waiting patiently in Kansas for him to get married and give her grandchildren, that he'd finally met a young woman as bright as he, a young woman whose magnetism had made everyone, including him, drunk with the feeling that she wanted only for their happiness. But he had, for these hot seven weeks, caught the energy almost buzzing off her in this fleeting period between high school and university. Faye basked in the light of youth as she readied to take off into a world of new ideas and experiences. Edward had, for these weeks, allowed Faye's moment to pull him back to the sense of an open road that had gripped him when he entered the doctoral program at Michigan. Back then, he had imagined his career unfolding in bursts of fame. He had tried, in these weeks, to teach her to make love like a man and woman do. He had pushed down her fear, opened her body to him, and filled himself with her eagerness.

He spoke to her.

"I do love you, Faye."

Faye sank back more deeply into Edward's couch. Her hand rested against the tender arch between Edward's ear and his hairline. She ran the tips of her fingers down to the base of his neck and back up through the thickening hair just above his shirt collar. She remembered Edward's tentative questioning the first night—*Is this the closeness you want with me?* he had asked.

This. This is what I want, she thought.

Faye wanted Edward's head in her lap like it was now, to feel the rise of his whole body as he slipped into the fitful sleep of a man who snores through the night, his mind deep in sleep while his body resettles with each breath. She wanted to curve her body to his in the worn blue sheets and to touch her leg against his under the table at dinner. Faye wanted to hold Edward's face with both her hands and kiss the tiny divot beneath his nose. She wanted to rub her lips across his eyelids and press her slightly open mouth against the smoothly shaved skin beneath his chin.

Faye had not wanted the fighting or the disappointment. Last spring, she would not have thought that fighting with Edward was possible. She had never expected Edward to turn his back on her in anger or to spit his words at her because she wouldn't do the things he asked. *How ridiculous it all seemed now!* Faye wanted to make love to Doctor Vogel's soul, not to Edward's pulsing, insistent body. *What a kid thing to think.* She hadn't known that Edward's desire would feel so threatening, that when he kissed her she would feel herself disappearing into the bed, her Faye-ness drifting away so that her body felt like a receptacle for an urgent explosion that could care only about its own need to erupt. She wanted to know that Edward loved her more than he loved all the others. And now, it was so. Here, enfolded by the messiness of his private life and the loveliness of his head in her hands, he loved her. She could be sure.

A warmth spread through Faye's limbs and up to her throat. It crept up to her ears and her scalp. Suddenly the double French braids felt too tight, her excitement too big for the quiet purr of Edward's sleepy breathing. Faye stepped outside to smoke and returned to a dimly lit living room. The slight imprint of Edward's body remained visible on the couch. A table lamp gave the only remaining light. In the bedroom, she found Edward awake and waiting for her.

This night, when Edward started asking again, when he begged her to put her mouth *there*, Faye capitulated without arguing.

Faye had long thought that Edward's conducting was not just sensual but sexy, his whole body moving with the music, his hands clenching and unfolding as the music got louder and more intense. She realized now that the sex was musical, too. He grabbed at her, the energy pulsing through him as he conducted her movements. He slowed and quickened in bursts, reminding Faye of *Musicians Wrestle Everywhere*, the extremely difficult eight-part concert piece Chamber Singers had performed senior year. As he pushed himself more forcefully at her, she tried to think of the words, remembered Edward shushing the sopranos and telling them to open their mouths into tall ovals instead of spreading the word *please* into a wide-mouthed screeching *pleeeeeease*. Edward mumbled to her as he focused his eyes upward.

"Tighter, tighter," he said. "Don't pull back."

Faye tried to follow his instructions. It was thrilling and disgusting and wonderful. She thought she might be hurting him and was sort of afraid that he might hurt her. Edward did not try to delay his orgasm this time. He was desperate to finish so he could believe this was real, so he could know they had done this *together*. Edward loved Faye with such intensity then. He loved her hot mouth and her messy braids and her expression so eager and a little scared like a bird caught up in a storm. She was vibrant and loved and so smart and had her whole life ahead of her. Faye had chosen him and had kept coming back to him. Edward shifted his weight back into his heels and grabbed Faye's shoulders. He wanted to watch himself and to see her sweet little mouth trying to contain him. His shirt hung down too long; with each thrust it caught over her head though he kept trying to pull it away. Finally, Edward tugged the shirt off, creating for Faye a rush of fresh air and putting them both completely unclothed together. Faye felt Edward's movement slowing down and then suddenly getting more urgent. With a deep staccato *oh—oh—oh* he pulled her head as close to him as it would go. She swallowed too hard and gagged when her brain sensed how viscous and sour the taste was. Now that they had stopped moving, the sweat at her hairline felt cool. Faye was afraid she would vomit, but she didn't. She pressed her open mouth against Edward's thigh. His lifeless penis was already shrinking back into itself.

Faye had been priming to please Doctor Vogel since they had met: acing exams, helping control other kids, modeling perfect behavior. She felt hollowed out and a little nervous, but she smiled. She had done it.

"Good job," Edward said.

His praise made Faye feel normal again.

Darkness and sleepiness disoriented Faye. She woke to feel Edward on top of her, his breathing heavy on her skin. She pressed her lips against his neck. The pungent sweetness of cologne lingered there; his breath was slightly soured by sleep. The heaviness of his body panicked her at first but then began to feel pleasant. She shifted a bit beneath his weight and wrapped her arms around him. Darkness enshrouded the bedroom. Faye wasn't sure how long they had been asleep. It had perhaps been an hour or two. Morning felt far away.

As Faye came out of sleep, only a mild sense of wakefulness rising to her consciousness, she remembered the night's triumph. She had done everything right, and she had not cried. Edward had been so pleased with her. Faye felt sort of proud of herself and ashamed all at once. She was glad to have made him happy, but lying under him now, tasting the saltiness of his skin, she hoped he would not ask her to do it again. When it went well, sleeping in Edward's bed was her favorite time. She coveted that stillness, waking and sleeping throughout the night, snuggling up against him and knowing he was there beside her. She could kiss him, then, without being kissed back. She could touch the parts of him that felt comforting without his expecting anything more aggressive and sexual. But that peace never lasted. She knew the drill from a long push-and-pull summer of argument and acquiescence.

"I want to be inside you," he whispered, his voice scratchy with desire.

Inside you. Edward's familiar script was set for stage. Through summer, he had begun each prodding with a honeyed tone. As Faye stiffened and pulled back, he would become more insistent, cajoling and then badgering until she let him wrap her hand around his penis or push himself into her mouth. *I want to feel inside you,* he would say, combing with his fingers the dark hair between Faye's legs. All Faye could think was she wanted him *outside, around* her and *enfolding* her so there was only them: no leaving for Sacred Heart and no people wondering if he loved her or why she loved him. She wanted to enjoy more of this stillness, this embrace, but she steeled herself instead for the routine to begin anew.

"I want to be inside you," Edward repeated.

The words finally clicked into place. Faye suddenly was alert and afraid. A jolt of panic coursed along Faye's arms to her fingertips. She felt a buzzing in her brain and a sharp pain at the base of her neck. Edward shifted his weight so he could push Faye's legs out on either side of him. He kissed Faye's mouth sweetly and looked into her eyes.

"Just for a minute," he said. "I want to feel inside you just a little."

Faye struggled to speak.

"Remember," she whispered. "I don't want to do that."

Edward's kissing intensified.

"It won't hurt," he said. "I promise it's okay."

Edward reached down unsteadily with one arm and re-positioned himself between her legs.

Faye's tongue felt heavy and the buzzing grew louder.

"I can't. I don't want to."

Faye looked away as the tears gathered. After last night's elation, she again was disappointing him.

Edward's voice dripped softly from his lips to hers.

"Don't be scared. I'll show you what to do."

Faye's breathing shallowed under Edward's weight. She readjusted her upper body and tried to stretch her neck. Edward rose up onto his elbows so she could untense her shoulders. He looked down toward their hips and tried awkwardly to push himself into Faye's body. With each push, Faye flinched and pulled back. Indecision seized her throat. Her ears pulsed with the sound of blood flowing through her body. The room began to waver as at the end of a vertigo spell. *Good job*, he had said, only hours ago.

She mumbled objections again.

"I can't. I'm supposed to wait."

Her strong-willed plans—so steadfast! So Catholic!—drifted powerlessly up to the five-cornered light she had used all summer as a point of separation, as an object that had held her gaze while the sounds and scents of sex had floated above and around her. Anxiety welled up from Faye's gut. He would pull back if she shouted at him. She was parched; a terrible dryness in her throat strangled her voice. Faye wanted Edward to stop. Edward knew she was waiting to have sex. He knew, but he was not listening now.

The pressure against Faye's body grew more insistent. Edward lifted himself up on his hands and rocked slowly toward her, then away. With each push, she felt herself twitch then relax, trying at once to brace herself against what was coming and to not upset Edward. It felt, she thought, like a clenched fist being pried open or a bramble of branches being pushed through slowly with a heavy tool. It was the persistent and steady uncobbling of a protective barrier. All summer she had feared he might suddenly stick his thing inside her without warning. Sex, she realized now, didn't exactly happen that way.

Maybe it won't work, she thought. *So he won't do it.*

"It's not working," Faye said.

"Yes it is," Edward said hoarsely, his voice dry and breathy like hers. "You have to let me in."

"I can't," Faye said a third time.

"Faye, it's okay." Edward leaned his head forward and locked eyes with her. "Shift your weight down toward your bottom," Edward said. "So your legs will open wider."

Faye followed Edward's directions and felt her pelvic muscles starting to loosen. Edward responded with a deep groan.

"That's it, Faye. Just like that."

Even as the tears came more quickly down Faye's cheeks, something about Edward's tone felt soothing and warm. Edward reached down to guide himself. He was instructive, Faye realized, exactly as he had been all those years at Aquinas Prep. Responding to his instruction was Faye's most coveted gift, the talent that Edward most loved.

Faye felt a concordant shift as Edward found his place inside her body. They both felt the transition, the pushing less driving now and more elastic. Once her body was broken open, after the natural obstructions had been untangled and cast aside, Faye felt hollowed out. She had fantasized about sex with Edward, thinking one day she might kiss the smooth skin by his nose and see his blue eyes glinting as he made love to her. Now, he closed his eyes and lowered his head. As Edward pressed on, Faye's insides moved frenetically, unsure when to tense or relax, to push back or to buckle. Faye looked above Edward's shoulder and counted the corners on the overhead light—*one, two, three, four, five*. She was as close to Edward now as ever she could be, her arms encircling him, their bodies knitted together. She felt further away, less visible, and more disposable than she had at Aquinas Prep.

Edward finished in an orgastic swell so quiet and intense it frightened her. Faye squeezed her wet lashes together. Edward kissed her hard then collapsed beside her, his sudden absence making her feel exposed and ashamed. Faye released a long breath she hadn't realized she was holding. Edward brushed a strand of hair from her forehead, smiled proudly, and kissed her sweetly, almost gratefully, before wrapping his arm around her waist and closing his eyes.

Before falling asleep, Edward kissed Faye just below her ear.

"I love you, Faye."

Faye cried fat, silent tears. She wondered if sex would always feel this way, her body an outwardly moving shell, the inside folding into itself like a defeated prize fighter cradling his head, trying to protect the last vestiges of life.

The night's enormous weight marked Faye's body. Her lips and mouth felt dry and gummy, covered in a hot, encasing film. She imagined scooping cold water and gulping it through her hands to get relief. Her hair was still braided but only barely so. Full sections of long strands stuck out, fuzzy and frizzy, from where they had been originally plaited. She twisted a bit with discomfort, overly aware of the summer heat emanating from her skin. Her whole body felt malnourished and dry. Down, between her legs, she felt sticky and raw, her labia slightly tender as if tiny matching bruises were forming on either side.

In Edward's bathroom mirror, Faye scrutinized her own reflection. Her cheeks looked plumper and pinker than she expected. Her eyes burned from so much crying, but they did not look puffy. She looked as she always did. But, Faye knew, she was not Faye any longer. Gone was the young Faye who had secreted a missal home from Mass and pored over the Eucharistic prayer in the quiet of her bedroom. Gone was the AP teen who skipped lunch with her best friends to serve as lector for afternoon Communion Service. Gone was the child who held her parents' hopes, she who would make them most proud because she would be chaste and proper when her brother and sisters had been otherwise. Faye had felt it predestined, not naïve, that she would maintain this kernel of dignity and grace, an inner treasure that justified the goodness adults had always seen in her. Adults trusted Faye. They took pride in her. Everyone lauded her and had great expectations for her. That Faye was gone now. Edward—*she* and Edward—had destroyed that girl. He loved her, yes! Still, joy eluded Faye this morning. At what cost had his love come? In binding herself to Edward, what had she sacrificed?

Faye felt ruined.

Dew slipped between her toes as Faye walked barefoot in the grass. Residual ocean wetness and the hot summer sun battled each morning in Citrus County, the result a mix of misty fog. Faye's fingers cramped from morning disuse. She clicked the lighter several times before a flame appeared and her cigarette caught fire. From the backyard of Edward's small lot, Faye sensed that Bonita Vista Drive was quiet. Many of the houses there were run-down and, at a glance, the beige, almost colorless exterior of Edward's house suggested shabbiness. Houses in Fulton were older than those in Osage Park where Faye lived. The city itself reflected slower times. Fulton seemed a relic now as Citrus County communities modernized and harried themselves. The whole world occupied itself with development and technology. Edward had told Faye once that most of his neighbors were elderly. Their restful retirements lent Bonita Canyon Drive a general stillness. Unlike the beach cities near Faye's side of the county, Fulton blossomed more lush trees and lengths of green grass. It suited Edward's temperament and midwestern sensibility more than the stretches of concrete and high reaching condos that dotted Vista View and had even begun to dominate Ian's rich Peninsula Pier community and the almost-as-affluent North Back Bay where Leah lived. Edward's front steps and yard were unadorned and unremarkable. They blended easily into the rest of the street. Faye never used the front door, and neither did Edward. Their outdoor life happened away from the street. Edward's back porch and his garage sat opposite each other. Both opened out toward a square yard lined systematically with trees and vines. After the drab ordinariness of the street's housefronts, Edward's back garden appeared a technicolor paradise.

As she walked, groggy but pensive, Faye found marks of Edward's handiwork framing the space. Gardening came easily and naturally to Edward. Though young Edward had balked and grumbled at farm labor, a homey comfort had risen up from the land as Edward matured. The longer Edward was away from his Kansas roots, the more earthiness had begun to steady him. Like composing, gardening stoked Edward's drive to create and beautify, if only something small, even fleeting. Tangerine trees stood single file along two sides of the yard's perimeter, a vine-covered lattice work obscuring the standard issue brick wall that divided Edward's property from the one behind. Against the garage, Faye examined several hand-made wooden enclosures latched with grates of intersecting wires. She ducked down to peer inside and found two fat rabbits, one black as tar, the other largely gray with muted white streaks. Still hunched over, cigarette smoke streaming up from the hand balanced on her thigh, Faye examined the next cage and pulled back with surprise. Upon seeing the birds housed there, Faye remembered Edward telling her freshman class that he raised chickens in his backyard. That she hadn't heard a squawk from them all summer seemed suddenly strange.

Faye felt momentarily how small a ripple she was in the ocean of Edward's life. Despite the summer's intimacies and Faye's free rein over the Fulton house in these weeks, experiencing Doctor Vogel's real life had unearthed truths she had never expected. Faye had thought Doctor Vogel a fledgling romantic, outwardly brusque to shield a wounded person inside. Now, she knew otherwise. Away from Aquinas Prep, Edward's abrupt and degrading tone in the bedroom, his emotional volatility, and his disregard for the boundaries she set disabused Faye of those notions. She could deny it no longer: there was almost nothing about Edward she knew for sure.

In the center of Edward's garden, a plum tree grew. Rich, ripe fruit hung heavy on the plum tree's branches. Muted gold specks dotted the plums' deep purple skin. Enticed in her thirst by the fruit's lush appearance, Faye reached immediately for a plum and tore into its flesh. The texture was ripe and juicy but deceptively so. Though the inside pulp dripped ruddy and rich, the taste was sour instead of sweet. Faye grimaced as the bitter fruit slid down her throat. She dropped the once bitten plum to the ground where other overripe fruit had fallen. Dewy droplets having wetted her feet, a chill passed through Faye. Suddenly, she felt exposed, her thin summer nightdress offering too little coverage. Thinking of the night's events, Faye rubbed her bare foot along the stones that encircled the tree's base. Faye shook her head with grave disappointment. *I never thought you would do this.*

But yes, he had done it. Edward had taken Faye's most precious stone when he knew, he must have known, how desperately she wanted to keep it. She willed back tears, too drained for more weeping. She vowed to forget. There existed no other way forward.

Faye stubbed out her cigarette as Edward appeared at the screen door.

"It's so early, Faye. Come back to bed."

Edward extended his hand. She took it, so warm and supple. She searched his eyes pleadingly. *Fix this awful feeling,* she begged. Faye could not name the sensations that swirled in her now. She could not be angry at Edward. Where would that anger leave her? After the night's loss, letting go of him would be certain death, an anguish too great to survive.

"I can't. I have to be home to make my grandma's breakfast. What time is it?"

Edward glanced behind him at the kitchen clock.

"Almost 5:30."

"I really should go."

"Always the good girl," he said. "Please, stay for a little while."

Two parts of Faye's psyche had been colliding all summer. Faye was young and inexperienced. She had hardly been kissed all through high school. But Edward wanted her! Edward had given Faye a sneak peak into adult life. It was thrilling, really, that a grown man like Edward would do such special, intimate things to her. In six weeks' time, though, the fantasy had darkened. Edward desired her too intensely and was too unforgiving of her youth. Now, it had come to this, an irreparable rent in her moral sense of who she was. Unworthiness blanketed her. Faye was not *good* anymore.

Fresh coffee percolating in the kitchen, Faye laid her head in her hands at the dining table. Edward appeared at ease.

"Did you not sleep well?"

"I guess," Faye said dully.

He reached down to massage her shoulders and kiss the base of her neck.

"I slept great," he said, smugly. "Last night was intense." His touch slid down her arms. He took both her hands in his. "And wonderful."

Pride surged in Faye. She let out a long sigh, trying to reconcile Edward's happiness with her own sense that something had gone horribly wrong. His serenity baffled her. *Blameless*, she thought. Edward looked blameless and unwearied. Resentment toward him roiled. How, now, could he seem so unbothered? Faye tried to enjoy his attention, but wooziness swept in and she thought she might faint. Edward talked over his shoulder as he poured his coffee.

"I picked up croissants from *Pain de Amis* yesterday. I know how you love them."

Faye perked up at this assertion.

"How did you know I love croissants?"

"You told me," he said, placing a pink pastry box in front of her. "In Paris."

"In Paris?" she asked, incredulously.

Parisian hotel lobbies sprang to Faye's imagination. More than a year had passed since Paris. They had spent the first three days of their European tour there, Faye eating nothing but croissants and tomatoes because she was too picky (and, frankly, too childish) to try the many vegetables and meats in the French buffets spread before her. Those were the earliest days of her flirtation with Doctor Vogel. The inkling of desire was just beginning to form then, and Faye had not yet decided whether to expel or embrace it. While Faye had been building her image of Edward, cataloging his history and memorizing each bit of him she could gather, Edward had, it seemed, been doing the same. She was stunned by the possibility that he had loved her so long. The thought increased her confusion. She had been plucking invisible petals for months. *He loves me. He loves me not. He loves me.* She could never be sure. Indeed, she would never be sure.

Fluffy pastry folds melted on Faye's tongue. The nutty aroma of Edward's coffee intensified her hunger. The velvety smoothness of the croissant lingered richly in her mouth, which began, again, to feel dry and uncomfortable. She felt parched and suddenly famished.

Edward tore a piece from a croissant and folded it into his mouth.

"Authentic, right?"

"Yes," Faye agreed. "Very French."

"A classic *le petit-déjeuner.*"

Faye smiled. A song melody dropped into her head.

"Hearing you speak French just reminded me of singing *Le Chant des Oiseaux* at the Park Newport competition."

"Lord," Edward cried, throwing his hands up in the air. "Don't remind me of that debacle. What a nightmare. Our one ignominious Chamber Singers failure!"

"It wasn't that bad," Faye said soothingly.

Edward chuckled. "Time has altered your memory. It's been too long since you've heard the recording."

"Maybe so," Faye remarked, melting another shard of croissant on her tongue.

The buttery flakes comforted her, as did the conversation. During their summer romance, it had seemed improper to remind themselves that Faye and Edward were essentially still teacher and student. Better it was to believe they had, from the heavens, been dropped fully in love into Edward's bed with summer's dawning. Just when Faye had been pushed to the brink of despair, this bit of reminiscing revived their intimacy. Faye could feel them both relaxing back into their roles. This was office floor talk, the type they had perfected in the past year.

Edward laughed a groggy chuckle.

"I felt like a plate-spinner trying to hold you all together."

The material had baffled the Chamber kids in the earliest days of their rehearsal. *You guys sound like Daffy Duck doing tongue twisters*, she remembered Edward saying. They all laughed then, all the kids, though to them it really was not that funny. Faye remembered because Edward had laughed so much. The joke had started small and, for some unseen reason, captivated Edward. His laugh grew from a light chuckle to a boisterous roar that brought a wet sheen to his eyes and deep pink color to his cheeks. The other kids giggled, too. Faye had watched Edward laugh and had felt her heart blooming at the sound of his delight.

"The French lyrics were too fast and too complicated. You said we sounded like Daffy Duck," Faye said, surfacing the time-worn memory.

Edward's eyes wrinkled in a smile at the remembrance of this past moment.

"I swear you remember everything," he said, embracing the safety of such familiar territory.

Faye wanted to stay here, too. "I know the actual French line, but what again is the translation?"

"*Réveillez vous, cœurs endormis,*" he said in French.

Edward cupped Faye's cheek in his hand and kissed her lips softly.

"Awake," he whispered into her mouth. "Awake, sleepy hearts."

Her question brought Doctor Vogel out from where he had been hiding behind Edward. She loved to hear him speak this way. With resolve,

Faye could push down the doubt. She wanted to stay in this cherished space, rife with ease and warmth instead of conflict. This love could erase the night's breach.

Edward's expression turned lustful.

"How is—" he paused, "—*everything* feeling this morning?"

Faye blushed, and her cheeks grew tingly. She shifted in her seat. *Fine* is what she would say. She could not tell Edward that she felt like she had peed herself (she knew she hadn't and that her period was still a couple weeks away), that even now, sitting at the table, her underwear felt so wet she feared whatever fluids were gathered there would start running down her legs. She couldn't ask Edward if this was normal. She thought something might be wrong and didn't know how she would find out. She could ask no one.

"Fine."

She added, in a whisper, "a little sore."

Edward brushed his hand across her breast and smiled playfully.

"Next time will be easier."

Next time?

Her stomach dropped. Anger rose. Faye eyed Edward sharply, then stood to leave.

"I better go. My grandma usually wakes by 7."

Faye gathered her things quickly from the bedroom, shoving last night's clothes down deep enough to seal her bookbag's stubborn zipper. At the back door, Edward stopped her.

"Call me later," he said. "I love you."

The morning sun had finally caught up with them. Bright light filled the kitchen and blazed in Edward's deep blue eyes, those beautiful depths she had been swimming in for months. Edward's face shone with optimism and self-possession. Faye did not know, yet, how fast feelings can flow after sex. Many times over she would learn this lesson, that sex could buoy and uphold the men she adored more than all her love ever could.

She smiled, wide and proud. "I love you, too."

Chamber Singer Summer Prep Week commenced! The new Chamber Singers flitted and flirted and laughed in great anticipation for the school year that was starting. Leah and Tommy pushed away thoughts of Faye and Ian and the whole mess of drama they had stirred up at graduation time. For Edward, turning this new page was a bit more complicated than usual. On these other teen-aged girls, Edward could smell the same bright, coquettish perfume that Faye wore.

The black leather seat of Edward's office chair cushioned and relieved him mid-day when the choir broke for lunch. Teaching after so many summer weeks off exhausted him. A din floated in from the adjacent room. The kids clumsily ate sub sandwiches and yelled to each other across the risers. Edward closed his eyes for a moment's rest and remembered Faye's visit to his office the previous week. Her shy tongue had lightly licked his lower lip. Her body, always so wet, had opened to his hands. The memory turned to fantasy. Edward pictured Faye on his desk, her perfect young nipple in his mouth.

Edward took a drink of lukewarm coffee from his morning thermos and eyed the phone. He picked up and replaced the receiver twice before dialing and getting Faye on the line. Instead of abating, his lust increased. *Bad idea*, he thought. A warm tingle spread across his abdomen and down between his thighs when he heard her voice. It was a puzzle, to be sure. Before this summer, Edward had prided himself on self-control. He had controlled his thoughts, his libido, and his emotions. Not for lack of trying, he could not determine now (nor would he ever) how Faye had broken through his carefully constructed restraint and had started this dangerous snowballing. He ended the conversation quickly to return to his waiting students.

"I've got to get back," he said. "I love you. See you tonight."

Fed up was what he was.

The argument began in the bedroom when Faye asked if they could, please, for her last night, keep their clothes on for God's sake and just spend time being together.

"Come on, Faye. Can we just have a good time tonight without all the drama?"

Old fears reared. She managed a weak apology.

"I'm sorry."

Then, with more strength, she begged. "It's my last night with you. Can we please, for the love of God, just not do all this stuff? I don't want you to take my clothes off. I just want time with you."

He did not concede.

"We're both stressed," Edward said gently. "We're both tired."

She fought against the rich, cajoling warmth of his voice.

"I love you, Faye. I thought you loved me. Let me make love to you," he cooed. "You'll feel better after. Trust me."

Unbelievable, she thought. *Look who wants to talk about love, now.*

"I do love you, but I don't want to do that. I told you that when this whole thing started. You knew I did not want to do that." Faye paused. "But you did it anyway."

Edward sat back and cocked his head. Hot, incredulous anger welled up.

"Wait just a minute," he said sternly. "Don't you dare say that."

A litany of protestations flowed forth.

"I don't like where this is going. I did not *force* you to do anything."

"I did not want to have sex. I wanted to wait. I've always said that."

"It sure sounded like you were enjoying it," he said snidely.

Faye was confused and embarrassed. She spoke quietly this time.

"I was crying," she said.

You are always *crying*, Edward thought, fear winding its way into his fingers and up his throat. Anger begot panic.

"Why are you talking like this? Are you trying to set me up?"
Edward was furious.

Faye balked.

No, Doctor, she thought with such great disappointment. *I have not shed all these tears and suffered all this humiliation so I could set you up.*

Faye's mind was a turbulent sea. Memories rose like rough waters tossing her about—Faye and her friends laughing with Doctor on the hillsides of Assisi, Faye basking in Doctor's praise in the Aquinas Prep choir room. And then, there followed the first night in his bed, the ravaging, the fear, and, my God, that first sleepover, an awful baptism by terror that had nearly destroyed her. Faye had learned quickly that summer: no, she did not want to do any of those things. And yet, she had kept on. She could not stop being a kid, and he could not stop being grown. She suspected too late that it was just that simple.

Edward rephrased and recriminated. "What are you trying to do?"

Faye spoke meekly, her tone tired. "I'm trying to love you."

Quiet enveloped them. The accusations stopped and frustrations receded. Faye tasted a salty tear on the corner of her lip.

Edward lowered her back to the bed, lay beside, and held her.

Her pulse slowed, and she smiled, the tension uncoiling in her limbs. "This is perfect, see? Now, can we make out like teenagers?"

Edward laughed and put Faye's fingers to his lips. "You really are keeping me young tonight, aren't you?"

Winding the blue ribbon back into Faye's hair, Edward sensed a fog of heaviness rolling in.

A sharp wrinkle of worry cut into Faye's brow.

He tried to cheer her.

"You'll be fine. In a few days, you'll wonder what all the fuss was about."

He finished tying a bow and draped his arms around her shoulders from behind.

"Call me when you get settled at school."

She questioned him.

"Do you love me?"

They kissed.

"Yes. I love you."

Faye pressed further. "How long will you love me?"

Edward sighed and spoke.

"Until I can't love you anymore."

Chamber Singer Prep Week ended with the annual Chamber Singer Reunion, a gathering of the elite group's alumni stretching from Faye and her friends back to Edward's first group of seniors who had graduated in 1989. The generally cold Aquinas Prep choir room humidified and grew clammy as more bodies joined in. Students and alumni littered the risers and stood in groups balancing paper plates so thin they grew transparent in the spots where greasy pizza sat. The current Chamber Singers and the newly-minted alumni, like Faye, looked with awe at the alumni in their mid-20s who came to drink flavorless orange punch from tiny paper cups and reminisce about the good old days. Edward conversed comfortably with these men (Faye recognized Phillip Van Der Linden from old choir room photos). With his operatic obesity and full beard, Phillip looked as old as Edward, though, Faye calculated, he could not be more than twenty-six even if he had been in Edward's first Aquinas Prep choir.

Unbelievable, Faye thought, watching Edward's constant twittering among his former students. It all seemed so easy for him. Sadness weighted Faye. Leah looked once in her direction, the caramel warmth of her eyes contrasting a pursed steeliness on her lips. Visions of their friendship had haunted Leah since the incident at the summer morning meeting. Leah had told no one about the fluttering paper carrying her teen-aged friend's flowery script from Doctor Vogel's bed to the foyer of Leah's house. She had prayed the morning of the reunion, had actually closed her eyes and clasped her fingers, in the hopes that Faye would skip the Prep Week festivities.

Leah expected that Faye would look triumphant, but her old friend oozed exhaustion. At first, Leah couldn't quite place the unusualness of Faye's demeanor. *Yes*, she thought now. *Faye looks like she wants to talk*. Leah's heart pulsed an extra long beat. The memory of their intimacies begged mercy from Leah. She could feel Faye's head resting in her lap while they lay in the AP Grotto. She could hear the loudness of the girls' laughter. *No*, Leah whispered. Faye had brought this on herself and on all of them, too. Leah turned on her heels and found Clara, a transfer student who now occupied Faye's second alto slot. There was no one left to listen to Faye, which was exactly what Faye deserved.

Edward, too, ignored her. Faye leaned against the risers' railing. The cool metal caressed her cheek and steadied her against the waves of anxiety that gripped her throat. She was Doctor Vogel's lover. Yet, Faye stood alone. Phillip Van Der Linden and Edward's first award-winning chamber choir; Leah and Tommy and their classmates, the last AP choir Edward would direct—they would know Doctor Vogel so much longer than she. They would write letters and stage rallies in his name, they would attend his wedding, and they would send compassionate notes of encouragement as cancer ate away the man they could never blame. Yes, they would know Doctor Vogel so much longer than she. Faye knew *Edward*, and knowing him meant losing everything else.

Faye approached the office door when Edward finally broke away from his fans. He met her eyes briefly then looked past her to the reunion revelry just beyond the threshold. Faye's pulse quickened and her voice came out cracked and scared.

"Can I come over tonight," she paused, "for a final good-bye?"

Edward sighed. The sigh continued beyond his breath into his words. He had looked ebullient a moment before, but such had faded now. Faye's neediness in this dangerous environment tired him.

"No, Faye. You can't. We had last week and we had last night. How many good-byes are we going to have?"

His words struck her, as if a blow.

"I need to go back out there," he said sternly. "We can't be in the office alone."

Edward's brusqueness perplexed her. She spoke condescendingly.

"You and I are *always* in the office alone," she scoffed. "I was Choir President three months ago." (*My God, had summer been that short?*)

Faye wanted to reach for him, but a strange immobility stopped her.

"It's different now," he said, leaving her behind and emerging into a sea of welcoming disciples.

The sky darkened as they walked in scattered clusters from the choir room to the chapel. The onset of dusk felt to Faye like the sky was falling. There, in the very place she had exalted him, Edward had denied her. They had changed, but Aquinas Prep had not. The chapel smelled of dust and incense. The sanctuary's smallness captured and held every scent. Dark tones created a consistent dimness that made the chapel feel like an unused relic. The new Chamber Singers sat apart from the alumni. Faye seated herself in the back row away from the crowd. Merton stepped in beside her and squeezed Faye's hand. She hoped he could not feel the nervous clamminess spreading across her palms. Amidst rich, angelic tones, Faye sank deeper. She felt herself coming apart. *Come into me*, the choir intoned. *And I will give you rest*. Faye recognized the deep, mournful pulling of the violin. The *Requiem* played often at Edward's house. Its harmonies transported her there now. *Come into me*, the music exhorted. Behind closed eyes she ran reels of the summer's intimate moments, feeling the pleasant warmth of Edward's head in her lap on the couch. She conjured the softness of his hair through her fingers and remembered the heat rising off his damp skin just out of the shower.

Even in that moment, when she had not yet lost him, Faye's mind worked overtime burying the trauma. *It will all be gone soon*, the protective voice inside her said. The nauseating smell of semen at that ghastly first sleepover. Gone. Gone the sounds of Edward's feet stomping away when she sobbed in his bed. All gone, the stifling terror of Edward's hot thighs pushing down on her while her mind flipped somersaults and looked for a way out from beneath him. The humiliation visited upon Faye that summer filtered down from her conscious mind to a place she could hardly find it. The panic soaked into the cells of her body, hiding in the very blood and tissue that comprised her existence. There, the trauma burrowed, waiting for another time to rise up and merge back into the Faye everyone else could see. *I will give you rest*, the voices repeated in a rousing fugue. Fatigue descended on Faye. She was tired of chasing Edward and so very tired of running from him and fighting with him.

Phillip Van Der Linden's faded AP Chamber Singer tee shirt stared Faye in the face when she opened her eyes. Its original AP red was a pinky white from over-wear, and the screen printed words looked strained from stretching for many years across his broad back. Still, Faye could read them: *To God Be The Glory*. As Faye stood musing, the opening prayer had become the *Kyrie* and led on to the *Gloria*. Tommy sang, and the bodies around her swayed ever so slightly in response. From wall to wall of stained glass and dark wood, Faye saw the faces of life's goodness. She saw devotion and excitement and desire and serenity. Here, in the Church and the chapel, Faye receded away from this peace. The glory of the *Gloria* eluded her as she let her eyes fall on Edward, still, for her, the consummate face of God. *When you sing*, Edward had always said, *you pray twice*. (Faye was passing the adage onto her own children by the time she discovered that the phrase had originated not with Edward but with Saint Augustine.) Faye did not sing, but, oh Lord, how she prayed. She prayed that Edward would notice her. Without his reassurance, Faye thought she might cease to be.

Gabriel Buford, his pimply face gleaming and eyes bright behind tiny-framed glasses, rang the bells too loudly for the small sanctuary. In unison, heads raised, then lowered. Eyes opened wide, then closed. The synchronization amazed and saddened Faye. On her knees for the consecration, she struggled to focus. When a teary film stretched across her eyes, the host wavered and became blurry. In their midst, a miraculous conversion announced itself. The consecration and *their* consummation and all the summer's trials suffused the fragrant air and the heat Faye felt flowing through her ears. A nervous apprehension stilled her. Yet, as she contemplated Edward's prayerful posture and the profile of his warmly tinged cheek, Faye felt a supple vibration move through her. *How she loved him!* They rose amidst the klanking of repositioned kneelers. Edward's eyes met Faye's. His countenance was more pious and aglow than usual. He looked away quickly without smiling.

At communion, Edward's throaty voice reverberated through the chapel. *The Body of Christ*, he said to each recipient, his voice and Fr. Jerry's a holy fugue as they distributed communion to the lines of kids snaking their way up the aisle. A litany of Catholic-school kids presented themselves before Edward. Gabriel and Thomas and Bernadette and Peter and each of three Sarahs and two Josephs and Joshua and Leah and Beth and Kathleen—each took the host in turn, receiving in their hands the very essence of Incarnation. As she approached, Faye felt both light-headed and unbearably heavy. At the front of the line, Edward stood, fully revealed, in front of her.

He spoke flatly.

"The Body of Christ."

She took and ate it. The Eucharist tasted starchy and dry, a lifeless cracker. There was no healing in it.

VII

DEPARTING FROM LOS ANGELES, FAYE sat between her parents like a little child. In the air over Chicago, Faye peered around her mother's shoulder and studied the ground below. The divided farmland stretched for miles in perfectly cordoned off patches. The neat angularity of it soothed her. She had cried so hard and so often before leaving. Now, Faye allowed this moment of calm and sank into it. As she did, a microscopic cluster of life began to grow, searching Faye's insides for fertile soil. From their two infinitesimally tiny seeds, Edward and Faye's child wormed and burrowed its way quietly and unobserved into the soft folds of Faye's uterus.

Faye collected phone numbers and danced to the 80s at the Sacred Heart Graffiti Tee Shirt Welcome Dance. Early evening nerves decreased with each new person Faye met. The people at Sacred Heart impressed Faye with their perfectly assembled outfits, big white teeth, and overflowing confidence. They seemed impossibly perfect. Still, they were friendly. Some of the boys reeked of too much cologne or slurred their speech under too many watery beers, but they were cute and excited and they made Faye feel a little excitement, too. Thoughts of Edward stood guard at the back of her mind, but maybe Sacred Heart could offer some balm, Faye thought, to soothe the ache of being away from home. Her tee shirt, bright white at the start, was almost filled now with names and numbers. Ben was the first boy to sign.

"As in *Ben there, done that*," he had said proudly, a hearty laugh balling up his dark, smooth cheeks to reveal a wide, glossy smile. "I'm in Disher," he continued, pointing at Faye's residence hall badge, "right next door. Looks like we're neighbors."

Ben stuck the purple cap of a marker into his mouth and wrote his four-digit student phone exchange in large font across the flat expanse between Faye's neck and her breasts. A sweet blend of cool aqua deodorant and cigarillo smoke rose up from Ben's Sharpie-covered tee. Faye's stomach flipped then settled. The electric energy at Sacred Heart easily overwhelmed her.

"Maybe I'll see you around, then," Faye offered as she turned to leave.

"Wait! I need your number, too!"

Ben offered his marker and turned his back to her. She wrote awkwardly in an open space across his left shoulder. A veneer of dampness pulled his shirt against his skin. Faye's fingers felt his warmth where she touched him to steady her writing.

As Faye headed back to her dorm, boys with mousse-slicked hair and ice-cream colored polo shirts ducked in and out of the crowds around her. The tangle of bodies only increased her loneliness. At first it seemed she missed Krystal and Ian and her parents and Edward. Really, though, the feeling was more than that. It was worse than that. Their voices on the phone rang hollow. The desperation that sat just behind her calculated facade grew more insistent, not less, when calls came in from home. Faye could not feel at home here.

The baby, unseen and unknown, flipped and floated and folded in on itself, multiplying by dividing from the smallest spark to an explosion of life inside her.

Ben never called Faye, and Faye never called Ben, and none of it mattered because she only wanted to listen to sad songs (from that summer), wallow under her bright canary comforter (the sunny color a mockery as the tears slid down her face), and wait for Edward to call. Sadness gnawed at Faye's stomach. A persistent queasiness settled in by the end of her first week at Sacred Heart. Eating turned her stomach but not eating left a sourness that spread out from her gut to the tips of her fingers. Faye subsisted on cigarettes and cherry lifesavers. She sat each night smoking on the cold concrete lions that guarded the South Quad residence halls.

"I know you're sad, but you need to eat or you'll get sick," Edward said, his fatherly tone reaching to her through the phone. "You need to get out there and make some friends."

Faye rejected Edward's advice. It was easy for him, she thought. Nothing had changed in his world. A new year started at Aquinas Prep. Leah and Tommy and dozens of other students stood in the same spots and told the same inside jokes as they had a year before. Of course life at Aquinas Prep would recycle each fall, but Faye was surprised when it actually pushed forward without her.

Peggy coaxed Faye out once or twice for fresh, doughy cookies with the other girls who gathered after midnight at the Sugar Shack in their dorm basement. The sweet aroma wound its way up the staircase to Peggy and Faye's second-floor room. The smell wobbled Faye's stomach muscles. Most days those first few weeks, Faye moved in a daze between her dorm room and the O'Casey Center for Language Arts. Three weeks in, Faye woke feeling peckish and strange. She stopped at South Dining Hall for a crisp Belgian waffle with thick cherry topping. She thought it might sit heavy in her stomach, but the more she ate, the hungrier she got. Filling her stomach felt satisfying in a way nothing had since leaving Citrus County. Having stacked her empty tray along the conveyor belt of dirty dining hall dishes, Faye noticed the time and hopped a bit down the steps into the quad. She was late for work at Golden Burger in the Sacred Heart Student Union. A few minutes later, Faye's stomach lurched as she stood behind the greasy counter tying her apron. The fullness of breakfast still stuck around, but she almost felt like eating again. An acidic liquid pooled in her cheeks and at the base of her throat. Faye wished she had a few more bites of waffle to sop up the nauseous fluid.

Debbie, an unassuming, thirty-something Potato Creek native with big eyes and a toothy grin, manned the register. A Golden Burger veteran, Debbie chatted away with Faye every shift they shared, and the two had become fast confidantes. Friendships did not spring up often between Sacred Heart students and the surrounding townsfolk. Debbie knew this well from six years working at the university. But something about Faye caught Debbie's eye. She seemed nervously adrift in the presence of other students and genuinely interested in the lives of Debbie and the other Potato Creek workers. What's more, Faye did not loaf around like most of the Sacred Heart students Debbie had worked with over the years. The two ladies moved in sync and laughed often as they worked. Faye wrapped burgers and scooped fries and called ticket numbers and handed extra packets of barbeque sauce to college kids who hardly looked up to notice the workers engineering their Student Union experience. As Faye rounded the corner to the front station, Debbie noticed a pale wave pass over Faye's face.

"You okay my little friend? You look a bit green."

Pushing her stomach out against her palm, Faye pulled air deep into her core to steady the nausea.

"I think I'm okay," she said. "Waffles aren't sitting well."

Debbie set a protective hand on Faye's waist. "I'll cover you," she said sweetly. "Go splash some water on your face or get some air. Air will do you good."

Debbie slipped the greasy plastic fry scoop expertly into a paper sleeve. She leaned over the hot fry bin. A small crowd of students milled about or waited for their burgers, but the open order ticket collection numbered only a few. Golden Burger's busiest rush wouldn't arrive for another two hours. After hesitating, Faye assented, a lump forming at the base of her throat.

"Good girl," Debbie called from behind. "You know," she added, "you've been queasy a lot lately. You're not pregnant, are you?"

A dome-shaped light, just smaller than a thimble, blinked on the dorm phone keypad in sync with the *brrrrrrring* of every phone call. Even when the phone was switched to silent, Faye and Peggy could see the light flashing through the night. She felt like smashing that light, Faye did, because not answering Krystal's calls was driving her crazy. She could not talk to Krystal now. Krystal, who had lost her virginity (unprotected) at fourteen, who had slept with three guys senior year (before Ian forced a modicum of chastity upon her), and who had done any number of irresponsible things in between, would react with the same capriciously dramatic tone she always did when Faye floundered. Nothing bothered Krystal. She was just confident enough and rich enough to stay untouched as she cavorted through life. Besides, this confession would unleash a cascade of other humiliations and secrets she had been hiding. Faye had to go it alone.

Summer felt years away. Forever, Faye had been burrowed under blankets in a stark, concrete dorm room, her head spinning, the baby (all those tiny baby particles) pushing acid up into her throat. Forever, golden stalks of corn had been whizzing by while Faye sat listlessly in Debbie's dusty Nissan station wagon, her forehead pressed against the cool window. For years, it must have been, the blipping and beeping of machines had been sounding frightfully through the Potato Creek Women's Care Center as Debbie's gentle hand held the tips of Faye's fingers.

Time stretched impossibly long. Faye remembered Ms. DeGroot's class on Christian Life. She heard Ms. DeGroot's deep, raspy voice now, reverberating in her head as it had bounced off the walls of her classroom in the 400 wing at Aquinas Prep: *All of time unfolds,* Faye heard her say, *forward and backward in an interminable succession and progression. We choose and we live and we die, but God is UP HERE.* Ms. DeGroot had held her hand high and lifted up on her toes. *God is up here, so far up here that he can see it all, past and future, as it unspools. He gave us free will. We choose the path,* she had said conclusively. *But God knows. He knows it and can see our choice already.* The memory sent a chill across Faye's exposed arms. Deep breaths followed shallow ones. She felt God watching her from above. Faye had not yet chosen, so how—how could He know whether she would throw away Edward's child?

Posters dotted the walls of the clinic. *Breast Is Best. Know Your Rights. You Have Options. No Means No.* This last sign caught Faye's attention. She narrowed her eyes to better read the smaller font beneath the glaring headline:

Unresponsive Means NO
Sick Means NO
Intoxicated Means NO
Silence Means NO
Crying Means NO
Date Rape IS Rape

The sour feeling of shame trickled out through Faye's limbs. She nodded ever so slowly. *Crying was supposed to mean no,* she thought. How many times, though, can a person say no? How small can a girl fold herself until the girl disappears and only the body remains? How does a girl's *no* stand up to a man's insistence? Edward loved her. She learned this summer that real love meant going along.

Faye flinched at the *click click* of the steel speculum as it cranked open inside her body. Her calves tensed. She pulled her insides as deep into herself as she could. Thoughts clashed about in her brain, flashing and dying out so she couldn't properly focus. She could hardly hear the doctor prattling on about precautions and procedures. The faces of the women at the Her Choice clinic in Citrus County swam into view now. The day of the Rite to Life protest receded in her memory. It must have been ages ago, all those ages ago when she had been a child. Soon, she would be one of those women whom she had wrongly shamed.

The baby inside her was, Faye had read, no bigger than a pomegranate seed and with hardly more potential. It had no thoughts, no heartbeat, no eyes. The baby was a lump of cells destined for miscarriage or growth or reproduction or deformity. There was no telling which. But of some fates, Faye was certain. If she allowed this elastic structure, this unfulfilled shell of a human to grow, Faye herself would slink away and become an empty shell of the girl she had been. No one could forgive her the wrongs that had brought Edward's child to life in her body. If her love of Edward had been unspeakable, this embroiling and embarrassing of her parents and her family and all of Aquinas Prep was unthinkable. The sin lay not in the snuffing out of this bundle (now digging deeper into her tissue for warmth, for life) but in the cowardice of choosing the life she knew over the life she knew God would provide. She had every advantage. Faye knew that her options, unlike some of those Citrus County women, were many.

Debbie's car squeaked and squealed when she pushed in the clutch. They drove back to Sacred Heart in a glum lack of small talk. An acrid smell, almost sweet but mostly bitter, drifted through town. The strength of it pulled a headache to the back of Faye's eyes. She lit a cigarette to refocus her breathing.

She questioned Debbie softly. "What is that smell?"

"It's leaves," she said matter-of-factly. "Burning."

Faye's eyebrows arched in confusion.

"When there's too many to pack and trash, people burn the dead leaves in big ol' piles."

A disbelieving grunt rose in Faye's throat. Television shows and wall calendars and screen savers showing fall in the Midwest had omitted this oddity. Everyone on the California coast imagined falling leaves in bright reds and sunny yellows. No one pictured a blazing pile of decay, the color drained, the stench spreading headaches across the bucolic landscape.

"I can't go through with it," Faye said weakly to the passing trees. Debbie's hand on Faye's arm brought her out of this daze. She turned to face her friend.

"I don't want to have an abortion." She paused. "Do you think that's crazy?"

Tears welled into Debbie's big eyes.

"I've had three babies myself," she said. "You won't regret it a day in your life."

The tip of Faye's cigarette glowed brightly. She blew a plume of smoke toward the window, unconvinced.

Debbie continued.

"Here's something else, my little friend."

Debbie looked Faye straight in the eye as if to say *this here is the truth*. "I had an abortion when I was about your age. And I don't never regret it neither. Not one day."

"Thanks for taking me to get checked out," Faye said. "I'm going to have the baby."

Peggy curled a lock of hair so tightly around her finger that the skin started to plump and redden. She hadn't signed up for this, for navigating a strange roommate's even stranger romantic *situation*. Crinkly worry lines dug into the skin around Faye's eyes. She came and went without much comment these days, and Peggy wondered if she were even attending classes. The Aquinas Prep Choir sweatshirt Faye often wore to bed started appearing outside the dorm as well. Worst of all, something seemed to have shifted behind Faye's eyes.

"That guy called," Peggy stammered. "He said to call him with your calling card around five California time and that he'd call you back."

"Thanks for the message," Faye said wanly. She plopped face down on top of her billowing comforter and buried her head in the pillow.

The seed that was a baby pushed tiny roots into Faye's inner soil. She talked to it inside her head and thought about getting to know it. She felt less lonely when she thought of herself as two rather than one. When Faye imagined the bud unfolding, a suffocating panic dried out her mouth and created a gagging sensation at the back of her throat. The seed was a secret that no one could keep. Its growth would consume Faye. The seed would be bigger than she, its babyness overshadowing every accomplishment she had worked for. Soon, when the world looked at Faye, it would see only the moment of baby's shocking creation. And what would Edward see? Two cigarettes first to steady her thoughts, then Faye would call Edward. She would tell him tonight about the baby.

Edward answered, then clicked the phone dead so he could return Faye's call on his dime. The phone bill had climbed up and up as calls shot back and forth among Faye's best friends now scattered to Virginia, Boston, and North Carolina. In the preceding few days, the conversations had dried up. Keeping food down and her spirits up were all Faye could manage while still dragging herself to early morning classes and flashing weak smiles to the other girls in her dorm.

"Give me the rundown," Edward said, the pause of a faint swallow halting his speech. Faye imagined Edward swirling his whiskey glass as he often did. "Will you go out with friends tonight?"

Faye answered with a shrug. The prodding about friendships and social activities annoyed Faye. Homesickness overwhelmed her. How could Edward be so blasé about it all? What was she supposed to find exciting about being so far away from the only person she wanted to be near?

She redirected. "This week has been reading intensive. I have another hundred pages of Victorian literature to get through tonight."

"You sound tired," Edward said sympathetically, "and that's saying something. I didn't think you ever got tired." He chuckled, pleased. "That's one thing I'll never forget about watching you at Aquinas Prep. You were my Super Girl in action."

Faye smiled into the receiver. The gleam from Edward's praise invigorated her.

"I miss those days," she said sweetly, "and I miss you so much."

A thoughtful moan rushed out from Edward's lips. "And what is it that you miss about me?"

Her stomach muscles buckled at Edward's lascivious tone. There was a rhythm to their phone calls. She suffered the small talk, the veiled arguments, and the dirty talk, waiting each time for the *I love yous* that brought absolution for it all.

"Sleeping beside you is my favorite part. I miss it."

He scoffed. "You like listening to me snore?"

"I like staying with you. I like not racing home for curfew."

"Ah yes, the dreaded midnight curfew," he said playfully. "I bet it's nice now not having it."

Confusion curled Faye's lips. Why would she dread curfew here in Potato Creek without him?

"There's no one here to stay out for," she said. "I miss holding you."

Again she sensed the swish of ice cubes in Edward's glass.

"I miss you holding me too," he said with a mischievous lift in his voice. "I wish you were holding me right now, but not the way you mean."

A quick pang swirled through Faye's thighs. Her throat tightened.

"I bet you do."

"I suppose I'll have to do it myself instead."

Faye let the line go quiet. The memory of that first sleepover never left her. It all stayed with her: the racing thoughts, the feeling of being trapped and then humiliated, Edward's deep groan, and the putrid smell of his semen on her shirt. It shocked Faye that she felt as scared now, holding the phone, as she had those days in his bed.

After a moment, Edward spoke again. "It can wait. Tell me more about your day."

Relief. Reprieve. Faye brightened.

"My day is boring. Tell me yours. What's going on in Chambers?"

She waited. "How are my old friends?"

Hesitation marked Edward's response. The cavern that had opened between Faye and Leah, between Faye and Tommy, and between Faye and everyone she had left behind brought as much hurt upon Faye as it brought relief to Edward. As he passed by that afternoon, he had heard Leah whispering to another girl. They stopped abruptly when they caught Edward half-listening. He assumed they had been talking about Faye. Their eyes darted quickly askance as they spoke. The words *summer* and *Indiana* stuck out in their conversation. The dread moved with Edward past the risers into the office.

Edward tried a sympathetic tone to pacify Faye. Honestly, he didn't want her keeping in touch with Leah or any of his choir kids. The sooner they all forgot about Faye, the more quickly he could bury the truth of what they had done and outrun the sense that the world was closing in on him.

"Do you mean old friends as in former friends or friends from long ago?"

A flush rose to Faye's cheeks. Leah and Tommy ignored her calls all summer. Sure, their friendships had fizzled out slowly through the second half of her senior year, the divide growing greater as Faye spent more time with Krystal and as Faye and the other seniors got ready to graduate and go off to college. But there was more to it. Faye sensed something more than mere indifference to her. It was more like hostility. Coldness came through in the few terse words Leah had spoken to Faye on the phone that summer. No, Leah did not want one last drive down the coast, music booming and cigarette smoke blowing, before Faye left for Sacred Heart. No, Leah did not think it was a good idea that Faye have a summer party with the whole gang of friends that had been so close in Europe and at Renaissance Pageant time. It was better, Leah had said, to just move on. Faye didn't know what could have made Leah enforce such a totalizing blockade against her.

"Both, I guess. Being so far away is surreal. It's like I've been cut off from everyone."

"Trust me," Faye recognized Edward's teacher tone here, "being cut off from those kids is the best thing for you."

Faye tired months before of this argument. It wasn't really true that she had chosen Edward over her friends, but that's how it felt. Her stomach dropped.

Oh God, she realized, *they will all know about the baby. All of them will know all the things we cannot hide,* she thought, *but no one will know what it was like. No one will know what he* did *to me.*

Faye stalled. "Tell me about the new kids. I want to know what everyone is working on."

The chair squeaked as Edward tossed his weight back and swallowed the remaining whiskey in one gulp. He tousled his hair a bit and spoke in an exuberant voice about the potential and passion of his new Chamber Singers. The familiarity of this subject comforted Faye. She had always liked being privy to Edward's thoughts about the AP choirs.

"If I had known this group was going to be so good, I would have added the Bach *Magnificat* to the Pageant."

"Next year, then," Faye offered.

An uneasiness descended on Edward. The school year had just begun, but even so, Edward had felt a sense of dread following him across campus these few weeks. Jaqueline DeGroot was poking around, sidling up where Edward did not expect her, and asking questions that rattled him. *A guilty conscience maybe*, Edward had scoffed the first time. Again two days later, though, Jaqueline asked if he had spoken to Faye at Sacred Heart. Jacqueline never showed interest in particular students, current or former. Now, she was talking about Faye. She was trying to get Edward to talk about Faye. He didn't bite. Still, he was unnerved. A leak was winding its way through AP channels. Edward didn't know how it had trickled its way to Jaqueline DeGroot, but certainly Faye must have been the original source.

"By next year, I may not even be here," he said with casual annoyance.

"You always say that," Faye responded flippantly, "but you always end up right back at Aquinas Prep for another year. You would never leave those kids."

Edward's tone sharpened. "Things have gotten considerably more complicated lately," he said.

And it's worse than you think, Faye thought.

It was time. She had to tell him. The baby divided and grew. Faye swallowed hard.

"Listen," she said flatly, "I need to talk to you about something."

Edward sighed. "Before you do," he countered, "you need to listen to me."

Faye sat up in her bed. Her scalp tingled; she pinched her thigh, an inch of hard flesh turning bright white between her tightly clenched thumb and finger.

"People have been talking at Aquinas Prep." Edward paused. "People have been talking about you and me."

Faye stammered. "I don't know what to say. I didn't tell."

Edward shook his head forcefully, glad not to have Faye standing in front of him.

"Really, Faye? You didn't tell? Then how do they know, Faye? Who did you tell? Who did you tell?"

"I told my friends." The confession came out quietly. "I told Krystal and Ian. Ian told James."

"What did you tell them? Did you actually tell them what we did?"

"Yes, but they don't care. I mean, Ian is mad, but he wouldn't tell anyone."

"You told them everything?"

Faye nodded, inaudibly. Edward continued ranting.

"Do you know how serious this is? Jesus, Faye. What did you tell them?"

His questions hung in the air.

"Did you tell your friends you gave me a blow job?"

Silence.

"Answer me, Faye."

Faye could not speak. Her tongue felt heavy, and she was afraid to swallow. An acidic bubble rose in her throat.

"Yes," she stammered. "I told them we did those things."

His heavy-bottomed glass broke in three parts as Edward banged it down on the desk.

"Damn it, Faye."

"But I didn't tell Leah or Tommy," she pleaded. "I didn't tell any of the kids who still go to school there. I swear. I absolutely swear. Don't be mad. Please," she begged. "Don't be mad."

Faye's voice was halting and weepy.

No, no, no, no, she thought desperately. Edward would get caught and he would hate her and he would leave her and she would be scorned and embarrassed and without him.

A long sigh echoed across the miles from Edward's semi-lit house to Faye's dorm room.

A hard edge vibrated in Edward's voice.

"Don't talk about me anymore."

Edward spit into the phone, drawing each word out.

"Don't talk about me any-more-to-any-one. I mean it, Faye. If anyone at Aquinas Prep finds out about this summer, you and I are finished. *For good.*"

The threat hit Faye like a punch to the stomach. The bud shriveled and grayed, its life sacrificed to the secret.

The exam room shimmered and blurred as Faye's vision went out of focus. An hour after the first dose of medication, the sedatives ran through her blood and the world softened. At first, the monitor's beeping reverberated in her temples, but now Faye could hardly hear it. Everything was fading to the background. She was vaguely aware of Debbie's presence in the chair beside her. *Your support person can be with you through the whole procedure*, the clinic brochure had said. *You are not alone!* While the room slowed, small moments announced themselves. The doctor's hand pressed gently on her abdomen. She felt a pinch at first slight then more forceful as the anesthetic swab found her cervix. The tables and wall art and jars of supplies pulsed behind Faye's closed lids. A confusing despair overwhelmed her. The abortion had only just begun. She wanted to imagine their baby, to sanctify it before it was gone forever. The bud that had been a seed that had grown because she loved Edward and because Edward always got what he wanted—the bud that had been a seed would never be a baby.

The doctor would insert a flexible tube, they had told her, to gently suction out the *pregnancy tissue* attached to her uterus. Faye imagined the abortion not as it was. She pictured warm water swirling through her body, the undulating waves lapping against a deep cave inside. Each time, the waves tugged gently at a wisp of seaweed as it tried to hold on to her, tried to bury deeper and ride out the swell. But the relentless surge continued. The water rose and loosened and cajoled with its inviting warmth until the seed and bud that was a precious flowering bundle and would never be Doctor Vogel's baby gave way and washed out of Faye in a warm push.

A dark abyss opened before her, and Faye imagined throwing herself headlong into it. She tumbled down unmoored in the blackness, not a glowing cartoon Hell but an endless darkness so deep it terrified and tore at her.

That Christmas, Faye's flight from Chicago scooted onto California ground in a series of bumps that jolted her awake. Having passed her first go from summer to fall to winter in Indiana, Faye understood why people called Southern California a land without seasons. Midwestern seasons bear little resemblance to each other, a phenomenon that leads to stark changes in temperature overnight and a neat alignment with the pictures that teach seasonal change to small children: bright orange leaves show fall is coming; see the majestic winter snow; flowers bloom in spring; the hot summer sun means ice cream in the afternoon! Seasons in Citrus County changed quietly, hiding in the quick falling of purple blossoms in spring and the high climb of the moon mid-winter.

A shiver ran through Faye's body. Everyone expected that Faye would feel warm in California because snow had blanketed the ground in Potato Creek when Sacred Heart broke for Christmas vacation. The scarf wound around her neck said otherwise. Faye could not shake the chill running through her from first step back onto Citrus County soil.

"You can't be cold," everyone from her brother to the parish priest had exclaimed in the past week when they saw Faye shudder and pull the folds of her peacoat more tightly together.

"It's a different kind of cold," Faye muttered each time in a weak retort.

Two days after Christmas, the night air hung heavy with ocean moisture. Faye stepped from one foot to the other to stay warm as she huddled against a callbox, the thick plastic pay phone cradled against her skin. She waited three rings for Edward to answer her call. Edward was at home in Fulton, but he had asked her not to come over tonight. Tiny pinpricks still dotted the tender skin around Faye's navel from Edward's bearded face rubbing across it four days earlier. She had spent the night with him three times during her October break and had found her way again to his bed two days after landing in Citrus County for Christmas. Tonight, though, he did not want to see her.

Something between Faye and Edward had shifted. Many things had changed since Faye's leaving for college. This night, dread wove its way into the recesses of Faye's mind. Bright white sun had poured through Edward's bedroom windows that winter day, two days before Christmas, when last Edward had foraged with his hands and his mouth over and through and into Faye's body, trying one final time to swallow her up. Tonight, though, he had asked her not to come back. Warning sirens pulsed through Faye. Again she had let him devour her. Now, she felt about to be spat out. The phone's ring reverberated in her skull.

Faye stood waiting, pay phone in hand, at a rather nondescript strip mall. Lights blared brightly from an open donut shop, a closed watch repair store slinked into the shadows, and a few elderly folks walked slowly into the corner pharmacy. Faye dialed Edward's familiar number on the stiff buttons of a pay phone keypad. She prayed for a moment that Edward would not pick up. But he did.

Pleasantries finished quickly. Edward described a lonely Christmas. Neither mentioned their intimate encounter only days before. Faye rubbed a hand across her stomach rash and felt an ache in her thighs where Edward had pushed them apart with his determined forearms. A flashpoint had arrived. Faye wanted to speak of her poetry and his music. Edward seemed to not want to talk at all. Faye drew deep breaths on her lighted cigarette. She could hear Edward puffing on a cigar as she and he sat quietly on the open line.

"Listen," he said after a long stretch of silence. "There's just too much talk at Aquinas Prep. Too much is at stake for me. Do not come here anymore. Please."

Three blows in quick succession assaulted Faye. The declarations stunned her. Edward delivered them effortlessly, unemotionally.

"I don't understand." She thought about the baby, about the lies, about how much of herself she had set aside because she loved him.

Her voice shook with panic and anger. "You said you loved me. Remember graduation?" Her voice dripped sarcasm now. "You could not bear to be separated from me. Isn't that what you said?"

Edward sighed, annoyed and unimpressed by Faye's desire to tie him down.

"That's not really how the adult world works, Faye. I have to worry about my job and my reputation. I should never have gone along with any of this."

Gone along? This phrase Faye understood. *So, it was her doing, was it?*

Edward's apathy disgusted her. There, holding the stiff, crunchy cord of the pay phone, Faye felt Edward pulling back. The empty space inside her pulsed insistently, the space where a baby should have still been growing, the Edward-shaped space that would dwindle and shrink and hide but would remain, would live as long as Faye did.

"You said you loved me," Faye repeated.

"I will always love you to some extent," Faye heard Edward say. "It just went away."

Silence thickened through the airwaves. Fat tears rolled from Faye's eyes. She shook them away, but their residue left her face itchy and bothered.

"I will never stop loving you," she heard herself say.

She meant it. Lord, how she meant it.

VIII

BY 2019, THE CHOIR AT MISSOURI'S EPIPHANY of our Lord Catholic Parish had for seven years held in its capable hands all of Edward's musical vision. After resigning from Aquinas Prep in 1999 (after Faye's accusations) and being fired from Meridian Community College in 2007 (after Faye's lawsuit), Doctor Edward Vogel had slinked in the shadows for a few years, working up the alcohol tolerance he had ceded during his daughter Amy's toddler days. He wanted to teach. His hands itched with the desire to direct. Jobs popped up here and there; Edward considered applying, but he feared interviewing in a way he never had before. When Jared McCombs called to revoke his spot on the American Choral Directors Association Board, Edward knew his career was finished. And so, after five years in the bottle, avoiding his wife's disappointed gaze, Edward had heeded the call of his parish and accepted the position of Epiphany choral director. From the mouth of God, the new role had lifted him from the abyss and breathed new life into his lungs. Seven years later, the parish was enamored with Edward. It was Aquinas Prep adoration all over again. Edward's piety and musical expertise pulled them all to him like a beacon, his music a soft glow of faith in their hearts. He and his wife Thuy tried to set their marriage back on track. Amy grew beautiful and strong, her voice sweet and well-trained by the time she entered high school. Perhaps there would be a life for Edward after all.

Church choir in Meridian, a suburb of St. Louis, was serious business. The singers' talent was on point and the singers themselves were on time for rehearsal despite having day jobs as engineers, farmers, and school teachers. For the last few months, the tenors especially had noticed that Doctor Vogel's voice was going. Out of respect for their director, they had kept quiet, but when Edward went from straining to downright laryngitis three times in a month, Bigsby Jenson asked if he had seen a doctor about the problem.

"I probably ought to go," Edward had said casually, a tiny ball of fear building in his core.

Something had been wrong for months, and it wasn't just Edward's voice that was affected. He felt fatigued but on edge, not quite deflated but rather like his tiredness intensified every other stimulus in his environment. His wife's questioning and his daughter's sluggishness and any lack of preparation on the part of even one of his choir members sent Edward reeling as if the world were closing down upon him. He was quick to anger and overly agitated. Worst of all, the soreness in his throat and the feeling that he was being strangled from inside his own voice box intensified. By the time Bigsby so compassionately approached him (Bigsby's dark eyes and cool demeanor reminded Edward of Merton, the young man from California that he had not seen nor thought of in almost two decades), the cancer had spread from his esophagus to his liver and was threatening his lungs.

The hits had just kept coming with this one. The first scan showing striated tears and a mass in Edward's esophagus was cause for concern but had not doomed him entirely. Even after the initial discovery, Edward had kept his fears quiet. After further testing, he had to tell Thuy and Amy.

"Bring Thuy to our next appointment," Dr. Anderson had said. "The more ears in here, the better. As the cancer effects worsen and the chemo effects pile on, it can be tough to keep everything straight. The chemo will be hard on you."

That man wasn't kidding around. Edward had never been so sick in his life. Chemo felt exactly like what it was, a toxin pumping through his veins. After the first dose he had felt surprisingly fine, but by lunchtime on the second day after treatment, his head spun with sweats and nausea so strong he clenched the toilet bowl and begged God for release. The vomiting started then, and Edward thought it would never stop. When the retching got so intense he nearly fainted, he stopped feeling humiliated and felt only pain. There was relief, then. Physical pain wasn't as painful as knowing how helpless and broken he had become. In the fog of sickness, Edward heard the heavy double doors latch downstairs in the cold, tiled foyer of the house, Amy heading away from the darkness out into a sunny day.

Crawling toward the bed, his head finally clear of nausea, his eyes heavy and sore, Edward let out a long, slow groan. The release of air and energy soothed him. A shard of something dug into the tender skin of his knee cap. It was unnatural, really, even if he had been feeling well, for a man of his age to be in this position. *A man of my age*, Edward thought. Age had swooped in quickly after Edward turned fifty. He felt every bit of his sixty-two years and then some. He gripped the cold bed frame, stood momentarily, then slid awkwardly into a pile of warm covers. Thuy had slept in the lushly padded Queen Anne chair in the corner of their bedroom so that Edward would have space to roll and writhe and sweat. A weaving of taupe and auburn paisley swirls peeked out from beneath a plush throw where Thuy had curled up the night before. Without another thought, Edward slipped into sleep.

"Here's a cold towel."

A refreshing wetness broke the cloud of heat Edward felt rising up around him. The soft skin of Thuy's wrist brushed his temple.

"How are you now?" she asked. "You were moaning in your sleep."

Edward inventoried his insides: legs weak, stomach weaker, mouth on fire, eyes runny.

On the second try, sound barely escaped his mouth.

"My glasses," he whispered, clotted saliva gluing his lips together.

Thuy placed her hand behind Edward's back as he pushed himself up to sit.

"You still have your contacts in," she said.

Edward blinked and rolled his eyes forcefully around in their sockets.

"I can hardly see," he said.

"Then close your eyes," she said sweetly. "You don't need to see right now."

Edward chuckled to himself. *If not now, when?* The room was dim, though he knew it was daytime. He felt suspended and unreal, like these were his final moments. This was not true. Edward knew that, too. Even his fast-moving cancer would not take him just yet. Still, instability discomforted Edward. He wanted to see, to move, and to take stock, but he couldn't. Thuy was there, and he was glad for it.

"Do you feel like waking up or going back to sleep?"

Edward blinked a few more times.

"I'd like to try some tea," he said hoarsely.

Thuy pressed the towel lightly to his cheeks.

"Please," he added in a whisper.

Before Thuy returned with the tea, Edward's body rejected the idea. After a few moments' waking, more nausea threatened. Though he felt only a small noxious lapping so far, he feared it would swell and surge, gaining momentum as he kept his eyes open and tried to sit upright. Edward looked about almost frantically, longing for the sleep he had been enjoying just a few minutes prior. He was dreadfully aware that the vomiting would return with a gnawing insistence. Edward closed his eyes and pushed his body downward. His feet found a cold spot in the sheets where the end of the mattress met the strong wooden footboard. (Edward had built the bed himself, carving lotus flowers on the headboard because Thuy liked them so much.) The cold on his feet and the warm covers on his chest brought just the perfect relief. *Oh thank God*, Edward thought. Every thought was a sincere prayer these days. Simple comforts reminded Edward that he wanted to stay alive. He closed his eyes loosely, letting the dim room carry him away. He wished for Vaughan Williams on the stereo but was too weak to get out of bed.

The next time he awoke, a haze disoriented Edward. Music played quietly. He thought at first that Thuy had just come back upstairs. He had slept but a few minutes, he thought, but the tea Thuy had brought (hours earlier) sat cold on Edward's nightstand. As his eyes focused in, he noted his mistake. It was Amy's slender frame, an odd mix of perfect posture and teen-aged malaise. Amy cradled a stack of old albums. She looked up expectantly when she heard her father's movements. Her voice felt crackly in the too quiet space.

"Hi. I didn't know what you might want, so I chose some Samuel Barber."

Edward caught his daughter's sadness and nodded, knowingly.

"I can change it," Amy said, "if you want something less melancholic."

"No," Edward paused. "Thank you, dear. It is a melancholic day after all."

Amy smiled without showing her teeth. A long black ponytail hung down her back. She pulled it nervously around beneath her chin and stroked the ends, a childhood habit.

"It's night," she answered. "You've slept all day. Do you want fresh tea?"

Sleepy saliva caked Edward's lips. He wanted his daughter to lie down beside him like she had as a child, her head against the side of his chest and long hair snaking down her back. He would never ask those things of her now. For years, that intimacy had eluded them. They lived, since the lawsuit, in a state of growing then waning hurt.

"Yes, let's try some more tea. Thank you."

She turned to leave, but Edward's voice stopped her.

"Can you start the song over?"

"Do you want the light on as well?"

"Just one lamp," Edward answered. "My eyes are burning."

The freshness of Amy's pale cheeks flashed upon Edward as she switched on a table lamp by the bedroom door. *So much life in her*, he thought proudly. A chill swept through him. The life was positively draining out of Edward.

Barber's *Sure on This Shining Night* filled the room softly but insistently. He knew it well and felt it heavily now. Yes, he wandered alone these days in a crowded life of so many who loved him. After the cancer diagnosis, a confusing but familiar loneliness blanketed him. The same feeling had defined the Aquinas Prep years, those years between Jane and Thuy during which he had been surrounded by admirers but existed in a fundamental loneliness. Edward went home alone each night to the house in Fulton while the Aquinas Prep families grew and thrived and went on without him. Living was lonely in those days. Dying, Edward knew now, was lonelier still. Everyone suffered, but death hunted Edward. The others knew they would go on without him. However painfully or dutifully or with whatever difficulty, they all—his mother, his brother, his sisters (little Millie had suffered so much already from the death of her husband and daughter), and the Epiphany church choir—would go on.

Even Thuy and Amy, his wife and teen-aged child, would go on without Edward.

Edward scanned the room. It was pleasing and comfortable. He had settled into it after all these years, though early on in the marriage its plushness had been off putting. A settee just beneath the east window was upholstered, like too much of the furniture in their home, with silk fabric. This particular piece was made of gray silk ornamented with roses of a crushed mauve color. Much of the décor was not what Edward would have chosen. Thuy's choices seemed less a matter of personal taste than of inherited style passed down from Edward's mother-in-law, an immigrant obsessed with a particular idea of what constituted the finer things of culture. Edward disliked the foreignness of their home. The objects were beautiful and well-placed, but, even after sixteen years, they felt impersonal because they had arrived on trucks and in moving vans.

Despite his struggles at Aquinas Prep, he cherished that California phase and loved the Fulton house best of all the places he had lived. He loved his California space because he had crafted so much of the Fulton house with his own hands according to his own vision. He longed now for the scent of wood shavings and lacquer, the very smell of possibility and creativity. Back in the '80s and '90s, Edward had remodeled the Fulton house piece by piece, tweaking and re-tweaking the artistry. Before he knew it was gone, the Edward of his 30s had squandered the unencumbered freedom of bachelor life. He had only half built new poplar shelving for his music room when all that nonsense with Faye had forced him to sell the Fulton house and go east. Letting the students down shamed him, and he raged at the unnecessary stain on his reputation as an educator. Most of all, though, he left the Fulton house with great regret because he had wanted to build something entirely of his own. When he and Thuy settled in a St. Louis suburb, he watched with apprehension as her things, her vision, and her money redesigned his life. Now, that life was closing in around him. *Advanced esophageal squamous cell cancer,* he mouthed. Since the diagnosis he had begun saying the words over and over in his mind, begging them to make sense or unspool or lose their power or just go away. *Advanced esophageal squamous cell cancer,* he mouthed again. Death was coming for him.

Amy returned with his tea and a slice of dry toast. Edward groaned deeply, sensuously, at the smell of food. He felt a change taking place in his body. He was a collection of basic needs, now. He almost lunged for the plate of food.

"What a lovely smell," he said politely instead. His exchanges with Amy had always been formal. The cancer had not changed that.

"That's my favorite scent," she said quietly. "Warm toast. I thought it might comfort you."

Edward held Amy's elbow tenderly as she set the plate at his bedside. The scent did comfort him. The toast and his daughter and a sudden knowledge rushed in—he had survived this round. Edward would live.

Faye could not shake the feeling that life was passing her by too quickly. Running through her neighborhood on a crisp morning, the wind shifted just so. Faye felt a swell of nostalgia and loss. As she hopped an extra long stride over a shallow puddle, not in front of the yellow house nor the brown house but right there astride the pale blue one in between, a subtle movement of the air brought Potato Creek to mind. The air felt fresh, light with new life but heavy with possibility as it had, her senses said, one spring morning so many years ago on the Sacred Heart campus. She had been a young woman then (a girl, really) tormented by her move across country from Citrus County and wracked with guilt because she had betrayed Doctor Vogel. The clean spring air and quickly melting snow had promised an expanse of new beginnings. And now, she felt its reappearance, the same bristling against her skin, the same sharp vibrancy in her nostrils as she jogged through the neighborhood where she had grown up and where she now lived with her husband and three quickly growing children. Across a thousand miles and two decades, a current of possibility flowed through Faye's limbs, but sadness followed after. With Teague in middle school and the other children asserting more independence every day, with a job that brought such tragedy to her office door, a chasm separated that young Potato Creek Faye from the woman whose skin hugged her now.

Faye kept running. A vibration buzzed her pocket. A call was coming through from Faye's best friend Megan, the woman who had been the girl who had succeeded Peggy as Faye's Sacred Heart roommate. Since meeting at freshman year's end in 1999, Faye and Megan had never looked back. Through thick and thin they had carried each other, and that was good because Faye's joy-filled life so recently blessed with three young children was getting thick again.

"I'm running," she answered breathlessly. "What's going on?"

"I'm booking my flight for the HPV conference in St. Louis," Megan began. "I'll be in sessions for two days but staying three. Do you want to come?"

Megan's question hung in the air. Faye slowed to a jog then an awkward walk. Thick stitches sutured Faye to Edward. They flexed and receded and reappeared and grew with her. Always, they remained. Twenty years had passed. Still, the wound would not heal. Faye needed to see Edward; she assumed he would not want to see her. Absolution by ambush was all that remained.

Faye wiped sweat off her upper lip with the ribbed collar of her worn Sacred Heart tee shirt. The silence stretched.

"I think you should come with me," Megan said.

Faye nodded, imperceptibly, for her own benefit. A few baby doves found their footing on the wire overhead. Her neighborhood was quiet. The children were at school; Daniel presenting to Kramer Foods headquarters in

Los Angeles; an old man watering his lawn while his wife troweled a newly turned flower bed.

Finally, Faye spoke.

"I should do it? It's not crazy?"

Megan scoffed. "I don't believe those two are mutually exclusive."

Faye chuckled. "Right. It's crazy, but I should do it. And what do you think will happen when I get there?"

"I haven't thought that far ahead," Megan began. "I don't know that it will go well," she continued, "but I do believe that you will regret not going. Maybe this is what you need."

Right, Faye thought. Because trying to let Edward go, revealing the affair to Ms. DeGroot, meeting with Aquinas Prep administration, smoking too many cigarettes, drinking a lot of martinis, having too much bad sex with too many strangers and just enough good sex with other people's husbands, marrying Daniel, calling an attorney, testifying under oath, staring Edward down for four days' worth of depositions, advocating for victims' rights, earning her Doctorate, quitting smoking, and pushing God's three most precious human beings out of her body had not been all she needed, maybe seeing Edward chased by death would plug this gape. Faye folded half over and searched the pink laces of her running shoes. *Fuck fuck fuck.*

"I'll talk to Daniel tonight," Faye said. "But yes. I think I should go."

Megan sighed. "What will you say to Vogel?"

His name through the phone roused a chuckle in Faye's throat.

Vogel is what Faye called him now. *Vogel is dying*, she had said to Daniel. When Daniel first met Faye, she had used *Edward*. *It's time I told you about this thing with my high school choir director,* she had said. *His name is Edward.* Even then, the name had sat strangely in Faye's mouth. Daniel could tell she was uncomfortable saying it. Several drinks in when she wasn't concentrating, Faye reverted to saying *Doctor Vogel*. Somewhere in the aughts, after the law firm of Hamilton, Shane, and Dupree had gotten involved, Faye had started calling Edward *the abuser*. By the lawsuit's end, everyone had settled on *Vogel*.

Faye never named *him* in her mind. She spoke to him as to God in internal, wordless confession. He was who he was, the one who had made and unmade her one summer. No name would ever contain him.

Engineering and architecture were the only non-medical fields Thuy found acceptable for Amy's academic focus. Even at seventeen, the girl walked through life heavy with expectation. Her future divided the family and drew a clear line between her parents. An orthodontist and a literal, scientific-minded woman from a cloistered immigrant home, Thuy judged success for her daughter through a narrow lens of financial security. *Painting is fun*, she would tell Amy for the millionth time. *Painting is a hobby. Art is not a career.* Edward sat silently each time, his eyes meeting Amy sympathetically over a steaming mug of coffee. *Art feeds the soul*, Edward thought. His daughter would be a great painter or exquisite performer.

Greatness flowed through Amy. He saw it in her posture and poise, in her melodic voice, and in the rich, contrasting colors of the thick oil pastels marbled into her black and white charcoal drawings. Edward did not understand Amy, exactly. She was a girl: a privileged girl with means, a half-Vietnamese girl tucked reluctantly under her mother's large, smothering wing in a nearly all white midwestern suburb, a girl with an alcoholic father who had broken his sobriety and had been accused of sexually abusing a teen-aged girl. No, he could not imagine what sharp thoughts swirled in Amy's head, but he knew the compulsion to create and to keep making beauty out of the red hot swells in one's soul. Yes, Amy's art would win out, Edward knew, because it had to. Despite her mother's obsession with practical discipline, Amy's art would heal her (*God, let it heal her*) after he was gone. After the cancer took him, Edward reasoned, Amy's art would live on and he would go on through her. Amy's creativity stood out in their small Missouri suburb, a feeling Edward well knew from his childhood on a Kansas farm in the 1960s. He was one of the lucky ones. His parents, not artists themselves, pushed him off the farm to find the songs in his head. He had been humming them and strumming them and hearing them in the cicada screams for as long as they all could remember. And so, they sent him in search of that which would fill him. Edward wanted that for Amy, but his advocacy meant little in a life her mother had taken hold of years before.

Thuy kept Amy's life closely trimmed and pushed Edward to the edges of the carefully manicured hedge that encircled Amy's childhood. For that, Edward blamed the lawsuit and all the nonsense following the incident with Faye. Yes, Edward called the whole mess *the incident*, a euphemism just vague enough to cover any number of sins and to ward off a litany of questions from curious but squeamish colleagues, acquaintances, and family members. The incident carried an ever-growing roster of penances, punishments, and, to be honest, bullshit that had followed him in the twenty years since. The formality between Amy and Edward, the distance between them, was the most regrettable of these. Born only five years before the lawsuit that had unraveled her parents' plans, Amy had no memory of the best years she and her father had shared. To Amy, Edward had always been a struggling composer and small-time church choir director. Sure, she heard tell of the accolades he had acquired in graduate school, knew he had an earned Doctorate, and had seen photos of him with the Pope who was now a flesh and blood Saint, but *that* Edward existed in a world she could never capture. That Edward had perished with her mother's trust in him and was buried in a whiskey bottle by the time her memories sharpened into focus. Thuy never spoke of the details and Amy never asked, but she had heard the rumors and had searched the web for newspaper clippings. The community disbelieved the accusations. The old ladies in Edward's church choir and the old men in Epiphany's chapter of the Knights of Columbus revered her father. Her parents were pillars of their community and she, their precious jewel, a spotlight in their small town. At home, though, her father's disgrace lived everywhere in her mother's hesitant affection. That her mother loved him was true. It was also true that Thuy could not feel wholly bound to her husband without the pang of sorrow. She and Amy, alone among their community, felt the moat that wound its way around Edward as they carried forward together.

Now the advanced esophageal squamous cell cancer went along with them. The cancer heightened their senses and gnawed at their vulnerabilities. Edward had continued conducting the Epiphany choir. Evenings, he still picked at his guitar. A slowness descended over the house. Each night since the diagnosis, Thuy had been sure to finish seeing patients at her orthodontic practice well before dinner so that she, Edward, and Amy could reconnect as the day dusked. Unspoken grievances hovered in air already rich with the warm steam of Thuy's fresh dumplings. Most nights, Amy pushed veggies around on her plate and let her dark hair hang obtrusively in front of her face. Edward detected a confused anxiety in her otherwise placid face. He had thought at first that she was pulling away from him. But, no. This was not a girl backing away from her father, Edward surmised. She was afraid to lose him. She was afraid to speak of the loss surely coming. He knew the fear well. It gripped him deep in the belly, fear pulsing like electric current whenever he dared speak the cancer's name: *advanced esophageal squamous cell cancer.*

Edward reached across the table and offered his hand. Amy took it, the skin of her fingers so much softer than his.

"How are the applications going?"

"Fine," she replied with a furtive glance toward her mother. Thuy looked down at her plate instead of meeting her daughter's eyes. "I'm a bit nervous, but the counselors say my application looks great."

"That's wonderful," Edward said with confidence. "Besides, the application essay is the most important part of the application, I'd say, and you've always been a great writer."

Because her father had taught high school in California for a decade before her birth and because he generally championed her abilities, Amy deferred to him despite her mother's incessant prodding about test scores. Her father held high expectations, but he also saw Amy as she was, an exceptional student with the heart of a true artist. She excelled in coursework, but it did not stir her. In the studio—painting, singing, and sculpting—Amy let the mess of creation frenzy her soul then heal her wounds. A distance sat between her and her father in so many places, but in this, they were kindred spirits.

Amy pulled a deep breath in through her nose.

"I've been working on my portfolio," she said quietly. "I'm still planning to submit to art schools."

Thuy exhaled sharply and set her fork across the edges of her plate.

"Can we please not talk about these fanciful art plans while we are focused on your father's health? Can we, please?"

Edward crossed his ankles under the table and reclined in his chair. The sickness was his, living and expanding like heat through his fast-pumping cells. The fear was theirs. An edge of impatience pounced back at him through the eyes of the women who had for all these years been so equanimous in their demeanor. Thuy and Amy controlled their emotions willfully, almost dutifully. Thuy had taught this prim stoicism to Amy, and she had exercised it well. But for their time together at the piano, Edward would not have known the passion that burned inside his young daughter.

Edward silenced Thuy with a pleading look.

"Come on, Thuy," he said with pity. "She's an amazing artist and she has a whole life ahead of her. Let's talk about her plans."

"No, dad. It's okay," Amy chimed in, eager to avoid an argument.

Thuy lifted the fork from her plate, pointing it toward Amy as she began to speak.

"I've spent my whole life working hard so you can make a career for yourself and be successful. You can be an engineer and still draw pictures in your free time."

The diminishing of her art riled Amy. Her mother didn't mean to slight her, Amy knew, but the unintentional blow made the chasm even more stark. Her mother just didn't get it. Amy felt the blood rising in her cheeks. Edward saw it too.

"You know," he said with a look in his daughter's direction, "I once had the chance to study orchestra in Rome."

Amy's eyes widened, visibly, like she was seeing her father for the very first time.

"In Rome? Like, in Europe?"

"Yes, in the Rome that's in Europe," he said, chuckling rather proudly through his nose.

Edward twirled a pile of noodles then let it unravel. Often he spent dinner appearing to eat without putting much into his body. Hunger felt better and less sickening than fullness did. The look now in his teen-aged daughter's eyes was filling him. She wanted to know him. For no earthly reason, he had hidden these ambitions under regret and the shame of failure.

"This was back in the '80s when I was finishing my Doctorate at Michigan. My final Doctoral composition caught the eye of several prestigious prize committees, and for a time I thought I might accept a scholarship to study and compose at the American Academy in Rome."

As Edward let out the long stream of information, a warmth expanded in the space between him and Amy. The delicate pink tips of her fingernails appeared at the table's rounded edge as she sat up with more interest, pressing forward in her seat.

"This was for *Expansions*?"

"The prizes are generally for a body of work, but since I was a Doctoral student, they focused almost entirely on *Expansions* because it was my Doctoral composition. I had written a few small orchestral pieces before incorporating marimba. The marimba focus really elevated my appeal because eclectic percussion use is unusual, especially in American classical."

A thin wetness stretched across Amy's eyes. She pursed and curled and smiled her lips as she drew a deep breath into her chest.

"That's amazing, dad. Really," she said, nodding to him, "that's amazing."

Edward ran a hand through his hair and enjoyed Amy's adoration.

"You never believed your dad had great talent, right?"

Amy slipped momentarily into her usual demurring self.

"Of course I did," she began. "But how could I really know?"

Edward sighed gently. If his daughter found his career disappointing or shameful, unfulfilled or beneath his talent, he would understand. He had played his compositions for her occasionally over the years, the scratchy recordings fading with time, the printed compositions themselves yellowing and becoming brittle along the folds. But she had never heard an orchestra perform them live, had never heard them resonate in a large auditorium, projected by a full choir, not even the likes of Saint Philomena or Meridian Community, the last two places he had taught between the incident and the lawsuit.

"I wish I had been able to see your works performed," Amy added, encouragingly. "I know how important they are to you."

Not as important as you, Edward thought. *Nothing as important as you.*

"You can't imagine the feeling," Edward said wistfully. "All the late nights and the false starts and the failures and re-creations all coming together at once is just," Edward searched for the word, "exhilarating. Creating brings its own joy, but sharing that new thing, giving it life and sending it out into the world—" Edward stopped, his throat getting tight.

Amy beamed with closed lips. "That's beautiful, dad," she interjected. "I hope I get to feel that some day."

Silence expanded to the kitchen's corners and under the table. The dreams Edward had once cherished for himself were planned for his daughter, now.

"You'll find out when you start showing your art," Edward affirmed. "It's magnificent."

The father's and daughter's eyes locked as they seldom did. A spark of recognition lightened the air and the room. For a moment, Amy seemed just a child, again, and Edward was happy. He remembered well those early years of Amy's childhood, the years when contentment poured over him like he had thought it never might. Resurrection had gleamed all around Edward: the liberation of escaping Aquinas Prep and California, of settling in Missouri and teaching young artists at Meridian, of tending a marriage, and of cooing at a new baby. He had gathered the new wonders hungrily and had spread their joy wide to the new community that embraced him.

Edward's memories of those days before the fall were vibrant and infectious. He could see Amy now as she had been then, a toddler with dark black pigtails and large, curious eyes. Late afternoons when Thuy was called to oral surgeries, Amy would skip playfully around the long perimeter of the

Meridian performing arts room, stopping to make faces at herself in the floor-to-ceiling mirrors that reflected back Edward's adoring choir. Fifteen years' worth of four-year families had given way to a middle-aged promised land in which his own family awaited him each night, the peaceful seesaw of Thuy's rocking chair reminding with each click that he had outrun disgrace (no thanks to Faye). He had created a child. Happiness had set down in his house.

The upstairs music room of their home held Edward's most precious memories of time spent with his daughter. Amy played piano with grace almost immediately upon touching fingers to keys. Even as a child, she worked tirelessly to perfect difficult runs, closing her eyes and letting the notes flow out from nimble hands. And then, she sang. Edward trained her from youth, transforming the sweet breathiness of her little girl voice to a rich soprano. Her confidence and poise carried Edward away, the musician in him proud, the father in him swollen with love. They inhabited the music. The strains themselves presented the only space in which they could see each other and see themselves. Amy found her father as she hoped one day to be; Edward met a daughter filled with the vigor he remembered from his own youth. But it was only there, apart from the world and from Thuy, that Edward felt Amy was his as much as her mother's.

As early as Amy's seventh birthday, she spent much of her time under Thuy's wing and on Thuy's schedule. As the days became weeks after his firing from Meridian Community, Edward had started drinking more and sleeping more, each day a long stretch from half-started project to half-finished composition. The *tsk tsks* of the Epiphany Church community and of the Meridian Community choir—oh, they could not believe the injustice of such false accusations!—would have buoyed Edward but for the mask he was struggling to wear. He welcomed their support, but self-righteous rage rose again each time he could not say what he wanted to say. *Yes, I did it!* he wanted to exclaim. *And there was nothing wrong with what I did!* Edward led his family up the Church steps each Sunday and held Amy's tiny seven-year-old hand in his. Inside, though, something heavy and consequential shifted. Thuy withdrew from Edward after the lawsuit. Worse, she took a part of Amy with her.

He felt restless and lost in a house that seemed more Thuy's than his, a house with halls he walked because there was nowhere else to be. His footsteps fell weightily with anger and resentment. The whiskey bottle tipped more heavily into Edward's morning coffee, and his afternoon water, and his evening snifter. Leaving Aquinas Prep had been one thing. After a few months' distance, he had been surprised to find how glad he was to go. But after the lawsuit—*Faye had no right,* the bitter voice in his head spat, *she had no right to take this new life away, too.* Years passed quickly with the small joys and great disappointments of ordinariness. The sluggish lack of routine felt worst of all. Love of music had driven him to teach. Without it, there was no salve but prayer: true, genuine prayer eluded Edward after the lawsuit. *When you sing, you pray twice,* he had always told his students. And so whenever Amy began to sing, Edward followed her voice up the stairs and listened. Often they would play together. Amy took the baby grand, its expansive mouth bouncing sound off the tapestried walls; Edward played the old upright Bechstein that he had carted across the country from Michigan to California then half-way back again to the new house in Missouri (after a quick year teaching at Saint Philomena Academy in Georgia). Amy's voice offered a peace that was just out of reach. She sang for herself and for a life she was building apart from her parents. Her teeth disappeared behind close-lipped smiles; she hugged Edward with caution, a fragile bird ready to fly the nest. Edward gathered these slight offerings greedily. Alone with Amy, he could at least feel the possibility of a world that would right itself.

Right itself, the world had not yet done. The advanced esophageal squamous cell cancer sat with them now. Amy readied for adulthood. Edward felt the thick noose of death winding around his neck.

Amy's voice, curious enough to break her father's serene countenance, brought Edward back from his reverie.

"Why didn't you go?" she asked. "Why didn't you study in Rome?"

"I followed a girl instead," he said, a new Edward having taken over, a dying man opening his past to the wide-eyed creature gobbling up its juices.

Amy's eyes, the same roundness as his, the deep almost-blackness of Thuy's, widened in disbelief.

"You? You followed a girl instead of your music?"

Edward chuckled. It was a million years ago, Edward knew, but like yesterday he saw Jane's wide-legged pants and tight blouse, stripes of yellow and pink fabric criss-crossing her breasts, her hair feathered out to frame her face. *Faint heart never won fair lady*, he had thought then, but both prizes had eluded him in the end. *Or had they?* Edward wondered. The warmth spreading through him now at the thought of Jane's coquettish posture and bright, innocent eyes said otherwise.

"Well, love can be magnificent too," Edward said casually. "While it lasts," he added more heavily, "it can be worth all the costs. I hope you get to feel that, too."

The decision loomed before a quite indecisive Faye. She chewed her nails and nervously sucked the insides of her cheeks. She ate one then two and then another handful of heart-shaped chocolates leftover from Valentine's Day. She swam laps in the morning and went running in the afternoon, scenarios traipsing her mind as her feet whacked the pavement. No matter how long she thought, the fog would not clear. By definition, this irrational impulse could not be rationalized. A need this desperate could not merely be figured out.

Your love is shallow, Edward had said, one long, warm night in 1999. She remembered him barking the words into the phone after his ousting from Aquinas Prep, his rage steeped in so much whiskey Faye could almost smell it across the states to Indiana. Edward wove his own story, then, of Faye's crazed obsession with him. *She wouldn't leave me alone*, he told Leah's mom and the other parents. *She's saying crazy things because I rejected her.* How easily they believed him! Leah's mom had patted Edward's hand, nodding her empathetic *humph* while Leah swallowed the secret of that summer. Edward had taken control of Faye's story back then. As the years stretched on, Faye risked settling into that role. Any flash of desperation condemned her to madwoman status.

  The lawsuit had given Faye voice, her court-reported confrontation with Edward bringing just enough vindication to allow a rebirth into motherhood. The births of her children followed quickly on the heels of the settlement, the years moving more quickly as she soaked up babies and joy. Teague and Louisa and Wyatt rescued Faye again and again until she forgot she had been hiding a damaged self beneath her altogether capable one. And so, by 2019, she had in some ways forgotten Edward, too. The recapitulation roared, now. *In the greatest symphonies, the opening theme always comes back,* she remembered Edward telling her class. *With a vengeance,* Ian had added, his tone caustically comedic. The time had passed for concerns about Aquinas Prep gossip or risks to her own image. Edward's illness swept all that pettiness away. Soon, Edward might be gone. Faye would have no chance of righting this wrong.

  Faye had never stopped believing how wrong she was. She thought herself wrong to have tempted him and teased him, wrong to have given in and wrong not to have given in more. *I was wrong to be so immature,* Faye sometimes thought, *and wrong to think I was so sophisticated.* There was only one right thing in the whole damn mess. She had loved Edward. She loved him, still. She loved Doctor still through her seventeen-year-old gaze, hungry for his approval, flushed and flattered by the desire shining in his eyes. In her mind, Doctor was still wearing a gray-collared shirt, the sleeves rolled up to his elbows amid the poorly circulating air of Aquinas Prep's modular choir room. Doctor was still forty-one (which of course he couldn't be; Faye was almost forty herself now). Faye folded herself into the love to escape the guilt of all those wrongs. Shame gnawed deep in Faye's core. *Worst of all,* the devil whispered, *you blamed Doctor Vogel so no one would blame you.*

  A week after Megan's proposition, Faye had still not talked to Daniel about a trip to St. Louis. At night she scoured the web, her face illuminated by the bright light of a screen. Silenced reruns of '90s television ran in the background; a glass of soda bubbled at her fingertips. She ascertained nothing of Edward's condition.

  This night, the youngest of her three children was still fidgeting in his sheets, pushing his bottom up in the air, and burrowing his face into the cold pillow when Donovan's message appeared on her phone.

  Check this out, Donovan wrote, *but with caution.*

  Faye furrowed her brows at Donovan's patronizing tone. Another line appeared.

  Don't let it overwhelm you.

Soothing voices floated out from the back of the house where Daniel was relaxing on their bed. The warm tones suggested documentary storytellers. Daniel consumed information the way most people took in reality television or bawdy dramas. This month had brought a series about food additives and dangerous changes in processing procedures in the dairy industry. A hesitant swipe of Faye's finger across her phone screen revealed a blue-fonted link embedded in Donovan's message. Faye winced at the title: *Prayers for Edward*. The muscles in Faye's chest spasmed. Her body collapsed in on itself, seeking protection. The dining chair creaked as Faye straightened up and looked to the back of the house. She didn't want to hide this from Daniel. But something about the page felt too private to share. She wished she were cocooned in her office, the wall-to-wall bookshelves an expanse of intellectual peace. She wished it were later so she could pore over the site, whatever it contained, without interruption and without judgment. Yes, that was it. Faye would wait until the whole house slept.

For now, she visited each child's bedroom and breathed in their scents. Each bed camouflaged a small Daniel-Faye mixture. Each child slept in a unique spread repeated each night. Wyatt smooshed his face down hard into the pillow, his neck turned only enough to bring in long, loud sweeps of breath. He slept now just like his infant self, his limbs tucked protectively under, his bottom pushed straight into the air. Louisa stretched her twiggy body as far as it could reach, her toes almost pointed and one arm extended over her head as if reaching for the wall behind her. Louisa talked in her sleep and chewed in her sleep. Faye had even seen a soundly sleeping Louisa rub her hands and forearms together over her head. Faye had just the same habit (as reported by Megan, who had been Faye's roommate three straight years in college). No boyfriends or lovers had remarked on the odd practice. Faye suspected she only did it when she was deep asleep and comfortable. She had never felt that way with a man in bed beside her.

Teague was blooming late, as Faye had. Puberty lurked in his changing face but had not yet swallowed up his little boy charm. Maybe he would shoot up dramatically in a few years, but for now, Teague's limbs were thickening and his height increasing at a slow but steady pace. It surprised Faye each morning that Teague filled so much space in his bed. At twelve, he slept curled and covered, clutching a giant, fluffy blanket. Watching him in the darkened bedroom, Faye flashed as she often did on an image of herself rocking Teague in his Illinois nursery. The image was blue lit from Teague's spaceship-shaped night light. Faye's hair hung long down her back. Her face was serene and unwrinkled. How she longed for the ease of early motherhood! Faye smoothed Teague's bright blond curls off his clammy forehead. He didn't stir.

Across the hall, Faye found Daniel sitting on their bed, a yellow pad and printed forms sprawled out across the unsmoothed sheets. Daniel held a pen in his mouth and a phone in his hand. He tried at once to study the papers, the phone, and the documentary. Faye sidled up to the edge of the bed. Daniel looked to Faye and began to gather the papery mess.

"Are you coming to bed? Here, I can clear these."

"No," Faye said quietly, walking to where Daniel sat.

Daniel wrapped his arm around her waist.

"Are you going to stay up and work?"

"Something like that," she said. "Donovan sent information I need to review."

It felt like a lie though it wasn't. Faye had long practiced the balancing act of deciding how much to tell Daniel about her work and her own healing. Faye was one of the lucky ones. Daniel's support was resolute. He was gentle but not patronizing; Daniel listened but did not prod. Victims who lacked support fared worse than Faye and often faced more terrible consequences like drug addiction and worse anxiety than Faye suffered. But often, support was not enough. She needed understanding, and no one, no matter how well-intentioned, could give that. Even between Faye and Donovan sat the reality that neither could fully comprehend or inhabit the other's experience. And so, the loneliness of recovery was immortal. Daniel gave more grace and space than Faye could have expected, but he could offer less understanding than Megan or Bridget or even than her mother. Because he was a man, a particularly invulnerable man who had never questioned his clear-eyed moral compass, Daniel could only meet Faye so far in her experience.

Sexual trauma imbued many of the Title IX complaints Faye processed in the schools. Her activism against sexual violence particularly as perpetrated by churches and other trusted institutions further narrowed the focus of her reading, writing, viewing, and other intellectual work. In every story set before her, shadows of her own experience hung menacingly. She feared their intrusion. Each revival of her own closed files (Faye vs Aquinas Prep, Faye vs Doctor Vogel, abused Faye vs madwoman Faye) meant discomfort for Daniel, a happy husband who preferred not to think of the indignities his wife had been forced to endure. Worse yet, Faye thought, what if the perennial narrative of blameless manhood secretly gripped Daniel, too? What if he blamed Faye for tempting her teacher and derailing the career that man had built? The terror of this thought stayed with Faye, and so she mentioned Edward as seldom as she could. It was embarrassing, really, that a woman like Faye would entertain such a scenario. Through years of work and study—in her office at Sunset Bluffs Unified, teaching literature courses at St. Anne's, at Gender Studies conferences, and in dorm rooms at Sacred Heart—Faye had told hundreds of girls (and a few dozen boys) that they were blameless, that they could not be culpable in their own abuse. *They* were innocent, Faye believed. But if they only knew her secret! If the world only knew that she had thrust herself headlong into Edward's arms, so giddy she might burst with pride. She had known exactly what he wanted. Hadn't she? *I should* have *known*, she mused, these twenty years later. And that was almost the same thing.

Faye sipped her soda and winced at its flattened, too syrupy taste. She clicked open *Prayers for Edward*. Rows upon rows of text appeared. The site was unadorned and crafted without expertise. *Please continue praying for Edward*, the headliner read. *He is battling advanced esophageal squamous cell cancer. Thank you for your support. Millie.*

The window shades wobbled. The room felt upended. An urgency suggested she must act, but there was nothing to be done. Faye thrust her fingernails hard into her thigh and waited for the sharp pain to ease her anxiety. This wasn't exactly news. Naming the cancer carved a space for it. Faye whispered the words slowly: *advanced esophageal squamous cell cancer.* Then again: *advanced esophageal squamous cell cancer.* She looked at each word alone then took the whole phrase in once more. The letters rose off the page and did somersaults in the air. Faye's estrangement from Edward stretched so long and with such angst that her stomach flipped and sloshed at the mere sight of his name. A familiar panic spread hot discomfort up into her throat and across her cheeks. Though Faye had never met Millie, she had heard much about her from Edward that summer of '98. Seeing their names together lured Faye into an uncomfortable, voyeuristic space. This plea from his baby sister touched Faye in a strange and unpleasant way.

Edward had esophageal cancer. A memory rose. Tears stung Faye's eyes.

"St. Blaise," Edward intoned.

"Pray for us," his students responded.

"Why do we pray to St. Blaise?" Santino had asked, six months into this established routine.

"We pray because St. Blaise is the patron saint of throats," Edward answered, touching the tender skin pulled taut over his Adam's apple.

Faye remembered the moment well, her weak-kneed reaction as Edward brushed the exposed skin with his strong fingers. Where had all the prayers gone? *Advanced esophageal squamous cell cancer.*

Scanning the screen now, Faye felt the shame of an intruder. Sure, the internet knew no privacy, but even so, some things were only for those on the inside. Faye had no business receiving this information, but, oh, how she wanted to drown in it. She wanted the page to swallow her whole, to pull her back into an intimacy with Edward that had been ripped from her when she was eighteen. *My mother would like you,* he had said that summer. But there had been no meeting of Edward's mother because no one had really wanted it then (*how would that have even gone?*) and because Faye had been ostracized by the following spring. Now, Mary Vogel was updating the friends and family who followed *Prayers for Edward;* Faye was reading those kernels of Edward's life furtively, with a racing heart, in her quiet living room a thousand miles away. *Edward had a good day,* his mother wrote. *We walked downtown for new guitar strings.*

Faye tried to visualize the image, but Edward walking with his mother, whom Faye had never met, in a city Faye had never visited was too foreign. Instead, downtown Fulton rose to her mind, the last place in which she and Edward had been Faye and Edward (*Faye and Doctor Vogel, actually*). She had always thought Fulton itself a quaint replica of the kind of midwestern Main Street Edward missed from the years before his Southern California life. A clinking bell announced a customer in the local music shop, a long thirty by twenty tunnel with dirty gold carpet flanked by bins of records and sheet music. The store's walls were tacked with album covers and concert posters; the ceiling was studded with hanging instruments and the love and peace flags of the 1960's era. Even this faulty mind's eye re-creation pained Faye. In the summer of 1998, Edward's normalcy had shocked Faye. How could Doctor Vogel eat taquitos and wear briefs and stack dirty mugs in the kitchen sink? Worse, how could he slink to the end of his bed and bury his face between a woman's legs? That feeling returned twenty years later. How could Edward, the larger-than-life presence that lived comfortably in the pit of Faye's stomach, walk gingerly down a tree-lined Main Street in a St. Louis suburb, linking arms with his elderly mother? For twenty years, this had been the hardest thing: the admission, the mere knowledge, that Edward's life went on in another place. Edward had a different skin that she never had touched.

Competing Edwards had traveled with Faye through all the phases of her life. There was the Doctor Vogel they had all known in high school and the one he had shown only to her and a few of her friends. There was the Edward who kissed her tenderly good-bye and the Edward who belittled and degraded her when she would not satisfy him. There was the Edward who had violated and embarrassed her (she never allowed herself to think about this Edward). There was the angry Edward who blamed and deflected and refused to admit his wrongs. Though she didn't know him, she sensed there was an Edward that his new community loved. It was easy for students and music-lovers to love such a talented musician and teacher. She knew Edward was father to a teen-aged girl, and she knew from experience that when he wanted to, Edward could listen with patience and grace to a seventeen-year-old girl's woes. After it all, though, a final Edward was finding his way into her mind. She met him in the guitar strings, in the pleading, praying mother, in the *advanced esophageal squamous cell cancer*: an omnipotent villain was collapsing into his frail humanity.

Yes, she would go to St. Louis. She would make peace with Edward, if only for her own peace of mind. But first, she needed to tell Daniel.

"If it's alright with you, I'm going with Megan to St. Louis for a few days next month."

Daniel only briefly glanced up from his notes.

"Of course it's okay, but what's in St. Louis?"

"A conference on the spread of HPV in teen-aged girls," Faye said flippantly, "but of course that's not why I am going."

"Given the state of things," Daniel said more seriously, "an HPV conference might be useful in your work as well."

Faye released an exasperated breath. "You're not kidding. That's about the only positive thing I can say about the Lewis Miller assault at Sunset Bluffs. We're not dealing with any STDs or pregnancy issues."

Daniel chuckled with annoyance. "The upshot of homophobic sexual pranks, I suppose." He waited a beat. "Really, what assholes."

"I don't disagree," Faye responded, "but the perps are kids, too. The question," she continued, "is this: what kind of ignorant jerks are running these families?"

"Look around," Daniel said. "It eludes me. It really does."

A pile of towels formed an amorphous mass at the foot of their bed. Faye plucked one up and began folding as she talked, eager to busy her hands and half-conceal her expression. Daniel would understand her wanting to see Edward (Daniel always understood), but the excursion felt too embarrassing and too exciting to share. So little of her relationship with Edward had stayed private (all because Faye had told, of course).

"Megan just invited me so we could get away for a few days on her hospital's dime. I'll catch up on filings and phone calls from the hotel during the day, and we'll go out in the evenings."

Faye stacked one towel on another and looked blankly at Daniel.

She continued, for good will. "My parents can take care of pick-ups and all that for the kids. Teague is between shows anyway, and the Walgraves can take Louisa to practice if my dad can't."

"Just let me check my travel calendar, but I don't think I'm gone again until May."

"Good," she said. "Megan will be thrilled to have a girl's getaway without my bringing our kids, even if she has to work through the days."

Daniel's agreement sealed it. Faye inhaled an obviously strained breath and smiled weakly. The room did a quick spin and rocked back into place. Daniel reached toward Faye and grasped the tips of her fingers.

"Are you worrying about the case?"

Faye's heart froze, momentarily confused.

"Oh," she stammered, "you mean the Miller case."

A switch in Faye's mind flipped away from thoughts of Edward and her own twenty-year-old file that never would close. Helping Lewis Miller would bring more good to this world than mulling a dead relationship with the dying man who had wronged her.

"Your office is doing everything it should," Daniel continued, "and that will make all the difference for that boy."

Daniel was right. Sunset Bluffs United had passed the case to SBPD immediately after the initial report from Lewis's parents. Formal authorities collected video surveillance of the Newport East locker room and witness reports from across the district. The only thing Faye and her colleagues could do for Lewis Miller was to shoulder his guilt. Faye did not believe Sunset Bluffs administration was at fault, but she would take the blame in a heartbeat to keep Lewis Miller from blaming himself. It was the bullies who planned the attack. They assaulted Lewis without hesitancy or remorse. But Coach Roland had done little to prevent the team's culture of toxic bravado and homophobia. The attackers' parents lined up behind their sons, lips sealed and attorneys in tow. Discomfort eked out from the puffy eyes and wringing hands of Lewis's parents, a well-meaning couple who wanted punishment for their son's attackers only slightly less than they wanted anonymity for themselves. Each meeting, Lewis seemed smaller and less interested in the platitudes batted around the office. Faye knew the process. Layers of feeling grew defensively around a victim's core and then thickened over time like an onion's protective skins. Without the justice of right action, of acknowledgment, of adult outrage, the folds roughened and toughened with exponential speed until finally they took the place of the child they shielded.

"I can't imagine charges not being brought," Daniel said.

Faye's brows twisted in surprise.

"That's cute. I think you're forgetting dozens of sexual assaults on the Aquinas Prep campus over seven decades."

"The incentive there is different," Daniel correctly countered. "There's no charges without police involvement, and there's no police involvement at Aquinas Prep without—"

"—an obviously dead kid?" Faye interrupted inappropriately.

Complementary sighs issued forth. Abuse culture exhausted Faye. Over the years, Daniel had thought about nudging Faye back toward teaching, but he knew this restorative work gave Faye more purpose than a classroom could. Dozens of Title IX filings and hundreds of conference presentations and school education campaigns had desensitized them both to the horrific details that had shaken Daniel's stomach during Faye's lawsuit.

"Charges may come, but I don't know that charges will help Lewis," Faye offered.

Daniel stood to meet Faye eye to eye.

"*You* are helping Lewis," he said proudly.

Faye dipped her head with closed eyes and nuzzled against Daniel's chest. A chirp sounded from the cuckoo clock in Wyatt's room. A tumultuous evening was closing, and with its end, Faye felt weepy and needed comfort. She laced her fingers together behind Daniel's back and held his body as close as it would go against her. She pushed their door closed with an extended right heel, and a few minutes hence they were making love in a darkened room. Faye positioned herself beneath Daniel, as she almost always did, and looked over his shoulder to the corner of their bedroom. She traced the outline of the painting on their wall, of the bureau, and of the mirror. Daniel's love making was generous and safe. He looked into her eyes and sometimes held her cheek in his hand. *I see you*, he always seemed to say. *I won't let you disappear.* Yet no matter his patience, Faye sank into her mind. After twenty years, she knew the scar that would not heal. Faye's sex life had never existed apart from Edward. Through the years, a vision of Edward had stood guard, lounging in the corner of every room where Faye had made love to a man that was not him. Now, after all these years, he was grooming her again, pulling her gaze over Daniel's shoulder. She wanted love and she wanted sex, but Edward's petulant outbursts and degrading accusations had sewn into her brain a pattern she could not unravel. During sex, a man could not love. *Love is love and sex is sex*, she thought, channeling Kipling. *And never the twain shall meet.*

The comforting sounds of her husband's settled sleep greeted Faye when she returned from the bathroom and climbed into bed. She kissed Daniel's temple; he nuzzled toward her in response. Faye stayed upright in bed, at first staring blankly at the running television. Postcoital reflections swelled in Faye's head. Tomorrow, she would tell Megan the good news. Next month, she would force a reunion with Edward. She had not seen Edward in twelve years, an expanse of time during which she had birthed three children, had moved back to Citrus County, and had thrown herself into the work of mothering her own kids and protecting everyone else's. And now here she was, planning to see Edward again. They had not touched in nineteen years..

In the half-dark, she closed her eyes and pictured her favorite Edward. The June night had been warm but breezy. The summer of 1998 had just begun; Faye had just graduated from Aquinas Prep. Vulnerability sat lightly in Doctor Vogel's folded hands that night. Faye and Doctor Vogel had been making small-talk in the piano room of his cluttered house. She had not yet seen Edward's bedroom or felt the smooth green and white tile inside Edward's shower. Faye remembered the baby pink tee shirt and baggy overalls she had worn to cover the parts of her she was afraid to expose: her teen-aged body was a mess of too-small breasts, shaving-nicked ankles, and too-bushy pubic hair. Behind trembling lids now, she could feel the heaviness of the air. Doctor Vogel had hooked his finger through her belt loop and tugged gently to pull her to him. He had spoken hesitantly, an unfamiliar uncertainty filling his voice.

"What is going on with us?" he had asked.

Two weeks after graduation, Doctor Vogel had asked Faye: "What is going on with us?"

Trumpets had blared in Faye's temples and blood had rushed to her head that night. It felt then like the start of a great adventure, the moment after which Faye would always know that Doctor Vogel really did like her. He *like liked* her, as Faye's friends had thought he did. The relief of finally being sure had been almost too wonderful to hold. She had accepted it like a long-awaited reprieve after too tiring a journey.

Daniel turned over abruptly in his sleep and slid his hand into hers under the pillows of their shared bed. The television hummed less quietly than Daniel's sleepy breathing. Her babies were tucked in bed and quieted.

Faye resurrected the memory of Doctor Vogel's fearful question. The start of so much, she had thought. She looked it over now like a gem in her hands, finally seeing the moment for what it was. It was the last moment she and Doctor Vogel would share unadulterated joy. A sudden bitterness rose in Faye's throat. Because of Edward, Faye realized, she would never enjoy the unrestrained sexual intimacy that was the birthright of her sacramental union with her husband. Each time they made love, Faye and Daniel moved intrepidly around her unhealed wounds. How she longed to be a *regular* wife. Was there such a thing? she wondered. Were there wives—were there *women*—who made love without the fear of violation and reproach? Her failures always standing guard, she turned her back to the present, sifting through the years for a long gaze at that younger, unbroken Faye.

Something about the blog bothered Faye. She couldn't quite put her finger on it, but something was missing. Millie and Mary didn't update *Prayers for Edward* very often, and when they did, the updates were usually technical in nature.

Edward has started a new drug called Opdivo. 3/2/19. Mary
Attendants reported no problems starting the line for chemo last night. 3/17/19. Millie
For anyone wanting to know more about the Opdivo treatment: opdivo.com/treatment61098. 3/28/19. Millie

None of the messages described Edward. The details instructed objectively, as a doctor's report would. They told of Edward's condition but not his mood.

Faye's inner voice pleaded with the screen. *How does he feel? How does he look?*

After his mother's personal note about buying guitar strings, the message board had gone dry and unfeeling. The women seemed to be relaying information from afar. A light sparked in Faye's head. She scrolled up and down the site, quickly scanning three months of updates. His wife was missing. There were no posts from Thuy.

IX

EDWARD COULD HARDLY BELIEVE HIS good fortune. All the niceties of family life had fallen into place by the spring of 2006. April in Meridian brought comfortable temperatures that invited outdoor gardening with neither the stifle of summer heat nor the threat of winter frost. On the eve of Edward's forty-ninth birthday, he nursed a home-brewed beer in the waning afternoon light and tended the brick-laid flower beds that flanked the front door of his family's modest but lovely two-story home on Green Arbor Drive. The home's burnt orange door complemented the warm exterior tones and made even more vibrant the expansive green lawn punctuated with multi-colored rose bushes and flowering greens that bloomed at this time each year. Amy's fourth birthday was just around the corner as well. For each of the past four years, Amy's birthday had overshadowed Edward's, which was just fine with him. Yes, he and Thuy had made a pleasant family. *Everything is relative*, Edward had reminded himself through the years. He and Thuy were certainly not partners in the way his parents had been, but measured against Edward's expectations, the life they had created was nearly idyllic. Edward tipped his beer bottle and drained its final swallow. Boy, did he feel how lucky he was. He was glad not to be mired in the mess that had been his exit from Aquinas Prep and Southern California. He had resigned at this time of year—St. Patrick's Day, in fact, it had been—but the crisp breeze of early April in Meridian was nothing like the high seventies heat of Citrus County that fateful week in 1999.

The first few months after his resignation from Aquinas Prep had felt chaotic at the time and were downright frenetic when he looked back on them now. Two Edwards had lived two lives in those early days after the explosion.

Dr. Edward Vogel had emptied his office cabinets under the cover of night (wondering if Faye had told Betty Frances about the day he had fingered her in the AP choral office) and had left a chocolate rose in the sheet music cubby of each of his Chamber Singer students. *I love you all and will miss you*, Doctor Vogel had scrawled on the movable chalkboard, flipping its blank green slate forward so that the musical staves tattooed on the opposite side reflected off the mirrored walls behind the piano. Doctor Vogel had maintained outward composure at St. Crispina choir rehearsal and had thrown out noncommittal responses to explain his sudden departure from Aquinas Prep. Doctor Vogel had helped AP administration find suitable candidates to fill his position and had sent AP choir parents letters of apology for his abrupt move. *Personal difficulties in my family need my attention*, his letter had claimed, *and I just cannot imagine staying on if the kids cannot have my most heartfelt effort.* So many calls had flooded Doctor Vogel's house in the wake of Faye's accusations that he had stopped answering. His telephone answering machine had recorded reel after reel of weepy, shocked voices.

When Doctor Vogel had exhausted himself with the stoic machinations of respectability, Edward had drawn the blinds in his front room and had drunk until the walls shook and his pores felt wet and invincible. He had cursed himself some, but, mostly, he had cursed Faye. She had baited him and begged him and promised him that she would not tell. He had risked everything for that girl and had listened through months of petty teen-aged dramas and for what? *What a joke*, Edward thought. The whole affair had been Faye's doing. That girl had gotten exactly what she wanted. He should have just told her *no* from the get go.

The alcohol had only helped until it didn't. Edward had then run through the remaining cocaine stuffed in the spare room. He had considered calling Diane to unleash the sexual frustration building inside him. But though he had wanted relief, the thought of another woman who might betray him (like Jane had; like Faye had) nauseated him. He had replayed his and Faye's relationship from every angle and still could not figure out why Faye had turned on him. *Ian must have put her up to it*, he had thought. But he couldn't be bothered with that in the immediate aftermath. He had to act fast to save his career. Edward had banked on his pending applications to a few community college jobs in the South and Midwest. If he could snag a new job for the upcoming school year and finally get out of this seasonless region where the cult of Aquinas Prep was his only root, he just might survive this stain and start the real career he had put off for too long.

Edward had denied the allegations to anyone brave enough to ask. Except, that is, to AP Principal Simon Murphy, head rector Fr. Steve Sandoval, Vice Principal Betty Frances, and that dreaded woman Jacqueline DeGroot to whom Faye had told all of their intimate secrets. Pride and shame had battled in Edward's mind the day of the personnel meeting. The usually pompous Dr. Edward Vogel had studied the tops of Fr. Steve's shoes during much of their conversation, avoiding his colleagues' expressions. Edward's shirt collar had felt tight around his throat as Simon Murphy read line by line from Faye's statement to VP Frances. Simon had been standing; Edward had shifted uncomfortably in a wooden chair, its design modern and uncomfortable. It had been humiliating, really, these men thinking the only sex Edward could get had come from a teen-aged girl.

Once he had realized he would not be fired, Edward had relaxed and an odd sensation had bubbled up inside. A strange pride had spread up to Edward's eyes, and he had raised his gaze to meet them after all. Sure, Simon Murphy had a wife at home, which meant daily access to real sexual intimacy and someone to partner with through life. But Edward, the faculty outcast at Aquinas Prep, not cool like Coach Martinez nor rich and slick like Mr. Windfield, had won the attention of a girl less than half their ages. She had thrown herself at him—everyone could see that—and he had satisfied her. Surely, they all knew he had every right to do it.

In his official HR interview on the matter, Edward had admitted what little he could without insulting the intelligence of his colleagues. Simon Murphy and Fr. Steve had nodded their heads slowly with folded arms in tacit agreement. *We get it*, they had seemed to say. *These girls really lay on the temptations. What, really, could you have done to avoid it?* VP Frances and Jacqueline DeGroot, who had heard the full story straight from Faye's mouth, had been less convinced. The women had scowled at Edward with contempt before falling in line with their male colleagues and agreeing to Edward's voluntary resignation.

"Resignation is best for everyone," Simon Murphy had asserted with a firm tug on his mustache. "Too much chatter would disrupt student learning."

"I agree," Betty Frances had chimed in. "We must think of the students first."

"I'd like to ask for one provision," Edward had boldly interjected. "My choirs are already booked for a tour of the Holy Land in June of this year. I'd like to stay on until the trip is complete."

Fr. Steve and Simon Murphy had eyed each other hesitantly.

"Well, I think it's possible that we could make arrangements," Simon had begun.

"Absolutely not," Jacqueline DeGroot had declared, her fist coming down loudly on Principal Murphy's desk. "I've gone along with my fair share of trickery and obfuscation around here," she had continued. "Faye Stoneman was a model student. She was our valedictorian and a superb athlete and an exemplary member of our community. And you, Edward, took advantage of her."

Jacqueline DeGroot had started perspiring then. Her hand had trembled as she stabbed at Edward's chest with her pointed figure.

"Let's all calm down," Simon Murphy had said placidly. "Penny—" here, he had nodded gently toward the school secretary who dutifully recorded meeting minutes. "Let's take this off the record, please. Jacqueline is right. If we want to get through this quickly without questioning and further investigation, Edward, you'll need to go now. Today. Faye is not the kind of victim that people will question. She comes from a good family and has strong credibility. She's attending Sacred Heart University for Christ's sake."

Fr. Steve had shifted his eyes down at this blasphemous exclamation.

"I'm sorry Father," Simon had continued, "but Dr. Vogel is not appreciating how important it is that we handle this properly. No investigation, no comment, and no special provisions. If you want to get out of here with your reputation intact, you will resign today, sir."

And so, it had ended there.

Thuy had appeared in Edward's St. Crispina adult choir a few weeks later when Edward had most needed to escape the stench of scandal at Aquinas Prep. And so he had capitalized on the desperation beginning to set in for Thuy who was thirty-five and unmarried, a condition her parents considered embarrassing if not out and out shameful. In 1968, four-year-old Thuy's parents had left war-torn Vietnam as refugees bound for a new world that promised safety and a bright future for their descendants. Four-year-old Thuy remembered naught from the trip but the feeling of relief upon the boat's arrival and the end of the near-constant sickness that had plagued her on the water. (*Why boat sick Thuy!* her father had exclaimed. *Water is her name's meaning!*)

When she and Edward met, thirty years later, the hope Thuy's parents had nurtured all those years was disappearing in the face of their daughter's inability to find a suitable husband. Though he wasn't Vietnamese and did not hold much wealth, Edward was Catholic, educated, charming, and interested in a quick courtship with their daughter. *God answers every prayer,* Thuy's mother had said. *And by God, Mrs. Nguyen wasn't kidding,* Edward thought. Thuy was exactly the answered prayer Edward needed after his mysterious ousting from Aquinas Prep.

Romance and, let's face it, relief had carried them through those first glorious months and had driven them to a dramatic display of sacramental perfection in the presence of God, family, and, to great effect, many of Edward's former Aquinas Prep students and their families. Merton had miffed Edward by neither showing up nor responding to his invite. *Well, forget him,* Edward had thought defensively, though Merton's slight had smarted. *If Merton wants Faye, he can have her.* The Fallons and the Laytons and the Fitzpatricks and the Gattos and dozens of other families had chosen Edward over Faye, a reality that still swelled Edward's ego every time he thought of it. Edward had even gotten Stu to sing at the wedding, the best *drop dead* to Faye if ever Edward could think of one. He knew Faye had always had eyes for Stuart Mendelsen.

The years he and Thuy had spent in Missouri had brought a vibrant life filled with colleagues and friends who complemented Edward's interests and opened for him a kind of community he had not experienced since graduate school. A few of the men in the Epiphany of our Lord parish enjoyed woodworking and gardening as he did. Edward quickly signed on with several of the opera lovers for quarterly trips to the Opera Theatre of St. Louis. The year after Amy's birth, Edward and Fr. Monihan had co-led an Epiphany tour of the Holy Land, Edward's history of organizing choral trips giving him instant status as the go-to parishioner for any number of Epiphany's major pilgrimages. Edward had clout with Peter's Way Travel Agency and his general worldliness enabled his navigation of spiritual adventures across the globe.

Amy's babyhood had been the consummate joy of both her parents' lives. Her jet black eyes and quivering red lips captivated Edward from their first meeting, a fifteen-minute cuddle during which Amy had slept fitfully and tried to wriggle her arms out of a tightly wrapped hospital blanket. Babies and Edward had mixed well if a bit awkwardly over the years. Anna, Millie, and Glen had given Edward a total of two nephews and four nieces during the years he had lived in Michigan and California. Many of his sisters' kids were teenagers by the time of Amy's birth, and Edward hoped they would dote on his little darling as he had on their mothers so many moons ago in Kansas. When his sisters and their kids seemed too distant to form much relationship with Amy, Edward was disappointed but not greatly so. He and Thuy needed only the new life they had built. After a few months off, Thuy had returned to her orthodontic practice, a career lucrative and fulfilling, especially in a small town like Meridian. As the local community had gotten to know the Vogels through Church and the college, Thuy's patient list had grown exponentially. A sweet young freshman from Edward's concert choir had swaddled and bottle-fed Amy in the mid-mornings while Thuy performed oral surgeries and Edward taught classes. In the afternoon, Thuy had pushed Amy in a stroller along the water's edge at Meridian River Park, stopping occasionally to rest on a wooden bench swing and wonder how she had been so fruitfully blessed in a short few years.

Amy's toddlerhood had gone on like this, a joyful though tiring season of life. (My God was it exhausting at forty-two years old to be mothering and treating patients and running the Church of the Epiphany's Women's Guild! Edward concurred. Forty-eight had not been easy. He feared forty-nine might bring more aches and more uncertainty about the world.) Still, *happiness* was a word too facile to describe Thuy's and Edward's existence: it was beatific and unclouded.

Edward folded both hands over the splintery wooden top of the shovel and peered up at the bright midwestern sky. April rarely brought thunderstorms, yet the horizon showed a smattering of dark forms moving westward toward Meridian. *Better to finish up now*, Edward thought, *and get these open bags of soil carted to the garage rather than risk a mess from a sudden spring downpour.* One last image of Amy ran through Edward's mind. His baby girl's squeal, her laugh, and her love of cupcake icing and balloons of all colors brought out a carefree ebullience Edward had not been capable of before Amy's birth. Life was really something, he had to admit. He was balancing a full teaching load at Meridian Community College, and his choir had recently been accepted for a solo performance at the summer's upcoming Windy City Choral Festival in Chicago. Edward, dare he think it, was happy.

Jack Hamilton, founding attorney of the renowned firm Hamilton, Shane, and Dupree, reassured Faye gently when her anxiety ticked up. Jack had made his fortune suing, deposing, questioning and generally putting in their place the cardinals, bishops, priests, nuns, clerks, teachers, and administrators who had for decades been abusing kids and covering up the Church's many crimes. Donovan Presley's case had been his most famous, garnering a seven million dollar settlement and turning more heads to the issue than other attorneys' haphazard filings had done over the previous few decades. Archbishops squirmed in their seats and lost their veneer of holiness under Jack's laser fine focus and comprehensive knowledge of the law. He was, as they say, a killer in the courtroom. Jack reserved his booming bravado for juries and cameras. With clients, Jack spoke in a compassionate father-knows-best tone. He was, in fact, father to three children and a confirmed Catholic. For obvious reasons, Jack was no longer devout.

Lance Shane, the perennial *bad cop* of Hamilton, Shane, and Dupree depositions, was ex-military, and it showed. After two tours in Afghanistan, Lance left the Corps behind but kept the closely shaved haircut and perfectly toned arm and chest muscles. A playboy rather than a father figure, Lance comforted victims by flipping the script on their abusers. His one-liners and stinging insults directed at the pathetic, perverted men (and some women) who manipulated the children in their care made Faye blush. Though his abrasiveness was off-putting at first, Lance's no-bullshit approach won Faye over after a few months of lawsuit lunches and deposition prep sessions. Hearing Edward belittled and mocked might be just what Faye needed. She told Jack and Lance all about Doctor Vogel (well, she held back a few details far too embarrassing to repeat) and tried on their flippant dismissal of the shame that accompanied her recovery. The fit was not right, but Faye wore it until she settled into it more comfortably.

At first, Faye didn't like that everyone involved at Hamilton, Shane, and Dupree referred to her relationship with Doctor Vogel as *abuse*. The word lived in every question they asked and every story they told.

"Did Vogel ever call your house as part of the abuse?" Jack asked.

Faye was used to this phrasing by now but she still shifted awkwardly at the word.

"He called my house a lot that summer and several times during my senior year at Aquinas Prep," Faye answered. "I don't know if you'd call that *part of the abuse*, though."

Jack softened his eyes and reached across the wide conference table for Faye's hand.

"Listen, sweetheart," he said with fatherly concern, "it's called grooming. The grooming process starts weeks, months, sometimes *years* before the physical assault. It's all part of the abuse. The calling during your senior year was to test your loyalty, to see how close he could get to you."

Faye nodded knowingly. Jack was right. Faye felt almost as small now as she had in Edward's bed that summer. All those protestations of love, all those confessions about his lonely nights, and all the complimenting of Faye's promising future were the perfect bait on Edward's line. She had swallowed it all, flopping happily along as Edward reeled her into his grasp. At first, the word *abuse* had not seemed fitting. Already, a few months in, the reality of Faye's victimhood embarrassed her. It was her narrative that no longer fit. Faye's romantic illusions and Edward's talk of lost love and of life's disappointments all made sense now as part of the play. How had she not seen it all these years? It wasn't just with Faye. Edward had been pulling all their strings. She and her friends had been mere marionettes dancing in his puppet show.

The acknowledgement nauseated but relieved her. Maybe she had been right to tell Ms. DeGroot after all. No wonder she had disappointed Edward those summer nights when the clothes came off and her body went numb with fear. She hadn't been ready. She had told him that, hadn't she?

"I don't know why I kept going there if I wasn't ready to do those sex things," she uttered weakly.

Seasoned, intelligent, important men and women in designer suits filled the sunlit room. Jack and Lance and their partner Marvin Dupree were there. Donovan Presley was there, too. In the five years since his own suit, Donovan had gone to law school, passed the bar, and been hired on by Jack's firm. A few victims' advocates and clerks rounded out the legal team. Faye raised her eyes to them. A tear slipped across her cheek to the folds of her ear.

"Faye," Lance said with authority. "You kept going because he was your teacher and you didn't want to disappoint him. You weren't ready because you were a child. He was forty years old, for fuck's sake."

Faye chuckled at Lance's usual irreverence. He was brazen, but he was right.

"When did you say he started spending time alone with you?" Jack asked.

Faye tried to think back. Her memory of their sexual contact was sharp. She remembered every outfit she had worn to his house, the sound of his conductor's alarm clock, and the smell of whiskey and cigar smoke wafting off the blue fabric of his bedsheets. The days at Aquinas Prep were less clear. They seemed to all run together. As far as she thought back, she and Doctor Vogel cleaved toward each other and away from everyone else. That couldn't have been true, though, because junior year she had spent all her time with Bryn analyzing their school-girl crushes on Stu and Santino.

"Europe rehearsals," Faye said with confidence. "Doctor Vogel always liked me, even from freshman year, because I was an excellent student. I was a do-gooder. I did everything right. He was proud of me. In Europe, Doctor Vogel started singling me out, and I liked it. I wanted to be on top, you know? I wanted to be Queen of the Renaissance Pageant. My friends and I all wanted to be close to him. We wanted to feel important, and we did."

Faye hesitated, remembering how wonderful Doctor Vogel's attention had felt. "He made me feel loved," she finally said. "I'm such an idiot."

Faye's words clung to the unmoving air. Donovan, quiet through most of his colleagues' questions, slid over to the chair beside Faye and looked into her eyes.

"Heald used to hold his palm flat against my chest," Donovan said without emotion, "here, at my heart, and then touch his forehead to mine. *God is working through you*, he would say. *You are God's love for me*." Donovan scoffed to shake off more unpleasant emotions. "What a rush, right?"

"What a prick," Jack yelled out.

"At fifteen," Donovan continued, "I thought I was the only person who could save this priest whom everyone loved. As long as I didn't scream when he was raping me—as long as I didn't expose his sinfulness to the world—he would love me, and he would be saved."

A swell of empathy surged in Faye. This wasn't academic for Donovan. The terror of his experience was unfathomable. *But*, she thought to herself, *Donovan didn't ask for it (like I did)*.

Jack's secretary caught his eye and pointed her wristwatch outward toward him. Jack nodded.

"We'll go through the detailed complaint after lunch," he said to Faye. "Let me just check this off, though. I wasn't sure after reviewing Donovan's notes."

The pages of a yellow legal pad crinkled loudly as Jack flipped through them.

"Honey, was there actual intercourse?"

A familiar tightening seized Faye. She swallowed to moisten her throat.

In every telling, Faye had denied it. Faye denied it in her Aquinas Prep revelation to Ms. DeGroot and in her informal interrogation with VP Frances. Faye denied it in the slow reveal to Megan over many drinks and many years. She denied it to Daniel during the unveiling of her traumatic past early in their relationship. In all those confessions, Faye denied that Edward had forced intercourse upon her. For seven years, the incongruity of the morning after Edward had taken her virginity had stayed sharp and present in Faye's consciousness. The lovely sensuality of dewy grass on her toes and warm croissants on her tongue wrestled with the disgust she had felt at her own body. She remembered squirming as warm sexual fluids gathered in her panties while she sat chatting with Edward at the kitchen table. And yet, she had been desperate that morning to hold onto him. Faye had never again allowed intercourse, and she had never told Edward about the pregnancy. She had spliced and shrunk and chipped away for so long at the memory of her abortion that nothing could bring it to the fore. The abortion was a wound too gaping. Faye never tended it because she knew it would never heal.

"No," she said in a hushed voice, "there was no intercourse."

"There's one thing that asshole will be thankful for when he responds to the complaint," Lance sneered. Faye read fierce judgment on Lance's furrowed brows. "Jesus," he continued unprompted. "This guy is a real piece of work."

Derision toward Edward was new for Faye. Everyone she had known (except, perhaps, her parents) had spoken of Edward with respect, almost awe. It was time to take off those protective Aquinas Prep blinders. Righteous anger, so much more than dollars, would be the lawsuit's real reward.

June 6, 2006 was Wallace Gormely's first day on the job. He rushed out the door, late already, and tried not to think about the malevolent aura of this day. As he scurried down the hall, Wally caught the incongruous opening of *The TODAY Show* blaring Matt Lauer's voice out from his grandmother's television set.

Coming up: the FCC says it is cracking down on obscene television content, five South Koreans abducted from an oil facility in Northeastern Nigeria, and believers around the world watch for signs of evil on this landmark day TODAY, 6/6/6.

Wally chided himself for being ill-prepared despite major excitement at this job opportunity. Sure, it wasn't glamorous. But when Wally's grandfather had said *get a job or get out of my house*, Wally knew he meant business. And so he had scoured the want ads and found this gem of a job that required only a high school diploma, a certified birth certificate showing at least eighteen years of age (certified copy allowed), a reliable vehicle, and a *clean and neat appearance*. At just eighteen and six months (and *always* clean and neat in appearance), Wally was the man for the job. His vehicle had always been reliable, but this morning en route to his first appointment, Wally had noticed windshield wipers not nearly up to the job of summer Meridian storms. Thunderheads were gathering in the east, so Wally had rushed back to his grandparents' house, taken the stairs two at a time to the second floor landing, had grabbed his grandfather's keys, and had re-started his first day of work in his grandfather's old Crown Victoria.

Thuy opened a sliver of light in the lace curtains to ascertain the identity of the young man hopping over puddles and up the brick-lined path to her door. An oversized black umbrella shielded his face. If the umbrella hadn't disguised the man, the sheets of driving rain would have. He looked to be a stranger. In anticipation, Thuy opened the door before he rang the bell. Amy was down for a nap and when four-year-olds wake from light sleep, they don't go back down easily.

"Hello there, ma'am," the boy said. Thuy could see that this young man was barely more than a teenager. Acne pocked his face, which was damp just from the car-to-door journey. "Is Mister Edward Vogel at home?"

Discomfort fluttered in Thuy's chest. Something felt amiss.

"It's Doctor Edward Vogel," she said so quietly the boy leaned in to hear her. "He's my husband. What is this regarding?"

"I have some papers to deliver for Mister, that is, Doctor Vogel ma'am. Is he at home?"

A creak on the stairs made Thuy's head turn. The boy looked over her shoulder and saw Edward walking proudly toward him, a tune in his head and the cozy feel of a rainy day in his heart. Edward sidled up by his wife and looked at the boy expectantly.

"What can we do for you?" he asked brightly.

Wally hesitated, making sure to get things right at his first appointment on behalf of ABC Legal Processing. He revealed a plastic-wrapped envelope from the inside pocket of his jacket, shifting his upper body in relief after pulling the papers from their spot against his chest.

"Mister Edward Vogel," he said in a clear, strong voice, "you have been served."

As a child, Faye had loved everything about the Church. She loved the priests swallowed into their heavy vestments, the old Latin phrases that punctuated the liturgy, and the expanse of Catholic Magisterium that reached along an infinite spectrum from the beginning to the end of time. She turned the words over in her mind: *apostolic, ex cathedra, transubstantiation*. Church history fascinated Faye because of its longevity and its mystery. The voice of God had descended on the bowed heads of Bishops reaching from early Church martyrs all the way to her own place in creation. Fourth grade Faye had prayed for a religious vocation, practicing daily prayers out of a missal she had borrowed from her family's usual pew at St. Cecilia's. This she and Edward had in common.

Edward, as a young altar boy, had longed for the priesthood. To the prepubescent Edward, nothing had seemed more joyous than the Consecration. Nothing was more satisfying than the reality of that transformation. The aging pastor at Holy Rosary, noticing Edward's unusually mature devotion and self-control, led him toward seminary. Edward abandoned this stilted vocation when adolescence brought sexual desire of equal urgency to his piety. Still, Edward and Faye both exulted in Church ritual and felt there a sense of being cherished. In this, they were quintessentially Catholic. They existed always with the certainty of being chosen and redeemable.

The legal complaint *Jane FC Doe vs the Roman Catholic Bishop of Fulton, the Diocese of Fulton Education and Welfare Fund, Aquinas Preparatory High School, and Edward Lee Vogel D.M.A.* offered redemption to no one. Jack's clerk filed suit with the Citrus County Municipal Court on June 6, 2006. By the evening news, the words *plaintiff* and *defendant* had lost all relevance. Faye learned quickly that a lawsuit's plaintiff did a great deal of defending. Faye chuckled, remembering Scripture: *When you are on the way to court with your adversary, settle your differences quickly.* The Catholic hierarchy missed its own message. The Church staffed itself several benches deep with mudslinging attorneys who accused the plaintiffs as much as they defended Church interests.

Faye stared blankly out the large windows of the Hamilton, Shane, and Dupree law offices. She could just barely see the ocean a few miles out. Its crashing white waves were subsumed into a generally blue haze from this distance. Three stories below, people in suits walked briskly across the office park, late for meetings in the few mid-rise buildings that dotted a plaza of glamorous shops and restaurants. A woman in an almond-colored skirt and blazer clutched her briefcase tightly and walked with her head down. A kind of pre-war equanimity flowed through Faye. She felt a bit like walking outside for a smoke but the desire was not urgent. Jack and Lance's handling of the lawsuit's initial days comforted and invigorated her. Aquinas Prep may have cast her from its glow of belonging, but she had a new tribe now.

The jovial boom of Jack's voice hung in the backdrop of Faye's thoughts. A change in his tone snapped her to reality.

"Are you saying he has new representation?"

Faye's eyes turned toward Jack.

"And he has actually filed with the court?"

Faye had not even thought about Edward hiring an attorney. These things had a structure to them. Sure, she was suing Edward, but she was really suing Aquinas Prep. Actually, Faye was suing the Church. The buck stopped at the Fulton Diocese, and the Bishop's purse—well, the Bishop's insurance, no doubt—paid damages.

"Give me her name," Jack said with annoyance. "I'll run the name around and see what I can find."

Jack scribbled illegibly on a notepad.

"It's Karen what?" he said. "Karen Fayland, with a *d*, or Karen Fallon?"

A lump rose in Faye's throat. She nearly jumped from her seat.

"Karen Fallon is his lawyer?" she asked, incredulous and panicked.

Jack held his hand over the receiver.

"Yes, Karen Fallon. Do you know her?"

The words caught in Faye's throat.

"She's my best friend's *mother*."

A year later, in the summer of 2007, Faye sat for a third round of depositions at the defendants' request.

"Enough of this bullshit," Jack said loudly into the phone. "If they want to grill her five more days—she's done nine days already for Christ's sake—tell them they can fly their asses to Illinois and meet us where she is. I am not making her come back to California again. Nine fucking days of questioning already."

And so Jack sent Lance to Tolono to fight Faye's battle, and Church lawyers settled their reservations for six nights at the Eastland Suites Hotel and Conference Center. Thick midwestern heat hung over Tolono at sunup and sundown in June, breaking only when the occasional thunderstorm erupted violently over the town before moving up to Chicago and across the lake to

Sacred Heart. Like the attorneys themselves, the heat moved in quickly that week and pressed on Faye an oppressive stillness.

Faye knew another week of depositions would mean more confrontation with Karen Fallon, the dreadful woman who was her former best friend's mom and Edward's new attorney. Mrs. Fallon had spent the previous spring peppering Faye with asinine questions about teen-aged crushes and making slut-shaming remarks that accused Faye of engineering a secret affair with Doctor Vogel and of making the whole thing up, though both could not be simultaneously true. *These perps hoodwink the parents even more than they do the students,* Jack had said. *They groom the whole community.* The blame had to fall on someone. After Edward's resignation in March of '99, Aquinas Prep had canceled the choir's planned trip to the Holy Land. Karen and Tom Fallon had gotten their money back as all the parents had, but their daughter didn't get what she had been promised. That selfish Faye had reached in and blown up all their plans. Leah and Tommy and Tiffany and all their friends missed out because Faye wanted more attention. And, too, there was the festering resentment Karen Fallon felt for the flippant, destructive girl who had broken her daughter's heart. For the childish sin of choosing Krystal over Leah, Faye was answering now. Karen Fallon exuded an incongruously happy mix of mockery toward Faye and pathetic allegiance to the man who had forced his adult hands into Faye's trembling, cocooning body before her Aquinas Prep diploma had even arrived in the mail. But none of that indignation compared to the real, unspoken horror. If Doctor Vogel *had* abused Faye, perhaps he had abused Leah, too. The catastrophe only got bigger when Aquinas Prep parents and Citrus County Catholics believed the victims instead of the adults.

Faye was ready to take on Karen Fallon again. Edward wasn't supposed to be there. No one had told Faye that Edward might be in her town eating in her restaurants, driving her streets, and smelling the slightly yeasty scent of macaroni from the Kraft plant by her house. But rushing through the lobby to Lance's room that morning, Faye had heard *his* voice. Though she may have glimpsed his figure—had felt his presence leaning heavily on the table, stirring weak conference center coffee with an impossibly flimsy stir stick—it was Edward's familiar voice that let her know he was there, mirroring physically in real time the massive space he occupied in Faye's consciousness. Again, eight years older, she and Edward had come together. Eight weeks of semi-secret California rendezvous had culminated in a run-down Illinois hotel and conference center. Lawyers and court reporters charted their movements. She heard him casually conversing with Mrs. Fallon.

"Feels like a real midwestern scorcher coming today," Faye heard him say as she walked briskly past.

"He's *here!*"

"Who's here?" Lance asked with far too little concern, stepping aside as Faye barreled into the hotel room doubling as an on location office.

"Vogel. He's *here* in the lobby. Why didn't you tell me he would be here?"

Lance sneered and flicked his head like he was shooing away an annoying gnat.

"Who cares? We don't care, okay? All he can do is sit there."

"Why didn't you tell me?"

"I didn't know." Lance pulled his collar out from beneath his suit jacket and grabbed a stack of files as he motioned toward the door. "His attorney has no idea what the fuck she's doing. What a stupid move. You never bring a perp to a victim's deposition. It will just make him look like a pervert who's trying to intimidate you."

Lance's forceful assurance was sobering. The lawsuit had made everything transactional. Faye felt thankful for this transformation. Rattling off abuse details over ordered-in sandwiches in the elegant Solita Beach high rise of the Hamilton, Shame, and Dupree law offices, Faye had slowly begun to let go of the teen-aged romance still gripping her well into adulthood. Jack and Lance, with their irreverent sense of humor and boisterous arrogance, had pried away Faye's delusional image of Edward like removing a pus-filled abscess. The lawsuit had become like a job, she a junior assistant to the men prosecuting her case. Edward's gray shirt and her burgundy ribbons, their private glances across the crowded choir room, and the tender way he had held her hands at the choral dance had all become evidence now. Faye was part of Jack's team, and seven years of reliving and fantasizing no longer felt humiliating or juvenile. Now, the journals stacked one on top of the other in the enormous Rubbermaid tub on her closet's top shelf proved her claims and increased her credibility, Jack said. Notebooks with crudely drawn 1998 calendars and sexual details scrawled in the margins were nothing to be embarrassed about, Jack assured her. Doodles and quotes and music notes stamped in glittery ink told a story all their own. They were the musings of a child processing her abuse the only way a child knew how.

Still, Faye put on this objective detachment like an ill-fitting coat.

If they knew the truth, Faye thought, *they'd realize that it was all my fault.*

Phrases like *sexual grooming, institutional negligence,* and *mandated reporting* were familiar to Faye now, their legalese assuring her she had done nothing wrong even as she remembered how desperately she had wanted Edward to want her and how terrified she had been whenever he hinted that they may have to end their affair. Lance's undiluted disdain for men like Edward, those he considered small and cowardly because they preyed on teen-aged girls, comforted Faye when she thought about Edward sitting in the conference room preparing his rebuttal. She remembered how in control Edward had always seemed, how unable she had been to direct their relationship. Lance was in charge now. Edward was quite literally on the defense. Even so, seeing Edward again seemed an event too emotionally momentous to share with Lance. But all her friends were gone, now, those who had loved him (not like she had but almost as much) and those who now hated her because she had destroyed their illusions. She and Edward's relationship was transactional now, too—a plaintiff and a defendant.

Mr. Weatherford: The time is 9:03am. Today is Monday, June 10, 2007. We are in Tolono, Illinois, recording the deposition of Faye Collins. I, Mr. William Weatherford, present myself for the defendants, the Roman Catholic Diocese of Fulton and the most reverend Bishop Ted Doyle. Also present are Mr. Lance Shane, counsel for the plaintiff, Ms. Karen Fallon, counsel for the defendant, and the defendant, Doctor Edward Vogel. These proceedings are being recorded as required by the Superior Court of Citrus County and counsel will refer to the assigned judge for adjudication of all objections that arise during questioning.

Faye appeared to stare directly ahead, her gaze in fact settling just above Mr. Weatherford's receding hairline and dark-rimmed glasses to where the tripod and camera stared back at her. Her tweed skirt felt a bit too tight at the waist but too large in the thighs. She wished Lance had let her wear something more form fitting and attractive. She had purchased a light gray suit on credit two days before, when her next round of depositions had been suddenly moved up, but Lance had asked her to wear something less professional and more traditionally modest. White tights and tan loafers made her skirt even less glamorous; she completed the demure look with a pale blue sweater, light and smooth, not itchy, and a gold crucifix affixed to a thin chain.

"I look like a nun," she had told Lance outside the conference room.

"Good. That's exactly what we want."

Faye tried to sit straight as the clerk administered the oath and Edward's lawyer shuffled papers almost silently where she and Edward sat on the straight side of the long oval-shaped conference table. At the table's narrow end, Faye clenched her hands together in her lap, wishing she could summon the strength exuding from Lance's posture. He leaned slightly forward in his chair and stared directly at Edward. In mere moments, Lance's intimidating gaze and almost palpable confidence put Edward on guard. A tingling sensation moved from his cheeks to the back of his tongue. Edward reached slowly for the bottle of water some hotel clerk had set in front of him and tried to appear natural as he unscrewed the thin plastic cap. He steeled himself against Faye's testimony, trying not to look at her too closely but also taking stock of the changes in her.

She looked older now, but not unlike her teen-aged self. Her skin seemed more clear and her cheeks a bit more full, but he could still see in her eyes the same sense of openness he had always found there. He had thought eight years in the world would have hardened her, but she seemed almost to be operating under this powerful attorney's lead in just the way she had followed Edward's. Her face was not made up. She wore only a slight bit of pale lip gloss and had not yet taken on the allure of a mature woman. Edward remembered how slow she had been to develop and thought now that she still seemed behind. He suspected that she wore sweatpants and Birkenstock sandals to the grocery store (unlike Thuy who, like his own mother, never left the house without full makeup), was still hesitant and too restrained in bed, and still thought of herself as a kid even though she was mid-way between twenty and thirty. Her hair was still long and she still dressed too conservatively, in his opinion. *Of course her lawyer might have told her what to wear,* Edward thought. Karen had instructed him to wear a dark suit and tie (not too loud). He regretted taking her advice. The other men were all attorneys and none wore ties. Faye's young attorney even had his top button undone revealing the collar of his undershirt. Edward had been sweating all morning and felt unnecessarily nervous. He was glad to be facing these charges like a man unafraid to show his face, but he also wished he had stayed away. Karen had insisted that he come.

"She won't be able to say those things if you are in the room," Karen had said. "I think having you there will at least force her to scale back these ridiculous accusations. She'll be too nervous to lie in front of you."

Karen had shocked Edward with her offer of pro bono representation in the face of such humiliating and tawdry charges. Her daughter had been one of Edward's students and one of Faye's best friends at the time of their affair, but Karen's indignation at Faye's filing suit had almost matched his. Her resolute belief in Edward's innocence and in Faye's duplicity sickened him because it was based in such self-righteousness and naivete. Karen hadn't asked him if he had *done* it. She accepted without comment that the girl had misread his affection and that his behavior had been harmlessly flirtatious. As rumors grew in the press and the public, Edward's scorn for his supporters had grown almost as intense as that for his accusers. The entire situation had him fuming. *Yes, he did it. She was basically an adult,* Edward kept repeating to himself. *What's the big deal?*

The whole affair was fuzzy to him now, coming back in bits and pieces over the years through a scent or a song as all former friends and lovers did. He didn't consider Faye much different from the rest of the women he had loved or lusted after through the years, all of whom—except his wife, of course—he had now lost. Edward knew Faye wasn't lying. Edward also knew he had done nothing wrong. He sometimes wondered if Faye and Ian had purposely sabotaged him, but looking across the table at her now, he knew that couldn't be true. Faye carried the weight of their affair on her now as she had then. It was her lawsuit, her *abuse*—as she was calling it in her testimony—but she didn't seem angry or vengeful as he'd expected. She seemed the same bundle of empathetic emotion she had always been. Edward shook his head almost imperceptibly and questioned Faye's profile as she stared across the table at the diocesan attorney: *Why, Faye, are you doing this to me?*

Mr. Weatherford: Good morning, Ms. Collins. Now that you have been sworn in, we will resume questioning in this matter. I will turn the questioning over to Ms. Fallon, representing the defendant Doctor Edward Vogel.

Faye breathed deeply, allowing the air to fill not just her lungs but her stomach. She was somewhat used to depositions by now, having answered questions inane, technical, irrelevant, and deeply personal for nine days in

California over the previous winter and spring. Depositions, Jack and Lance had explained, were not about finding the truth. Depositions were designed to confuse and obscure, to sully the victim's reputation and therefore buoy the abuser's credibility. She had become somewhat comfortable with discomfort and knew to expect the unexpected. The day would bring convoluted questions and illogical strings of inquiry that required her to jump years apart in her memory.

Who was your history teacher freshman year at Aquinas Prep? To whom did you lose your virginity? Did Merton attend your wedding at Sacred Heart? What was Doctor Vogel's phone number at the house in Fulton where he lived when you were his student? Who is your dissertation director? Did your tennis team win the CIF championship your senior year? Does Doctor Vogel have any distinguishing marks in his genital area?

She had told them several times how to spell her best friend's last name—Bryn A-p-p-a-m-m-a-r-a-f-f-i-l—and had sketched out Edward's flirtatious behavior during school days at Aquinas Prep. She had clarified obscure references and inside jokes that appeared scribbled in her yearbooks and had described the inside of Edward's bedroom. All of this information she had culled and crafted, bringing to life a complete picture of her high school years and the role Edward had played in attaching her to him before exploiting and abandoning her. She had woven this narrative in the safety of Mr. Weatherford's California office. Mr. Weatherford, a man stern and precise in his examination of her, ultimately felt unaffected by her presence. He had deposed dozens of victims over several years for the sake of defending the Church. For Karen Fallon, this suit was personal. Something was driving this woman to put Faye in her place.

Ms. Fallon: Tell me Ms. Collins, is Doctor Vogel circumcised?

Faye's mind went blank. A sharp pain stabbed at her throat. The ticking of a wall clock clicked in her ears. *Tch. Tch. Tch.*

Ms. Collins: I don't recall.

Leah's mom balked (unprofessionally, as far as Faye was concerned).

Ms. Fallon: How is it that you claim to have been intimately involved with Doctor Vogel but you do not recall if he is circumcised?

Condescension dripped off Karen Fallon's words.

Ms. Collins: At the time that Doctor Vogel exposed himself to me, I had never seen a man's penis before. I was also scared and nervous. I don't think I would have known whether it looked circumcised or not.

Ms. Fallon: Is your husband circumcised?

Ms. Collins: Yes, he is.

Ms. Fallon: Thinking back now, then, can't you say whether Doctor Vogel was circumcised?

Mr. Shane: Objection. Asked and answered. She does not recall.

Ms. Fallon: I'll move on. I just wanted to give her an opportunity to explain herself.

Faye thought Leah's mom smirked. Edward had not once looked up from the legal pad on which he was writing.

Ms. Fallon: Does Doctor Vogel have pubic hair?

Faye almost shivered in the air conditioned room. Her body felt hot; her hands, cold. The hair on Faye's arms prickled against sweat dimpled skin. Why didn't she know these answers? Edward had pushed himself into her hands and her mouth, straddled her against her will, forced himself slowly through her body's defenses and deposited that thick, sticky fluid all over and inside her body. She could not picture his body. They were trying to trick her. Faye could not see it (the pubic hair) in her mind's eye just now. And so, she could not say for sure.

Ms. Collins: I don't recall.

Ms. Fallon: Does Doctor Vogel have chest hair?

They won't believe me, she thought frantically. *How can this be happening? He's right there and he knows. He knows it happened.* She could remember his gravelly voice and the insistence of his tongue in her mouth. She could remember the smell of his sheets and the cloud of shaving cream he had smeared on his cheeks in the bathroom with the checkered tiles and green towels. But no, she could not recall his chest hair (though surely it must have been there).

Ms. Collins: I don't recall.

Leah's mom sounded exasperated this time.

Ms. Fallon: Does Doctor Vogel have hair anywhere on his body?

Hot tears pushed against the back of Faye's eyes. This hateful woman was breaking her, and Edward was watching. *Tell them*, she wanted to scream. *Tell them you loved me and so you did those things to me. Tell them what you did!* Faye gathered herself and spoke slowly.

Ms. Collins: He has hair on his head, yes.

Ms. Fallon: Is that it?

Ms. Collins: He has hair on his arms and sometimes on his face.

Ms. Fallon: What size is Doctor Vogel's penis?

Ms. Collins: I don't know how to answer that.

Ms. Fallon: You allege that you have seen Doctor Vogel's penis, so I'd like you to tell me what size it is.

Ms. Collins: I don't recall.

Ms. Fallon: Was it about five inches long?

The questioning was just ridiculous, now. Faye's limbs felt heavy. Panic pushed her heart against her chest. Girls like Faye did not think about penis size then. Nor did she think about it now. She had no idea the size of her husband's penis (which she saw every day, had seen that morning while he towel dried in their room just out of the shower).

Karen Fallon's disbelief tumbled out of her mouth and covered the table. Faye put herself back to that bedroom. Her breathing was so tense she was almost holding it in. She remembered Edward taking her hand and wrapping it around that part of his body, even after she had told him how much it scared her. His hand had enfolded hers, the pressure stopping her each time she tried to pull away. In the dark of that room she could smell Edward's familiar cologne and had tried to take solace in it. His features and his eyes had been dark though she knew in the light they were vibrant and kind. She had squeezed her eyes tightly and tried to float away. She remembered the long groan of his orgasm, the sourness of that awful wetness.

Ms. Collins: I don't recall the size.

Ms. Fallon: Was it three inches long?

Ms. Collins: I don't recall.

Leah's mom pressed, enjoying herself now.

Ms. Fallon: If I showed you a ruler, would you be able to tell me if it was shorter or longer than three inches?

Ms. Collins: No, I do not think I could.

Rage sent a dull buzzing between Faye's ears. *Maybe if you shoved the ruler down my throat,* Faye wanted to say.

A smirk spread across Lance's face when Edward glanced in his direction.

Karen Fallon hardly recognized her own voice. All this talk of penis size and pubic hair sickened her. But it was the only way, she had told Doctor Vogel, to expose this girl for the liar she was. In Karen Fallon's opinion, Doctor Vogel was being far too reticent. He was probably embarrassed (*the poor man*) by this little slut's overwrought accusations.

Humiliation spread outward to Edward's face, feet, and groin as Faye struggled to respond to Karen's attacks. *By God, this line of questioning had better end soon!* Edward resisted the urge to shift in his seat. Faye had begged him and teased him and promised she would not tell. Here she was—*telling!*—and the most intimate details at that. Edward braced himself for what shaming might follow, but Faye seemed genuinely confused by Karen's questions about his features. Faye's earlier depositions exploded with details Edward had forgotten. *Had he really worn the same shirt at her graduation and on the first night they went to bed together? Had they eaten popsicles in his garage, the door half open so as to conceal Faye's presence so late at night? Had he stocked his fridge with Cokes and bought packages of the fudge-striped cookies that so delighted Faye?* Faye had unfurled the scenes with vivid allure. Edward remembered none of that. (He believed her. Faye would not lie, though obviously she misinterpreted a lot of what happened that summer.)

Plenty *had* stayed with him. At times through the years, Edward had fantasized about that sweet girl's belly, slender but soft, the skin a bright white luminescence in contrast to the deep tan of her arms and legs. He traced in his mind the fleshy part of her thigh that slightly flattened against the bedsheet as he pushed open her legs, and he remembered the sharp angularity of her tailbone as he raised her up to take her in his mouth. After a parade of women his own age whose bodies bore striations and stretch marks, whose skin carried the damage of experience, whose breasts and bellies slumped with the weight of forty years' living, Faye's body thrilled Edward so intensely he could not look away from it. And so he had returned to it as often that summer as he could without concern for Faye's tears or his own safety. Her flesh had addicted him, to tell the truth. Her body was an unmarred playground offering a high more intense than whiskey or cocaine. It wasn't that she was beautiful, though Edward had found Faye lovely and worth loving. It was that she was untouched, her skin not yet weary, her body not yet spent. An improbable shame pricked at Edward. Why had Faye found *his* body so forgettable?

Therapists in California, at Sacred Heart, and in Illinois had told Faye that a person's brain used memory loss as a protection against trauma. *That's for sure*, her subconscious said. So little of Edward's body was imprinted on her visual memory. The person of Edward Vogel did not exist for Faye as he did for all others who had known him. His aura was part of her now, a nameless, disembodied idea incarnate in the fear and guilt that sat palpably under Faye's ribcage. Edward was a feeling, and feelings did not have pubic hair or distinguishing moles or measurable genitalia. She had seen him without clothes dozens of times. She had showered with him, had shimmied her nude body up against his in her sleep, and had felt the panicked suffocation of his thrusting at her mouth while she struggled to breathe. But she could not see those images anymore.

All these years, Faye held only one image of that part of Edward. The scene, like a gory photograph, reeled in Faye's mind. She had seen Edward's naked penis, looking wet and puffy, by the light of the refrigerator in Edward's Bonita Vista kitchen. It had been dark throughout the house, though it had not necessarily been the middle of the night. Faye could not remember if she had been sleeping over or merely staying until curfew that night, but it had been common practice for Edward to extinguish the house lights before carrying or coaxing Faye to his bedroom. After they had *fooled around*, as Edward called their sexual encounters, they walked together to the kitchen for a cold drink. Faye remembered covering her naked body with the bedsheet, its blue fabric a long train following her through the piano room into the kitchen. She had not thought about Edward's nakedness (he almost always kept a tee shirt on during sex) until a splash of light from the open refrigerator revealed the shocking reality of his exposed penis. The fleshy mass jutted out at an odd angle between Edward's thighs as he crouched before the open fridge door. Faye had looked quickly away, intrigued and repulsed by the sight. Edward rummaged through the crisper choosing a can of fruit juice. Faye knew no one else who kept aluminum cans stacked sideways in their vegetable drawer. She had never seen fruit juice in a can.

Lance would not agree that the morning session had been a disaster.

"It's fine," he said, with his signature head shake. "Those questions are bullshit anyway. They don't matter, and they make that woman look as horrible as she is. The judge will not be happy when he hears the tone she used toward you."

"I looked like an idiot."

"Give yourself a break. Your answers showed that you are conscientious, that you want to get it right."

Faye blew a stream of smoke out the window of Lance's rental car. "But I did not get it right," she said with an edge of hysteria in her voice. "Now they're going to think I'm lying."

"Faye," Lance said soberly. "Calm down. You freaked out when Vogel showed up, and you let them fluster you. They know you're not lying. This is your tenth day of a ton of questions and a ton of answers."

Confidence by proxy stirred in Faye. She nodded and dragged forcefully on her cigarette.

"Do as much storytelling as you can," Lance reminded her. "Give details. Set the scene. That kind of stuff frightens them because they know juries love stories. Juries care that you had Barbie Doll underwear or whatever."

It was Hello Kitty, Faye thought, but she got Lance's meaning. For nine days' worth of questioning in California, Faye had sprinkled colorful details into her answers, her strength growing as she recounted the warm breezes and musty scents wafting through Fulton in July of 1998. When testimony resumed after lunch, Faye would lean into her narration, bringing back to life Edward's dusty wood flooring and the click of the security light above his back porch. Many of those encounters sat fully embalmed in the front of her mind, unchanged after a nine year gag order. The best part of the lawsuit wasn't reparation or reward, it was the permission to talk about Edward. The story of Faye and Edward was the story of her life. Faye's existence had perpetually stalled in 1998. Now, thanks to the lawsuit, everyone else was talking about those days, too.

Ms. Fallon: When was the last time you allegedly had sexual contact with Doctor Vogel?

Ms. Collins: December 23, 1998.

Ms. Fallon: And that was when you had already graduated from Aquinas Prep, correct?

Ms. Collins: Correct.

Ms. Fallon: And you were already eighteen years old, correct?

Ms. Collins: Correct.

Ms. Fallon: What happened on that final occasion when you claim you had sexual contact with Doctor Vogel?

Faye felt like smiling. *She's diving in*, Faye thought, *because she thinks I'll be embarrassed to describe the sex in front of him*. But asking Faye to describe her final intimacies with Edward was a gift to her case. Faye's mind flashed immediately back to that bright December day. She had arrived at Edward's house just as the sun rose highest in the sky, its light blinding but its heat mild. She began slowly to set the scene, each detail unfolding the way she had remembered it all these years. She had revisited it often as one might cling to a worn blanket that had once given comfort but now only gave the memory of that solace.

Ms. Collins: I arrived at Doctor Vogel's house about noon that day. I was home on Christmas break from Sacred Heart and had told my parents that I was going out to do some last minute Christmas shopping. The back door was open, so I walked right in, like I always did. He was sitting in the front room at first, flipping through some papers while making cassette tapes of music for the students. He told me that his mom and dad had just come to visit from Kansas but had flown home the night before. A bit later, he moved over to the computer and started clicking around in his files while we talked. He almost never just sat while I was there. He was always tinkering with something in the garage or working on something related to school at his computer desk. Eventually, maybe after about twenty minutes, he grabbed my hand and pulled me onto his lap, and we started kissing. I remember it felt strange and a little funny because he had grown a full beard for the AP Choir Renaissance Pageant, which was held the week before Christmas. I had never kissed anyone with a beard before. He carried me into his bedroom. He put me down on the bed and performed oral sex on me. I remember looking toward his bedroom window as he did it, trying to see through the slats in the blinds to the backyard. It was a really bright day. After a while of that, he took off his shorts—he had been wearing sweat shorts or just cozy house shorts—and his underwear, and he climbed up to where I was. He kind of straddled me with his knees on either side of my legs and looked down directly at me. I remember that the room seemed really bright though it still felt kind of like winter. I remember thinking that the brightness made his eyes look really blue. We were kind of laughing. He reached over to a bottle of lotion on the nightstand to the right side of the bed and squeezed a few pumps of the lotion onto his hand. Then he masturbated until he ejaculated on my stomach.

Faye stopped speaking and tilted her head slightly, her eyes locked on Leah's mom's stare. *It happened*, her eyes said to this woman who was both her former friend's mom and her abuser's attorney. *It happened just like that. I know it, and he knows it.*

Mr. Weatherford found himself holding his breath. The stories he had heard in depositions were stomach churning. Victims had described a priest who assured adolescent Catholic boys that he could cure their homosexuality by giving them orgasms while they watched porn, coaches meeting teen-aged girls for sex in locker rooms during passing periods, pastors paying for abortions, and Catholic school administrators telling fourteen-year-old girls that they shouldn't be tempting men by wearing their skirts too short. He had actually vomited one day in the tiny restroom off his office. He had been suddenly overcome when re-reading testimony from a man whose parish priest had ejaculated on the man's chest when he was eleven years old. The priest had traced a cross in the semen and then forced the boy to do the same. The boy's mother was a divorcee who had sent him to the priest every Saturday afternoon for an ice cream treat and some fatherly influence.

Faye Collins, the woman before him now, had filed suit with accusations that were comically dull in comparison. He believed she had not been forced and he couldn't imagine she'd really been harmed, but the exactness of her memories and the steadiness of her tone as she recounted them impressed him. In a dozen years of taking depositions, he had never seen a defendant stare down his victim. Any good attorney knew that bringing the perpetrator to a deposition would make their client seem controlling and insensitive, if not desperate. But there he was, only one in a slew of stains on Aquinas Prep and the Diocese of Fulton, showing up to dispute accusations so commonplace against the Aquinas Prep of the 1990s that Mr. Weatherford had no doubt they were true. Each interaction had happened, he knew from experience, exactly how this young woman was describing. But here they were, again, to poke holes in her memory, question her motives, and ultimately shave as many thousands as possible off the settlement they all knew the Church would eventually pay to this victim and all the others.

Karen Fallon received Faye's monologue like a slap to the face. She seemed in disbelief at this girl's audacity and hoped the incredulous tone of her own response would somehow discredit Faye.

Ms. Fallon: Did Doctor Vogel say anything during this alleged encounter?

Ms. Collins: Do you mean during the sexual contact?

Ms. Fallon: Yes. Do you remember anything Doctor Vogel said to you during this alleged sexual encounter?

Faye's shoulders slumped a bit and her courage waned. She had hoped never to repeat these humiliating words. She had not even told her lawyers this little story.

Ms. Collins: Yes. After we had cleaned up and were getting dressed, he kissed me again and I said something like *it feels weird and prickly kissing you with that beard.* And he said, *Now you know how I feel.*

The conversation about Edward's beard had been seared in her memory. So often, Edward had spoiled their time together with remarks that seemed intended to embarrass her, and she had never understood why. During the Renaissance Pageant her senior year, Faye had fantasized about kissing the bearded Doctor Vogel, cupping the scruff of his cheeks in her hands as she touched his soft lips with hers. When the time came, a year later, the feeling had been awful. It had been bristly and abrasive and off-putting and surprisingly scary. And then he had made that horrible remark about kissing through the beard, and she had fought back tears of shame. At a time when she was so young, Faye was still self-conscious about her pubic hair. She had begun senior year to wear boys' swim trunks over her bathing suit so no one would see the dark hairs curling out from beneath the hot pink spandex of the women's suit she wore underneath. She was surprised to realize at this moment, casting her eyes down to the itchy tweed skirt, that she had never forgiven Edward for making this remark, for confirming her fear that men would see her as a collection of body parts that weren't as sleek or sexy or perfect as they wanted her to be.

Lance kept his eyes trained on Edward and saw a flash of recognition cross his face. *Of course this prick remembers*, Lance thought. Such a small moment it had been, but even nine years later, Edward did remember. He had thought the joke such a clever thing to say and had enjoyed watching Faye squirm and blush at its meaning.

Ms. Fallon: What do you think he meant by that remark, Ms. Collins?

Faye let out an exasperated breath before speaking. Mrs. Fallon was there to watch Faye's discomfort. Faye had told everyone's secrets. Leah's mom planned to make her pay.

Ms. Collins: He was saying that kissing him with a beard felt for me like he felt when he was performing oral sex on me. Because of my hair. Down there.

Ms. Fallon: How did this alleged encounter end?

Ms. Collins: After we got dressed, we talked a little. He told me he did not want me coming to his house ever again because students and teachers at Aquinas Prep had become suspicious and thought he might have been having sex with me.

Ms. Fallon: Doctor Vogel told you that other teachers at the school thought he was having sex with you?

Ms. Collins: Yes. He told me that Jaqueline DeGroot, a religion teacher whom I also had been close with when I was a student, had made some comments to him about rumors she had heard.

Ms. Fallon: After this discussion, did you leave?

Ms. Collins: Yes.

Ms. Fallon: Did Doctor Vogel walk you to your car?

Ms. Collins: No. Before I left, he stood outside with me on the back porch while I smoked a cigarette. When I was finished, I told him that I loved him, and he kissed me on the top of my head, on my forehead, and then on my lips. And I left.

And now, Faye thought. *Here we are. Nine. Years. Later.* Narrating these final moments, Faye could see herself driving away down Edward's tree-lined street, tears beginning to stream down her face, the jarring sounds of too-giddy Christmas carols pumping through her car stereo. She could feel again the emptiness of that day, the hot knot in her stomach that had started growing like a ball of fire from tiny embers of fear to a raging blaze of panic. She sensed that Edward did not love her anymore. The absence of love was palpable.

Faye remembered feeling that day like she had lost him. She had not yet known that she would revisit this loss through the years, that each milestone they crossed in their now separate lives would leave a parallel trail of what ifs, and that before she was the age Edward was then, she would have lost him forever to the cancer. Almost glaring at Edward now, watching his performed indifference, Faye had already become used to his presence and took for granted that the loss of Edward might always be followed by reunion. She did not know now, as the court reporter typed, that Edward would be dead when a dozen more years had passed.

Ms. Fallon: How many times did you sleep over at Doctor Vogel's house?

Ms. Collins: I slept over on seven different occasions.

Ms. Fallon: Let's start with the first occasion. When did you first spend the night at Doctor Vogel's house?

Faye felt strangely relieved this tenth day of depositions as the details poured out of her. Edward knew what had really happened between them. Karen Fallon had hoped Edward's presence would unnerve Faye. Instead, Faye started looking toward Edward as she talked, showing him a strength that came from knowing the truth.

Over dinner and drinks at the end of day one, Lance assured Faye and Daniel that Faye was hitting it out of the park.

"You can tell Vogel is fucking terrified beneath that asshole veneer," Lance said, stuffing a fat carne asada taco in his mouth. "Does he always look so fucking arrogant and pissy?"

Faye sipped her margarita and tried not to look at Daniel's reaction. Daniel had never seen Edward. Truthfully, he had spent nine years hoping Faye's trauma would finally just go away. Daniel was more than prepared to support her if it never did, but he wished it away all the same.

Faye tried to sound flippant.

"Yes," she replied to Lance. "He always looks arrogant. Extreme haughtiness is his thing."

"I can't fucking see why," Lance responded. "He even looks like a perv."

Daniel chuckled. Faye did not. Blaming Edward instead of herself felt good, but the whole situation reeked of humiliation either way. She had developed theory one in 1998, and it had carried her for better or worse until her first meeting with Donovan, Jack, and Lance: Faye was a tease and a fraud who had betrayed a man who needed her love. She was still getting used to theory two: She was a fool who had been assaulted by a serial abuser set on manipulating whichever vulnerable students he could get his hands on. Both theories unfolded toward the same conclusion. Faye was a failure. Faye pushed her plate aside and lit a cigarette, blowing smoke up toward the brightly colored plastic roosters lining the ceiling of *Dos Reales Restaurante*. Her mind flipped somersaults while Lance and Daniel kept talking in the background. She had to man up and get angry. Matching Lance's disdain was the only thing likely to carry her through.

"I wouldn't worry about Vogel leering at you any more," Lance began.

Lance continued, motioning toward Daniel with his beer. "Your wife kicked their asses today. Vogel won't show tomorrow. He'll go back to wherever the fuck he came from and his attorney will finish out the week alone."

Wrong. At nine o'clock the next day, Edward was right back in his seat.

Lunch at Hickory River Smokehouse settled Faye's nerves but upset her stomach.

"Finish up that cigarette," Lance said with forced equanimity. "We have to be in our seats in three minutes."

Edward patted his tie and looked down his nose at an outstretched palm. Leah's mom looked fresh. Raw bitterness pushed her forward. William Weatherford regretted not bringing co-counsel. Karen Fallon would have been a poor lunch date under good circumstances. William found her chummy allyship insufferable. Imagine equating her client with his. William Weatherford represented the Bishop of Fulton, a man magnanimous enough to recognize the Church's flaws and savvy enough to look out for its assets. Karen Fallon had chosen, for reasons William could not understand, to wade waist deep in the actual perpetrator's sleaze. William put on a serious face and let Karen Fallon resume her questioning. He half listened and half thought of his two children back home in California.

Ms. Fallon: Has Doctor Vogel ever hurt you?

Edward had grabbed her wrists the final night she had seen him. They had been fighting, and he had been pushing her away as she tried to embrace him. It hurt, but she knew he had not been trying to hurt her. The sex had hurt, too. That summer, the tender folds of her labia had been sore from so much probing. The day he ejaculated into her she had felt bruised and swollen. Adult Faye knew pain and discomfort weren't entirely abnormal during and after sex. She hadn't known that, then. Faye forged an answer to Mrs. Fallon's spurious question.

Ms. Collins: Do you mean physically?

Mrs. Fallon paused. She resumed her questioning with a sneer of disdain.

Ms. Fallon: Is there some other way that he hurt you?

Faye fought the urge to shrink down in her seat. Lance had told her to hold steady, no matter the question. Her confidence waned. She nearly whispered her response.

Ms. Collins: Emotionally. I would say he hurt me emotionally.

Annoyance shone on Mrs. Fallon's face.

Ms. Fallon: Did you file this lawsuit because you were angry that Dr. Vogel got married?

Faye was visibly confused. Lance scoffed.

Ms. Collins: No.

Ms. Fallon: Were you angry when Dr. Vogel refused to keep seeing you?

Ms. Collins: No. It wasn't like that.

Ms. Fallon: You weren't angry?

I was a kid, she wanted to scream. *I was scared and angry, and I was a kid and so were my friends, and I missed him and loved him and wanted to be near him, and I was just so scared and so young. So young and so scared.*

Faye dropped her voice.

Ms. Collins: I felt hurt.

Faye's righteous anger slipped away. The memory of his rejection suddenly stung her.

Ms. Collins: It just hurt so much.

Ms. Fallon: Is that why we are all here? Are we here because Doctor Vogel hurt your feelings, Faye?

Mrs. Fallon's head bobbled with incredulous outrage.

Maybe, Faye thought. Lance interjected.

Mr. Shane: Objection, argumentative. And misstates her testimony.

Lance argued with Leah's mom about the validity of his objection. Faye tuned them out, hoping for a cigarette break and thinking about all the hurt that had passed between her and Edward. He had hurt her so thoroughly that summer. Since then, Faye thought, only she had been doing the hurting. Edward started it, but Faye had spread that hurt around. Edward's job, his reputation, and her friendships were all casualties of Faye's betrayal. How much and for what did her love mitigate the pain? If Edward's love did not matter, if his love were no excuse for the harm he had inflicted on her, then why should her love excuse all the trouble she had caused him? Maybe twenty-six was still too young for Faye to understand what had happened to her. The attorneys at Hamilton, Shane, and Dupree talked a good game, but all their legalese about grooming and consent and accountability could not break through Faye's guilt.

Ms. Collins: No, that is not why we are here.

Ms. Fallon: Why did you bring this lawsuit, Ms. Collins?

Twenty-six-year-old Faye and seventeen-year-old Faye butted heads in her brain. She had thrust herself at Edward because he had needed her. Doctor Vogel had convinced her of that. She had given him all the love there was. *He shouldn't have taken it*, grown-up Faye said. *It wasn't his to take.*

Ms. Collins: They were supposed to protect me. They did not protect me.

Ms. Fallon: Who was supposed to protect you?

Ms. Collins: Aquinas Prep, Mr. Murphy, Fr. Steve. All of them. Doctor Vogel should not have done this. He should have stopped himself. The adults should have stopped him before it happened.

Faye narrowed her eyes and pushed the final words out of her mouth.

Ms. Collins: You were my best friend's mom. *You* were supposed to protect me.

Ms. Fallon: Did you ever talk with Dr. Vogel about having sexual intercourse?

Ms. Collins: Yes, he talked about it all the time.

Ms. Fallon: Did he ever say that he wanted to have intercourse with you?

Ms. Collins: Yes, he did.

Ms. Fallon: When did he say that?

Ms. Collins: He said it whenever we talked about sexual stuff. He told me on the phone a few weeks after I graduated from Aquinas Prep that he had been fantasizing about having sex with me. During the summer of 1998 when he was performing oral sex on me and doing other sexual things, he would say he wanted to make love to me. He always said he wanted to be inside me. He wrote emails to me at Sacred Heart and said he was thinking that if I were back in Fulton with him that we would be making love. I asked him if it hurts to have sex and he said it would probably hurt a little the first time we did it. I told him I wasn't planning to have sex with anyone until I got married.

Ms. Fallon: Did he say anything else about having sexual intercourse with you?

One of Faye's most vivid abuse memories sprang to her mind. It was still early, maybe the second week of July. The heat was not yet scorching, and the breeze through Edward's bedroom window chilled the air. It was evening but not full dark, and in the gloaming, Faye and Edward could make out each other's features without a lamp or the overhead light. Faye was wearing a tank top. Its baby blue fabric was printed with tiny violet and pink flower buds. Her jeans were a size too big; a patch from the JFK Presidential Library was ironed onto her back pocket. Edward lay on his back; Faye straddled him and laid her head against his chest. *Sit up*, Edward had told her. *Sit back and let me look at you.* Edward had reached his hands up and cupped them over Faye's breasts. Her cheeks blushed. A whoosh of adrenaline rushed between her thighs. *This will be one of your favorite sexual positions*, Edward had said. In her head, Faye had filled in the phrase Edward omitted. *When you grow up*, she had thought. *This will be one of your favorite sexual positions when you grow up.*

Ms. Collins: Yes. He said that being on top during sex was going to be my favorite sexual position. I took that to mean when I grew up and started having sex.

Ms. Fallon: But he did not say that, did he? He did not say *when you grow up?*

Ms. Collins: No, he did not.

Ms. Fallon: Did you have sexual intercourse when you were in high school?

Lance called out before Faye could answer.

Mr. Shane: Are you asking if she had intercourse with the defendant or in general with anyone?

Ms. Fallon: Did you have sexual intercourse with anyone when you were in high school?

Ms. Collins: Absolutely not.

Ms. Fallon: You say that with conviction. Did you believe in high school that having sex before marriage was wrong?

Ms. Collins: I'm not sure I would characterize it that way.

At twenty-six, it was difficult for Faye to believe she had passed such judgment. Edward's sexual history had not bothered her, but Krystal's had.

What an idealist Faye had been. Waiting until marriage had been a quiet crusade for Faye long before virginity crusades were in vogue.

Ms. Collins: Actually, let me revise that. Yes, I thought at that time that sex before marriage was wrong.

Ms. Fallon: Did you tell Dr. Vogel you thought sex before marriage was wrong?

Ms. Collins: We never talked about sexual activity as *right* or *wrong*. I told him I intended not to have sex until I got married.

The sneer in Leah's mom's voice returned. Faye felt an attack on the horizon.

Ms. Fallon: Did you wait until you got married to have sex?

Mr. Shane: Objection, relevance. My client's sexual history is not relevant to her abuse by the defendant.

Ms. Fallon: The case records show, Mr. Shane, that these questions have already been ruled admissible. Your client is claiming damages relevant to alleged sexual trauma. The defendant has the right to show that this alleged trauma may have derived from other sexual encounters rather than from any conduct of my client.

Mr. Shane: Clearly, you intend to use these questions to humiliate this girl.

Lance spoke aside to Faye.

"Go ahead and answer," Lance whispered. "Slowly. Don't let them rattle you."

Ms. Collins: Can I have the question again, please?

Court Reporter: question by Ms. Fallon: Did you wait until you got married to have sex?

Ms. Collins: No, I did not.

Ms. Fallon: With how many people have you had sexual intercourse?

Ms. Collins: Do you mean other than my husband?

Ms. Fallon: Yes, Ms. Collins. Other than your husband, with how many men have you had sexual intercourse?

Faye counted a three-second breath before answering.

Ms. Collins: Eleven

Ms. Fallon: Okay, well, let's go through each of these separately. When did you first have sexual intercourse?

Heat cascaded through Faye's body. The room shimmered like Faye might faint. Across the table, Edward raised his eyes in anticipation. His lips parted a sliver, silently drawing extra oxygen. Edward folded his hands atop the legal pad in front of him. The fingers of his right hand trembled slightly.

Ms. Collins: I first had intercourse in August.

Faye paused. Edward's eyes met hers.

Ms. Collins: I first had intercourse in August of 1999 with a co-worker named Jeffrey Paulson.

Without expression, Edward turned his gaze back to the notes he'd been taking. His heart raced; his mind searched frantically for an explanation. She brought this circus. Why was Faye protecting him?

Ms. Fallon: And that was eight months after the last time you saw Dr. Vogel?

The summer of 1999 had been a blur of active passivity. Her first days home from Sacred Heart for summer vacation, Faye and Merton had driven the streets of Citrus County all night until the sun came up, smoking cigarette after cigarette. Tears had streamed down Faye's face. Her stomach twisted knots upon knots. A few weeks into summer, Faye picked right back up at Cal's to earn spending money. There, she had met Jeffrey, a plump, grinning twenty-five-year-old waiter who was waiting tables while waiting for his big break in the art world. Faye and Jeffrey drank screwdrivers and played lawn darts, smoked marijuana out of homemade bongs, and swam naked in the backyard pool while his parents were away in Europe. At the end of the summer, Faye rewarded Jeffrey's fun-loving, goofy courtship with a week of sex before she returned to Sacred Heart for the fall semester. Like Jeffrey, the sex was playful and kind. Faye told everyone, herself included, that it was Jeffrey to whom she had given her virginity. Sex with Edward, her abortion of their child, his disdain for Faye, and his resignation from Aquinas Prep all sank in a sea of vodka and frivolity. Later that year, Merton proposed to a girl he had known only two months. In Edward's absence, Faye remembered feeling that she and Merton were running some kind of cathartic, chaotic race, trying to fill their lives with whatever might calm the raging storm Edward had stirred in them.

Ms. Fallon: Tell me about your relationship with Jeffrey Paulson.

And so two hours passed with this line of inquiry. After Jeffrey there had been a one-night fling with Dillon DeLeon in the off-campus house of the Sacred Heart Lacrosse Club and then Ned, the friend of a friend of Peggy, Faye's freshman year roommate. Faye and Megan had met Brad and a few months later Brandt (Faye didn't know either of their last names) at bars in Potato Creek. The on-again-off-again affair with Charlie Bartlett, her married boss at Vino's Supper Club in Pepper Creek, Michigan, elicited the greatest number of questions from Leah's mom. The usually inexpressive Edward raised an eyebrow when Faye recounted the Labor Day weekend sex-fest she had shared with Griffin McCabe, a visiting Professor of Irish Studies whom Faye and a colleague had offered to show around town. Of course there was Daniel, and during Faye and Daniel's brief break up there had been a musician from Rum Runners Dueling Piano Bar and a few businessmen who blew off steam with martinis at the T.G.I.Fridays a few miles from campus. The court reporter click-clacked, Lance listened stoically, his chin balanced between thumb and forefinger, and Leah's mom wrote furiously as Faye talked. Edward stared ahead, his mind unwittingly conjuring images of the timid girl who had hidden her naked body under his quilt every time he stepped away from the bed. *How quickly they grow up*, he thought. Edward chuckled to himself. *What was all the waiting for?*

Edward didn't remember telling Faye that she would prefer to be on top during sex. It sounded like him, though. He had probably said it. Wistful predictions aside, he was hearing all of it now. All the details of Faye's sex life, about the men whose chests she had stroked and whose balls she had fondled. Karen pulled from Faye every detail about the men who had been on top of and inside her, had enticed and exhilarated her. Faye's testimony forced into Edward's consciousness the men who had massaged the tender undersides of Faye's limbs and had licked the salty sweet crevices that Edward had been the first to explore. As for Faye, she spoke calmly. The names and dates and habits poured out of her in a litany of exhausted regret. Faye named and narrated them all, all the men she had wanted so much less than she had loved Edward.

Ms. Fallon: You performed oral sex on some of these men, is that correct?

Ms. Collins: On a few of them, yes.

Ms. Fallon: And did having oral sex with them make you feel afraid?

The corner of Faye's mouth turned up in surprised confusion.

Why would I feel afraid? Faye thought. *I hardly even knew them.*

The afternoon of day three was a bore for Faye no less than for everyone else in the room. Lawsuits that seek financial damages run on endlessly with detailed questions about financial circumstances and lost wages. Again and again Faye answered inquiries about missed college classes and bouts of depression. Many days freshman year, depression had bound Faye to her bed. Stomachaches and back pain plagued her. Recurrent heartburn seemed unusual for a girl her age. Faye had learned from a therapist that survivors of forced oral sex often felt a perennial sourness in their mouths and throats. *The body remembers*, her therapist had said. *The body feels trauma when the mind refuses to acknowledge it.* Faye had done well for herself, graduating Sacred Heart with honors and completing a master's degree before entering the doctoral program at the University of Illinois. The attorneys' questions were insufferable and largely unanswerable that afternoon.

Mr. Weatherford: If you had not had this relationship, we'll call it, with Doctor Vogel, do you believe you would have performed more successfully in your undergraduate studies at Sacred Heart?

Ms. Collins: I would say so, yes.

Mr. Weatherford: Bear with me here because I do not know much about doctoral programs. If you had not suffered from what you are calling depression and anxiety during your undergraduate years, might you have been accepted to a doctoral program of a higher caliber?

Ms. Collins: Possibly.

Mr. Weatherford: And if you had been accepted to a doctoral program, let's say, that had a higher ranking than the University of Illinois, would it then be more likely that your career would be more lucrative financially?

Faye hesitated. Edward's damaging of Faye defied quantification, a circumstance ill-fitted for a civil lawsuit.

Ms. Collins: It's hard to say.

Mr. Weatherford: Would it be fair to say that because of the relationship with Doctor Vogel, you feel hardship in your personal life and your relationships with others?

Ms. Collins: Absolutely.

Mr. Weatherford: Please tell us about those hardships.

The click-clack followed Faye's voice as she tried against reason to delineate the struggles Edward's abuse of her had caused. On Faye's long-running but incomplete list of abuse-related consequences, the most graphic and gross and vile details—that moment, for example, when Edward had stood over Faye's prostrate body and forced that thing into her unwilling mouth—ranked at the very bottom. None were as bad as the pervasive feeling, deep in the tissue of her soul, that she had failed to save Doctor Vogel. She had condemned him instead, and herself along with him. The scars had long ago burrowed into the soft folds of Faye's fleshiness. The guilt ate away at her intestinal lining. Fear pulsed against her dry throat when Daniel, however lovingly, pushed himself into her.

Even now, in the dissertation phase of graduate study, married and happy and thriving for all anyone could see, Faye spent an average of three nights each week pacing and swearing, smoking and thumping her chest with a closed fist to redirect the anxiety rising up behind her tongue. A scar like an inchworm, its ridges puffy but smooth, flashed its translucence when Faye caught sight of her thigh. Two years prior, she had stabbed herself with a steak knife during a panic attack. Megan and Daniel had been frantic with worry ever since.

Clarity had come to Faye slowly after the abuse. *Here's what happened,* she explained to herself. Faye, famous for her *yeses* and do-alls, became difficult when she started saying *no* to Edward's sexual requests. And so, quite quickly in fact, Edward had tired of her. If unquenched sexual need could make Doctor Vogel cast off Faye, his Super Girl, his star pupil, the one shimmer in a life so stuck in the gray, what had Faye to offer? Faye's own worth fizzled and starved under the weight of the secret adult knowledge Edward had shown her. *Men seem to see you,* Edward's repudiation of her said, *but they see only their own desire.* In the eighteen months that stretched between Freiburg and the end of Faye's first college term, Edward had made and then unmade her. He had given, and he had taken away.

Ms. Collins: The intimate relationship between me and my husband is as strong as it can be, given the circumstances. It's difficult for me to make my own sexual choices. My body clams up. Sex confuses me. Some parts of sex panic me, and I don't know when or why that panic will come.

A sheen of wetness stretched across Faye's eyes. On the blurry edges of her vision, Faye sensed Edward's stillness. He listened though he did not look. Leah's mom barely concealed her annoyance. Every word irritated Karen Fallon.

Bright summer light splayed the conference room though late afternoon approached. The June heat of Tolono burned Faye's nostrils as she stepped outside for a smoke and a chat with Lance.

"Today is awful," Faye said, cupping a hand around the cigarette as she flicked a flame to it. She blew smoke toward her beige Mary Jane loafers.

"Talking about the abuse is fine. It feels good. The questioning about my life after the abuse drains me. I hate having Vogel here for all that. I look weak, right?"

Lance rebuffed Faye's self-effacement with a quick head shake.

"You've succeeded in school, gotten married, and made an amazing life. And more, you are standing up to that asshole. I work with a lot of survivors, Faye. Most of them can barely hold down a job. They're on drugs. They cannot manage their pain."

So we call this managing, Faye thought, glancing over her shoulder to see Edward and his attorney huddling at the hotel coffee cart. Away from their familiar seats and the now familiar table, the sight of Edward sent her stomach buzzing nervously. Faye's head shook side to side with slight motion. She and Doctor Vogel, litigation, lawyers, shitty hotel coffee, the court reporter's sensible tweed suit, Leah's mom's holier-than-thou prudishness, an on-the-record airing of Faye's medical history, and her account of Edward's stilted orgasms—how could any of this be real?

The isolation and dullness of Tolono was getting to Lance four days in.

"Fuck, it's hot here," he said with a laugh. "I need to find some place cool to stretch out with a beer tonight."

Lance's nonchalance bounced right off Faye. She grimaced.

"Come on, buck up," Lance encouraged. "Besides," he continued, returning to Faye's earlier remark. "If there is anything holding you back, it's that sorry excuse for a man."

Lance pointed toward their opposition just as Edward looked Faye's way.

"And he knows it, Faye. And he'll pay for it."

Day three questioning ended abruptly in a flurry of emotion. Faye's anxiety bubbled up when Karen Fallon asked a dozen questions about Faye's Aquinas Prep crushes as evidence of Faye's instability and hysteria. Evidently, Karen Fallon could not decide whether Faye was too naive or too whorish. She attacked from both angles to cover all defenses.

Ms. Fallon: Did you and your friends used to drive by Stuart Mendelsen's house?

Ms. Collins: Yes. Bryn, Krystal, and Leah—your daughter—used to drive by Stu's house with me and smoke cigarettes and play loud music. Just for fun.

Ms. Fallon: Did you have a name for this activity?

The voice inside Faye's head groaned. *We were high school kids, for fuck's sake.* She could hardly look at Leah's mom. She remembered Lance's admonition against sighing and eye-rolling. She lightened her tone.

Ms. Collins: We called it *stalking*. We *jokingly* called it *stalking*.

Ms. Fallon: So you thought stalking someone was something to laugh about?

Mr. Shane: Objection. Misstates her testimony. She said they jokingly referred to it as stalking, not that she thought stalking was something to joke about.

Ms. Fallon: Well, I heard her say they thought it was funny to stalk Stuart Mendelsen. Did you think it was funny to stalk Doctor Vogel?

Mr. Shane: Objection. No foundation.

The video camera focused squarely on Faye with a partial view of Lance and total view of the flowered wallpaper behind them both. Leah's mom was off camera and visibly irritated. She had no such injunction against eye rolls.

Ms. Fallon: Did you ever stalk Doctor Vogel?

Mr. Shane: Objection. What do you mean by stalk?

Ms. Fallon: I think she knows what I'm asking, Mr. Shane.

Lance smiled, enjoying Karen Fallon's increasingly pissy tone.

Ms. Fallon: Do you think this is funny, Mr. Shane? Do you find something funny about allegations of stalking and harassment?

Lance had toed the line with his derisive tone, keeping his mockery of Karen Fallon just civil enough to pass a judge's assessment of appropriate decorum. At this, he nearly leaped from his seat.

Mr. Shane: Ms. Fallon you are wholly out of order. The only allegations we are here to litigate are those against your client. Certainly, I find the juvenile behavior of teen-aged girls comical when it is being purposely misinterpreted to appear as something it quite clearly is not.

Mr. Weatherford: Shall we take a five minute break to quell tensions?

Mr. Shane: No, we would rather not. Counsel previously agreed that Ms. Collins needs to leave thirty minutes before our scheduled end of day to visit her doctor's office that closes at five o'clock. We need to wrap up for the day in the next twenty minutes.

Ms. Fallon: Will the court reporter please read back the last point before Mr. Shane's outburst?

Court Reporter: Ms. Fallon: Did you ever stalk Doctor Vogel? Mr. Shane: Objection. What do you mean by stalk?

Ms. Fallon: Let me rephrase. Ms. Collins, did you ever drive by Doctor Vogel's house?

Ms. Collins: Of course I did.

Two can play this cheeky game, Faye thought with glee.

Ms. Fallon: Have you ever driven by Doctor Vogel's house at a time that Doctor Vogel was home but he did not know you were driving by?

Ms. Collins: Yes, I have.

Ms. Fallon: Tell me the first time you drove by Doctor Vogel's house when he was home without telling him you were there.

A memory flashed into Faye's consciousness. Rain was drizzling into her car window, left open for the sake of her cigarette. The FOR SALE sign on Edward's lawn rose into view before his green sedan or the weathered south side of his home. The effect had been immediately stirring. Faye's head swam with panic and terror. She would surely lose him for good.

Ms. Collins: It would have been in June of 1999.

Leah's mom shuffled a few papers then cocked her head with confusion.

Ms. Fallon: Do you mean to say June of 1998, the summer after you graduated from Aquinas Prep?

Ms. Collins: No, it would have been June of 1999.

Ms. Fallon: You never drove by Doctor Vogel's house in the summer of 1998 to stalk him, as your friends would have jokingly called the practice of driving by people's houses while they were home?

A defensive posture turned Faye's shoulders rigid. *That woman just won't stop*, Faye thought. Leah's mom wanted them all to see Faye as a fatally attracted teenager who had stalked and begged then retaliated against a man who rejected her. After everything Faye had sacrificed for that man, the suggestion incensed her.

Ms. Collins: No. In the summer of 1998, I had a standing invitation from Doctor Vogel to drive by, come into, or spend the night at his house any time that I wanted. If I had been driving by the area, I would have come in to visit.

Ms. Fallon: Why did you drive by his house in the summer of 1999?

Truthfully, Faye had driven by Edward's Bonita Vista house just three weeks prior (in May of 2007) while home for her brother's wedding. By late summer 1999, Edward had moved to Georgia before settling with his new wife in Missouri. Faye knew from some internet digging and a robust Aquinas Prep grapevine that the two had a daughter, now, of about five years old. Seven years after that summer (and for how much longer, Faye couldn't have known), Faye still drove down Bonita Vista whenever she visited Citrus County. The new owners had relandscaped the front yard several years earlier. They had planted variously sized palm trees and torn out the front grass in favor of water-saving succulents. A year or two ago, they had painted the house blue and erected a wide white gate that blocked any view of Edward's garage or backyard. Pachelbel and Vaughan Williams still blared from Faye's stereo. Smoke still curled into the driver's seat from Faye's shaking hand. So quickly, Faye's conscious mind had extinguished the memory of Edward rebuking her on his toilet-papered front lawn. The reverberating sound of her own screams was forgotten now, as was the thumping boom of her fist to her heart as her tires had peeled away at dawn after Edward ejaculated on her body without consent (actually, after she had explicitly said *no*).

Faye still cruised Bonita Vista because she felt close to Edward there. Moreover, she felt near to the Faye she had been at seventeen: happy Faye, Faye on-the-go, Faye the AP rising star off to spread her wings. Eight years she had been driving by. As Edward looked on, Faye hoped to God she would not have to confess this embarrassment.

Ms. Collins: I drove by his house because I missed him.

Ms. Fallon: How did you feel about Doctor Vogel in the summer of 1999?

In deposition prep, Sasha, the firm's Victim Advocate and herself a survivor of an abusive AP teacher, had cautioned Faye against the use of certain phrases. *Don't say you loved him*, Sasha had intoned again and again. *Say you thought you loved him.*

Ms. Collins: I loved him.

Edward raised his eyes but not his head.

Ms. Fallon: Did you promise Doctor Vogel that you would not tell anyone that you and he had been having a relationship in the summer of 1998?

Ms. Collins: Doctor Vogel gave me permission to tell Merton about the relationship. Other than that, yes, I promised not to tell.

Leah's mom set her head bobbling again, a sign of her contempt.

Ms. Fallon: If you promised Doctor Vogel you would not tell, why did you break your promise?

Faye pursed her lips and nodded. Spiritual exhaustion covered her. Leah's mom spoke for Edward now, and both resolved to make her answer for this most traitorous deed.

Ms. Collins: I was reeling. I felt pierced.

Faye searched for the words. So often she had tried, in the dark of night, to untangle this very contradiction. She had betrayed Edward, whom she so loved.

Ms. Collins: Despair deflated me. I knew, in a way I cannot describe— I knew that what he had done had broken me. I needed to tell.

When Mr. Weatherford adjourned the deposition—the court reporter noting the four thirty-two timestamp—Faye pushed her chair back with a burp of the buckling carpet and headed without Lance for the double doors that led out of the conference room. The quickly closing door snapped back, depositing Faye in a tube-like passageway that connected this meeting room to the rest of the hotel. Her doctor would hold the prescription only until five o'clock, but she could honestly go another few days without it if necessary. An after-glow of energy chased a rumbling of sadness through Faye's veins. These public x-rays of Faye's demons shook her. Instead of hustling toward the outside, Faye planted her feet. She held a hand to her breast and tried to re-center, pulling a deep breath in through her nostrils. Her eyes closed, Faye released the captured air with her face lifted heavenward. *Steady me*, she prayed. *Another day is done.*

Back in the room she had just left, Edward rose slowly, resisting the urge to flex his arms in a much needed stretch. He felt like an ass for thinking so, but Faye's depositions taxed him as much as they did her. To sit still while she accused and defamed him was maddening. Every fiber of Edward denied her characterization of their affair. Of course he knew she was hurting. For God's sake, if he remembered anything about that summer (besides the pleasure of the girl's soft, timid mouth wrapped around him) it was all the crying Faye had done. Some tears were expected, though. His years teaching at Aquinas Prep had schooled him in the volatility of teen-aged emotions. They were up then down, grown then childlike, sexually developed but wonderfully inexperienced.

Impatience with Karen Fallon had also been nibbling at him since the start of day two. He saw to his left that she was anxiously shuffling papers and trying not to engage Faye's attorney, a young gun who clearly enjoyed flustering a prudish woman like Karen. Edward needed air, though the breeze outside would be dry and stifling at this time of year. The hot stickiness of midwestern summer would be preferable just now to the artificiality of the hotel's air conditioned coolness and to the manufactured outrage masquerading as shock and concern. No one in that room could possibly have cared this much whether Edward had spent the summer of 1998 with his head buried between his star pupil's thighs. Cameras and court reporters were done for the day; Edward rolled his eyes, sighed, then nearly groaned at the thought of teen-aged Faye in his bed, curls falling down her shoulders, a tear creeping into her smile.

"I will meet you back here in a moment," Edward said flatly to Karen Fallon. "I need to grab some air."

The court officials and attorneys, including Lance, all remained packing and chatting. Faye had run out a few minutes earlier. She was late, her attorney had said, for a doctor's appointment or some such interference that had ended the questioning thirty minutes early. Edward left his briefcase and over-used legal pad at his spot near the table's curve and pushed through the doors to be alone a moment.

Still counting breaths though she should have been driving down Cunningham Avenue by now, Faye spun around quickly at the sound of the conference room doors. This would be Lance, she was sure, trying to catch her with a last minute question. Edward had emerged with downcast eyes, expecting an empty hallway. A length of six feet stretched between them. Faye's senses slowed. Raising his head, Edward raked his fingers through his hair. He dropped his arm when Faye's eyes locked with his. Faye detected in Edward's eyes the same look of wistful surprise he had offered at the back door as the July sixth sun had dropped in the sky. But there was no Citrus County sunset now. The suspense of romance and the thrill of forbidden pleasure had long ago died. All that remained was this moment. They were plaintiff and defendant, now. They had been lovers and friends. They had been teacher and student.

Faye and Doctor Vogel stood in silence on the matted industrial carpet of the Tolono Inn and Suites. In the air between them, Faye felt a gentleness as sweet as their peach pie picnic and as precious as Doctor Vogel's wet wisps of hair in a Freiburg storm. She could feel, now, that Edward was not angry with her. He had absorbed his wrongdoing though perhaps not atoned for it. Edward's face was more round than nine years before, his cheeks more ruddy still, and his eyes a bit tired at their corners. Faye stared a fleeting second at the soft divot above his mouth. How she had wanted to touch him there as a comfort to his wounds. In mirrored synchronicity, Edward and Faye smiled with closed lips and chuckled inaudibly. Each thought for a moment they might throw up their hands. *What did you expect?* they both seemed to ask. *This*, each told the other silently without words. *We were headed here this whole time*. Edward tilted his head and nodded to Faye with an unexpected grace so strong it took her breath. Because her children had not yet been born, Faye thought she might never again know as great a love as this.

The glow on Amy's face gave the child an angelic appearance. Amy smeared a wet thumb on Thuy's leg and leaned against her mother, speaking in a sweet voice.

"What are you reading, *má*? Why are you sitting without the light?"

Full darkness had fallen in the past hour while Thuy had been too preoccupied to notice. She peered wordlessly at the child now. Amy had her father's big, round eyes. It was hard not to notice their perfectly rotund shape when compared with Thuy's delicately squeezed expression. The girl quizzed her again.

"What are you reading on the computer?"

A sheen of saliva still lingered on Amy's upper lip. She pressed her thumb back against the roof of her mouth and waited for her mother's response. Thuy's mind said to close the document and rise from her chair, but the weight of her body would not concede and move away.

"I am reading grown up material. It would be boring for you. Amy, where is *ba*? Have you seen him after dinner?"

The girl moved her head in an exaggerated back and forth motion.

"It is time for going to sleep now *con gái*. Are you wanting some fruits before bed?

"I want toast before bed," Amy declared. "I need *ba* to make my toast."

Thuy gathered the strength of a thousand women inside her. The task ahead seemed that monumental. She felt on her shoulders the immense weight of the words she had just read. But now, Amy needed tending. Tending was Thuy's job.

"I will get you grapes instead tonight. You can have toast for breakfast."

The girl's obsession with toast bothered Thuy in the same (shameful) way her European eyes did. Amy's way of being Vietnamese was not Thuy's way. Five years she had still not quite learned how to navigate this difference. Thuy had not eaten toast growing up and disliked Amy's affection for it at any time of day.

"Fruits will make you much stronger." Thuy spoke to the child with authority but not without kindness.

At bedtime, after her mother extinguished the overhead light, Amy remained in a purplish haze from the papier mache lantern hanging above her bed. She wriggled a minute in her sheets, wanting to sneak down the hall to her father's music room, to check one last time that he was protecting them. Instead, she tapped her fingers in the air, striking invisible piano keys and humming a tune. Easily, she drifted to sleep.

Thuy pulled a damp sponge across the kitchen counter and re-sealed the red grapes that distended with their bulbous mass the flimsy plastic bag from the grocery. She choked back a sob and touched a hand to her mouth. What else could she do to distract from that taunting screen? The computer still hummed in the den. Twenty minutes was all the difference in the world. If only she could go back to the moment before she had opened the email. Edward did not like Thuy managing his affairs, but she had checked to make sure the water bill had been paid. And now, such an everyday matter had led to this awfulness. Thuy was not a snoop. She did not pry, nor did she mistrust. But as if a spirit operated independently of her own mind, she had clicked open Karen Fallon's email and just kept on clicking. The deposition transcript had downloaded while Thuy rolled pink-polished fingertips nervously across the desk. The sun had been merely starting its descent, then. Now, in the darkness, Thuy sat, heavy with the knowledge that her husband was a liar. Her life was a lie.

The tears sliding down Thuy's cheeks tasted warm and salty when they pooled in the corners of her mouth. She looked side to side with a panic, afraid an unseen audience was witnessing her humiliation. Oh Jesus, the shame of it. She had believed Edward's story all these years. *That girl kept coming onto me*, he had said. *I told her to leave me alone*, he insisted, *but she forced her way into my house and she kissed me*. Every time Edward told the story to his soon-to-be-wife, he hung his head at this part as if in deep remorse and embarrassment. *I shouldn't have kissed her back*, he would say then. *It was just a moment. It was just habit. I pushed her away almost immediately. That was it.* His tone became triumphant here. *That's all there was to this whole thing.* That one moment in which he had kissed back only slightly and only out of politeness had escalated, Edward said. He said it had snowballed into a witch hunt because the girl's father worked for the Sheriff's office and wanted Edward fired. Messy tears, too many to ignore, were coming now. Thuy reached for a scarf to wipe her face. How easily she had believed him! How desperate she had been to get married and have a child.

A quick button push whizzed the file back to full screen. Thuy swallowed the words this time, feeling them congeal in the pit of her stomach with tonight's *bò lúc lắc*.

Mr. Weatherford: Can you describe any specific sexual habits that you observed in Doctor Vogel?

Ms. Collins: I'm not sure what you mean by habits.

Mr. Weatherford: Is there anything he did sexually that you think might be unique, might give clear indication that you are familiar with his sexual behavior?

Ms. Collins: Yes, though I'm not sure how to explain it. I mean, Doctor Vogel had this tendency to kind of restrain himself during sexual activity. I mean, he would be getting close to having an orgasm and so he would, kind of, stop. He would wait a minute and sort of stave off the end. And then he would start over. It was awful because I was always hoping that it was over. Just when I thought it would end soon, it was like he would start again. I don't think that's typical. I've never experienced any other man do something like that. It was like he had this immense amount of control and wanted to squeeze as much anticipation as he could out of every sexual encounter.

Thuy wanted to vomit, but the knot of disgust stayed resolutely lodged in her gut. Undoubtedly, this girl had slept with her husband.

The settling of Faye's lawsuit brought unwanted fame. A few notes of support trickled in.

> *I'm sorry this happened to you!*
> *I always thought something was* off *about Doctor Vogel.*
> *You are so brave for coming forward!*
> *There was* so much *abuse at Aquinas Prep! Right under our noses!*

But these well wishes could not hide AP's general disdain. Overwhelmingly, in 2007, people were *mad*. At twenty-six, though they would never admit this, Faye and her Aquinas Prep classmates had not yet *grown*. They had aged only slightly, and their kids were just babies (if they'd even had children yet; Faye and Daniel had not). Sex and sexual harassment still seemed easy, breezy, almost unnecessary topics of discussion. Everyone still blamed Monica Lewinsky for the Clinton affair and no one talked about consent. No one was saying *me, too!* because women were still choked with shame. The job Faye would hold at Sunset Bluffs ten years later had not yet been invented.

And so Faye was suspicious at first when Donovan mentioned Jane.

"She says she was engaged to Vogel twenty years ago," Donovan reported. "She's asking to be put in touch with you."

And that's how Faye and Jane came to meet.

If he could see us now, Faye thought sarcastically. Two contemptible, ruinous women seated opposite each other, smiling. Coffee sloshed in Faye's mug as she set it unsteadily on the table. She lifted her opposite hand as a shield, but at the last moment, the coffee dipped back toward the rim and did not spill. Jane Willoughby reached across the table and covered Faye's shaken hand with her own slightly more worn hand. In the face of this sweet woman,

Faye could see traces of Edward's ex-fiancé, the shy, pretty girl with the feathered hair and the photographer's keen eye. Until this moment, Faye was saying, she had not been sure that this woman was flesh and blood *real.*

"I knew you existed," Faye clarified. "He showed me pictures of you from when you lived in Ann Arbor, but I only had his word that you had been engaged."

Jane inhaled deeply with a self-deprecating smile to show that those days were too long ago.

Jane's smile stretched wide and irreverent now. "It's all true!"

She raised her hands in an animated gesture. The clanging of two bangle bracelets on her slender wrist mesmerized Faye. When teen-aged Faye had first heard about Jane, everything about this mysterious woman had fascinated her. She remembered peering into the polaroid's grainy image, a fortune teller trying to find and heal Edward's ailments. Now, Faye felt drawn to the sophistication and aplomb of this older version of herself.

"Oh," exclaimed Faye sarcastically, Jane's energy drawing her from nervousness into excitement. "So you did leave him to a ruined life in the wake of your abandonment." She paused, the truth evident to both coffee-cradling women.

Jane touched Faye's hand again. Heat from Jane's coffee spread across Faye's arm.

"I see. He used my story," Jane said with a lilt of sadness. "He used that sad story of loss to attract you."

A familiar anxiety gathered behind Faye's eyes. After a chorus of scorn from Jack and Lance and Daniel and victims' advocates and self-help books, Faye could not stomach one more re-telling of her life as a silly, helpless victim. Jane squeezed Faye's wrist firmly, without pity.

"That's not why it happened, though," she said knowingly. "It wasn't because he trapped you."

Tension eked out from Faye's pores, but she could not speak.

"You loved him," Jane continued, "because Edward can be so loveable. We want to love him," she said. "Don't we?"

Like a dragon-slaying goddess from Edward's mythical past, Jane swooped down and carried Faye up above her hurt. Jane had leaped out of Edward's photo album just in time to affirm that Faye was, indeed, alive and alert. She was not alone.

"Yes," Faye agreed.

"I came here today because I wanted to see that you were alright. And you know what—"

Faye leaned in. She wanted more of Jane's solid, reassuring voice. "—I can tell just by the way you talk, the way you hold yourself aloft in the face of your sorrow, that you are alright. You are strong."

Faye believed her. Faye had not believed Jack or Lance or Daniel.

"I'll bet Edward liked your strength. He wants to dominate the people around him, but that domination is only worth it, it only feeds him, if the people he controls are strong willed. He likes smart women who can match him. Do you see what I mean? Do you see that being strong actually made you appealing to him?"

"Tell me what happened with you two," Faye said matter-of-factly. "I'm certain you did not abandon him as he claimed."

"I want you to know something," Jane said by way of introduction. "I did not mean to hurt him. I suffered a lot when I was with Edward, but I did not leave him out of vengeance or ill will. I left him because I knew that I would not be happy if I married him. I just want you to know from the start that I would not have purposely hurt him."

Between the lines of Jane's assertions, Faye knew where this was going. She spoke out of reverence for Faye's feelings. She spoke as if she were afraid to debase Edward's memory.

"I really did love him." Jane sipped her coffee, then added: "I know you loved him, too."

The hours ticked by and coffee disappeared. Sandwiches arrived before cheesecake, and both women—one twenty years senior but the carbon copy of the other—got up to stretch their legs and use the restroom and order a fresh cup of coffee once again. Faye stepped outside to smoke. Jane stood beside this girl (at twenty-six, Faye seemed girlish and unspoiled to Jane) even though Jane disliked smoking and knew the stale cigarette smell would cling to her clothes and follow her home. Back inside, the air thickened then thinned. Anxiety rose then was quelled.

In hushed tones, they whispered the secrets of sex with Edward, feeling like men as they compared notes about this absent lover's body.

Jane told Faye about the violent kissing, the suffocating feeling that Edward was sucking the breath right out of her throat. Faye knew exactly what she meant.

Faye told Jane about the night she first slept at Edward's house, how she had lied to her parents so she could stay all night and cuddle with him. She told Jane that instead of cuddling, they had fought because Faye was on her period and wouldn't let him touch her. She showed Jane with imitative gestures how he had pinned her against him while she slept and ejaculated on her without her consent.

Jane cried then.

Faye told Jane that she had never told anyone about that before. She had testified about it, but she had never told her best friend or her husband. She'd been too embarrassed even to tell her therapist (no wonder the therapy hadn't worked).

Jane told Faye that Edward insisted they have sex even when Jane was ill. Once when she was battling a stomach flu, she soiled the bed because she could not push him off her quickly enough to get to the bathroom. He had shamed her and had refused to help change the sheets.

Faye cried, then, because she knew (without being told) that Jane had gone back the next day and apologized.

"In case you've ever wondered," Jane said confidentially, leaning in and checking the tables around her. "Edward has a kind of practiced stamina to keep him from finishing. It wasn't you, is what I'm saying. Edward controls everything about sex with Edward."

An acidic fear rushed to Faye's throat when Jane said this last bit. Her stomach flopped and she said she needed to go back out for another cigarette.

Certain refrains stalked their stories.

"I get it," Jane would say with a tap of her fingers on the dark wood table.

"He was the same with me," Faye would say, shaking her head in astonishment.

"When Edward and I met," Jane told her, "I was eighteen and he was twenty-four. Our circumstances were much different than yours, but he knew I had faced trauma in my youth, had been abused before and was not confident enough to resist his charm. He knew I was desperate for a man who would love me. And oh boy—" Jane positively beamed as she spoke these words. "—Boy, did he know how to woo a girl!"

Years later, after Edward had passed away, after Faye had birthed, raised, and sent her children off to college, after the choir room at Aquinas Prep had been torn down and rebuilt, the thought stayed with Faye that Jane was the only person in all the world who understood her. Jane and Faye had known the same Edward. Doctor Edward Vogel was a narcissist as volatile and hurtful as he was charismatic and talented. And, as Faye did, Jane still loved him.

X

THE NEW STRINGS RESISTED EDWARD'S fingers, as new strings always did. The tightness would give way eventually. *If there's time*, Edward thought. Fear squeezed Edward's throat. The strings might outlive him. Edward's bent head inclined toward his guitar as he picked out a familiar melody. On the settee beside him, Mary Vogel reclined ever so slightly, tired from a long day of quiet worry. Soft, fading light shone through the sheer green curtains that framed the music room. Amy, Mary's youngest granddaughter, struck a pianist's perfect pose on the baby grand's sleek black seat. Mary Vogel was not often invited to her son's family home. Each time she visited, Mary found the place a bit cold and austere. Even in winter, no hearth blazed, no slippered feet tucked themselves up under blankets on a comfortable couch. Mary and Elias Vogel had raised two sons and two daughters in a country farmhouse suffused with affection and warmth. Her other three children had replicated this intimacy in the homes they now kept. Edward's home diverged. There was something performative about the place. The silk fabrics and sheer curtains were unexpected in this traditional brick house on this traditional, cottonwood-lined midwestern street.

  Edward's marriage was formal, too. Mary could not tell whether Edward or his wife were to blame. Edward had always been fastidious and self-controlled. It did not surprise her when Edward went off for his Doctorate and Glen stayed home to work the farm. Edward's eyes were always up, in search of bigger things. And so, he shocked her, then, when he settled in Meridian, a community as small as the Kansas town he had left behind in young adulthood. Years later, she understood. That girl from the high school—he had moved to outrun that nonsense. Mary suspected, then, that he had married Thuy for the same reason. Edward had hardly mentioned Thuy when suddenly, that Christmas, he had announced their engagement. The news had thrilled the whole family. A few years into their marriage, Mary sensed a change in Thuy's demeanor. She was aloof though pleasant. Something heavy but invisible sat between Edward and his wife. Mary did not enjoy her daughter-in-law's condescension.

Edward's daughter echoed her mother's formality, but Mary could see that her spirit was soft and beautiful like her father's. These past years, Mary had seen Edward truly happy only when he was with his daughter. Their intimacy was different from the closeness Mary shared with her children. Edward and Amy did not embrace; she spoke softly to him, with a deference that befuddled the Vogel family. Still, Edward loved the girl and she sought his admiration like a thirsty bud hoping to bloom. At the piano, they shared a secret love language. Despite Amy's shyness, Mary found her granddaughter striking. Amy's eyes were almost black (like Thuy's), but they were not almond-shaped as her mother's were. They were big and round, like her father's. There, the physical resemblance stopped. Compared to Edward's easily tanned skin, Amy's was fair and fragile. The hearty Vogel stock evident in Edward's strong stance and solid frame gave way to Amy's waif-like limbs. A serpent of black hair hung half-way down Amy's back, the hair as fine and thready as it was dark. Mary Vogel looked softly upon her son's face and wondered when both of them had gotten so old. Her heart thumped against her chest. *Where has it all gone?* her heart exclaimed.

Edward held his palm gently across the strings to quiet them. His mother's smile was soft and genuine.

"That was lovely, dear," she said, reaching a hand toward her son.

Edward took the hand his mother offered. He held it lightly, its weight a feather even in his weakened health. His mother's fingers felt soft and unfamiliar. Her papery wrinkles showed patches of discolored skin from sun or injury. Dark blue veins puckered the tissue-thin folds here and there. They looked painful, though Edward knew they were not. His mother's hands were old. That was all. *And why shouldn't they be,* he thought wistfully. Mary Vogel had carried a mother's burden for sixty years, all the way to the cancer bed of the first baby who had nursed at her breast. The feeling of Edward's hand on hers now overwhelmed her. It filled an enormous chasm that opened whenever she was away from her children.

Edward breathed in the soothing amber scent that floated off his mother's perfumed skin. The whole of their life together stretched long and wide in Edward's vision. For so many of those years, Edward's mother had been in quiet remove from the life he was building. She had released him into the world and watched from afar. Now, as the cancer was closing in, she had come to imprint on her heart the indelible image of her son, a perfect being whom she and Elias and God had brought into a world determined to test him. Mary squeezed her son's strong hand then rubbed her palm along his forearm.

"Bring Amy to Kansas for Christmas if you can. She hasn't seen her cousins in quite a minute."

The unsaid truth hung between them. In her son's blue eyes, mirror images of her own, Mary saw a glint of fear. She was Edward's mother, and she would mother him until God took him back.

"You'll be alright," she said in a shaky voice. "Everything will be alright."

Mary Vogel left Meridian on a Thursday afternoon. By nightfall, Edward stood with bowed head in the master bedroom's smooth marble shower. Steam filled the large space; curtains of hot water stretched down from Edward's head to his ears and across his shoulders. The waterfalls traced paths down his arms to his fingertips. The longer he stood, the more full and splashy the shower became. Matted clusters of Edward's hair raced each other toward the drain and stopped there, damming the tiny silver holes and turning his shower to a dirty foot soak. He thought to clear the mess away, but he could not move. That is, though he easily could have moved, could have swooped down and cleared the water's path, Edward did not want to move. The streaming water obscured all but the vision of his own body. Three rounds of chemo had not only stripped most of Edward's hair but had shaken his general steadiness as well. Many days the previous week he had used the shower's marble bench, sitting for spells like a feeble old man. He could hardly believe it. Today, though, he stood strong, his feet planted resolutely. Edward watched as they slowly disappeared into the growing pool of water. He had lost some weight since starting chemo. He noticed now a reduction in his waistline, an area that had plagued him since middle age. Edward rolled his head a few times around to stretch his neck. The water hugged him like a hot embrace, comforting and almost sensual. He felt a stirring in his thighs and watched as his penis bobbed slightly.

Thuy and Edward had not made love since the chemo started, though his sex drive had not diminished much as the oncologist said it might. He generally still woke to erections in the morning and still ran his hands along his penis a few times each night as he prepared for sleep. Thuy had been sleeping alternately on the chair in their room or in the guest room. Edward liked having the bed to himself again after all these years. One of marriage's greatest gifts had been the comfort of his wife beside him every night. Even when they were arguing or in long stretches of sexual inactivity, Thuy's soft, sweet-smelling skin soothed Edward. But now his body and mind were out of whack. The chemo caused intestinal disturbances and sudden flatulence. His throat felt hot and bubbly; his skin sometimes seemed papery and uncomfortable. And so he was glad for the privacy his wife's absence afforded him. The advanced esophageal squamous cell cancer had taught him this lesson, too: we are alone with our bodies. Only we can feel them and suffer them and love them as they are.

Edward reached down and cupped his testicles in his hand. His erection intensified as he remembered the exploits of his younger self. He pictured a snowy day in Michigan, he and Jane holed up in his living room, the sun bouncing bright white rays off the piles of snow that had blanketed Ann Arbor the night before. They had made love four times that day and eaten peanut butter and banana sandwiches for lunch and again for dinner because it was the only food he had in the apartment. They were just kids, then. He thought about sex with Faye though he hated himself for remembering it. Bitterness toward the whole awful Aquinas Prep situation competed with his memories of that time. Because he had lived alone in Fulton and because he had known Faye right before his marriage, his time with her overlapped the final months of that younger self, the last single-man Edward who had composed late into the night and lived entirely as he pleased. Of course, his months with Faye were also the last in which his arousal had carried him away. Reckless desperation drove him in those days, Edward realized now. The price he paid had been steep, but so too had the pleasure of Faye's soft, young flesh been overwhelming. All these years later, he still thought about her and felt flutters of desire.

Thinking of her and of all the women he had loved and satisfied over the four decades from his teens until now, Edward enjoyed a kind of buzzing arousal that warmed and pleased him. He had been chasing these small ecstasies all his life as boys and men do, lusting after warm chocolate chip cookies and cake batter spoons until the teen years when new cars and new tools had fed his insatiable and unidentifiable needs. Manhood stretched before him, then, a series of placeholding intimacies, drowning in the suppleness of lovemaking, feeling always in that space a fulfillment so intense that each time he could not believe it would be fleeting. But always, it was. And now the advanced esophageal squamous cell cancer was ravaging him as he had devoured so many of life's most satisfying carnal pleasures. Steam filled the bathroom. The air hung hot and thick around him. He remained still and leaned his forehead against the shower wall. Edward held his penis loosely in his hands, enjoying the sensation of hot water engulfing his tired, sick, old body. The peace of it, the beingness of just being here and remembering all that loving, struck him more intensely than any orgasm could.

When Edward's mother had been two days back in Kansas, an intense soreness scraped inside Edward's throat and made swallowing unbearable. He tried at first to ignore it, choking down in forty-eight hours only a few cups of ice chips, a spinach and banana smoothie Amy had brought to his bed, and a few pours of whiskey he had secreted after Thuy had fallen asleep. Intaking the smoothie had backfired at first. Its thick richness had immediately kicked his digestive juices into gear. Eventually, though, the nutrients took hold and the chewing sensation of his knotted stomach had calmed. The whiskey burned going down Edward's destroyed pipes, but once it passed that obstacle, its potency coated Edward like a great salve on a wound, winding its way through his limbs and seeming to pool in hot relief in his lower back. He closed his eyes, then, and was able to sleep. He did not dream and so was surprised a moment later to awake and find that a new day had already come.

A quick test. Yes, his throat still ached, and now his eyes pained him too. His eyes felt crusted shut with a sticky film, a realization that panicked him. For Edward, the cancer's worst feature was near-constant fear that something else was about to go rogue. Advanced esophageal squamous cell cancer involved much more than the esophagus, and in bad weeks it seemed his whole body was crumbling into ineptitude. A few months in, humiliation still weighed on him. Edward's discomfort oscillated between the psychological degradation of a broken body and the concrete agony of that body's sickness. Both monsters beset him at the moment. He didn't know what was worse, the painful puffiness of his eyes or the horrifying thought that he might lose his vision.

He forced a word through chapped lips to check his ears.

"Amy."

His voice was weak but still there, thank God. *God*, Edward thought, considering a prayer. No words came. The impulse for prayer would have to suffice.

Sun burst through the windows, refracting bright beams across the room. He had forgotten to close the drapes, or Thuy had opened them earlier in the morning. The urge to sleep fought his desire to get up and be alive. His garden needed tending. His near-finished psalm needed an oboe line. Through eyes half-opened and half-caked with goop, the ceiling light fixture wobbled and the doorframe looked rubbery and about to collapse. Clearly, he would not garden or write today. Edward rolled to his side and gingerly pulled his knees to his chest. He heard the teardrop jewels on Thuy's bedside lamp clinking together before he faded to another time.

Instantly, his eyes cleared and a cold wind brushed his face. Glen's strong, cowboy's voice rang in his ears.

"Grab that auger and get drilling! That hole's nowhere near deep enough, Ed!"

It was his father's farm. Edward could smell the earthiness and the Kansas heat. Sweat ran along his hairline and spread damp patches across his back. Edward dragged the heavy tool a few yards and plunged it into the earth. His muscles quaked under its weight, but the heaviness felt satisfying as well. Glen's laugh bellowed toward him.

"See, Eddie Van Beethoven—" Glen cupped a hand to his mouth, throwing his voice to his brother. "You can do it."

Dream Edward chuckled and looked down at the strong, virile hands holding the tool. He was young again, maybe twenty years old. Glen, Edward's little brother, the baby of the family, was younger yet. Dream Edward nodded knowingly, placing the memory. He and Glen had built the fence on Edward's summer break from Kansas State. Those had been his final days on the farm before graduate school and prestigious awards and love and life had taken him so far from his childhood. Aging Edward—*cancer* Edward—did not often think of those days. The vision thrust itself upon him now. The sun on his back was a magic balm. He turned his face to it and closed his eyes.

A clap of Glen's hand against his back brought Edward to attention.

"Back to it," Glen called out. "That sun'll be gone soon. It'll be thundering before supper."

"Then let's go!" Edward responded. "*Tide and time* and all that."

(Dreaming Edward laughed. They lived by his mother's aphorisms, stolen from Chaucer and Shakespeare then passed down to her country kids. My God, how wonderful his mother was.)

Edward smiled broadly in his sleep, his brother's voice and his mother's memory building confidence in him. Thuy's lips returned Edward's sleepy grin. She reached to caress his face. The mumbling had ceased but the dimpled skin on his cheeks felt hot to her touch. Amy peeked her head in the door.

"Is he awake?"

Thuy moved her hand instinctively away. Seldom did she show her husband affection in Amy's presence.

"No. He is sleeping," she said flatly to her daughter. "Would you like to sit with him?"

Amy considered. Her father's stillness scared her.

"I'd rather wait until he wakes," she said softly, shamefully, to her mom. "He would want music," she added. "I'll play something for him."

Thuy's eyes followed her daughter's slender fingers as Amy picked through Edward's albums, intently searching for his recording of The Robert Shaw Singers.

As the tenors announced themselves, Thuy countered. "Put on something sacred," she instructed.

Amy chewed the end of her braid. She stared at her mother's nose as she spoke.

"It is," she replied. "It's *Hymn to St. Cecilia.*"

Amy replaced the album shell and slipped out of her parents' bedroom. She paused on the landing a half flight down. Her heart raced but her body slowed, her foot suspended between two steps. Something tugged her back. The thought rose to her throat but she would not speak it. *He's dying,* she thought. *We're dying with him. What, then?*

The Shaw Singers were there, now, in his dream, their melodies trading and fugueing and wrestling each other. Rich music filled the humid air. The Kansas sun was gone. Thick drops careened down from the sky. A sheet of rain obscured Edward's view. His feet sank into muddy ground. He called out for Glen, but he knew Glen was gone. The fence post was gone and the auger and the sense that he was home. The landscape changed quickly. Raindrops jumped back up from the stone street. A flash of lightning revealed a towering cathedral in Freiburg. Edward's Aquinas Prep choir was there, their bodies swaying to the hymn, their mouths a sea of undulating *o*'s.

Tears wetted the seams of Edward's closed lashes. The skin around Thuy's eyes crinkled into a slight smile as she absorbed his silent features. What feverish thoughts was her husband having now?

Edward's lips moved and a hoarse voice escaped. "Freiburg," Edward said in his sleep.

The pit of Thuy's stomach hardened. Her body, a trapped animal, froze in alarm. Freiburg was on her husband's mind. Hot anger supplanted the fear. She saw the thunderstorm in Freiburg as vividly as if she had been there. Edward never spoke of those days, but Thuy knew. She had read that girl's testimony. Thuy lived her own version of Edward and *the girl*. That horrible girl and her gossiping friends had danced carefree and sweet on the cobblestone streets of Europe, teasing and tempting Edward just to break him. That whorish Delilah had forced her way to his bed and stolen his future. And now, in his fever dreams, he was with those kids. For what did Thuy deserve this, a dying husband mired in thoughts of his most ignoble desires?

A time traveler in his own past, Edward saw himself, too. The forty-something Edward was soaked to the skin, his Aquinas Prep tee shirt stuck against his frantically conducting body. It moved him, this vision of his own passion. He could watch his students, now, as he never had before. He scanned their faces. Some of the students held hands; others were crying. So many times on that trip, Edward had tried not to look at Faye, to avoid her temptations, to ignore the pleading heart she was thrusting toward him. He saw her now, as she must have looked then. Her baggy jeans hung awkwardly on a girl's narrow hips. A ribbon was wrapped around her messy hair braids. Her face held not a stitch of make-up. Childish drawings graffitied her dirty tennis shoes. Edward thought of Amy, and mourning draped his heart. How had he ignored Faye's girlishness?

Dream Edward exhorted his choir as the storm raged on. Cancer Edward prayed in his deep sleep.

"*Drip down O Heavens from above.*"

An urgent email from Paul buzzed through to Faye's phone in the wee morning hours. Faye was still in bed but awake; Daniel breathed heavily, half-way to a snore. The awareness of morning, but not quite the light itself, seeped through their bedroom shutters. And then, Faye's phone pinged and Paul's name appeared.

I know you fly out this morning, the message began, *but you need to get in touch with Marilyn before you go off the grid. SBPD is dropping the assault charges in the Miller case.*

Faye groaned. Sunset Bluffs had followed procedure to the letter, but still Lewis Miller would be denied justice. She knew the drill. Roland Fagan, the Newport East football coach, had friends in high places. The courts, the police, and the media would brush off the assault as locker room antics. Citrus County would soon forget (until it happened again); outrage at Newport East would turn to snickers and whispers (*they wouldn't have dropped the charges if the assault had really happened*, naysayers would repeat like truth); Lewis's parents would decide that lawsuits and media blitzes would do more harm than good; Lewis would pull his chin up and laugh. *It wasn't as bad as I made it sound,* he would tell his parents just to ease their pain. *It's not even a big deal.* Worst yet, the attackers would do it again, not at Newport East, but during pledge week at their fraternities or in locker rooms at Spartan University next year or the year after that. Their assault on Lewis injured everyone: the school kids, the parents, even the attackers themselves. But Lewis's wound would fester and blister, puff, seep, and scab before it finally scarred and never fully disappeared.

The shower door squeaked and clanged though Faye moved it gingerly to avoid waking the house. She had emailed Marilyn a few thoughtful suggestions, including the names of highly recommended restorative justice experts, so SB Unified could start planning for educational activities in light of the new legal circumstances. Later, Faye would worry more about Lewis and about all the victims whose cases she cataloged in her brain, whose ashen expressions rent her heart. Today, Faye would seek her own justice.

Still wrapped in a towel, her skin damp and hot, her teeth biting nervously on her lower lip, Faye opened *Prayers for Edward* for a final pre-flight update.

Edward has been hospitalized for dehydration, confusion, and migraines of undetermined origin. He is stable. We're hoping for a new PET Scan soon. Keep the prayers coming. I'm sure he would enjoy letters or calls. SSM-St. Clare Hospital, Meridian. 4/5/19. Millie

"Who's Edward?"

Louisa's cold hand on Faye's bare shoulder sent a shock to her chest. A scream jumped out without warning. Louisa's little body doubled over and laughed.

"Sorry, mom. I thought you heard me walk up."

Faye recovered and laughed a bit, too. Her pulse still pounded in her throat.

"Oh goodness, Weesy," she said, whirling around in her desk chair. "You scared me to death."

"When are you leaving?"

"Not for about an hour," Faye said sweetly, brushing back the dark, stringy hairs that swooped across Louisa's forehead. "So why don't you go back to bed for a while."

Louisa shook her head. "I don't think so," she said, looking around.

Faye tilted her head and considered. "How about I start a movie and you can just rest on the blue couch?"

"Yes," her child began, "and I'll take some dry cheerios and raisin toast, too, please."

Louisa turned confidently and walked away. "With butter," she called back over her shoulder.

Little girl blithesomeness followed Louisa to the worn couch in Faye's very lived-in living room. She carried Faye's heart there, too. Louisa's sweetness brushed away the news Faye had not yet absorbed. Edward was in the hospital. Terror and relief wrestled in Faye's head: terror that Edward was getting worse, relief that she would know where to find him. It seemed a blessing, really. She and Megan had not developed much of a plan beyond scribbling down Edward's last known address and mapping their route from the OB Convention in St. Louis to the tree-lined street that looked on Google Earth so typical it could have been a movie set.

An hour later, Louisa and Wyatt vied for Faye's attention as she pushed, pulled, and zippered her suitcase. Packing for the Midwest always challenged Faye. This April day, a puffy vest threatened to catapult the contents of her bag back out and make her start anew. Spring time in Missouri would not be unlike spring in Potato Creek or Tolono, which meant that Faye might feel leftover winter chill, spring renewal, cool winds, humid showers, and warm sunbeats in her three days away from Citrus County's sunny and seventy-three standard. Teague slurped cereal at the table and watched his phone.

"When are you coming back?" he asked between swallows.

Faye spoke over her shoulder while wrestling her luggage.

"Thursday night after Megan's conference. I think we land at 8:00. You can come with dad to get us if you want."

"Yes!" Wyatt and Louisa jumped and cheered. Teague picked up his phone and began tapping.

"I'll probably stay home," Teague responded, "but I'll be up when you get back."

Faye let out a deep breath and started the good-bye rounds. She snuggled each toasty little child, saving Teague's more sturdy, robust shoulders for last.

"Please help out while I'm gone," she whispered in his ear as she kissed the side of his head.

Daniel pulled Faye in for a kiss just as a car pulled into the drive.

"Be safe," he said. "Try to relax while you're there."

Faye smiled and hugged him close.

"You can save the world when you get back," her husband said proudly.

Louisa rushed out the door behind Faye.

"One more kiss!" she called.

A familiar sadness trembled its way up to Faye's lips.

"I hate to leave you," she said, her face burrowed into the crook of her daughter's neck, "but I'll be back before you know it. And I'll bring you something from St. Louis."

Louisa smiled big. "A snow globe for my collection!"

"Play with Wyatt while I'm gone," Faye continued, "so he won't be too sad."

Louisa skip-stepped her bare feet back to the house as full light came to the Citrus County morning and Faye headed off to chase Edward across the sky.

Window shutters made faces at Faye as rows of clapboard houses flew by on Interstate 270 from St. Louis to Meridian. She had seen this drive before in other places. Chicago to Tolono, Indianapolis to Potato Creek—each journey from place to place in the Midwest mirrored drives past and those not yet considered. The homes stretched tall and narrow, windows and doors impersonating jack-o-lanterns to passersby. Faye watched the homes whizzing by, their siding made dingy by rough winter weather, their yards rolling one to the next in solidarity. (In Citrus County, fences and walls cut squares around every suburban house. Property began and ended in easily digestible borders.) Every twenty miles or so, another town crept into view, its yellow framed stoplights swinging on suspended wires. Flying J gas stations and Shoney's restaurants reminded Faye that Citrus County was far behind her now. Familiar patterns presented themselves. Flat farms gave way to rolling hills which dipped into bustling towns, each equipped with an extended row of restaurants, home improvement depots, nail salons, discount stores, and mega-super-center markets pressed one against the other in a densely compressed capitalist smorgasbord. Since college at Sacred Heart, Faye had referred to these midwestern eatery and shopping hubs as Daisy Drives because they exactly duplicated Daisy Drive in Potato Creek: Home Depot across from Menards next to the Cheddar's across from the Lone Star Steakhouse next to the Dollar General. Less visible from the highway were the towns' *main drags*, as Faye's mother would say. These Main Streets and Riverside Drives housed local antique shops, mom and pop one-stop shops, locally-owned hardware stores, hand-dipped ice cream parlors, Catholic churches with their stained glass Madonnas, and Protestant churches with their unadorned church halls and simple lawn marquees. Mile markers winked at Faye in the bright sunlight. They were half-way to Meridian. Faye's stomach flipped. The back of her neck felt flushed.

"Looks like the next Daisy Drive is coming up," Megan said brightly. "Do you need to stop for anything?"

"A Xanax," Faye joked. "I'm starting to freak out."

St. Clare hospital sat just over the river from Meridian River Park, a collection of small green patches cut out by cement pathways that reached along the river and up a slight slope to a park entrance flanked by two lamp posts. A few of Meridian's senior citizens occupied two of the three bench swings that swayed slowly under their weight as they looked out over the barely moving water. Faye and Megan approached the empty bench but did not sit. Rich-smelling steam wafted up from Faye's coffee cup. Her eyes followed a small bird that flew over the bridge and disappeared behind the repeating pattern of identical windows. Behind the glass lay the patients of St. Clare's many medical units.

Even this far away, the hospital's entrance hidden from view, the windows appearing opaque from outside, Faye struggled to contain the excesses of her body. Too much vomity saliva pooled in her cheeks, but just as suddenly, her mouth went dry. Faye's tongue felt swollen and hot, a sensation almost as unpleasant as the one it replaced. Her arrival in St. Louis had brought with it an existential fear. Here at the park, it came into focus. Since the depositions in Tolono—*had it been twelve years already?*—she and Edward had not been so physically near. She breathed his town's air, now, her shoes imprinting her presence on the short grass at Meridian River Park. Heat bled through from the coffee cup to her hand. She studied the logo's deep brown ink and its smiling coffee bean. Perhaps Edward was a patron at Jed's Grind and Grain, as Faye had been this morning. The invisible thread that kept Faye tied to Edward was slackening now. The closer she got, the more it gave way. If she kept walking, she could place it, a tender pile of unspooled color, into his hand. Oh, how wonderful it would be, to unburden herself that way, to feel a Faye untethered.

The drive up and over Meridian's Bud Weil Memorial Bridge to St. Clare Hospital revealed a downtown strip that charmed Faye against her will. Too many American flags waved in the light spring breeze. Too many white Americans (there were bright white and dirty white but no specks of color among the townsfolk) sat casually on benches beneath the front windows of crowded breakfast diners and walked arm and arm in and out of Phil's Pharmacy and Meridian Hardware. They could stall no longer, so Faye and Megan parked in visitor parking and scanned their flimsy white ticket stub, its weight suddenly unbearable in Faye's shaking hands.

St. Clare buzzed with a level of activity unfitting a small-town hospital. The whole town seemed present. Faye saw old men wearing the same black Vietnam Veteran hat her father always wore, toddlers toddling and laughing despite the somber setting, and women with big glasses reading romance novels with their legs crossed at the knee, doing their level best to escape the slow ticking clock that separated them from a surgeon's announcement. Icy blasts of air pumped out of painted metal vents that lined the room's floorboards and ceiling trim. The slightly antiseptic aroma comforted Faye because it brought thoughts of her babies. For most people, hospitals are rife with worry and uncertainty. *If a person is seeing me,* she had once heard an ER doctor say, *that person is having the worst day of his life.* This did not hold true for Faye. Her grandparents were all gone, but each had passed either before she was born or after long illnesses that left them languishing in convalescent hospitals or in palliative care in the comfort of their own homes. Her parents and her children had been exceptionally lucky; none of her three precocious and largely free range kids had landed themselves yet in the emergency room; neither she nor Daniel had ever broken a bone or had even minor surgery. And so, every hospital stay had brought Faye another child, each unbelievably soft and warm, a salve for all of life's woes.

A sudden terror gripped Faye's throat. The chair at her fingertips skidded a bit as she fell into its under-padded seat and tried to disappear into her handbag. Megan quickly took the seat adjacent and whispered urgently in Faye's direction.

"What happened? Did you see someone?"

Faye's stomach quaked and churned. She needed to swallow but thought she might gag if she did.

"His sister," Faye responded. "I can't look up. His sister is over there."

Faye tried to nod in Millie's direction but made a movement too small for Megan to interpret.

"Okay," her friend said softly, setting a hand on Faye's shoulder and looking, as was Faye, down into her cluttered purse. "Take a deep breath. No one is looking our way. Everyone is focused on their own things."

Faye's mock digging unearthed a peppermint. She twirled the cellophane with trembling fingers and popped the candy in her mouth. The cool burst of flavor wetted her throat. Faye set her purse gently under the chair and smoothed her pants with flexed palms and wide fingers, pulling a deep breath to her lungs as she looked up. She recognized Millie from a photograph on the *Prayers for Edward* blog. Well, she recognized *little Millie*, as Edward had always called the younger of his two sisters, because Millie looked just like Edward. Her cheeks were ruddy and full (like Edward's); her nose showed just the same mix of angularity and flare. Her posture was strong and solid (like Edward's). Faye imagined Millie walking with the weight pushed back in her heels as Edward always had. Even in these uncertain circumstances, Millie sat with her feet flat to the ground. She projected balance, stability. Faye thought Millie looked unbothered, though not unworried. It was a practiced posture, perhaps. Millie seemed, like Edward always had, conditioned not to break. Just sitting there—just being Edward's real sister from a real life that had never included Faye—Millie forced doubt to the edges of Faye's consciousness. Edward loomed large in Faye's story; Faye wondered how much space she occupied in his.

Crowding in where she did not want it was the unmistakable realization that she was doing something wrong. She felt desperate in the face of her separation from Edward. But for the gray strands in her hair and deep wrinkles around her eyes, Faye might have thought herself seventeen again, wanting only to show that she loved him, trying to save a man who didn't need saving. *I will love you,* she remembered Edward saying, *until I can't love you anymore.* A tear snaked its way down Faye's face to the corner of her mouth. She nodded slowly in confirmation of her own suspicions. Perhaps Edward had stopped loving her twenty years ago and had never looked back. She was a blip, really, in a long life that had never been about her. Edward's life was about Millie and Glen and Anna, about his parents and his wife and his child. That, Faye could understand. Faye was a motherwoman now, as Chopin would write. Faye's motherness *was* she. At home, her three children awaited her return. She had left them to go grasping at the love of a man she did not know and had hardly ever known. It all seemed so silly. Still, the thread tightened, harkening Faye to

Edward's bedside. Oh, how she longed to see him once more. How could Edward be so instrumental and so fleeting all at once?

Megan leaned in. She spoke in a low voice.

"Is she the lady in the purple?"

Faye looked with quickly darting eyes.

"No. The one in the flowery shawl."

Megan stared in Millie's direction but spoke to Faye.

"She looks nice," she said calmly. "Do you want to go talk to her?"

The mere thought dizzied Faye.

"Absolutely not," she said. "If any of them know anything about me, they hate me. All there is to know is that I ruined his life." Faye swallowed hard. Great anxiety was bubbling up in her again.

Megan smiled sympathetically.

"Why don't we go drive around and get some air? We can come back later."

"In a few minutes," Faye responded. "Let me just be here a little while."

Megan pulled two novels from her bag and handed one to Faye. She let the book fall open on her lap, a decoy so she would blend in with the other waiting room waiters. Faye found levity and annoyance when she thought of this ruse. *I'm a grown woman for God's sake,* Faye thought, *acting like a teenager driving by a cute boy's house. And Edward?* her musing continued, *well, he had always been too old for this, hadn't he?*

Panic and calm toppled each other in the ocean of Faye's mind. She did not belong in this hospital or in this town. It was time to go, but she could not leave him behind. Even without seeing Edward, Faye felt a familiar mix of comfort and apprehension because he was so close. She had felt this contradiction every day that summer. Faye would move mountains to be near Edward, even if that intimacy compromised everything else she knew to be true and good. A clock over the Nurse Station ticked loudly in the quiet room. Faye would wait three more revolutions, and then she would leave. She remembered Edward conducting in the St. Francis crypt in Assisi. She thought, as she often did, about the last time he had kissed her good-bye (on the back steps of the Fulton house in December of 1998, a kiss on the top of her head, one on her forehead, and a final one on her lips). She saw them both in the hotel hallway during deposition week, alone with their unspoken disappointments, a shared sigh asserting that the stitching still held.

Faye studied Millie, taking her in like a disappointing replica of a prized gem. She held a rosary in her hand. Faye could see it now, the crucifix dangling out of Millie's closed fist. Faye held her eyes closed and uttered a quick prayer. The allotted three minutes had almost passed when a teen-aged girl emerged from the corridor opposite Millie's seat. The girl walked airily, almost on the balls of her feet. Her posture approximated a ballerina's poise. Her slender fingers caressed each other in lightly folded hands. A long ponytail of dark black hair lay flat against her back, the tips swaying slightly as she moved. She cast her eyes down, watching the tops of her Aunt Millie's shoes.

Faye fidgeted in her seat, nudging Megan without taking her eyes off Millie and the girl.

"That must be Amy," Faye said. "His daughter."

Across the room from them, Faye could not hear the voices of these people whom Edward loved, but this, she could discern. They were awash in a quiet sadness, an exhaustion seeking relief, seeking hope. The girl lifted her pale face to meet her aunt's eyes. Faye saw the girl's shoulders shake with a sudden sob. Tears collected in Faye's throat. Through blurry eyes, Faye saw the girl turn away from Millie and look absentmindedly in Faye's direction. Faye managed a weak, empathetic smile that the girl did not see. Clearly, she was overcome with distress.

Faye sucked in a long stream of air, a singer's breath that filled her abdomen. She focused on the wall directly opposite her chair. Strips of paint had chipped off unevenly along the margins where the wall met its trim. Faye cocked her head and allowed her eyes to unfocus. The pinky-peach paint reminded her of the bathroom in her childhood home. This bathroom in the back of the house, between Joy's room and Faye's, the family had called the *cat bathroom*. Faye chuckled to herself as she remembered this. It could more appropriately have been called Joy's bathroom since it was closest to Joy's room (and since Joy had spent so many hours there teasing her bangs in the '80s and plucking her eyebrows in the '90s) or the square bathroom, as the linoleum flooring sported a design of pink-toned squares of many sizes interlocking like puzzle pieces. But just over the toilet, in a cheap plastic frame, Faye's mom had hung a novelty picture of a scruffy calico cat. There weren't ten cat pictures (or even two cat pictures) or feline-shaped soap dispensers or hand towels embroidered with fluffy kittens. Still, the phrase stuck. Even now, though the bathroom had been remodeled and painted blue (and of course the frame and the cat were long gone), Faye held to the name in her mind. *Go wash up in the back bathroom*, she would tell her children after lunch with their grandma. *The cat bathroom*, she would say to herself.

These were the intimacies of daily life, the details too ridiculous or nonsensical to share, the stories too embarrassing or too *personal* for outside the home. Together, these details, the trivial and the private and the disgusting and the silly, made a family. Only a family could share them, and Faye felt now more than ever that a cavernous distance stretched between herself and Edward's family. When she was seventeen, desperation had overpowered Faye. When she was twenty-six, the fiery righteousness of her attorneys had fueled Faye's staunch pursuit of justice at the expense of Edward's reputation and career. She was thirty-eight, now. Marriage and motherhood and the harshness of a self-obsessed world had taught thirty-eight-year-old Faye something about mercy and restraint. Edward belonged to his family like Faye belonged to her children. She would not intrude on his space in these last precious moments.

Faye rebuked the young girl's voice in her head, the frantic teen giddy with Edward's attention and thirsty for his affection. *He does not belong to you*, she told herself. Faye would bank on the mercy of God, hoping the bond she and Doctor Vogel had built all those years ago would shepherd them toward mutual forgiveness, even if they never spoke of it. The Victoria *Ave Maria* sprang to her mind. Faye felt the tune and its Latin pleadings resound in her heart though she made no external sound. It was Edward's favorite rendition of the prayer. She imagined him on the other side of that pinky-peach wall, his body motionless in a hospital bed, his head swimming in the sacred music that had sustained and fed him in defiance of his flaws. Her only hope of salvation lay in this. If she prayed and so did he, they were in fact praying together.

The flowery hotel bedspread wrinkled beneath Faye's weight as she scooted to a seat against the headboard and dialed home. Wyatt's slobbery face filled Faye's phone screen as they connected with a swoosh of sound and a flash of light.

"Mama!"

Faye's living room blurred by as Louisa pulled the phone away from her brother.

Louisa talked through a mouthful of granola. "Today we ran the mile at school," she started without introduction, "and I got first in my class but second in my grade and Hunter got third in our class."

"That's amazing Weesy," Faye responded. "I didn't realize you were that fast."

Louisa snapped off another bite and continued. "I sometimes get first in the whole fourth grade but today Gus got first but Mrs. Carillo said that our times were only three seconds apart or something close like that, so I'll probably get first when we do the mile test next month."

"Amazing," Faye repeated. "What else am I missing?"

"Nothing, really. Last night Wyatt was crying a whole bunch before bed because you weren't here but I asked dad if I could make a bed for Wyatt on the floor in my room and he said *yes* so I did that and we had a movie night and he stopped crying almost right away and he slept all night in my room."

Louisa's storytelling was energetic and detailed. Faye loved that she relayed her daily life in this manner, each intricately told event running into the next, each phrase jumping from her mouth desperate to be shared with her audience. As Louisa talked, she darted her eyes left and right to ward off interruption from her brothers. Teague's nascent adolescence had introduced a sense of privacy to her eldest son, a sense of separateness Louisa and Wyatt did not yet possess. Faye could see in her middle child's eyes that Faye's attention was everything she wanted. And so Faye listened each evening as Louisa described her fourth-grade world. She drank in the experience of a nine year old racing on the grassy field, of a young kid and her comrades playing handball and making dioramas. That her children had a life apart from her was thrilling as it was scary.

"How's—Wyatt bring my water bottle over!" Louisa yelled, contorting the right side of her mouth toward her brother off screen. "How's—wait, where are you mom?"

"I'm in Missouri," Faye said instructively. "That's about half way across the country, not quite all the way to Sacred Heart."

Wyatt appeared in the frame and reached a hand toward the screen.

"Let me talk, too!"

"Hi baby Wy," Faye cooed.

Louisa retook control after a swig from her water bottle.

"How's Missouri? Are you and Megan having fun?"

"We *are* having fun," Faye answered. "I have some good news for you."

Four eyes widened as they bore into the screen.

"Did you buy my snow globe?" Louisa asked.

Wyatt joined in. "What about for me?"

Faye laughed. "Better news. Well, I think it's better. I'm coming home early. I'll be home tomorrow."

Squeals of delight followed.

Louisa projected her voice far beyond the family room. "Teague! Mom is coming home tomorrow."

Teague stayed off camera, but an audible whoop issued from elsewhere in the house. Its residual sound barely reached Faye through the phone.

"Where's your brother?"

Louisa swallowed another big gulp then poured a drink into Wyatt's gaping mouth.

"He's playing *Flight Simulator* in his room. He said he can't stop right now."

"Let me talk to dad so I can tell him the details. You can come with dad to meet me at the airport, or you can stay at papa's while dad goes."

"Watch the planes," Wyatt squeaked. "Planes, planes, planes!"

Louisa nodded in agreement. "We'll go see the planes coming in. We can watch from Jupiter's Pizza by the airport before you land."

Faye's lids grew heavy as she hashed out arrival details with Daniel. A siren whirled outside her hotel window; a pair of chunky shoes clopped down the hallway.

"You seem awfully tired for being on vacation," her husband said with a frustrated smile. "I was hoping you'd be able to recharge a little, especially with the Miller case hanging over Newport East."

"It has been nice. I had two margaritas at dinner," Faye confessed. "They're just making me a tad sleepy."

"Are you in for the night?"

"I'm not sure. Megan is finishing up notes for her presentation tomorrow. We might go grab one more drink in the hotel bar. We won't be going back out into town, though."

"Okay, be careful. We need you to come back to us."

"Well I'm coming tomorrow," she said sweetly, the butterflies in her heart beginning to still their wings.

All her life, it seemed, Faye had been saying good-bye to Doctor Vogel. She had left him behind as she came of age into each room of her unfolding life, only to discover in a puff of cigar smoke or a sharp July breeze that the door had been propped open all that time. Another good-bye to Edward had come. Faye could wait unseen in the hospital corridor no longer, would cease to plot deathbed reunions, must stop seeking dramatic reconciliations.

A Faye-shaped absence was calling her home. Most days, Faye simply could not believe she ran a household of five people. Five living, breathing, eating, talking, fully human *people* relied on her for clean pajamas, packed lunches, homemade waffles, scrubbed toilets, full boxes of tissues, and every other emotional and material need their minds and bodies could conjure. What's more, they loved her. They loved Faye more than they loved their favorite stuffed animals and more than a brand new car or a Hawaiian vacation. The love and the need burdened her. Yet, the need and the love buoyed her. They were hers, and she was theirs.

The door creaked slightly at about one-third open (two-thirds still closed). Edward fluttered his lids when Amy re-entered. He tried to look her way with just his eyes. Dilation tubing in Edward's throat kept his head too still for much movement. A burning spread along the walls of his eye sockets from the effort to meet his daughter's expression.

"Aunt Millie wanted me to bring you this rosary," his daughter said quietly, her natural shyness befitting the hospital's melancholy air. "She said it belonged to Grandpa Elias."

Her father's trembling palm raised an inch above the pea green hospital blanket. He curled his fingers in assent. Amy placed the heavy, dark beads in her father's hand. His skin felt just the same as it always had. Under the tremor, Edward's skin was smooth and taut. Amy could not reconcile her father's recent vivacity (hadn't they just been planting gladiolus the week before?) with the stench of death permeating the room. The incessant beeping of machines pulsed an angry chorus in her head.

"Let's say a decade. Where do you want to start?"

Edward pointed to the bedside table. Amy handed pen and paper to her father, watching carefully as he scribbled a few letters.

Glori

Amy covered Edward's hand with hers and smiled.

"Got it," she said nervously, straightening herself back against the padded chair. "I'll count, dad, so you can just relax."

Edward nodded.

"The first Glorious Mystery," Amy began, peering intently into her cupped hands. "The Resurrection of Jesus."

The rattling of Edward's rosary pulled Amy's gaze up when she reached the first *Hail Mary*. She stopped and handed her father the pad once more.

Sing, Edward wrote.

"The Victoria?" Amy asked knowingly.

Her father nodded.

Amy imagined her fingers on the keys of her father's worn Bechstein. She seemed to feel the warmth of a summer sun beaming through the music room windows of their home. For many years, they had focused on his iniquity. It was time to be loosed of those chains, to cast off the resentment she had learned from her mother and the doubt she had turned on herself. Many days, she and her father had sung their prayers together. *When you sing, you pray twice*, her father had always said. In a hushed soprano, Amy began to sing. Blood circulated warmly from chamber to chamber through Edward's still-pumping heart. He felt strength returning.

The tear-swollen eyes won out. Faye fell asleep waiting for Megan to be ready for last call at the downstairs bar. Air that was too cold and too loud was pouring out of the cooling unit when Faye awoke to the phone buzzing beneath her thigh. She reached sluggishly for it and blinked her eyes into focus on the screen.

I wanted to tell you when you came home but I can't wait.

Today Maya asked if we could hold hands

Faye sat to attention and tapped back.

What did you tell her?

Two genderless yellow figures holding hands appeared beneath Faye's question. A thumbs up followed.

Faye chuckled and responded.

Sounds like a great day.

Her baby boy, who wasn't a baby, kept writing.

I miss you mom.

Thanks for helping me talk out all that Maya stuff.

She imagined Teague's bright blond curls and saw his shy pre-teen cheeks beaming. Yes, still in Edward's hometown, still reeling from the unanesthetized abscission, Faye's heart bloomed anew.

The gaunt face of Lewis Miller looked especially sallow on Faye's computer screen. As a last move before closing the file, Faye checked in via video chat to make sure Lewis no longer needed services from her office.

"Do you mind telling me if you have been seeing a therapist in Aspen?"

"I don't mind," the boy said flatly.

Faye smiled warmly, wishing she could reach through the screen and pat the shoulder of this precious overgrown child. His eyes showed both distraction and boredom.

She asked directly this time. "Have you been seeing a therapist?"

"Yes, ma'am." He spoke without optimism or derision.

"I hope you will find therapy useful." Faye winced at her own empty words. She sounded far more clinical than she intended. There was nothing worse than sterile comfort.

A bright splotch of pink drew Faye's eyes to the blurry background behind Lewis's seated figure. The ill-defined shape sharpened into Lewis's mother as she walked toward the camera and materialized on Faye's screen.

"I would have liked Lewis to continue at Newport East until the end of the term," his mother said, clasping her chunky gold necklace and letting out an exasperated breath, "but he prefers to stay in Aspen at the new school."

While his mother spoke, Lewis pulled his arms into his sides in a protective motion. Faye watched him get smaller in the frame.

"I like the doctor here," he interjected. "He's easy to talk to."

"I'll give you some privacy, honey," Mrs. Miller said. "I just wanted to pop in. Thank you Doctor Collins for your help. I know we are all ready to have this behind us."

"It will take some time," Faye responded. "I'm open to chat any time Lewis needs. You and your husband have my card as well," she added. "We're not dropping you just because Lewis has left the district."

The bright pink splotch retreated. Lewis turned his head to see his mom out. His head swiveled back to Faye. Then, she spoke to the boy alone.

"What happened when you came back to Newport East? It wasn't okay, was it?"

Lewis shook his head. Since the assault, it was like every conversation needed a translator. His parents didn't get it. His teachers didn't get it. Even Doctor Bell, the therapist, didn't really get it, but Doctor Bell was laid back and smart. Lewis could tell he was trying to understand.

"It felt awful being back at school, being back in the locker room."

"Everything had changed, right? The other kids were treating you differently?"

Faye thought she knew the feeling. Lewis fluttered his eyes. He puffed a quick burst of air out his nose.

"That's not it at all," he said flatly. "Nothing was different. They acted like nothing had even happened."

In 1992, just as summer became fall and Faye turned twelve years old, a sudden onset of stomach cramps, nausea, and general panic had derailed her usually smooth schedule and left her parents grasping for explanations and cures. After two years of Faye's journaling (emotion charts and food diaries), special diets (no dairy then a lot of dairy, nothing spicy then spice in moderation, no berries then extra fruits of all kinds), stool sample tests, blood draws, barium x-rays, and finally an out-patient endoscopic exam, Doctor Narajanset Shah had located two tiny ulcers in the duodenum, a small forgotten organ linking the stomach to the small intestine. A camera had snaked its way through Faye's digestive track taking photos. *There's your problem*, Doctor Shah's nurse Bruce had said, pointing toward two shadowy swirls against the wet, pink tissue of her stomach. Faye's siblings had always said she would worry herself sick, and here she'd already done it by the start of high school.

Clearly, Faye was no stranger to worry. She kept intimate comfort with anxiety, a relationship that grew more familiar as Faye (and her parents and her children) aged through the tumult of life. Those early years after it happened—Vogel, the abortion, the whole AP mess—were covered in so many new memories and altered retellings that Faye had lost access to the raw angst of those days. Instead, Faye awaited each dawn with surety. *Joy cometh in the morning*, she told herself and told her children. After each night of fitful sleep, morning light crept across the darkness, birthing a world of new possibilities. Each day the children greeted Faye with wet morning smiles, their soft skin dimpled from deep, unmoving sleep. Thoughts of her babies consoled Faye because what she and they shared was unspoiled.

On the morning before Teague's thirteenth birthday, Faye wrapped her arms around the children in the front pew at St. Cecilia's, seeing in their stratified youth incarnations of herself as she had grown from toddler to child to the many stages of young adulthood. In church—in *the Church*, wherever it was—there was God and (still!) there was Edward. As Faye had grown, Edward's presence had grown with her. Some nights Faye would sit straight up from a dead sleep and fight back a vague sense of dread that knew no relief. She would take stock of her life, then, her mind journeying back through so much love and success to the house on Bonita Vista and the knowledge (however foolish) that she had failed herself and failed Edward. *To God Be the Glory*, Edward had said. In a blink, twenty years had passed. Faye still felt Edward with her, sometimes as a shiny scar that blended smoothly into her skin, others as too-tight sutures that felt about to burst open and bleed. What worried her most was the awful possibility that she would feel this way at fifty. At sixty. For as long as she lived. The thought of being healed terrified her almost as much.

Louisa squeezed Faye's hand, so she bent her ear down to the child's lips.

Louisa spoke quietly. "Are we going out to breakfast after Mass?"

Faye's mouth turned up in a smile. "Of course," she whispered back. "Any place you choose."

The easy touch of her daughter's hand was everything.

Looking askance, Faye rested her eyes on Teague, his head poking up above Louisa's, almost as high as her own. Life's angels were marching Teague ahead to adulthood and were hurrying Teague away from his mother.

Beneath Faye's knees, the patterned fabric rubbed abrasively against tender skin. St. Cecilia's wide sanctuary and bright windows swallowed the incense as it rose from the golden thurible beside the altar. The diluted aroma of other Masses drifted in through Faye's hungry pores. Her body feasted on a store of memories—Edward giving Eucharist in the dark, somber closeness of the Aquinas Prep chapel; she and Daniel praying alone on their wedding day, their tiny human figures mere ants beneath the high, painted ceiling in the Basilica of the Sacred Heart; teen-aged Faye smoothing her hand across the cold marble of St. Peter's foot in Rome.

Oh, how she wanted to wrap herself in the Church. Faye eyed the dirty, shoe-traveled carpet of the St. Cecilia aisleways and wished she could stretch her body out against it, prostrating herself like young seminarians dead to the world and reborn to the priesthood. There was so much to be grateful for, and yet a gnawing hunger still roiled beneath her satisfied upper layer. Squished together on their knees between her and Daniel, their children seemed at once too much joy to contain and somehow not quite enough to hold the darkness at bay. In churches everywhere, modern churches and Victorian cathedrals, beneath ugly, unadorned windows and intricately patterned stained glass, Faye imagined the candles, altar cloths, and wooden pews stretching into amorphous pools and swallowing her up. She could not quite pin down the feeling, this unspeakable desire to be submerged in the holiness and ritual that had shaped the contours of her life. Even when the Church's sanctity seemed more smoke than substance, Faye wanted to drown herself in it.

Right at the edge of her field of vision, Faye could see Trina Hendricks hovering in the office doorway. Faye waved her hand toward the plush chairs opposite her and Trina bounced in with more energy than Faye expected. The girl wore the same clothes Faye had usually seen her wear around campus–torn jeans, black boots, a glittery pink tee shirt that reflected different colors of light as Trina moved. On her wrist, Faye glimpsed a rainbow the girl or some friend had recently inked with semi-permanent markers. Though she must have been about fourteen weeks along, her body seemed firm and strong as ever. Oh, Faye thought, how even our bodies cling to childhood as long as they can!

"You look well!" Faye said. She stretched her arms out with exuberance toward Trina.

"I feel so much better these days," the girl said. "I've only thrown up once in the past couple of weeks. I think my body is kind of used to being pregnant now."

Faye smiled and questioned. "Does the doctor say you are healthy?"

It was natural to think about the baby, Faye thought. Everyone asks about the baby. Faye wanted Trina to know that she was concerned about *her*, that the baby was only secondary to the first child in this equation. Trina was a child, too. She needed rest and support and to feel like her messy life had as much value as the perfect, unspoiled life of the baby inside her.

"Yes, the doctor says my weight and my labs and all that are just perfect. I'm really proud of myself for everything."

Faye received Trina's confidence with great exultation. In the days after their first meeting, Trina and Faye had discussed terminating the pregnancy and had considered Trina keeping the child with or without her boyfriend's help. Faye's educator instincts and motherly nature had suited up in full gear. She helped Trina research local women's crisis centers, abortion procedures, teen-aged parenting, and colleges that offered special housing for students with young children. Most of all, Faye centered Trina's experience.

"You have many options," Faye had said that first day. "You have the power and the right to make whatever decision you believe will be best."

"For the baby?" Trina had said softly.

"For you," Faye had said sweetly, taking Trina's hand. "And, if you choose to continue this pregnancy, for the child, too, when the child comes."

She had held Trina's hand—literally—through a tense conversation with her parents and had stood by on speed dial when Trina had told the baby's father and had begun meeting with adoption lawyers. Yes, Faye also was proud of Trina. This sweet child had climbed out of a deep well of fear and given herself more love than she knew she had in her.

"So," Faye began, folding her hands placidly over her own breast, "have you settled on an adoptive home?"

Faye was careful not to say *parents*. Trina was the child's mother, Faye kept thinking. When Trina was twenty and thirty and forty, her body would bear the scars of carrying this seed to life, even if she never shared the joy of its youth, the pain of its heartbreak.

A glowing smile spread across Trina's face.

"That's what I came to tell you," she said with uncontained joy. "I have big news."

Faye sat forward in anticipation.

"I've decided to keep the baby," Trina announced proudly.

Trina smiled expectantly, waiting for Faye's response.

"That is news!" Faye said too loudly. "What changed?"

Trina sat up with more presence now.

"I thought about what you said," Trina answered with a smile. "You told me to make this decision based on what I really wanted for myself and my future. From that first day in your office, I looked at you and at the picture of your kids." Trina motioned to the photo of Faye's children. "And I knew I wanted to be a mom. I wanted to be a mom now, to this baby."

Faye nodded encouragement. Trina's words came more quickly, with more excitement.

"I decided adoption because I was afraid I couldn't afford to raise the baby. I finally told my parents the other night that I wished I was keeping the baby, and they said they would take out another mortgage or maybe we would move inland to Greenview County so they could help me until I get through college and get a better job."

"Your parents love you a great deal," Faye affirmed. "Your child will have an awful lot of love, too."

Trina exhaled a big breath and reached for a candy from the dish on Faye's desk.

"I almost can't believe it," she said with such cool aplomb that Faye was taken aback. "In my whole life, I never thought I would be excited about getting pregnant in high school," she laughed, unwrapping a chewy pink taffy. "But I just can't wait to start feeling the baby move."

A colleague covered for Faye so she could catch up on paperwork. I'm drowning in forms and half-finished reports, she had said with fake alarm. After the meeting with Trina, Faye canceled her afternoon meetings and sat quietly in her office with the door closed. Her weight sunk heavily into the thick seat of the office chair. She was glad, really, for this girl. And yet, Faye felt a discomfort pressing itself against her skin. She had not in years thought about her own abandoned baby, about the ride with Debbie to the clinic with the cold exam room, about the burning leaves dotting open spaces along the highway in Potato Creek. Faye felt small, now, in the face of Trina's resolute maturity. *Choice*, Faye felt her mind saying. The word hovered in her mind's eye in thick, dark lettering. Faye had chosen out of fear. Trina chose in spite of it.

That was the best thing, really, about working with high school kids these days. It was like they could do anything they wanted. Faye meant this in a good way. Just when the outside world said that kids didn't talk right and that their noses were stuck in their phones, Faye would see before her eyes a life force that flowed beneath this generation like a wellspring of infinite strength. Their strength was different than hers had been. On their tiny screens, these new kids saw a world of diverse people, desires, lifestyles, and perspectives. The old guard hung on as it faced extinction, rising up through bully culture and homophobia and misogyny, but waves of resistance slowed its momentum. Some days, the bigotry won. But on other days (oh, so many other days that Faye had seen), kids like Lewis Miller and Trina Hendricks chose for themselves and demanded to be seen. Slowly, knot by knot, this massive ship would turn and sail toward the sun. Faye's own children—please, God!—would bring forth a world of compassion and inclusivity that was absolutely fearless.

At 2:20 each afternoon, Cor Jesu Academy was a flurry of activity. Preteen girl giggles and harried parents competed for attention amid the din of loudspeaker announcements and of idling cars in the pick-up line. Edward did not pick Amy up often, but today had been a special day, and he felt hopeful though certainly not strong. He could see Amy coming out of the gymnasium, her crisp white blouse and blue Phys Ed shorts barely crumpled, her red and blue plaid skirt folded over her arm. Three or four girls jostled each other, rambunctious and carefree, as they emerged from the building on this bright June day, the final days of high school receding quickly. Their bobbing heads moved back and forth as wide smiles crossed their lips. Edward waved his hand hesitantly in their direction, pulling it down slowly when he realized Amy could not see him. She slipped from Edward's view amid the crowd of students searching for their way home.

      Edward's pulse raced as an uncomfortable sweat dampened his chest and his hairline. *Step*, he thought, willing his body forward despite an uneasiness that quickly engulfed him. A strange sensation beset him, a cleaving of himself into two Edwards. One Edward felt panicked and uncertain, losing consciousness and bodily strength with each move toward the cascade of steps leading up to Cor Jesu Academy. The other Edward was calm. This Edward began to let go, shedding the tired skin so rash-dimpled since the chemo. Edward felt a surge of eagerness, as he sloughed with relief the weight of worldly unhappiness and exhaustion. Effortlessly, his heart embraced a deep peace that promised a journey to a safe place. A seraphic vision rushed over him. *Pray it three times*, Edward remembered, *and the words will be absolute.* Edward's long day in this body was ending. He spoke resolutely in his mind. *Holy. Holy. Holy.*

      Edward did not think of Faye. He did not curse her or love her or forgive her or beg her mercy. He thought neither of Faye nor of Thuy, not of lovers abused, rejected, or adored. He thought not of Jane in an Italian piazza or of little Millie over the casket of her daughter taken too young. Edward pictured himself as a vulnerable young boy, feeling death embrace him tenderly like his mother's warm terry cloth bathrobe on the darkest days of Kansas winters. He could smell the heady jasmine of his mother's Imari perfume. Soothing. Comforting. Forgiving. But most of all, he thought of Amy at the piano, her porcelain skin almost sparkling in the fading light. Her soft music ushered him away from the pain.

      He hoped the real Amy, the vibrant teen-aged girl with a life of love and art ahead of her, was shielded from him now, could not see him falling, could not hear his final gasp. Yes, he thought only of Amy, hoping that his child would carry him with her.

      Meet us at the Zipper at 7 so you can take Louisa.
      Maya's mom is letting her stay until 9 and we want to be alone.

      Teague's text lit up Faye's phone as it lay on a faded green lunch table at the Our Lady of Sorrows outdoor cafeteria. Faye sipped a soda and fed a greasy piece of funnel cake into Wyatt's gaping mouth. Plumes of powdered sugar leapt up from the table as Wyatt shimmied and bounced in his seat. The summer evening was still bright, the din permeating but subdued. Faye hadn't been to the OLS Summerfest since 1998. Anticipation buzzed through her toes and up to her fingers. Darkness would bring intensely bright lights, louder screams, and a melee of activity. Faye looked forward to the vibrant bumping of adrenaline-hyped teens and tired parents as Citrus County Catholics poured into the festival to feel each other's company. Faye's family had no friends in the OLS parish, but she had driven the kids over for the festival because Maya's grandparents lived just around the corner.

OLS had been Ian's old parish. Faye's adventure riding the OLS Zipper was a legendary tale in the Collins family. Everyone knew the half story of that night, how Faye had been forced to flip and flop and scream in that terrifying cage by Krystal, Ian, and James, three kids who had been Faye's best friends of a summer and whom Faye's children had never met. Krystal knew more of the story, that Faye had given Edward a blow job that afternoon and had then vomited the disgusting contents of her stomach on the OLS field. No one (but her lawyers) knew the full story. No one (even her lawyers) could really know what that day had been like. Other people didn't know there could be fear without any real danger or dizzying disorientation in a familiar place. The incongruity of that day had lodged itself in Faye's consciousness. That was the day Faye realized that sex could make a person—a *woman*—invisible. The memory humiliated and incensed her. She could still conjure the look of concentration and euphoria on Edward's face, him grasping at nirvana while the room collapsed and Faye prayed for it all to stop.

And so for twenty years she skipped over that part. It had been a beautiful day at first. The sun had streamed through the open windows. Edward had talked about falling in love with her. She and Krystal had held hands on Top Spin, and Faye had lived to tell the tale. She and her teen-aged friends had danced down the midway, tossed dimes, won goldfish, ate nachos, and smoked clove cigarettes until Faye's embarrassment had been washed in the glee of being a teenager with the whole world open before her. Delight returned to her now in the face of baby Wyatt, his cheeks full and sticky, his eyes big and curious.

"Can we go ride the flying bees now?"

Faye swooped Wyatt up with one arm.

"Absolutely. Pick any ride you want. It's just the two of us for another hour before we meet Teague and Louisa."

Wyatt threw his arms in the air. "The three of us, Mama! Don't forget Baby!"

"That's right," Faye said with resolute happiness. Wyatt pushed his fingers, skinny and frail like a sparrow's claws, against Faye's stomach. "Just you, me, and Baby."

Maya was glad when Louisa went off with her mom and baby brother. She liked Teague's sister alright, but she and Teague couldn't really *talk* talk in front of a little kid.

"Do you want to take popcorn out there with us?" she asked.

Teague pointed at his mouth and grimaced. "I can't eat popcorn because of my braces," he said, "but I don't care if you get some."

"Cheese fries?"

"Definitely, cheese fries," Teague said. "I think I have seven dollars left."

Dust kicked up from the baseball field as Teague and Maya shuffled across. They headed for the dugout. They'd had enough of the lights and the rides for now.

They talked guinea pigs and Battle Bonds as the cheesy potatoes cooled quickly in the night air. The hot summer day had turned to night without their noticing. Teague's shoulders shook in a quick shiver. Maya was always warm. Teague noticed at school that Maya wore shorts even on the coldest mornings when the marine layer covered the town in a wet sheen.

"Do you want my sweatshirt?" Maya asked. "My grandma made me bring it even though I'm never cold." Maya's middle school growth spurt had left Teague well behind. Her sweatshirt was roomy and comfortable. The fleece lining felt good against Teague's goose-pimpled arms.

"How do I look?" he asked with a smile.

"Like you don't know how to spell," Maya said with a laugh.

Teague looked down at this chest. The screen-printed *k* and *i* had peeled off from *Osage Park Middle School*.

The noises of Summerfest felt far away.

Maya broke the silence. "Listen," she began, "I think I'm ready to try."

Teague's face brightened. He straightened his shoulders and almost jumped off the cold concrete bench.

"Do you mean the Zipper," he asked. "Do you really want to go this time?"

Maya laughed so wide Teague could see the darkness at the back of her throat. She doubled over and grabbed his wrist.

"I don't get it," he said.

Maya gathered herself and tried again.

"No, silly," she said with her eyes trained on Teague's. "I'm ready to try a kiss."

Suddenly the fleece was too warm. Teague felt sweaty in the crease of his elbows.

"What about you," Maya asked. "Do you still want to do it?"

Yes. Teague wanted this kiss. He bit his lip and peeked his head around the dugout to check for stragglers from the carnival.

"I really like you," Teague said. "But how do I know if I'm ready? How do you know that you are?"

Maya took Teague's hand. He hoped she couldn't feel the clamminess that had spread across his palm in mere seconds.

"I used to feel more nervous than happy when I thought about it," she said with authority. "Now I feel calm." The wide smile returned. "That's how you know. Being close to you makes me feel calm. Like, you understand who I am, so I don't have to be nervous after all."

Teague and Maya leaned toward each other with their eyes wide open. Just as their noses touched, Teague saw Maya's eyelids flutter closed. He shut his eyes tightly, then, and enjoyed the indescribable delight of Maya's soft lips pressed against his. It was the only first kiss they would ever have, and it was perfect.

A loud groan jumped out of Faye's throat as she stretched out on top of the bedspread.

"What a marvelous night!" she exclaimed. "It's exhausting, though, all that traipsing back and forth. Even with Teague having a phone, it's just a nightmare to meet up at carnivals."

Daniel breathed relief as he untucked his shirt.

"I thought I'd get there for at least part of it, but you know how Tracy can ramble in manager meetings. How many fish did Louisa bring home?"

Faye laughed at the ceiling.

"You know her too well. She only brought home three, thank goodness. She won six but gave three to a little girl who didn't win any."

Faye tilted her head back uncomfortably far and met her husband's gaze.

"The fish are still in the bag on the counter by the tank. Can you mess with it before you go to bed, please?"

Daniel's silence meant of course he would since he always did. Daniel took care of pet fish and pet birds and plants and the lawn and really all the living things that hadn't come out of Faye's body.

"How's Baby," he asked, leaning over Faye and touching his lips to her nose.

"Baby is achy," Faye said, "in a good way. I don't remember it being like this before. It's like I can feel the baby already."

Daniel spoke with surprise. "You can feel the baby? This early?"

Faye reframed. "I can't feel the baby, but I can feel my body growing and making room. There's a pressure right here—" Faye cupped the vee between her belly and thighs—"that feels like roots spreading out through my middle. I've never felt anything like it."

Faye always thought it odd to say that women had babies *in their tummy*, but in truth, pregnancy grew from the stomach out, the torso becoming soft and the softness emanating out slowly to the upper body, arms, and face until, in the final months, Faye became a swollen version of herself, the change happening so slowly that it was only noticeable when looking at photos of her pregnant self a year after each baby's birth. Daniel loved this early pregnancy stage when her body had just begun to soften and he was able to mold his flesh into hers in a way her slight stature usually did not allow. Faye hurried to bed before Daniel this night and closed her eyes lightly as if she were asleep. She wanted Daniel to press his chest up against her without expecting her to turn over. He wrapped his arm over her stomach and buried his mouth beneath her hairline at the base of her neck. Faye took a yawning breath and filled her lungs with the familiar stillness of a sleeping house.

XI

THE BITTER SMELL OF BURNING CRUMBS reached Thuy's nose a moment before smoke started curling up from the toaster.

"Oh no! Where does this smoke come from?" she exclaimed.

Amy yanked the plug from its outlet and opened the kitchen window wide. Cold air rushed in. The tiny kitchen curtains billowed out over the sink.

"Don't worry about the toast," Amy said. "We need to get going. My flight leaves at 3:00, and the international terminal is always a mess."

The click of Thuy's heels resounded in the empty foyer. Her husband was dead. Her daughter was flying across the world. The day was hers to do with as she pleased. Thuy did not enjoy this feeling. An old white lady at Church had suggested that Thuy find stress release in swimming or yoga or crafting. *You must have hobbies that relax you,* the woman had said. *Repetitive activities like knitting can really help in the grieving process.* Thuy did not have hobbies. Edward had played guitar and piano; he had grown vegetables and raised chickens; he had done woodworking projects and brewed his own beer. Thuy kept a home and managed Amy's schedule. Thuy made sure her husband had the things he needed. That was a Catholic wife's hobby.

There had never been anything bustling about the Vogel home, but since Edward's death, the stillness inside Thuy's house was palpable and exhausting. She couldn't blame Amy for wanting a distraction. (She did blame her for traveling halfway around the world to chase romantic notions about her father, the great artist.) Most of Edward's family had come and gone quickly in the few days surrounding his burial. Millie and her son were the last to leave, heading back to Kansas on a muggy Wednesday evening. The next day, Amy began scouring the internet for opportunities to study abroad. Thuy had suggested a classical piano course taught by a Juilliard trained composer in New York, but Amy wouldn't hear of it.

"I want to go to Rome," Amy said stoically. "I want to study in Rome, like dad should have done."

Now, six months later, here was Thuy. Alone.

Thuy tackled the toaster after cleaning the counters. The cord curled awkwardly away from the wall where Amy had dropped it. Thuy had grown up in a Vietnamese culture that ate mostly vegetables, fish, and noodles. She never made toast and couldn't remember how Amy had grown to love the crusty bread so much. Edward had started each day with only coffee and an egg or a grapefruit, but most days he made toast for Amy. That girl ate piles of whole wheat and nine grain and sourdough. Thuy remembered Amy rushing out the door on hurried high school mornings balancing books and keys and a napkin full of toast teetering in a buttery stack. She peered into the toaster now, hesitantly checking its various parts. When she pushed lightly on the chrome-plated underside, a retractable tray popped out and sprayed toast fragments across the counter, the floor, and up onto Thuy's sweater. She jumped in alarm at the sudden burst of burnt crumbs. Her heart raced a moment, and then she laughed. What a sight she must be, cowering amid whizzing crumbs.

She realized then, what she had not known. Edward had been emptying this tray for Amy's toast. All the years–Edward had been cleaning the toaster. Thuy wept now, the rising tears fat and sharp. Edward had done awful things, and he had done this for their child. All the small acts–those Thuy had seen and those she would never know–made a family. Her husband had been a man who liked to be pleased, to be catered to. And so, this service toward their daughter felt especially precious. It did not make everything okay. It did make Thuy feel better.

Edward's brother Glen would arrive in three days to sort through the boxes that had accompanied Edward from place to place and never been unpacked. *Nothing in them would interest you,* her husband would say whenever she mentioned the boxes. *I don't even know half of what's in there.* Church rummage sales came and went over the years. At First Mid Bank and Trust, Edward and Thuy took a safe deposit box. Through it all, Thuy never touched Edward's boxes, and for the most part, Edward didn't either. Some five or so years back, Thuy had heard Edward hunting around as she was tucking Amy into bed. At breakfast the next morning, Edward showed Amy and Thuy a photo of himself shaking hands with Pope John Paul II, who had been canonized the day before. Thuy examined the photo more closely when she was alone in the house that day. Edward's teen-aged choir beamed wide and tall behind the two men. There to Edward's right, Thuy could see that girl who had brought such shame upon their family.

Don't let that girl take your peace, Thuy had scolded herself that morning.

What a marvel it was, one ordinary morning eating eggs, to find that Edward had been touched by a saint.

The text of Camus's novel jumped and jiggled with Amy along the twenty-minute bus ride from the American Academy of Rome to St. Peter's Square. The yellowing, dog-eared copy of *The Plague* had been passed to Amy by her Aunt Millie after her father's funeral. This was your father's favorite novel, Aunt Millie had said. I remember your dad reading it in high school. He used to sit with his back against the hackberry tree out along our property line.

Amy was sure her father had never mentioned Camus, but she recognized his handwriting on the inside cover and in a few of the margins. *All suffering is unique*, he had written on one page. *No suffering is unique*, he had written just below it.

Amy had started *The Plague* in Meridian before heading across the ocean to a six-week seminar in Roman Pottery Studies at the same elite academy her father had passed over thirty years earlier. The first few days of reading disappointed her. Amy wanted to love this book because her father had, but the story of a deadly, pervasive disease sweeping the nations felt out of touch with the world that buffered her. It probably should not have felt so aloof, Amy thought. Her father's illness had jolted everyone he knew out of complacency. They hadn't thought death would take her father so soon. Her dad wasn't particularly healthy, but he was *there* and he was *theirs*. People just didn't imagine that those standing solidly before them could be torn up and carried away with the capriciousness of a child plucking dandelions.

A burst of spring breeze rushed against Amy's cheek as she exited the bus. The grandeur of Rome stretched long and wide before her. God's beauty lay bare. Indeed, her suffering was not unique. She would learn in time that her father's crime had been like a stone around her family's neck, that she would view her lovers with suspicion, that the world she inherited still protected a man's desire instead of a girl's dignity.

Amy's mother had caught her one night looking online at pictures of her dad's accuser.

"Turn that off," her mother had yelled.

"I'm sixteen," Amy had said with the righteousness of an entitled teenager. "I think I should know what happened."

The rage in her mother's eyes scared Amy.

"Your father did nothing wrong," she spat. "That girl is a liar."

Amy found the photos again on a rented PC at the library and in her school's computer lab. Faye Collins did not look like a liar (but how did a liar look?). She wasn't glamorous like Amy expected her to be. She looked plain and professorial. Amy's mother almost never spoke of that woman, but when she did, it was as though Faye Collins were a cartoon vixen. Amy had pictured Faye with high heels and a pouty mouth thick with red lipstick.

Amy's father loomed in her memory like a giant whose musical genius and superior intellect made them all seem small in comparison. But Amy did not know her father as a real person. She did not know who he had been or what demons he had battled. Of course Amy loved her father. She wanted him back at the piano with her, wanted to hear his rich baritone and believe that one more time he would brush her long braid away from her neck and tell her how proud he was that she was an artist and a thinker, just like her dad.

But Amy thought the lady deserved to tell her story, even if her father didn't like it. Too many women had been silenced through the years. Amy and her friends did not want to become the silent women their mothers were.

Amy sat in the east nave of St. Peter's during High Mass. Latin chants rolled off her tongue from years of study at her father's knee. Amy felt aglow with energy. Her eyes desperately drank in Bernini and Michelangelo and all the masters whose gilding moved the artist's soul in her breast.

After Mass she watched a group of protestors gathered along the thick white columns encircling the piazza. They held signs that said *Believe the Victims* and *The Pope Protects Pedophiles*. Amy noticed a handful of Catholic priests among the crowd. One with big, weepy eyes gave her a gentle smile. A woman stood beside him in a simple nun's habit. Her sign said *Abuse Hurts Everyone*. After some time, the protesting marchers began moving toward the St. Angelo Bridge. The women, men, teens, children, and consecrated religious heaved along as one massive body, chanting and singing as they walked. Amy watched them get smaller and smaller until she could see them no more. Faith filled their resolute, united voice. Amy almost followed. The Church confused her. Where was a girl like Amy supposed to stand?

When she learned of Edward's death, Faye was lingering leisurely outside Louisa's classroom, the too-green fake turf unmoving in the late March breeze. Faye's fingers scrolled absent-mindedly through her phone, scrolling as she and everyone else seemed apt to do these days, so seldom merely standing and waiting, more often scrolling and checking, bouncing between emails and news sites, friendships and advertisements, almost never merely waiting. So it was in this moment of nonchalance, Wyatt singing to himself—"Jesus loves me. This I know!"—and tumbling on the scratchy grass, in this moment, that Edward died for Faye. The real Edward had been dead many months. Edward had been buried. Edward's real life mourners had mostly moved on and accepted the new normal of their lives without Edward. But only that morning, as Louisa's fifth-grade class prepared for dismissal, did Faye open Jane's email and find the news. A few hours earlier, a friend of a friend had told Jane, Edward's ex-fiancé, about the obituary she had discovered in an old, discarded newspaper, only hours since Jane had drawn her breath in sharply, pulled her fingers instinctively to the collar bones jutting out beneath her blouse, and thought immediately to write Faye with those awful three words: Edward has died.

"Enjoy the weekend!" a cheery young voice called from Louisa's classroom door.

Faye looked up from her phone but did not move. The clouds spun quickly around and resettled. Faye hugged her giant belly as if to keep her almost-grown baby from spilling out. Wyatt ran past her toward his sister. Faye could think only one thought. Finally, these twenty-some years later, it was over. *It is finished,* she thought, not with relief and resentment. With regret and longing. She was struck suddenly by the realization—somehow at once surprising and expected—that she had buried a hope within her, protecting it like a precious, sprouting tendril. She had hoped to see Edward again. But now, he was gone.

Against her will, a prayer rushed into Faye's mouth. *Pray three times and it is absolute,* Edward had taught them.

Mercy. Mercy. Mercy.

A look of terror crossed the medic's face as he positioned Faye awkwardly in a wheelchair and headed from the ER to the third floor.

"Park the car and meet us upstairs," Daniel shouted to Faye's mother, who had already slipped behind the wheel and closed the door.

"The baby is coming," Faye grunted. "He's coming right now."

"It's alright," Daniel cooed in an exasperated whisper. "We're in the hospital now. We made it."

Panic was still apparent on Daniel's ashen face as relief settled down beside it. *Thank God for uncluttered freeways at dawn,* he thought. Faye's water had broken eight miles back.

Baby Wren came forth in a nauseating and frightful push. Messiness and confusion and pain—oh, the enormous pain—thrust him into life.

"He's here!" Daniel exclaimed.

Faye's insides rose into her throat and poured out of her womb. She was overcome and weeping with fear.

"I'm not ready to hold him," she said to no one and everyone in the room. "I'm shaking too much. I'm afraid I will drop him."

No one seemed to hear her amidst the rush of new life.

"I'm not ready," she said to Daniel, feeling a surge of doubt and desire as her husband cradled baby Wren in a warm, bloody blanket and lifted him toward her. She needed him, this final baby, who had come too fast and at just the right time.

"I can't take him yet," she said aloud, feeling her strength return.

Faye pulled the baby to her like a lifeboat.

Acknowledgements

AN ESPECIALLY HEARTFELT GRATITUDE TO Nicole De Leon, Ellen Friend, and Kara Jacobi—this cohort of smart, courageous women has served as readers, confidantes, spiritual directors, and partners along my journey. Their friendship nourishes me, and for that I am eternally rich. I have been immeasurably blessed and buoyed on life's seas by the quiet encouragement of so many family members, friends, and colleagues. Among these are Holly Haynes Nicholls, Jamie Koottarappallil Asdorian, Marilyn Dancey, Luck and Elizabeth Luckey, Joanna and Todd Ventura, Matthew and Alison Luckey, Merton Lee, Austin Riede, Carol Baker, Jim Hansen, and Kelsey Keyes. Many thanks to Angela Yarber at Tehom Center Publishing and to Jennifer Owens-Jofré who directed me to the Tehom community.

My writing and all that I do are made possible by the love of my husband and our three children. They save me from the world and show me the joy of being in it.